Stealing VENICE

Stealing VENICE

HEATHER REDDING

Matador
9 Priory Business Park,
Wistow Road, Kibworth Beauchamp,
Leicestershire. LE8 0RX
Tel: (+44) 116 279 2299
Fax: (+44) 116 279 2277
Email: books@troubador.co.uk
Web: www.troubador.co.uk/matador

ISBN 978 1783064 465

British Library Cataloguing in Publication Data.
A catalogue record for this book is available from the British Library.

Typeset by Troubador Publishing Ltd, Leicester, UK
Printed and bound in the UK by TJ International, Padstow, Cornwall

Matador is an imprint of Troubador Publishing Ltd

For Ben

Contents

Foreword

Readers with a knowledge of Venice may realise that I have taken some topographical liberties, primarily with the location of Ca' Melisa. Certainly, there are some charming residences where I have placed this fictional house, but none possessing its splendour. Ca' Melisa is my own invention, although it does exist in part, if not its entirety, in many of Venice's public and private buildings. Izzy and Anna's flat, however, and Raffi's apartment are rooted in reality, and I have spent happy times in both.

Sadly, the Church of the Misericordia has not been accessible to the public since the 1970s. The small houses adjacent to it spring from my imagination.

Of the Cima paintings I describe, all but one exists. The exception is the Virgin and St Catherine. The two that feature a youthful John the Baptist, for which Giacomo models, are in the Fitzwilliam Museum and the Brera.

I am fortunate in that there is a wealth of source material available regarding early sixteenth century Venice, and I have provided a full bibliography. However, for a non-historian to write an historical novel is a challenge, as I very soon discovered. Any errors are all my own, and I hope will be forgiven.

Thanks to the National Gallery in London for their prompt and helpful replies to my many emailed questions. And to artist John Frederick Black for generously giving permission to use his painting as the cover image. I am also particularly indebted to Jeff Cotton's wonderful website, Churches of Venice, which is a mine of information, and provided me with photos of the Misericordia's interior.

I remain eternally grateful to my ever-patient readers, who throughout the process of committing this story to paper provided me with advice, assistance and encouragement. So to Alan and Sally Burton, Sarah Hamilton, Lin Holridge and Viv Day – thank you again, I could not have done it without you. I also owe a special debt of gratitude to my friend, Pat Roberts, for choosing to live in Venice, and who always made me so welcome, showing me a city that I would otherwise have never seen. Without those memories this book would not have been written.

And finally, and above all, to my ever supportive, ever loving husband Ben Redding – Venetian location spotter extraordinaire – and apologies for all the missed meals, burnt meals and computer hogging. Thank you for giving me the freedom to write; thank you for giving me everything.

In her own Words

Still, after all these years, I remember that first day in Venice: the pressure of the blindfold; the firmness of gloved hands guiding me through the crowds. Robbed of sight, my other senses are newly sharpened, so that even now, a scent or a sound can evoke memories of that morning in colours brighter than anything my eyes can see.

It is nearing midday. Visitors and residents alike are mindful of lunch calling, as savoury effusions beckon from countless restaurants. Apartments, high above the shop fronts, join the ritual and the winter air is heavy with a pungent trinity of onion, tomato and celery sweating in hidden kitchens. Beside me, Izzy smells of lemon and patchouli; Will of cigarettes, and the vast amount of garlic he threw into last night's supper.

Around us, I feel the surge of bodies; scurrying humanity crammed into ancient thoroughfares. Venetians, concerned only with getting from A to B; the slower, unpredictable pace of tourists who peruse menus, peer into shops and halt mid-stride, creating mini incidents as those behind bump into them. And protective in their closeness, is the warm press of my companions and captors.

And the noise. We hardly speak, but an incessant babel surrounds us: Italian, French, German, Japanese, the shock of pure Home Counties: 'Darling, do you think we could do both the Doge's Palace and the Accademia this afternoon? And for lunch, the guidebook says...' But she is out of earshot before I hear anything further. And then, above the din, noon is heralded from numerous bell towers. A huge clamour of sound, as each *campanile* unleashes its own distinctive peal: near and distant, some tinny, some mellifluous, but rising above them all, unmistakable and unnervingly familiar, although I have never heard it before, is the deep, reverberating call of what can only be the bells of San Marco.

'Are we there yet?' I whine, like a fractious child on a car journey.

'Nearly,' comes the reply, as I sense a palpable thinning of the crowd and a lightening of the air. It feels much, much colder. A rogue breeze catches my hair, whipping it into my mouth. I lick my lips and taste salt.

As the second peal of the noontime bell fades, fingers tug at the blindfold and it is whisked away.

1

I am at first blinded by the pure white light of the midday sun and stand blinking in amazement. Nothing has quite prepared me for the mirage that unfolds; the audacious, vast Piazza. I've seen photos of course, but here is the stuff of dreams – or at least of my dreams. At the far end crouches the Basilica di San Marco, a glorious, gaudy confection of cupolas and turrets, shifting marble and sparkling mosaic. Towering over it is the Campanile, a monolith of terracotta, green and gold, pointing towards God and His heaven. Sweeping around us are Renaissance arcades, the white marble streaked grey by time and pollution. Hiding behind the graceful arches are shops and cafés from which music filters. At my feet, pigeons coo and flap, squabbling for food: overhead seagulls squall. I sense that somewhere, very close, is the wide-open sea.

While it astounds and delights me, I have the strangest sensation of having been here before.

'*Eccola!*' Izzy circles on the spot, her head thrown back, arms outstretched. She is jubilant, the ritual complete. This is what she does with her Venice virgins; leads them, compliant and unseeing, so she can relish their reaction when they are faced with all this beauty, all this splendour.

For a second I am tempted to say, 'It's smaller than I imagined.' Just to tease her. But I know that my rapturous expression has given me away, and I feel a surge of gratitude that she finds such pleasure in showing off this magical city – her home and workplace.

Will breaks the silence. 'There you are, Anna. Napoleon's drawing room.'

'Napoleon?'

'Yep. He called it the finest drawing room in Europe. Mind you, as soon as his armies marched in, they started shipping the best bits off to Paris. Not that the Venetians had much justification in complaining. Half the stuff in Venice had been nicked from Constantinople during the Crusades: the horses on the Basilica; the columns on the Piazzetta – that's where they held public executions, by the way, so don't ever walk between them, it's very bad luck.'

I have a photograph; the three of us, frozen in time. I remember it being taken. Will hijacked a passing tourist, a serious young German, who spent an age composing the shot.

'You vill now smile, pliz,' he ordered in such commanding tones that we could hardly suppress our laughter.

It is a good photo, and I'm grateful to that earnest boy for taking his time. We stand, arms linked, under a great arc of blue sky. Izzy, tiny and yet voluptuous in a black velvet coat, a halo of blonde waves framing an elfin face. Will, scowling into the camera, raven hair falling over round spectacles; a cigarette dangles from

2

a petulant mouth and he affects boredom, somewhat unsuccessfully; he enjoys these jaunts as much as Izzy, but does not like to let on. And then there is me, their willing hostage, smiling – no, I am more than smiling; I am beaming. Light slants across my thrown back face, the wind whips my dark curls, and I am caught in the midst of uninhibited laughter. I tower above Izzy, standing shoulder to shoulder with Will. Around my neck hangs the red blindfold, a vibrant gash of colour against the London drabness of my pigeon-grey coat. Around us teem numerous people we will never meet, but look very carefully, way to the right, and you will spot a small figure meandering towards us. If you enlarged the photo you would see a fur-trimmed coat, auburn hair and huge sunglasses. She has just disembarked a *vaporetto* and is heading for a restaurant near La Fenice, where a man is waiting. It is an important meeting, and not wanting to be late, when she saw the approaching boat, she ran. And so, Patrizia, over punctual, who should still have been on the Lido, saw us, spoke to us, and so it all began.

When I look at myself in that photo, I see a young woman with such joy imprinted on her face that anyone would assume she is on the brink of something wonderful, which, I suppose, for better or worse, I was…

We Three

…or that is how she remembered it, years later…another life later.

And it was, of course, Tom, the wordsmith, who made the suggestion. 'Face your demons, Anna. Turn them into words. Then you have power over them… it's as simple as that.'

'They're not demons,' she protested. 'It's just that there are some things I'd rather forget.'

'But you don't have much choice do you? The old boy still writes, I presume?'

'Yes,' she replied. 'Always at Christmas, and once or twice throughout the year.'

'So there's no surprises waiting for you?'

'No, no surprises. Look, I can cope with the reality of things. It's the unreality that's difficult…all the jumbled up dreams. Like the opening chapter of *Rebecca*: "Last night I dreamt…" etc, etc. I think I'm all OK, and then…'

He tried to read her face. Their tongues were loosened by wine and sentiment, but in her eyes he detected the usual defensiveness.

'Anna, I'm a writer, not a psychoanalyst. But I am one of your best friends, and I was there to pick up the pieces, if you remember. So I think I'm qualified to give my opinion, and I say, write about it. Or even better, bloody face those demons head-on, and go there!'

'No, Tom…not that. But if you really think it'll help, I will try writing about it, just for you…OK.'

It was a promise she honoured, beginning with an account of that first visit to Venice, but she soon abandoned the task and consigned her scribblings to a bulging case of other *memento mori*. And Tom was wrong – it didn't help; the dreams still came. Only with the passage of time did their frequency diminish, as gradually she remembered less and less – except when Vittore's letters arrived, and then she could not help but recall that watershed summer and wonder what if…?

She had always been the unadventurous one of their ill-matched trio: Izzy, Tom and Anna, inseparable since their first day at primary school. All were only children and perhaps because of this they immediately formed a bond, becoming surrogate siblings. Whoever else flitted in and out of their lives, they always came back to each other.

In their teens they joined a local youth theatre: Tom wrote plays, Izzy acted, and Anna stage-managed, painted scenery and designed the posters. They whiled away hours on the riverbank, sneaking into the more tolerant pubs for illicit drinks, and dreamed about their futures. Only when the sea change of further education loomed did they acknowledge that their ways would part.

One weekend, revising for their French O level, Tom announced, 'I've decided. If my grades are good enough I'm going to have a stab at Cambridge.'

'Thought you might,' said Izzy. 'Well, if you do get in, I just hope you'll still deign to talk to us poor plebs.'

'Oh, I'll consider it. And what about you two?'

Izzy frowned, trying to look serious. 'Anywhere with a great social life and lots of rich men. Bristol? Exeter?'

There was a moment's silence, then Anna said, 'I'm not altogether sure I want to go to university. After A levels I rather fancy getting a job and earning some money.'

Her friends gazed at her, incredulously, as if she had announced an intention to take holy orders.

'But think of all the fun you'll miss,' Izzy said, and as an afterthought. 'You'll regret not stretching yourself academically.'

'I'll have fun here. It's not as though there's nothing to do in London. And my brain isn't going to atrophy just because I'm not doing a degree. I'm quite happy living at home, and if I save I may even be able to buy my own place.'

Sensing that Tom and Izzy remained unconvinced, Anna threw out a challenge. 'Bet you, in five or six years, I'm earning the most.'

'But it's the long term you should think about,' warned Tom. 'Graduate pay almost always outstrips non-graduates.' Having a degree is the only way to get onto the best company training programmes, you know.'

'Honestly, Tom, you sound like my careers teacher,' said Anna.

He shrugged, a little embarrassed. 'And what about your parents? Won't they be disappointed?'

'Well, I haven't discussed it with them yet. But as neither of them went to university, I don't see it'll be a problem.'

'Oh, come on,' said Izzy. 'It was a bit different in their day. For one thing there was the slight disruption of the war. Anyway, I'm sure you'll change your mind,' she concluded, with her sixteen-year old confidence.

But over the next two years Anna stood by her decision. Her parents, ever supportive, greeted her determination to forgo further education with surprising equanimity, and so after A levels she allowed herself a few weeks holiday, spending time with Izzy and Tom before they disappeared to Bristol and Cambridge.

That summer the country basked in a holiday humour, buoyed up by warm weather, royal silver jubilee celebrations and street parties. They took life easy but were each aware of the separate paths that would soon lead them to the next stage of their lives.

Whenever Anna recalled those days, she would forever associate them with Elvis Presley songs scratchily played on her cheap stereo. Tom had arrived one morning, clutching a battered collection of his mother's long un-played LPs.

'The King is dead,' he announced.

'I didn't know you liked Elvis.'

'I don't, particularly. But it's… well…it's the end of an era, isn't it?'

"Tis for my mum,' said Izzy. 'She won't stop crying.'

And so, long forgotten songs that had once been part of their childhood were reborn as a soundtrack to their last weeks together. Then, as summer surrendered to autumn, and the house martins disappeared from the pallid London skies, Tom and Izzy were gone. Anna was alone.

One golden October evening she lay on her bed, staring at the whitewashed walls, as a weakening sun pricked out patterns through the turning leaves, and wondered what on earth to do with her life. Her exam results had been better than expected, and if she applied to university for next year, entry was virtually guaranteed. She was tempted, but at the same time faced an unpalatable truth. It occurred to her, with a frightening verisimilitude, that the real reason she had not applied was because she feared failure and rejection. It was not a trait she admired in herself – a coward soul was not something to be proud of – and so she determined to prove that her instincts were correct. She would go out into the world and work, forge a career and fulfil her prediction that in a few years she would overtake Tom and Izzy on the monetary ladder.

And so, barely a month later, Anna walked through the impressive marble doorway of Hartland, Hyatt & Co to commence a career in finance. Despite two lengthy interviews she still found it difficult to summarise exactly what her job entailed.

'Initially, my role will be very junior,' she explained to Izzy during a long telephone conversation. 'But I can work towards gaining professional qualifications. I'm so lucky that Dad introduced me. Normally, they only take graduates.'

'Hmm. The advantages of having a bank manager for a father.'

Anna knew that Izzy was disappointed to be living in lodgings rather than a hall of residence, but despite this she had seemed happy enough during their previous conversations. In the face of her continued reticence, Anna gently probed, 'Well, how is everything? Still enjoying student life?'

The silence was shattered by a noisy sob. 'Oh, God, I can't pretend any longer. It's bloody awful. My digs are miles away from the University, and when I get off the bus I have to walk along this really dark road with a park on one side and the sort of houses where no one would come out even if you were screaming blue murder. My landlady's not had the heating on once yet, and my room's freezing. I go to bed with two hot water bottles, and believe me, that's all I ever will go to bed with in this dump. I'm trying to find somewhere else, but I've had no luck. And… and I really miss you and Tom.'

'Oh, Izzy, I'm sure it'll get better. Look, why don't I come down for the weekend? Tell you what, I'll treat you to a couple of nights in a nice warm hotel, and you can show me the sights. We'll blow some of my first pay packet.'

So Anna booked a B&B in Clifton, and found Izzy much jollier, having just secured herself a flat for the following term, and a date with a "scrummy" second year. They ate in a cheap and cheerful bistro and glowing with red wine and moussaka, strolled over the Suspension Bridge. It was a mild night and as they watched the river snake its way along the gorge, Izzy said, 'Why don't you apply here, for next year? We could share a flat. It'd be brilliant. Much better than Hartland whatsit.'

'How do you know? My first couple of weeks have been great. It's not just students who enjoy themselves. Seriously, Izzy, I've made my decision and whatever you and Tom say, I'm going to stick with it.'

Izzy turned and looked into her friend's eyes. 'All right, I give up. We both will. But promise me you won't change. You've always been the sensible one, but please don't get boring. I'd hate that.'

'I'll try. But I might disappoint you. I really don't think I'm destined for a very exciting life.'

'Don't you believe it.' Izzy pointed an index finger to the heavens. 'I predict that you, Anna Elizabeth Fleming, will surprise us all and have a strange and extraordinary life. Nearly as extraordinarily wonderful as mine's going to be. Now let's get back. We've got another bottle of wine to finish before bed.'

But Tom and Izzy, complicit in their mission to change Anna's mind, launched one more attack. This time it was Tom, home for the weekend to celebrate his mother's fortieth birthday. On the Friday, he and Anna met at a quiet pub in a Putney back street.

'God, that's good,' he said, gulping back his beer. 'I've missed the local brew. How was Izzy?'

7

'A bit frenetic. Got completely pissed on Saturday night and spent most of Sunday nursing a hangover. We had to leave the guesthouse by ten, so she curled up in the student union while I traipsed round by myself. She was just beginning to perk up by the time I had to leave.'

'She'll settle down,' said Tom, draining his glass. 'Want another?'

'Not yet, I've hardly started this one. God, you students! Is your degree in drinking too?'

Tom grinned: a flash of uneven teeth, his bony, large featured face lighting up; kind eyes crinkling. He peered into his empty glass, as though answers lurked there. 'It's just because it's…you know…there.'

'What? Alcohol?'

'Not just that – freedom. For the first time in our lives we can go out, get filthy drunk if we like…come back at whatever time we please. No worried mother hovering by the front door, convinced you're dead in some back street when you're not back by eleven. No having to get up for school.'

'What about lectures?'

'Mostly at very civilised hours. The thing is, all my life I've towed the line, and no doubt when I've graduated I'll do the same. I'll never lead this sort of privileged existence again.'

'You're very enthusiastic. Is there a downside?'

'Well, I can't say I'm mad about doing my own laundry. And I do miss Mum's cooking.'

'I bet you live on cheese and biscuits,' laughed Anna. 'And the other students? What are they like?'

'All sorts really. A lot are public school, obviously. There's a bloke on my staircase who actually lives in a stately home. Not just a house that's big and old, but one they open up to the peasants. He can trace his ancestors back to…I dunno…God! But they're totally broke. In winter they live in a tiny annex to save on the heating. Now, the guy opposite is from Newcastle way. Lives with his mum in a tower block; went to the local comprehensive, but he is a fucking genius. I've never met anyone with a mind like his. The other night we sat up till four in the morning discussing…well…everything…the metaphysical poets, Bob Dylan lyrics, the Grunwick strikers, which of us the barmaid at the Anchor fancies most…'

'It sounds great, Tom. I'm really happy it's everything you'd hoped.'

'It is. And it's what you're missing, Anna – out of sheer stubbornness.'

Anger bubbled up inside her. 'Tom, I really don't want to hear all this again. I had it from Izzy a couple of weeks ago – at least when she was sober enough to speak coherently. And how dare you call me stubborn. Look, I've made my decision about what I want to do with my life and just because it's different from what you and Izzy have chosen, it doesn't mean it's any less worthy. So if you don't like it you can...'

'What, Anna?'

'Stop seeing me. After all, you've found all these stimulating new friends. Perhaps I'm already too – what's the word Izzy used? Ah, yes – boring.'

'What?'

'Well, she asked me not to *become* boring. It was only afterwards that I realised how bloody insulting it was.'

'Silly cow. I'm sure she didn't mean it like it sounded.'

'Look, all I ask is that you don't denigrate what I'm doing. A university education, even at the best of universities, isn't the be all and end all, you know.'

Tom cleared his throat. 'I'm sorry. We've no right to try and shape your life. It's just that we go back a long way, don't we? We three. And we want the best for you. But whatever happens, we'll be there for each other, won't we? To give support if things are ever bad. You know...pick up the pieces.'

'OK, it's a deal. In sickness and in health!' Anna toasted the air with her empty glass. 'You can get me that drink now. And let's hope there's not too much picking up of pieces to be done, eh?'

'Oh, there probably will be,' said Tom cheerfully.

His prediction was correct. Over the years, Anna lost track of the number of times she comforted Tom and Izzy as they suffered the pangs of disprized love, or worked through the guilt of ending a dying affair. But, surprisingly, it was she who suffered the first cut.

The Christmas after her friends left home, she met Martin, a second year student at London University. Their relationship quickly assumed an easy permanency but then, Martin, who had set his sights on an academic career, went to Manchester to study for his MSc. By the end of term he had fallen in love with someone else – Janie. Anna was devastated. He was her first love; the only man whose bed she had shared. His betrayal left her inexplicably ashamed. What was wrong with her, she wondered, that she could not keep him? Was she not sufficiently attractive, intelligent, interesting? Was she, as Izzy had once intimated, boring?

She threw herself into work and this, together with the support of her parents and friends, gradually eased the hurt and humiliation. A few months later, celebrating a well-earned promotion, she realised that an undeniably attractive broker was chatting her up. As she gave him her number, she concluded that perhaps it was for the best that Martin had left her. She had no wish to abandon London, and all it offered.

In the meantime, Tom and Izzy, both still single, graduated, found jobs, lived in a series of rented flats (although, probably wisely, never together) and Anna stayed at home and saved and saved…until one autumn evening the three friends were gathered in an airy studio flat high above a South Kensington street. They stood, raising glasses of champagne, as dregs of sunlight filtered through grime-speckled windows.

'To Anna. A woman of property,' Tom and Izzy chorused.

Anna wore a black linen dress that looked, and indeed was, expensive. Her hair proclaimed the attention of an expert stylist, and she glowed with barely concealed self-satisfaction.

'Wow, your own place – in Kensington.' Izzy drained her glass, not bothering to hide her good-natured envy. 'You always said you'd be the richest of us.'

'I'll have you remember, the building society is the major shareholder in this property. No more posh frocks for me. From now on I'll be shopping Chez Oxfam.'

'Even so, it's more than Tom and I have. Makes me wonder why I spent all those years slogging for a degree.'

'You didn't slog,' said Tom. 'That's why you got a third!'

'All right, Mr Clever-Clogs-I've-got-a-first-complacent-bastard. No need to rub it in. I can't help being thick.'

'You're not thick, just too fond of partying,' retorted Tom.

'Hey, no fighting, you two. I don't want bloodstains on my new carpet.'

'Oh, all right,' muttered Izzy. 'It's his way of telling me off. On the way here, I told him I've handed in my notice.'

'But I thought you liked this one,' said Anna. 'It's your third job since graduating; your CV is going to look terrible.'

'Bugger the CV. I've had enough trying to get on in publishing. I'm going to do something completely different.'

An expectant silence followed, prolonged for maximum effect before Izzy announced, 'I'm going to teach English…in Italy.'

'When? Why Italy? Where?' were the questions that rapidly followed.

'I start in January. And why Italy? Well, it's a beautiful country: the booze is cheap, the food's gorgeous, and so are the men. And I'm going to…wait for it… Venice! Whatever George Orwell predicted, I think 1984 is going to be a brilliant year.'

'Venice?' said Anna. 'You know, I've always wanted to go there.'

'Well, now's your chance…you can stay with me.' Izzy turned to Tom. 'You're very quiet. What d'you think? And please don't tell me off again. You know I hate my job, probably almost as much as you hate yours.'

Tom's expression was inscrutable; then he hoisted himself from his chair and hugged Izzy. 'I think it's great, kiddo. So bloody great I may do it myself.'

'Yeah!' whooped Izzy. 'Come with me. It's high time for a bit of fecklessness, and you may even finish writing your novel.'

'It's very tempting, I must admit,' he said.

'Hey, you can't both bugger off and leave me,' protested Anna.

'Well, why don't you come too?' said Izzy, disengaging herself from Tom. 'You could…if you really wanted.'

'No, I couldn't!'

'Well, there you are then. Look, let's face it, gallivanting off abroad isn't exactly your scene, is it? For one thing, I can't see you leaving your mum and dad for so long, especially now they're getting on a bit.'

'What? They're not exactly ancient.'

'OK, OK. But, you know, last time I saw your dad he was looking a bit peaky… is he all right?'

'Yes, of course,' snapped Anna. 'Oh God, I think I can smell dinner burning.' And she dashed to the kitchen.

But she had noticed a change in her father: a creeping weariness, a greying of the complexion, and a rounding of the shoulders. She reasoned that these aberrations signified nothing; after all, he was over sixty, not old, as Izzy had intimated, but at an age when he had the right not to be so boisterously energetic. Surely there was nothing to worry about? And so, wrapped in the security of her friends' companionship, Anna reassured herself that all was well.

Hugh

Hugh Fleming sat by the window, basking in the reluctant warmth of a December sun, letting its tired light play on his neat features and sandy hair. He closed his eyes – just for a moment – and when he opened them, and looked into the garden, he saw Guy, his long dead brother.

Hugh watched as the boy dug deep into the bark of the old apple tree, strong brown fingers wielding his new birthday penknife, dark hair falling across his eyes. He flashed an exultant smile at the child that had once been Hugh. He is twelve years old, happy and heartbreakingly innocent of the fate awaiting him.

Then time snapped back into focus. It wasn't Guy, of course; it was Anna, Hugh's daughter. Wrapped up against the cold, she was picking rosemary, and in her hand was a pair of kitchen scissors – not a penknife.

Rosemary…that's for remembrance, thought Hugh, remembering; and wondering, for the umpteenth time, what throwback gene had emerged in both his daughter and in Guy.

Both were so different from anyone else in the family, but so like each other; the slender, yet athletic frame. The same long, straight nose and olive skin. They were the two that could have been taken for father and daughter, even down to their light blue eyes and mass of dark hair. Guy had tamed his with a short back and sides and lashings of Brylcreem, whereas Anna's grew in Pre-Raphaelite abundance. That morning, Hugh had noticed one or two white strands threading through those dark curls, and had imagined the same early silver brushing Guy's temples. Anna was twenty-six; Guy had barely made it to twenty.

Hugh took a restorative swig of his G and T, making an effort to activate the positive button in his brain. He suspected that this alien thing rebelling in the depths of his body would kill him; perhaps not this year, or even the next, but that eventually it would win. He did not fear death – never had done – just the journey to that undiscovered country. And until there was no denying it, he was determined to carry on as normal; to avoid, for as long as possible, the tiptoeing around death's gloomy shadow. What he wanted, more than anything, was to forget the last two gruelling years and for things to be as they had been.

And anyway, perhaps this brush with illness was merely a blip; perhaps he would be one of the lucky ones. Hadn't he always been? And whatever happened, he was certainly luckier than Guy, shot down in 1940.

They never had found his body, so their mother forever hoped that her son would return. Her uncompromising grief had hurt Hugh, but he understood. Guy had been so very special. And when both his parents died in short succession of each other, it was this, more than anything that had compelled Hugh to move back to the family home in Putney. He could not bear to abandon the house where his brother had grown from child to adult; the garden where that tree still bore Guy's initials:

GRF

6.9.1932

Three years after Guy's death, Hugh had also joined the RAF, but unlike Guy, he emerged unscathed, the only testimony to his wartime service being a long, whitened scar on his right palm where he had grabbed a broken glass in the mess. By then, the Battle of Britain was long over, already the stuff of legend, and the war waged in the skies of Europe had taken on another dimension. It was now Bomber Command, attacking the enemy on its home ground, on which the hopes of Britain and her allies rested.

Hugh was chosen as a pilot and like most of his fellow airmen, he never questioned, even towards the end of the war, the nightly blanket bombing. But now, after all these years, it hurt and angered him when the actions that had resulted in the death of so many of his friends were condemned; as if they were personally responsible for the obscenity of those mutilated towns; those lost lives. So he skirted over his wartime service, and when he mentioned serving in the RAF, people usually assumed he had been one of the Few. He did not disabuse them, but let them hold on to the idealised fiction of fighter pilots and solo dogfights.

And Hugh was not one to chew on life's bitter pill; not like Dougie Forster, the only one of his old flying comrades that he saw on a regular basis, mostly because Dougie lived in nearby Wandsworth. Dougie had been their rear gunner, and ever since the war had suffered recurring ill health, which he put down to long and lonely hours spent in a freezing turret, scanning the night sky for Luftwaffe fighters. After the war, competition for jobs amongst ex-servicemen had been fierce. Dougie, unlike Hugh, was not blessed with a good grammar school education and this, combined with his all too obvious mental scars and fragile health, meant he had been forced to accept a series of low paid, menial positions. He had never married, fearing that no woman would want to sleep with a man who woke up screaming on a regular basis. He remained obstinately solitary, convinced that as he did not love himself, no one else could.

'And what, in God's name, was all the fighting for?' he would routinely demand as they sat in quiet corners of dismal pubs. 'I mean, the country's gone to the bloody dogs, hasn't it? You know my neighbour, old Freddie? Fought in the trenches in the First War, was a firefighter in the last? Well, a couple of days ago, he's coming back from the Post Office, with his pension, and these little bastards surround him. One trips him up and when he's on the ground another of them robs him.'

'Poor old boy,' murmured Hugh. 'Is he OK?'

'Amazingly, yes. Just a few bruises. Well, the police come to interview him. Can he identify the boys? Course he can't. He was on the bloody pavement, wasn't he? And anyway,' Dougie made no attempt to lower his voice. 'Half of them were, you know, black lads. I mean, to old Freddie, they all look the same, don't they?'

Dougie fell silent, chewing on his misery, unaware that the barmaid was tuning into their conversation. They often drank in this pub, and Hugh had discovered she was studying medicine. She was brainy, beautiful – and black.

'Your round,' Dougie announced, holding up his empty beer glass.

'Yes, of course.'

Hugh made his way to the bar. 'A pint and a half of Special, please, Zoë. Oh… and, er…one for yourself.'

For one awful moment he thought she was going to tell him to fuck off, and then she flashed him her amazing smile. He knew she would not have the drink but would pop the 80 pence, or whatever, in her tip jar, which was fine by Hugh.

Encouraged, he leant conspiratorially forward. 'Sorry about Dougie. He doesn't mean to be rude.'

'Oh, that's all right,' she said. 'There are plenty of bad boys around here, black and white.' Her voice was deep and melodious, with just a hint of the West Indian accent her parents had brought with them when they left their own warm shores for the alien pavements of London. 'You know, I was observing in a geriatric ward the other day. All male patients, and all white, as it happened. And do you know, to me, they all looked the same: sans eyes, sans teeth, sans everything.'

Hugh had a sudden, and awful vision of himself and Dougie, twenty years hence, propped up in a battery farm of a hospital, turkey necked geriatrics gobbling inanities, while Zoë – now a consultant – white coated, and even more beautiful, wafted down the hope forsaken ward, quite oblivious to their existence.

His hand struck his chest; his horror only partly feigned. 'Touché, Zoë!'

'Only,' she continued, with a wicked smile, 'I would not be so rude as to say so.'

'But, Zoë, you just did.'

'Only to you,' she beamed. 'Because I knew you wouldn't be offended.'

And Hugh realised that he wasn't, not in the least. On the contrary, he found himself thinking how splendid it was to share such a joke, with such a girl, in a local pub. And how very glad he was to be part of a society where young women like Zoë could flourish and make the most of their talents. If, for twenty of the little bastards that had robbed old Freddie, there was just the one Zoë, all the fighting had been worthwhile. At the time, admittedly, his motivation had had little to do with the desire to create a safe world for the Zoës of the 1980s. Rather, his compulsion had stemmed from a fierce need to defend these mundane South London streets; for a night out in the West End, and the occasional trip to a corny English seaside town. That is what inspired most of the boys; they battled for their own little patch of sceptred isle, for their friends and families; not for a nebulous future generation. Half the time they hardly considered tomorrow, let alone the next thirty or forty years. But whatever their reasons for fighting, thank God they had.

Hugh was musing on these thoughts, this December afternoon, as he watched Anna in the garden. He had reconciled himself to not living to a great age, but he did so yearn for a few more years. A book of Betjeman's poems lay on his desk and he recalled an interview in which the late poet famously declared that his main regret was: "not having had more sex".

What Hugh regretted was not having had more adventure. The war, certainly, had been an awfully big adventure, but what he longed for now was the sort of experience kids enjoyed on what they called a "gap year." Fat chance of a "gap year" in the 1940s, but some interesting holidays would have been a start. Apart from a few months training in Canada, he had hardly left Britain, and he was now assailed by an overwhelming desire to see the world – or at least a bit more of it.

In the years immediately after the war, however, he was content not to travel. England had become intensely precious to him. How could it not? He had looked down on it time after time, returning at dawn from missions in the skies of Europe. He recalled the rolling Lincolnshire landscape hurtling up through the early morning mists, gently warmed by soft slants of hazy sunlight, his aircraft flying so low over the patchwork quilt of fields that he could see the old men saluting, and the white, upturned faces of pretty land girls, waving and blowing kisses. Then he landed the plane, and they were home and safe, for at least a few hours. They spilled out onto the tarmac, exhausted and hungry, taking great gulps of the sharp, green air, and nothing was as beautiful as the windswept grass and trees, the church spires and sleepy villages that lay all around them. Each time he returned, he imagined how, when peace reigned, he would bring his crew home one last time, drink warm beer in a local pub, sleep a dreamless sleep on a soft mattress and never again leave the safety of his native shore.

And so it came to pass. Hugh returned, surprised and grateful that his whole life lay ahead of him, but humbled and puzzled that he should survive when so many had perished. He toyed with the idea of university, but the prospect of mixing with kids fresh out of school deterred him and so, like his father, he went into banking. It was a secure and predictable profession, eminently suited to Hugh's new status, for only weeks after the war's end, he had married, if not the girl next door, the girl from the next street.

Millie was tiny and blonde. She had spent her war years typing confidential reports in a central London office, and to Hugh's amazement, 1945 saw her still single. She had once told him that so many of her friends had been left bereft and broken-hearted, that it seemed best not to fall in love. And so, with a flinty hearted resolve she had not – not until the war was over, and Hugh was safely home. Forty years later he still adored his wife, and staying alive to spend more time with her, and their daughter, Anna, was all that mattered. He was three years from retirement and although he was now back at work full time, and glad to be so, he found it exhausting. It was a young man's game and he had a sneaking suspicion that someone soon might be suggesting an early departure.

Whatever happened, Millie would be financially secure. His pension would ensure that she was more than comfortable, and in the event of his death before retirement there would also be a substantial cash payment (one was usually worth more dead than alive). Bearing this in mind, Hugh had taken a decision that may just alter the whole course of his daughter's life. He hugged this warm secret, and found comfort in imagining her future, even though he would not see it. Hopefully, it would not be relevant. He did so want to live; to be well again and to see those places of which he now dreamed. They could take Anna with them. Manhattan perhaps, or New England in the fall. Millie did not care for flying so their family holidays had been confined to Britain and northern France, but there was still Provence, central Spain or Italy to explore.

From the kitchen came an optimistic clatter of pans; lunch would soon be ready. Having Anna at home for the weekend was like old times, for although he was delighted that she owned her own place, even after two years he still missed her. When his unmarried sister-in-law had died he had persuaded Millie that they should give Anna the money she left. Not that there had been that much, after all those nursing home fees, but together with what Anna had accumulated, it proved sufficient for a substantial deposit.

Anna was ecstatic, and soon found the perfect place – a little eyrie at the top of a rambling building, a stone's throw from South Kensington underground station. It was right in the hub of things, buzzing with an eclectic mix of peoples. Shops stayed open till all hours; Polish and Middle Eastern restaurants rubbed shoulders with the traditional French and Italian establishments, and there was even an English restaurant where one of Anna's school friends, a struggling actress, occasionally worked. The night Hugh dined there, the place appeared to be entirely staffed by an ebullient bunch of thespians, as intent upon staging their own dramas as attending to the customers.

One evening, shortly after Anna had moved into her new home, he left the train at South Kensington, and armed with a bottle of champagne, pressed the entry-phone bell to her flat. She had taken the week off work, so there was a good chance she would be in. After a few moments he heard her voice.

'Hello?'

'It's Dad. Can I come in?'

'Of course. What a wonderful surprise.'

There were a hell of a lot of stairs, and by the time he reached the top he was panting heavily.

'Dad, are you OK?' Anna immediately hustled him to a chair, then waited till he got his breath back.

'Yes, fine, darling. I thought I'd check out what I needed to bring this weekend.' He had promised to hang pictures and put up shelves. 'Shall I open this?' He held up the bottle.

'Bubbly! Oh, thank you. What a treat.'

Champagne poured, they stood side by side, gazing out of the window. It had begun to rain and they watched the buses en route to the Fulham and King's Roads, extravagantly red against the cellophane grey streets.

'You made a good choice here,' said Hugh. 'Property should always hold its value in this part of town.'

'Hopefully. But that's by the by. You know, I've always wanted to live here. When I was a little girl and you took me to the museums, I used to think how marvellous it would be, to be all grown up and have a flat in Kensington. And now I do. Of course, I'll always think of Putney as home, but even though I've lived here such a short time, this feels like home too.'

Hugh felt a prickling sensation in his eyes. His baby girl, all grown up – where had the years gone?

'Well, think of Putney as your country pad. It'll be yours one day. Have you ever thought what you'll do with it? Sell it I suppose?'

'I don't know. I mean that's not going to be for years, is it? You and mum aren't planning to run off and retire somewhere in the sun, I hope?'

'Good Lord, no. Can you imagine your mother on the Costa del Geriatrica, miles from an M & S and Peter Jones?'

'It would be a fantastic house if I had a family,' Anna continued. 'But there's no prospect of that at the moment, so…'

'So, I take it that you don't think Chris is going to be the one?' And then, before he could stop himself. 'No sign of wedding bells?'

'Dad! I've only been seeing him for three months. It's far too early to say.' Anna was instantly defensive, and he realised he had overstepped the mark.

Hugh had met Chris twice. He was a bluff and hearty solicitor of thirty-three, well over six foot, athletic, but with a tendency to the portliness that threatened to overtake him if he continued to wine and dine so enthusiastically. He had a shock of golden hair, tinged with red, a florid complexion and his face just missed out on classical handsomeness due to the disproportionate smallness of his nose. There was something about him that made Hugh think of a young Henry VIII. Although he doubted that Chris would treat his wife – or wives – in the merciless fashion of the monarch, he sensed that behind his affability the man possessed a ruthless streak.

Hugh correctly guessed that Chris thought Anna the perfect partner: a thoroughly nice girl, reliable and kind; attractive, but not in a showy way. She was bright, but importantly, not too ambitious, for Chris made no secret of the fact that whatever career aspirations she may hold, they must, perforce, be subservient to his own.

Over the years Hugh had observed his daughter with various young men. He noted that since the failed romance with Martin, she was, not exactly hard-hearted, but seemingly determined not to give all the heart until she was certain she had found the real thing. Having seen the way she looked at Chris, he wondered if she now believed she had found it. He rather hoped not.

Hugh drained his glass, glanced at his watch and seeing how long he had lingered, stood to go, when a sudden, sharp pain shot through his body, causing him to almost double up. He forced himself upright. 'Oh, the champagne. A bit fizzy. Gives me heartburn.'

'Bit too much of it too,' Anna laughed. 'Chris is taking me to San Frediano's tonight. I'm squiffy already!'

'San Fred's, that's a treat. Have a lovely time.'

He kissed her goodbye, then began the long descent downstairs, feeling a little light-headed but perfectly well. Yes, he was sure that it was no more than a surfeit of champagne. Looking up, he saw Anna waving to him over the banisters. 'See you Saturday. Thanks again for the bubbly, Dad. Love you.'

'Love you too, sweetheart.'

Anna did indeed see Hugh on Saturday, but not in the circumstances she anticipated. On Thursday she was painting the walls of her bathroom when the phone rang. It was Millie. Hugh had collapsed at the office and been taken to hospital.

Anna had remained icily calm. She ordered a taxi, changed out of her paint splattered dungarees, even put on a bit of makeup, and was then violently sick. In the half painted bathroom, she stared at her white face, as the newly applied mascara ran down her cheeks, and knew that nothing would ever be quite the same again.

She coped with her father's prolonged ill health by convincing herself that modern medicine and the skill of his doctors would triumph, and all would be well. But it was an uneasy peace, for she always suspected that he was protecting her from some dark truth, and she constantly scrutinised his face for indications that the disease had returned. So, two years later, walking into his study, on this wintry Sunday afternoon, his broad smile provided instant reassurance.

'Mum says lunch will be ready in ten minutes. She forgot to put the carrots on, so I think the lamb is pretty much incinerated. A nice bottle of red?'

'Of course. I've already opened one.' Hugh indicated a bottle warming by the radiator.

'Chateau Talbot. Very nice.'

'Don't want to risk it going over the top,' he said.

They both knew that the Talbot had at least another ten years.

He poured her a sherry and asked, as he did every month or so, 'And how are Tom and Izzy keeping?'

'Izzy's renewed her teaching contract, again. And moved in with her latest man.' Anna remembered the opening line of Izzy's letter: "Reader, I shacked up with him!"

'And Tom's over the moon about how well his book's selling,' she continued. 'The second one's nearly finished, so he's been given a big fat advance on the third. And he's up for some crime writers' award thing.'

'So, no sign of him returning to London?' It amused Hugh that Tom, who now earned his living writing about a detective working in war-torn London, should choose to reside in Paris.

'No, but he can't wait for them to build this channel tunnel. Then he'll be able to pop back in no time.'

19

'Yes. I think it may really happen this time.'

'I know. It's brilliant. Just think – we'll be able to leave London in the morning, have lunch in Paris, and be back home that night. We must do it when it opens.'

'It's a date, sweetheart. Let's hope it happens this century.'

As soon as he made the quip he saw the panic in Anna's eyes, and was not surprised when she asked, with feigned casualness, 'How are you feeling these days, Dad?'

'Oh, Anna, love. Can't I make a little joke without you worrying about my health? I did say the end of the century. Let's change the subject, eh.'

'Actually, I have a reason for asking.'

'I'm fine, Anna,' he lied. No need to let on about that nagging ache that had been troubling him for the last few days.

'Are you sure? Because I was thinking of visiting Izzy. She's been inviting me for ages. Her new flat has a very comfortable sofa bed apparently. And I'd love to see Venice, and meet her bloke. His name's Will.'

'I think it's a wonderful idea. When are you off?'

'As soon into New Year as I can. No later, because February and March are always so busy at work.'

'You deserve it, sweetheart,' said Hugh. 'Bring me back a bottle of something nice. Grappa, perhaps.'

Then a call from Millie summoned them to lunch and, following the scent of burnt lamb, they made their way to the dining room.

Twelfth Night

Anna arrived at Santa Lucia, Venice's railway station, shortly before eight in the evening, thirty hours after Chris had dropped her off at Victoria Station. Industrial action by Italian rail workers, coupled with a national holiday, had resulted in a six-hour delay. She had shared a compartment on the overnight sleeper with five Italian students who were bound for Milan, where the train, it was announced, would terminate. Following this unexpected ejection, her travelling companions tracked down an alternative service to Venice; gave her *gettoni* for the telephone so she could alert Izzy to her late arrival, and presented her with a bag containing *panini*, fruit and a small bottle of red wine, purchased from a trolley that trundled up and down the platforms.

At last, safely ensconced on a Venice bound train, Anna waved them goodbye and settled down to the final stage of her journey. She was captivated by everything: the place names; the fleeting glimpses of small towns and villages; the terracotta pantiles and skeletal vineyards; the gardens full of scurrying chickens and scampering goats. Her fellow travellers, who piled on and off at almost every station, were as varied as the scenery. Most regarded her with friendly but silent curiosity, although some attempted to engage her in conversation, despite her protestations of, 'Non parlo Italiano.' And a few even insisted on sharing their provisions: sweaty cheeses, salami hacked into jaw breaking pieces with a rusty knife, and earthy red wines of staggering potency.

Darkness had long since fallen when the train reached the inky waters of the lagoon and snaked along the causeway connecting the ancient city to modern day Mestre. Anna, now alone in the compartment, pulled down the window, hoping to catch a first glimpse of her destination. All she could see was a smattering of lights indicating where the water ended and the city began. A fine rain was falling, and the chill of the night stung her cheeks, but the salty, sea-spiked air was invigorating and laden with promise. It seemed to her that it was a scent she had known for a very long time; that it was interleafed with her earliest memories but forgotten, like a flower pressed in the pages of a long-unread book.

As the train drew to a halt, she ventured into the corridor. A man, wearing a weary expression, trailed past.

'Venice?' she asked, just to make sure.

'*Si, signorina*,' he replied and then, somewhat pointedly, '*Venezia.*'

Duly corrected, Anna lugged her case off the train and surveyed her surroundings. It was just a railway station, constructed of modernist 1950s grey concrete. She had expected oak panelling and Belle Époque wrought iron, not this bland ordinariness.

Izzy had promised to meet her in the station bar, but it would be at least ten minutes before she arrived, so, with suitcase in tow, Anna trudged down the platform. The vast booking hall milled with people, and for a few moments she lingered by a souvenir shop, fascinated by the tacky riot of hideous glass, gaudy masks and plastic gondolas. Then she spotted the bar, its windows opaque with steam. Pushing open the door, she was engulfed by heat and babbling conversation. The place was heaving, but its conviviality and booze-laden shelves contrasted happily with Anglo-Saxon counterparts, and she decided that, for all its austere functionalism, Venice's railway station had much to recommend it.

'*Café, per favore*,' she said.

Into her waiting palm was deposited a vast quantity of change and a slip of paper, but no coffee. Eventually, she realised this receipt must be surrendered to the barman. Only then did she receive her drink, which was of such minute quantity and such searing bitterness that it almost took her breath away. She was just wondering whether she could face the imbroglio of purchasing another – milky – coffee, when she was engulfed in the bear hug of damp black velvet and spilling golden curls that was Izzy.

'Oh, God, you poor thing! Has it been complete hell?'

'No', laughed Anna, extricating herself. 'But it's been quite an adventure. I'm whacked. Please lead me to a hot bath and a very large drink.'

'Your wish is my command. Let's go!' Izzy made a token attempt to lift Anna's suitcase, then thought better of it. 'I should have warned you about travelling on a national holiday.'

'What holiday is it?' asked Anna, as they made their way out of the station. 'Someone did tell me, but I was none the wiser.'

'*Epifania* – Epiphany. In England we take down the Christmas decorations, sing *We Three Kings of Orient Are*, and that's about it, but in Italy it's a huge celebration. Well, here you are. Welcome to Venice.'

The sight that greeted Anna was at once a revelation, and yet strangely familiar. Dominating the vista, on the opposite bank of the canal, was a floodlit building sporting a classical portico and an oversized green dome.

'That's San Simeone Piccolo,' said Izzy. 'There's a painting of it by Canaletto in the National Gallery. The dome used to be black and Ruskin hated it. But I quite like it, even if it does resemble some sort of bizarre birthday cake.'

Anna abandoned her efforts to drag her luggage down the steps. Nothing had prepared her for this. She had anticipated the elegance; the silhouetted facades of fantastical buildings; the lights that sparkled and shifted on the reflecting water; the majestic sweep of a bridge. But the sheer animation of the scene was totally unexpected and strangely disconcerting. The canal was as busy as Brompton Road, the large vehicles chugging up and down its waters as laden with passengers as a number 14 bus in the rush hour.

'It's amazing, Izzy. I love those big boats. What a fantastic way to travel.'

'They're called *vaporetti*. And talking of which, look who's just got off one.' Izzy began jumping up and down, waving madly. 'Will, Will! Over here.'

Anna spotted him at once – a gangly young man wearing an oversized tweed coat who, having spied Izzy, broke into a run and headed towards them.

'Sorry I'm late.' He planted a kiss on Izzy's upturned face, his long dark hair brushing her cheek. 'Got held up.'

'Well, never mind, you're here now. Just in time to be luggage-wallah. Anna, this is Will. Will, this is Anna. Give each other a hug, and then let's get home. I'm freezing.'

Anna and Will did as commanded, and with ice duly broken, they set off, weaving through the crowds.

Izzy's flat was a short walk from the station along the Lista de Spagna, which according to Will, was quite the tackiest street in the whole of Venice. Enchanted though Anna was with her new surroundings, even her inexperienced eye could tell that the shops were aimed at the tourist market, and that the waiters' constant attempts to entice them inside did not suggest restaurants favoured by the cognoscenti.

'It's a bit late for Halloween, isn't it?' she said, peering into the window of a *pasticerria*. Over the glistening mountains of chocolates and candy, a puppet was suspended – a hook nosed witch astride a broomstick.

'Nothing to do with Halloween,' said Izzy. 'That is *la Befana*, the reason for today's holiday. And probably why this shop is open so late, hoping to sell a few more sweeties. It's rather a sad story. Once upon a time there was an old widow who lived all by herself, her only child having died. Well, one night three visitors arrive at her humble dwelling, who are none other than the three wise men. They ask for directions to Bethlehem and invite her to join them, but she's so busy she says, "no". Anyway, a bit later the shepherds arrive, and they too ask her to come along, and again she refuses. But then she sees a great light in the sky, and decides she will go with them after all, and take all the toys that had belonged to her own child and give them to the baby who's just been born, but…'

'But typical woman,' interrupted Will. 'She gets lost. So, to this day, she hurtles around the skies on her broomstick, trying to find the Christ child, hoping to give Him her gifts. She never does find the manger, of course, but instead she brings pressies to other children, if they leave a stocking out.'

Izzy resumed the story. 'But only if they're well behaved; naughty kids just get a lump of coal. You can even buy sweets looking like coal to give as a joke. And there's this insane regatta, entirely made up of old blokes dressed as *la Befana*. It's like hell's grannies. They row down the Grand Canal and when they reach the Rialto they hang a huge stocking over the bridge! But the best bit is that the bars by the Rialto give out free hot chocolate. I actually had two, one after the other! I mean, when it's free, it's rude to refuse, isn't it?'

'Piglet,' laughed Will, hugging her.

'Isn't it brilliant? I've lived here for two years now and things still happen that take me totally by surprise.'

She skipped along, face gleaming, holding onto Will's arm; happier than Anna had ever seen her. A few minutes later they swung into a dark alley and came to an abrupt halt.

'Here we are. Home sweet home.'

The flat was on the fourth floor, up a dark and uneven staircase. Paint peeled from the walls; the tinny strains of televisions drifted from the other apartments, and the frozen air was clammy with damp and the smell of cooking, but when the door was unlocked and Anna stepped inside, she was pleasantly surprised. It was warm and welcoming, unmistakably Izzy's domain, full of colour and quirkiness, books and brightness.

'As you can see, this is both the sitting and the dining room,' announced Izzy, in her best estate agent's voice. 'But for the next two weeks it is also your boudoir. The table usually lives there.' She pointed to where a beige sofa, its mundane personality relieved by an array of brightly covered cushions, nestled in the smaller part of the L-shaped room. 'But we've moved things round a bit so you can have some privacy. *Eccola*! Like so!' And with a flourish she pulled at an extravagantly patterned curtain, so that the sofa was hidden.

'Sorry it's a bit basic. There's not much space for your things, I'm afraid.'

'Izzy, it's fine. If you can stand me taking over your sitting room, I can stand living out of my suitcase. It's just wonderful to be here. And thank you too, Will.' She met Will's eyes, sea-green and glinting behind John Lennon spectacles, hoping that he was not feeling imposed upon.

He returned her gaze, steady and warm. 'No problem. Any friend of Izzy's is

24

a friend of mine. Now, do you want to freshen up, as they say, or eat?'

'I'm dying for a bath.'

'OK, while you're soaking yourself, I'll start supper. It'll be about forty-five minutes.' He disappeared into the kitchen but they heard his question clearly enough. 'Does Anna know about the loo?'

'Er, no. Look, we have one house rule here, and that is, you must always, always put down the lid.'

'OK. But why?'

Will reappeared, a knife in one hand, a bulb of garlic in the other. 'We have, in the past, had a little visitor. An unwelcome little visitor.'

'Mice?'

'Oh, much worse,' shuddered Izzy. 'Sorry, there's no easy way to say this. A bloody great rat!'

'Specifically a *pantegàna*...a sewer rat.' Will's voice rose over the sound of furious chopping, almost as if he were dismembering a despised rodent. 'One of the less attractive aspects of a city being built on water.'

'Just after we moved here, we went away for the weekend and came back late on the Sunday. I was busting to go, and just as I was about to plonk myself down, I caught sight of this beady little face looking up at me. Well, you know me, if it's furry with four legs, I'll find a place for it in my heart; but not that bugger.'

'You should have heard the screaming,' said Will. 'She wouldn't go to the loo for a month without plunging down a toilet brush followed by gallons of industrial strength bleach.'

'Yeah, well, do you blame me? *Imagine* the damage those sharp little teeth could do! Bye bye, sex life. Anyway, we've seen neither hide nor hair of it since, thank God, but I'm not taking any chances, so do NOT leave that lid up. But apart from the visiting rodent, it really is quite a nice bathroom.'

Two hours later, bathed, fed and replete with quantities of red wine, Anna sat curled up with Izzy on the sofa. Will had disappeared, announcing that he was, 'Going to the *altana* for a ciggie.'

'OK, Izzy. Two questions. What's an *altana*? And what happened to your vow never to have anything to do with a man who smokes?'

Izzy shrugged. 'I don't know. It wasn't as though I didn't know from the first. But I was just completely bowled over by him, and it didn't seem to matter. I mean, he is gorgeous isn't he? So Byronic! And he does only smoke rollies.' She lowered her voice. 'Actually, I can cope with the ciggies. It's the other stuff he smokes that worries me.'

'I know how much you hate drugs, but the occasional joint isn't...'

25

'Yeah, yeah, I know…and I know he's not going to end up a heroin addict like that girl I knew at Bristol. You remember? Penny. She started with the occasional joint, moved on to the hard stuff, dropped out and ended up in a filthy bed-sit – dead, after an overdose. OK…that's not going to happen to Will, and he insists cannabis is harmless, but at the end of the day, the stuff is illegal. He says the police are no more interested in busting someone for having a bit of dope for personal use than they are in England. But I still think that…'

Izzy was interrupted by the front door slamming. She changed the subject with startling dexterity. 'An *altana* is a sort of wooden balcony, of varying degrees of rickety-ness built onto the roof, which is…'

'Absolutely bloody freezing now.' Will burst into the room, the sharp tip of his nose glowing red from cold. 'But a God send on a hot summer's evening. Not many people have access to a garden here, so it's a way to get a bit of private outdoor space. And a spectacular view.'

'I can't wait to go sunbathing up there,' said Izzy, lifting her face to an imaginary sun.

'Something Venetian women have been doing for centuries,' said Will. 'They used to smear their hair with bleaching paste, stick on a special hat, called a *solana*, which was crownless but wide brimmed, and let the sun do its work on lightening their hair.'

'Think I'll try it,' said Izzy.

'Has to be cheaper than highlights,' murmured Anna, her eyelids beginning to droop.

Izzy jumped up and grabbing Will by the arm, made for the door. 'I think we ought to let you turn in. Any thoughts about what you want to do tomorrow?'

'Not really. Obviously I'd like to see the major sights at some point, but…'

'You know what I think?' said Will. 'It's your first visit, so don't spend ages in museums. Just walk around, getting a feel for the place. Everywhere you look there'll be something to delight the eye. With luck, it'll stay dry and if it gets too chilly, pop into a bar and watch the world go by.'

'But I warn you, if you fancy a quiet stroll through the *calli* and *campi* of Venice, don't go with Will,' said Izzy. 'He's only been here a few months, but he knows ten times more about the art and architecture than I do. It's like being with a walking guidebook. I, on the other hand, am an expert on the really useful things, like where to buy the best olive bread, the best pumpkin *gnocchi*, the cheapest *prosecco*; the things that make for the real Venice! We're not working tomorrow, so I suggest a leisurely breakfast, and then we'll take the day as it comes.'

Anna leaned back on the sofa, sleepy and content. 'Sounds perfect.'

* * *

The next morning, she was nudged awake by a sharp blade of sunlight slicing through the curtains. Somewhere a door banged; heels click-clacked on the pavement below; voices greeted each other; a bell struck the half hour. Grabbing her dressing gown, she clambered out of bed and pulled back the curtains. Facing her was a crumbling wall, haphazardly embedded with tightly shuttered windows.

'Admiring the view?' Izzy asked, padding into the room, her skinny pink-kneed legs emerging from what could only be one of Will's sweaters. 'Make the most of the one bit of sunshine that manages to penetrate each day. This flat has some good points, but natural light and the *bella vista* is not one of them. However, the bread shop round the corner IS. I've sent Will out for breakfast.'

She meandered into the kitchen, intent on making coffee, chattering as she did so. 'It's such a shame you didn't come a day earlier. All the churches have these amazing cribs, and you could have seen the Epiphany celebrations.'

'Not to worry. There's always another time, isn't there?'

'Hopefully. It's funny; a lot of people visit Venice, enjoy it, even say they love it, but once is enough. Then there are those who just keep coming back – again and again. It gets under your skin, takes you captive.'

'And what about people like you, who come for six months and are still here two years later?'

Izzy's chocolate drop eyes grew distant. 'Dunno. I was actually ready to go home, but then I met Will and he's still so head over heels in love with the place, I can't see him tearing himself away for a while yet. So for as long as he stays, I stay. Talking of which, here he is with a big bag of *corneti* – croissants. Hopefully the almond ones, they're divine.'

A couple of hours later, they spilled out onto the narrow *calle*. Despite the sun and deep blue sky, the cold air cut like a keenly sharpened knife. Their progress was slow, as Will could not resist providing a running commentary: a perfect Gothic window here; the remnants of a Romanesque doorway there; an Istrian stone relief on the Strada Nova. His list was endless. Izzy's tour, on the other hand, centred on shops: the shop of outrageous furs; the shop of ridiculous articles for dogs; the shop of the flimsiest underwear. But soon she was complaining of the cold, and remembered there was a cosy bar just off their route that sold particularly good *prosecco*, and surely it was not too early for a fortifying little drink?

When they emerged, slightly tipsy and blinking in the jubilant light, a short walk led them to a busy *campo* near the foot of the Rialto Bridge. It was presided over by the statue of a jolly man in eighteenth century dress, caught in a mid-stride so energetic that he appeared poised to jump down from his plinth and join the chattering crowds.

'That's Goldoni,' said Will. 'Venetian playwright. Particularly famed for his comedies. Wrote hundreds; some still very funny. And this *campo*…'

'…is where today's drama kicks off,' interrupted Izzy. 'Roll up for the magical mystery tour!' And beaming like a magician's assistant, she produced a long red scarf from her bag.

'Oh, not the blindfold routine,' groaned Will. 'I'm sure Anna will appreciate the beauties of the Piazza without all that melodrama.'

'Don't be such a spoilsport. I always do this with my first timers. She wants to, don't you Anna?'

'Well, yes, OK. But it does sound like one of those awful trust exercises that Jennie Quinn used to do at drama school.'

'Yeah, well…this is Venice, not bloody Earls Court,' said Izzy, tying the scarf over Anna's eyes. 'Is that comfortable? Can you see anything?'

'Yes, it's fine, and all I can see is red…Venetian red!'

'How appropriate,' laughed Izzy, taking one of Anna's arms, while Will took the other.

Anna would forever remember that walk along the Merceria, and the moment when, for the first time, she stood reeling at the beauty of San Marco. She was at once possessed by it, as though it had been unveiled for her sole delight, and standing in the huge airiness of the square she had a sense of time shifting. It was as though she were part of a vast jigsaw puzzle that had been broken and dispersed across the centuries and was now slowly mending itself to become a coherent whole, as the fragments settled back into a familiar pattern. In an effort to banish the unnerving sensation she focused on the prosaic: the wheeling pigeons, the noisy crowds, the trestle tables incongruously stacked near the basilica.

'Is there going to be some huge street party?' she asked.

'What? No, of course not,' said Izzy. 'They're *passerelle* – walking on them is the only way to get around when there's *acqua alta*.'

'High water,' explained Will. 'The water in the lagoon and canals laps onto the *fondamenta* – pavements to you and me – and bubbles up through the gratings. If it weren't for the *passerelle*, we'd all get very wet feet.'

'Come on, you're joking.'

'I wish we were, it's a real pain. Quite exciting the first couple of times; then deeply inconvenient. Usually only lasts a couple of hours, but sometimes, especially when it's combined with the *sirocco* wind, the flooding's really serious.'

'It's a ridiculous way for a city to behave,' said Izzy. 'But that's Venice for you. Come on, let's get someone to take our photo with the *passerelle* in the background. I want something to remind me of Anna's street party gag.'

They were still laughing, minutes later, post photo, when a voice hailed, 'Izzy. Izzy. *Ciao!*'

Trotting towards them was a young woman dressed in a full-length suede coat, lavishly trimmed with fur at collar and cuff. She greeted Izzy with an enthusiasm bordering on rapture, and a brief conversation followed in rapid Italian. The girl turned to greet Anna, as Izzy, switching to English, said, 'This is Patrizia. One of my very best students. She's even picked up my south London accent. I'm insanely proud of her.'

'I am so pleased to meet you,' Patrizia beamed, holding out a hand encased in a soft leather glove, which Anna took in her own woolly mittened paw. 'I cannot talk long because I must meet my uncle Vittore for lunch. And first I am buying a book for him, as a thank you gift. He is giving me the usage of the Ca' Melisa for my birthday party...' She stopped. 'Oh, but Izzy, you must come. And Will and Anna. This Friday. I do hope you can.'

Izzy immediately pealed, 'Yes! We'd love to. Thank you so much.'

'Fantastic. I see you Friday. And please, absolutely no presents.' With that she drifted away, leaving a trail of perfume and a prickle of excitement.

Will was the first to speak. 'What a coup. Ca' Melisa is, to coin a phrase, an architectural gem, and with luck I'll get a guided tour.'

'And if Vittore Anzelieri is there,' said Izzy, 'I may be able to put out a few feelers for a job at the University.'

'And, you, Anna,' Will continued, 'can count yourself very lucky to be invited into such an illustrious Venetian home. Not many tourists can claim that privilege.'

'Don't call Anna a tourist!'

'We're all tourists,' said Will. 'Even those of us who've been here for years – we'll always be strangers – *foresti* – as the Venetians call us. And talking of tourists, how about a turn around the Basilica? Now's the perfect time with all that sun pouring in.'

So Izzy and Anna linked arms, and with Will leading the way, they set off towards the glowing, gaudy jewel box of a church, watched by the indifferent eyes of saints and sinners; prancing horses and winged lions.

Venice: December 1514

I was seventeen years old when I became my father's eyes; when the creeping blindness that robbed him of sight, granted me undreamt of freedom. His loss unfurled, for me, a world of colour and light: the gold and the blue, and the shifting shapes and reflections of the place that made me. For I am a child of *la Serenissima*, the most serene republic of Venice, where art and beauty reign supreme. So splendid is our city that sometimes I find myself supposing that angels, homesick for the world, must have absconded from Paradise and during their truant hours, passed divine hands over these stones we call home. There is no other explanation for such perfection on earth, and we, her people, are also much blessed. Thus, I always assumed my life would be prosperous and peaceful…until the day I realised what ailed my father. Then everything changed.

On that day, *papà* and I walked arm in arm through the hustle bustle of the Piazza, winding our way around the mountebanks and moneychangers, wig sellers and wine merchants. A troupe of tumblers was about to perform, and I was urging *papà* to watch. It was then, in the merciless winter light, that I looked into his eyes…his poor eyes. And I saw what I had hitherto refused to acknowledge; that his new spectacles did not help him see one bit. How could they? The lenses were akin to the bottle glass in our windows, thick and opaque. Their only use was to disguise the telltale milkiness that floated over the once piercing blue. But I saw through them, and through his deception. And it chilled me more than the wind screaming off the lagoon.

My father is a doctor, the best physician in Venice, with the possible exception of Jakob Solomon. Jakob is a Jew, but we are, of course, Christians. Well, I say, "of course", but living in Venice we could just as well not be. We Venetians pray to our Lord Jesus Christ and build the most beauteous and noble churches in which to glorify and praise Him, but we will happily do business with the Turk and the Jew. This city is built on trade, and if infidel gold provides some of the glister, so what? We are good Christians, but first and foremost we are Venetians. And is this to be wondered at when you consider how Pope Julius waged war against us? His League all but destroyed our Empire and threatened this very city. Venice owes nothing to the Church in Rome, but everything to the protective waters of the Lagoon, to St Mark…and to trade.

Go down to the Rialto and you will see how we trade – in silks and spices; sugar and salt; and even slaves. As a respectable woman I should not be there, for wives and daughters are hidden away, and it is more often their menfolk haggling at the meat and cheese stalls. I believe it is not so in other Christian cities, and strangers to Venice are surprised to see so few women of good character out and about.

The only time women enjoy freedom in Venice is when we are children. As little virgins we can play in the *calli* and *campi,* protected by the fact that we are too young to be possessed by any but our fathers. But after our breasts begin to bud and our monthly courses start, everything changes. Soon we must become wives; there is little else we can do. And for girls born into the nobility, dowries are so high, that only the richest families can provide for more than one or two of its daughters. The youngest – or plainest – must submit to another sort of wedlock; they become brides of Christ.

Thus, it is whispered that the convents of Venice are bawdier than the whorehouses of other cities. Some are so corrupt that the priests themselves have been known to pimp for their supposedly virgin inmates. I cannot comprehend why they take the risk, for if they are caught, the punishment is fiercesome. I remember one such man of God, who was stripped of his vestments and then heartily whipped, all the time crying upon Our Saviour to give him strength. *Papà* hurried me away from the Piazzetta before the man's torments worsened, but I hear that he was strung up by the one foot, and the crowd threw stones at him until, after much pain, he left this world…a bloody, beaten thing.

But despite such harsh punishments these crimes continue to fester, and many tiny corpses, fruits of sinful liaisons, are found floating near these sad convents. I pity those unfortunate girls and cannot find it in my heart to condemn them for seeking pleasure, and I thank God that I am not born rich.

I once asked *papà* what punishment awaited the humiliated priest in the next life and he confessed that he did not know, but that he truly believed the Almighty was more merciful than the Venetian state. Sometimes he says the strangest things. Fortunately, he says them only to me, and to Jakob. It is not wise to voice such critical observations, otherwise one's name may be scribbled on a denunciation slip and slid into the jaws of a *bocche dei leoni* – the fierce stone lions with gaping mouths that leer from the walls of our city. They say such accusations are rarely sufficient, on their own, to bring a man before the authorities, but still, it is best to be careful…

I am my father's only child. He and my *mamma* had been wed some six years when I burst into the world, but by the time her belly again grew large I was nearly eight years old. I remember the excitement and the certainty that the child would be a boy – a boy who would learn all my father's skills; who would study at the University of Padua and be a great physician too.

And indeed it was a boy child, but that child was not a healer. By refusing to enter the world headfirst he brought only death. He tore my mother apart and so much blood was spilled that she could not hang onto life. My little brother filled his lungs and screamed for milk, as she lay dying, too weak to hold him to her breast. I have never hated a thing so much as he.

As the day of his birth slipped away, she held my hand. 'Look after your brother. Be a little mother to him. Promise me.'

I nodded, but later, when she was no longer there to hear, I whispered into the night, 'Let him die too. Please, God, let him die.'

And maybe God did hear me, for my little brother's lusty cries faded to a whimper, and just days after my mother left us, he breathed his last.

I remember standing at the newly opened grave as they laid the yellow faced child next to the pitch sealed coffin of its mother. Whilst the clods of earth fell, I contemplated the punishment God would send to mortify me, for surely I was a sinner beyond forgiveness. But perhaps God is more merciful than we think, or perhaps my torments are yet to come, for although I still grieve for my mother, my life has been untroubled. Even the misfortune that has visited *papà* has been a blessing for me.

You see, if my father had not begun to lose his sight, I would most likely be married by now, or at least betrothed. But the fact is, *papà* needs me; needs me too much to let me go to another man's house. I am the only one he trusts with his secret. And he is right to be cautious, for although he has a reputation as one of the finest physicians in Venice, would his patients still consult him if they knew how little he sees?

It started by my assisting him with the preparation of tinctures and potions. Even then, he did not admit his growing infirmity but made out that he allowed me to measure the grains and liquids because he knew it would interest me. And it did, for I longed to learn the secrets of his profession. But he had never before thought to tutor me, as he would have done had I been a boy. So after my first joy at being permitted to assist him, I began to question his motives. Also, other incidents had begun to arouse my suspicions.

My father is a methodical man, neither clumsy nor careless, but he started to knock things over, and sometimes he would overfill his glass, so that the contents spilled onto the table. He became agitated if I did not replace jars in exactly the place from where I had taken them. Then, on that winter's morning in the Piazza, my keen eyes looked into his fading ones, and I saw everything…

I was aware of others who suffered this affliction, but they were much older than *papà*. Why should he suffer thus when his years were still so few? Was this, at last, the punishment I deserved? Because of my transgressions, was God hurting the person I loved most? I had no idea how wealthy my father was. We are *cittidani*, which means our names are engraved in the city's Silver Book, but that would not fill our bellies or warm us in winter. As well as the cruelty of his blindness, perhaps we were also facing destitution.

The next time he asked for my assistance, I first had to complete some household chores, so was a little delayed in joining him. Then, as I made my way to the place at the top of our house where he keeps his workshop, I heard what sounded like a muffled sob. When I pushed open the door, I saw *papà* slumped over the worktable, his head resting on his arms, whilst the contents of an upturned vessel dripped onto the floor.

I made no sound, but my little dog, Cesare, scampered off and rising onto his haunches, laid a paw on my father's thigh, as if in comfort.

Startled by Cesare's touch, *papà* looked up. The room had darkened, so I do not know how he read my expression, but he said, 'I see you have guessed my secret, Ginevra.'

'For how long?' I asked, kneeling by his side.

He gazed past me, ruffling Cesare's spiky fur. 'Many months, but only in the past few weeks has it hindered me.'

'What is the cause?'

'Part of my ailment is simply age. Although I grant you, I am young to be afflicted. But there is something more, I fear. The mistiness through which I now view the world is, of late, combined with great gaps of…of nothingness, as if the object, or person, I know my sight should be fixed upon has been torn away, and I am looking at a blank.'

'Will it worsen?'

'I fear so. And when that happens I do not know if I will be able to see patients sufficiently to identify their ills. I rely upon other senses of course, touch and smell, and what they tell me. But think how little they will trust my judgement when they realise that I am all but blind.'

'But if someone were to describe to you what you cannot see, surely that would mean you could make a diagnosis?'

'Possibly,' he conceded. 'But I believe they would still lose faith, and whom could I trust to keep my secret? It would be common knowledge in days.'

This was true; gossip steals its way through our Venetian *calli* like the stink from a rotten egg.

33

We both fell silent. My father lost in his thoughts, and I pondering the best way to tell him of the idea that had presented itself to me. It was so outrageous that I could barely bring myself to speak, but his next words gave me no choice.

'Ginevra, you must not worry. I am not a rich man, but I have never been extravagant and over the years I have saved. There are sufficient funds to keep me for the rest of my days, and to provide you with a dowry appropriate to your station.'

I could not help but recoil from the hand he laid upon my arm. The world was tumbling about our ears, yet he thought my only concern was my dowry. I did not know whether to laugh or weep that he knew me so little. Had he not guessed that I had no wish to marry? I know what happens between a man and a woman, and it seems to me that it is not something so very fine. And what is the end result of that union? A child. Well, I had seen what childbirth can do and if there was any other way for me to live I wanted none of marriage. Even a convent might be preferable. But if I possibly could, I intended to avoid both.

'My dear,' he continued. 'I do believe it is time for you to wed. What do you think to Bartolo Artuzzi's boy?'

I wanted to say that I thought nothing of him: that I thought him plain and dull, and that he looked at me with eyes that belonged to a spaniel rather than a man. Instead I said, 'No doubt he will make an excellent pharmacist one day. And I am sure he will be a good husband and father, but I do not want to be his wife.' I took his hands in mine. '*Papà*, you need me. I cannot leave you.'

'But you must,' he said. 'I will not live forever, my dear. And when I am gone what will become of you? Unless she is financially secure in her own right, a woman needs a man to protect and provide for her. I am sorry, but if I no longer receive an income, I will not be able to leave enough for you to be independent.'

'The answer is simple, *papà*. You must continue working!'

'Ginevra, I have just explained that without my sight no one will want me as their physician.'

'They will, because I know someone who will accompany you and who will never, never betray your secret.'

'Who?'

'Me, *papà*. Me!'

He shook his head and had our situation not been so tragic, I believe he would have laughed. 'You are a good and brave girl but what you suggest is impossible. It would be difficult enough with my female patients, but how do you think men would react if a woman examined them. And I certainly could not expose you to such immodest sights.'

34

'But in the countryside where there are no doctors, people, men as well, consult wise women.' I could not remember where I had heard this, but I was sure of its truth.

'This is not the country, Ginevra. This is Venice. And such women are matrons. I could take a young man with me, but not a maid.' His voice trailed off, and I knew he was thinking of his son, my long dead brother; the child I had wished dead.

Then suddenly the guilt that had slept for so many years reared up, like one of the fiends from Hell that torture poor souls in pictures of the Last Judgement. I must have made some desperate sound, for *papà* asked if I was well, and Cesare, sensing my distress, ran from the corner of the room where he had been snuffling for spiders, and jumped onto my lap.

I shook my head, trying to banish the awful thoughts, only able to rock back and forth, hugging my little dog for comfort. When I could speak, my voice was a hoarse whisper. 'It is all my fault.'

And so I told him. The secret so heinous, I had never been able to speak of it, even in the confessional: how I had wished a tiny baby dead, and how God had heard me. When I finished, my father said nothing. It was like the hush before thunder shakes the earth. He has never raised his hand to me, but I thought perhaps now he might strike, so when he half rose from his chair, I flinched in anticipation of the blow.

But there was no blow. His arms wrapped around my shoulders and he pulled me towards him, so that my head rested in the warm fustian of his robe. I could hear the beat of his heart. God may not have forgiven me but I knew that *papà* had. The realisation made me sob with relief. He let me weep awhile, then gently pushed me away and peered into my drenched face.

'Oh, my poor child. You have borne the burden of guilt all these years? And such senseless guilt. Nothing you felt about little Adriano would have made any difference. Ginevra, there is much about Our Father I do not understand, but I do think that our prayers, noble or base, are sometimes totally unheard. If prayer could move God to give or take life, I promise you, the strength of my prayers would have preserved the lives of both your mother and Adriano. God listened to neither you nor me. You bear no responsibility.'

But I was not so easily comforted, and still clinging to my excruciating guilt, I persisted, 'But it was a wicked thing to wish, was it not?'

'Perhaps. But you are not the only child to have felt so. You were simply unfortunate in that it seemed your prayers were answered. Do not forget, my own mother died giving birth to Carlo.'

My uncle Carlo, his wife, Cecilia, and their two children had all perished in a plague that swept through Venice nearly five years ago. We had loved them dearly and the pain of their loss was still great.

'I am going to tell you something I have never told anyone,' said my father, his voice lowered to a confessionary whisper. 'When my mother died and I saw Carlo screaming in his cradle, I wished him dead. Like you, I begged God to take him, but I was fortunate, he lived and became my greatest friend. Even so, I used to sometimes remember for what I had prayed, and be terrified that he would die.'

At first I did not dare speak, but eventually I said it. 'But, *papà*, he did die.'

'Yes, but from the plague, not because of a child's prayers. I grant you, many people believe plague is a punishment sent by God, but I am not so sure. And I am not so conceited to think that God would send a pestilence for the sole purpose of punishing me.' Then his voice softened and he asked, 'Do you feel reassured now?'

'If only I was a boy. Then I could accompany you. I am sorry.'

'For what?'

'For being born a girl, a useless burden.'

'Gina, do not be sorry for who you are. You are all the sons I could ever wish for. I would not exchange you, my daughter, for a whole tribe of boys.'

I was not sure if I really believed him, but he sounded so sincere that I laughed with delight. Then an idea sprang into my mind, so audacious that I felt the words would burn my mouth unless I spoke them.

'I am more than common tall. Let me dress as a boy. You could say I am your nephew, come from Verona.'

'Are you quite mad? You would fool no one.'

'Oh, I think I would.' I leapt up, pressing my hands to my bosom, or to what passes for one, for I am almost as flat chested as a youth. 'Some binding here, and I could cut my hair.'

It was inevitable that he would shy away from the suggestion. Whilst it is not unusual in Venice to see females garbed as men, it is something no respectable woman would do. Those who resort to such an exhibition are courtesans, and they do it to display their wares all the better. Sometimes they dress as a youth: sometimes in gowns that are split, or cut short at the front, so their customers can see their pretty legs encased in brightly coloured hose, and no doubt imagine all the better what is to be found at the top of those legs.

Hoping *papà* was not thinking of such women, I murmured, 'I would dress modestly,' and dropping my voice, added, 'And I can speak very low if need be.'

He replied with just the one word, 'No.'

But I, who knew him so well, sensed the smallest of hesitations, and prayed that behind his gritty pronouncement there was a soft heart that might, in time, relent.

36

A Cradle

Ca' Melisa, the venue for Patrizia's party, teetered on one of the long *rii* that snaked through Cannaregio. Compared to many patrician residences it was of modest proportions, and perhaps that was why no one had ever sought to call it a *palazzo*. According to Will, "*Ca*", meaning house, and "*Palazzo*", were now interchangeable, their usage having more to do with the self-aggrandisement of owners than the buildings. But at the time of Ca' Melisa's construction there was only the one palace in Venice – that of the Doge; every other residence would have been deemed a house.

The day after meeting Patrizia, Will and Anna stood before its exquisite façade. It was late afternoon and although the skies were gravid with rain, its rosy brickwork lent warmth to the wintry backdrop. From the *fondamenta* they watched the rising waters of the *rio* lap against its crumbling underbelly – a salty kiss of death insidiously eating into its vulnerable old bones.

'When was it built?' asked Anna.

'Oh…a long, long time ago. It's been added to over the years, but see the watergate…the carvings are Byzantine, so I reckon its been here since Marco Polo's time.'

'Which was?'

'About seven hundred years ago. This part of Venice was developed later than the rest of the city, so the houses on either side almost certainly wouldn't have existed then. It would have stood alone on its own little island, looking out onto reed banks and the lagoon. Even now, it's still detached, which is unusual. Just look at…' And Will reeled off a list of architectural terms: Venetian Gothic, five-light polifora windows, quatrefoil traceries, ogee arches. His eulogies, however, were quite superfluous. Anna's entranced eyes told her just how very special this place was.

While the ground floor was solid, almost fortress like, with only the watergate and two barred windows punctuating the brickwork, everything above was a riot of invention. There was a profusion of balconies, not just on the building's façade, but also at its corners. They hung, like filigree earrings, and were so finely and intricately carved that they seemed fashioned out of thick, white lace, rather than marble. Their delicate spindles, in colours borrowed from a sweet shop, supported creamy balustrades on which cavorted prides of stone lions, their once belligerent faces rubbed into benevolence by the hands of time.

'Shame about the fourth floor,' said Will, reverting to comprehensible language.

'What's wrong with it?' She lifted her eyes to where hardly visible windows winked behind a long terrace.

'It's a much later addition. Lots of *palazzi* have them. Expertly done, I admit, but it spoils the proportions, don't you think? Makes it too tall.'

Anna imagined those rooms, intimate and low-ceilinged, looking out to the pearly lagoon and distant mountains. 'Seems fine to me, Will. It must be lovely up there. Think of the views.'

'I suppose so,' he conceded. 'Hey, don't mind me. I'm too much of a purist for my own good.'

'The upkeep must be phenomenal.'

'God, yes. The Anzelieris used to be very wealthy – American money apparently. They bought the house at the turn of the century from the Sartorani family. On some maps it's still called Ca' Sartorani.'

'So they're not rich any more, the Anzelieris?'

'Well, it's all comparative, isn't it? But Patrizia's uncle Vittore certainly doesn't sit around on his backside all day. When he's not lecturing at Ca' Foscari – that's the University – he's writing books about the city. And they use Ca' Melisa as the base for art history holidays. His wife, Rosina, is in charge of the catering. The food's supposed to be out of this world.'

Even as they watched, someone in the house decided that night had won its battle over day, and light flooded from the five arched windows of the first floor, paddling onto the canal below.

Conscious that they were staring into another person's home, Will took Anna's arm. 'Come on, let's go and warm up with a rum punch. Plenty of time to see more of Ca' Melisa on Friday.'

On the night of the party, the two women had spent much of the afternoon, as Will put it, titivating. Anna had not anticipated attending any formal events, but at the last moment had packed a flimsy chiffon bolero peppered with sequins. She had intended to team this with a black camisole and trousers, but Izzy persuaded her to wear it over one of her own dresses, a stretchy black velvet number, that on Izzy modestly brushed her knees, but when worn by Anna was a great deal more revealing. In London she would never have countenanced such a short skirt. To complete the ensemble, Izzy had talked her into buying a pair of new shoes from a little shop by the Rialto. Unused to the value of *lire,* Anna later realised they had cost nearly a week's salary. Still, they were rather beautiful, made from soft patent leather with a very high heel.

'I don't know if Chris will approve,' she mused, teetering before the looking glass. 'Wearing these, I'll be nearly as tall as him.'

In reply Izzy snorted, but then softened. 'If you want to phone him, feel free anytime.'

Anna had contacted Chris just once to assure him of her safe arrival and since then had been surprised by how little she missed him. It made her feel slightly guilty.

'I'll call tomorrow. Then I can tell him all about the party.'

'I'm sure he'll approve of you mixing with all these nobs…even if they are Johnny Foreigner.'

Anna ignored the bait. She had reconciled herself to Izzy's dislike of Chris, knowing it largely stemmed from his dismissing her long sojourn in Venice as "playing at life", because she had failed to forge a "proper career". Izzy, in retaliation, condemned him as a parasitic moneymaker, feeding on people's misfortune or greed.

Chris was due to join Anna for a long weekend at the end of her stay, after which she would fly back with him. She was now anticipating his arrival with mixed feelings, hoping the antipathy that existed between him and Izzy did not result in another acrimonious confrontation.

'Do you think Chris would like to take us all out for a slap-up meal?' said Izzy. 'Somewhere really expensive.'

'You little gold-digger,' scolded Anna.

'Excuse me! You're the one with the moneybags boyfriend. Will's as poor as a church mouse. Right, let's have a quick drink to fortify ourselves before we brave the elements.'

Ca' Melisa was so situated that it was not worth taking a *vaporetto*, so they made the journey by foot, turning onto the Lista di Spagna and past the church of San Geremia, home to the desiccated remains of St Lucy. Here she lay, in a glass coffin, her face hidden behind a shimmering silver mask, finally at rest after being moved from her titular church, long since demolished to make way for the railway station.

After crossing over the end of the Cannaregio Canal, they progressed along the bright curve of the shop lined rio terra Leonardo, where men chattered together outside smoky bars; dogs barked; market stall-holders called to each other, and women bargained for the ingredients of their evening meal. Then abruptly, they entered the labyrinth of northern Cannaregio. Here lay another world, hushed and empty, inhabited by dark shadows and skulking cats.

The winter skies were clear and star studded; the night so cold that their breath hung heavy on the air. Trying to forget her frozen knees, Anna concentrated on Izzy's chatter.

'I suppose all Patrizia's cousins will be there,' she said, as they threaded their way into a *calle*, so narrow that they had to walk single file. 'And Raffi, of course – Vittore's nephew. Vittore and Rosina don't have any kids of their own, but they've brought Raffi up as their son.'

'Why's that? Did his parents die?'

'Suppose so. Patrizia's never said, and I don't like to ask. But he doesn't live at Ca' Melisa anymore; he's got a place of his own, right by the Arsenale...'

'Arsenal?'

'The site of Venice's shipbuilding industry,' said Will. 'At the height of Venetian power...'

'Raffi's an architect.' Izzy switched the subject back. 'A very clever boy, by all accounts. Oh, and that reminds me, Will, I saw Vittore's new book on Cima da Conegliano today, hot off the press.'

'Cima? Didn't he paint that lovely Nativity you showed me?' asked Anna, proud of recalling the artist's name.

'That's right, well remembered. Vittore's the world expert on Cima,' said Will, as they stopped before a *portone* set into the alley wall. It was topped with a semi-circle of frosted glass, reinforced by an ornate metal grill, through which light filtered, together with the sound of laughter and soft music. Beside the door, embedded in the crumbling wall was just the one bell, indicating that a single family occupied the building.

'Well, here we are,' said Izzy, leaning on the bell. 'Isn't it a shame it's not like the olden days, when we'd have arrived by *gondola*, all wrapped up in our furs?'

The door sprang open and they stepped into a spacious courtyard garden. Suspended from trees, coloured glass lanterns swayed like ripe fruit, casting blushing shadows over sleeping flowerbeds and shivering marble statues. The house lay to their left, with the entrance to the first floor accessed by an external staircase that hugged the inside wall of the *calle*. This led onto a balcony, bathed in light spilling from floor length windows. At that moment, Patrizia appeared, resplendent in crimson velvet. She beckoned them to join her. 'Ciao, welcome. Please to come inside and be warm.'

Accepting her invitation, they bounded up the stairs and entered a room that Anna realised ran the entire depth of the house, for facing them were the five arched windows that she and Will had seen from the *fondamenta*. For a moment, she was dazzled by her surroundings: it was as though they had stepped into a masked ball. The revellers' clothes, although conventionally fashionable, were rainbow bright, creating a shifting kaleidoscope of colour, as exotic as a souk. Vast mirrors, tarnished and age spotted, reflected this radiance again and again into hazy infinity, while shadows, cast from haphazardly scattered nightlights, trembled and danced on the walls. The illumination was supplemented from above by two huge, but elegant chandeliers, whose delicate twists of calla lilies lifted or dipped, their graceful heads, as multitudes of crystal droplets, hanging from their stems, stirred and glinted like frozen raindrops.

Through wide double doors lay the dining room. Here stood a long table draped with white cloths on which was spread an edible tapestry. Glistening green and black olives; creamy salt cod heaped onto squares of bright yellow polenta; robust little meatballs; tangy slivers of *grana* cheese; twirls of salami and an array of unidentifiable pink, white and coral seafood, all presided over by a small dumpling of a woman with a radiantly pretty face.

'That's Rosina, Patrizia's aunt, the lady of the house, and a brilliant cook. She organises all the grub for the posh holidays,' whispered Izzy as someone handed them flutes of ice cold *prosecco*. 'God, this is good. Probably from the family vineyard. I think this is going to be an excellent party.'

Izzy's prediction was correct, and the *prosecco* slipped down and the hours slipped by. At some point Will disappeared, having persuaded one of Patrizia's cousins to give him a guided tour of Ca' Melisa. Izzy meanwhile, with Anna in tow, happily meandered, until tired and a little tipsy, she draped herself over a chaise longue and waited for people to come to her. Anna perched on the few unoccupied inches, and even though most of the conversations were conducted in Italian she felt at ease, listening and watching. Then she became aware of a man gazing in their direction.

At first she assumed that Izzy was the object of his interest, but when their eyes met for the third time, she whispered, 'Don't look now, but there's a guy over there who keeps staring at me. I thought it was my imagination but...'

'My God, you've pulled! I knew I shouldn't have lent you that dress.'

'Pulled? I don't think so, it's not that sort of stare. He looks more shocked than anything, as though he can't quite believe what he's seeing. I know this skirt is short but I didn't think I looked that outrageous. Izzy, I told you not to look!'

'How am I supposed to know who you're talking about if I don't? Ah, I take it you mean the silver haired fox, not the poser in the tight red jeans? He's one of my pupils – red jeans that is. I teach him to say useless things in English, and he schools me in the invaluable art of swearing in Venetian. His name's actually Carlo

41

Felice but everyone calls him Carlo *Faràle*. *Faràle*'s Venetian for spider. The red jeans are his party dress, but he normally wears all black, so with those long thin legs he looks just like a spider. But *signor* Fox, he's Patrizia's uncle Vittore, our esteemed host. Now, I'm going to have a chat with Spido because rumour has it that he's just become very friendly, and I mean friendly, with a senior member of staff at the University, a man to whom I need introducing.'

'Oh God, Izzy. He's coming over.'

'So he is! I'm sure his intentions are entirely honourable. His wife is here, after all. Good luck.'

'Don't you dare leave me. I won't understand a word he says if you aren't here to translate.'

'Oh, don't worry about that,' Izzy beamed. 'He speaks better English than we do. *Ciao carissima.*' And she was gone, waving happily to Carlo *Faràle*, eager to extend her already extensive collection of profanities.

Anna considered fleeing the room, but before she could do so, the man she now knew to be Vittore Anzelieri was at her side.

'Did I do something to frighten your friend?' he asked with a small smile, seating himself next to her.

From a distance his appearance had been a little intimidating. Tall and very slender with a shock of swept back grey hair, his high cheekbones and aquiline nose gave him the air of a Venetian patriarch gazing haughtily from a portrait of yesteryear. Yet, close to, his eyes were warm and gentle, surrounded by a light tracery of laughter lines.

'No, no, she needed to speak to…' Anna gestured to where Izzy and Carlo were giggling.

'I gather, *signorina* Anna, that you are from London. Please allow me to introduce myself. I am Vittore Anzelieri and I am delighted to welcome you to Ca' Melisa.'

'And I'm delighted to be here,' Anna said, as he took her hand, his lips not quite brushing its surface.

'And what do you think of our little city? After London it must feel quite tiny?'

Anna drew breath, searching for the right words. 'You can't really compare them, they're so different, but I think Venice is the most beautiful, amazing place I've ever been to. Not that I've been to many places, but…' She paused, struggling to describe her feelings without resorting to banal clichés, '…it's as though it's been always waiting for me. I keep feeling I've been here before, seen things before. This house for instance, the first time I saw it…'

'Ah, déjà vu?'

'Not quite. It's not as…as elusive as déjà vu. What I've been experiencing seems natural, almost ordinary, which in itself is strange. Sorry, I'm not making much sense.'

He did not reply but held her gaze, a strange expression in his grey eyes. Then he said, 'Tell me, do you like paintings? Our Venetian painters that is?'

'Yes, of course. But I don't really know anything about art.'

'Who does? I have spent a lifetime studying the work of our forefathers, but sometimes I look at a painting and know that I will never be able to pluck out the heart of its mystery.'

'But there must be very little that you don't understand. World expert is how you were described to me on Cima da Con…' She stumbled over the unfamiliar name.

'Conegliano,' he interjected. 'People are kind enough to say so, but in the world of art, especially of Old Masters, one is always making discoveries. Something as apparently insignificant as an ancient receipt hidden in a forgotten archive can blast apart all the theories accepted to date; repudiate a painting's provenance and monetary worth. And so, history constantly reinvents itself. In a hundred, even fifty years, my work will have been superseded, or even discredited. But at least I will not be here to experience the embarrassment.' He paused. 'May I ask you another question, Anna? Do you have any Italian blood?'

With her dark hair and olive skin, Anna had been asked the same thing more than once in the last few days.

'Not a drop that I'm aware of,' she said. 'All my family are English, apart from my father's mother. I never knew her I'm afraid; she died before I was born, but she was from a little place outside Bruges. My grandfather met her there just after the First World War, and brought her back to England, which created a bit of a scandal, as he was already engaged to another girl.'

'Ah, the occasional family scandal is a healthy thing. It provides the descendants with a little impunity if they, themselves, transgress. We Anzelieri have many. Perhaps you would like to hear them? But first, I wish to show you something that you may find even more interesting. Please, come with me.'

Before Anna could reply, he took her arm. As he led her from the room, she caught a glimpse of Izzy, eyes and mouth wide with surprise.

They left by one of the single doors that punctuated the long walls of the *sala* and ascended flight after flight of narrow stairs. When Anna guessed they had reached the top floor, Vittore flung open a door and flicked on a light switch. The room was scholarly rather than luxurious, the furniture being limited to two single beds with simply carved headboards, an *armadio*, a writing desk and a couple of easy chairs. Books provided the only decorative touch, together with a profusion of paintings. A clock ticked, and white muslin curtains stirred, very slightly.

'This is one of our guest rooms now, but it used to be Raffi's – my nephew. It still shocks me to see it so tidy. When he came to live with us, we let him have whatever room he desired for his own, and this was the one he chose. Partly, I think, because this was here.'

And turning, he indicated a painting, his hand outstretched, almost in a gesture of benediction. The wooden panel was unprotected by glass and, even to Anna's inexperienced eye, clearly very old.

'You mentioned Bruges. That is where I bought it. Have you any idea what it might be? The shape should give you a clue.'

Time shudders, then halts; and in those frozen moments Anna gazes at the picture – quite transfixed. Its base is straight, the top curved and significantly wider. She has never seen it before, but like so much in Venice it has a disquieting familiarity. A young woman kneels before a crib in which a baby lies. Next to her is a shepherd. On the other side of the crib stand an angel and a small boy. A white and sandy coloured dog sits at their feet. The boy holds a line from which dangles a single, silver fish.

Eventually, Vittore broke the silence. 'Well?'

Anna turned and with absolute certainty replied, 'It's the end of a cradle, isn't it?'

'Correct, bravo!'

'I've seen it before. Well, not IT. But something very similar. In a church?'

'Yes. Cima's Adoration of the Shepherds in the Carmini. Admittedly, here, some of the figures have been eliminated and the placement of others modified, but I find it inconceivable that the painter did not know the Carmini altarpiece. This is roughly painted but it has a vitality and sweetness that makes me think it could only be the work of a very young man with little formal training.'

'Perhaps it was someone working in Cima's workshop,' Anna suggested, showing off the knowledge she had acquired from Will.

'Possibly, but here is the strange thing. I had it analysed and the wood and pigments all point to it being Northern European. But the composition, the features of the Virgin's face and gown are pure Venetian. Also, if you look very carefully you will see a date, 1520. Three years after Cima died, so it is unlikely the young man who painted this was his pupil.'

'Or young woman?' She registered the surprise on his face, but somehow convinced that her words could be true, continued, 'Why not? I know women artists were few and far between but there were some, weren't there? Will was telling me about one – the daughter of someone really famous, I've forgotten who. She dressed as a boy so she could have access to her father's workshop…'

'Ah, Marietta,' said Vittore. 'The daughter of Tintoretto. They called her La Tintoretta. She lived and worked just a few minutes from here, although I imagine the story of her cross-dressing is a myth. Tintoretto was, by all accounts, an irascible old fellow, so if he had wanted his daughter in his workshop I do not believe anyone would have dared object. And yes, she was very talented, especially as a portraitist. She could have travelled the courts of Europe to paint monarchs and princes, but her father insisted she remain at his side. He did not permit her to marry until she was nearly thirty, a decision I daresay he regretted.'

'Why, what happened?'

'She died in childbirth; aged thirty-four. Her gravestone is in the Church of Madonna dell'Orto. You know, I always think that if I had had a daughter I would have named her Marietta.'

They both fell silent, contemplating the long dead woman whose talent had been extinguished so many years ago, and whose mortal remains lay beneath the floor of a great, cold church.

'I do believe I can detect her hand in some of Tintoretto's later works,' Vittore eventually said. 'And even though her contribution was never officially acknowledged, at least she was allowed to develop her talent. You see, women were barred from art academies, and although girls from the nobility received drawing lessons, and nuns produced illuminated manuscripts, that was the extent of female opportunity.'

'What a waste. Was it the same everywhere?'

'Fortunately not. In Bruges, for example, where I found this cradle, the records of the Guild of St Luke, which was the artists' guild, show that a significant number of its members were women. So perhaps you are right, Anna. Intuition, especially feminine intuition, is very powerful, and if you are so certain that it was painted by a woman, perhaps it was. But I am afraid we will never know.'

'Never know what, *zio*?' a voice asked. It was a voice, soft and low, with just a hint of Italian accent, tinged by the same transatlantic cadence that Anna had detected in Vittore's speech patterns.

They both started at the sound and turning, Anna saw a young man standing in the doorway. From his relaxed stance – he leant against the frame, his arms loosely folded, one leg crossed in front of the other – she suspected he had been there a few moments.

When, in months, or even years ahead, Anna recalled her first impression of Raffaele Anzelieri, she always remembered that, despite the added inches lent by

45

her new shoes, she had to lift her face in order to meet his eyes. He did not immediately smile and in the seconds before he did so, she experienced an irresistible urge to raise a finger to his mouth and trace the line of his upper lip. Perhaps she did begin to lift her hand, for the next moment he had taken it in his and held it firmly in a gesture both formal and warm.

'Anna, my dear, this is my nephew, Raffi, who is supposed to be entertaining clients, but has presumably managed to slip away to grace us with his company. Raffi, this is Anna, and as first impressions are so important, tell me, does she not remind you of someone?'

The long moments that ensued, during which Raffi studied Anna's face, meant that she, likewise, could gaze without inhibition. His wide apart eyes were a clear, pale hazel above high cheekbones, giving him a slightly Slavonic appearance. He wore his light brown hair brushed back from his forehead; thick and glossy, it fell in soft waves, just long enough to curl over the back of his collar. His jaw, though strong, tapered to a surprisingly delicate chin, and although his nose hinted at the aquiline, it was not prominent and was slightly biased to one side. As his face broke into a lop-sided smile, Anna noticed that his teeth, though well-shaped, were slightly crooked. The sight of these small imperfections unaccountably plucked at what the fanciful would call her heartstrings. It was a face, at once strong and sensitive, far from perfect but one that Anna felt she could look upon for a long, long time.

Raffi glanced back to his uncle, shrugging his shoulders, obviously nonplussed. Vittore made a small clicking sound in frustration at his nephew's lack of perspicacity. 'Anna, turn your head towards me. Yes…like that. Now look again, Raffi.'

Anna was beginning to feel a little uncomfortable, when, out of the corner of her eye, she saw both surprise and recognition flash across Raffi's face. He opened his mouth to speak, but Vittore silenced him with a swift gesture.

'Please do not tell her. I do so wish it to be a surprise. Anna, I would very much like to introduce you to someone. How much longer are you in Venice?'

'Till a week on Sunday.'

'Excellent. Perhaps you could come here on Tuesday morning at eleven-thirty. I promise that the meeting will not take long and afterwards I hope that you will join me for lunch. And you too, Raffi, if you can?'

'Possibly. I'll have to check my diary. But, *zio*, the party's breaking up. Everyone's beginning to leave.'

'Oh, how remiss of me,' exclaimed Vittore, clapping a hand to his chest in a gesture of contrition, but not sounding in the least contrite. 'I must bid farewell to all these beautiful young people.' And he headed towards the door, abandoning

Anna and Raffi, but then turned and fixing them with an expression both amused and intrigued, said softly, 'Well, *ragazzi*, come along. Or are you going to stay here all night, gazing into each other's eyes?'

With no choice but to scurry after him, they descended the stairs and Raffi whispered, 'I do apologise on behalf of my uncle. He loves a little drama, but please don't be alarmed about this "meeting". I'm sure you'll enjoy it, and I do hope I can be there.'

'I hope so too,' said Anna with more coolness than she felt. And then, as they re-entered the *sala*, their brief moment of intimacy was gone, engulfed by the party hubbub.

Izzy immediately sashayed towards them, flashing her best 24-carat smile at Vittore. '*Dottore*,' she cooed, the slight slur in her voice probably only evident to Anna and Will. 'I thought you'd kidnapped my friend!'

'No, indeed not, *signorina*…?'

'Jackson. Isabelle Jackson, but Izzy to my friends. Anna's staying with me.' Izzy proffered her hand which Vittore took with due deference.

'I am charmed to meet you,' he said, and after being introduced to Will, continued, 'Anna has done me the honour of agreeing to lunch with me next Tuesday. Perhaps you could both join us?'

Izzy's eyes widened. 'I'd love to. As it happens I'm free on Tuesday, and I'm sure Will can be too.'

'Excellent. I will look forward to seeing you. But now, if you will forgive me, I must make my goodbyes elsewhere. Goodnight.' And he was gone.

'I too must say goodbye,' apologised Raffi, helping Anna into her coat. 'I hope I can join you all on Tuesday, but if not, it's been delightful to meet you, Anna, and perhaps our paths will cross again on your next visit to Venice. I'm sure there will be a next visit.'

Then he too joined the crowd of departing guests, moving amongst them with a loose-limbed easy grace.

Having departed Ca' Melisa, Izzy was no longer obliged to keep up the appearance of sobriety, and whooped and giggled all the way home, as she insisted on hearing again and again the details of Anna's encounter with Vittore. The entire city seemed to be sleeping, so there were few witnesses to her increasingly extravagant theories as to the identity of the person to whom Anna was to be introduced.

By the time Izzy tottered into her bedroom, she appeared to have, at last, exhausted the subject, but later, as Anna drifted into sleep, a small tap-tap broke the silence and Izzy's face peered round the door.

'Sorry to disturb you. Will's out for the count, but I can't sleep. Every time I close my eyes the room spins round. Christ, it's cold! Can I come and cuddle up?'

Without waiting for an answer, she dived under the duvet, her feet like blocks of ice.

'Well, well,' she mumbled, after making herself comfortable. 'Who'd have thought it. A date with Vittore Anzelieri.'

Feeling rather more sober than she had at the party, Anna was beginning to experience misgivings about her "date". Why should this urbane Venetian wish to be friends with her? An English tourist; a friend of a friend, in a borrowed, too short dress.

'Does he often do this?' she asked. 'Pick up – no, that's the wrong word. Adopt complete strangers?'

'Dunno. But I do know that he seems a genuinely nice man. Manages to keep his head above the Machiavellian politics of Ca' Foscari; doesn't flirt with his students, and is devoted to his wife. A real gent.'

'And what about Raffi?'

'Ah – the lovely Raffi. Has he set your heart a-flutter?'

'Not in the least,' Anna lied. 'Anyway, I wouldn't describe him as lovely.'

'Oh, I don't know. I think he is rather – in an unshowy, boy next-door sort of way. Not that he knows it, which is part of his charm. Most Italian men think they're God's gift, even if they look like the back end of a *vaporetto*. Sadly, however, he is taken, with a capital T. He's been with the same girl, on and off, for ages. Actually, I'm surprised she wasn't there tonight, making sure no one else got her paws on him. What's more, her daddy is a very senior *carabiniari* officer, so no flirting with Raffi, or you'll find yourself in jail, my girl.'

'You seem to know an awful lot about them all.'

'Yeah, well, Venice is like a village. It's really quite tiny, so you do get to know other people's business. A girl I used to work with got herself a job at the University, and she tells me all the Ca' Foscari gossip. Patrizia, who for some reason thinks I'm her best friend, is Raffi's cousin. Spido is Patrizia's gay confidante – except he knows less about confidentiality than quantum physics. And me, well I just love gossip, and if they want to tell me, I'm not going to stop 'em. Anyway, I'm feeling a bit better, so I'm going to shut my eyes and hope that God loves me enough not to give me a hangover. Sweet dreams, precious.'

Stopping the Clocks

The only telephone in Izzy's flat was in the bedroom, so it was Will who broke the news next morning.

Slightly hung over, Anna found herself dragged from a place of sweet dreams to the hard reality of a nightmare conversation with Millie. Hugh had complained of acute pains earlier in the week and was now in hospital. He had, at first, asked Millie not to contact Anna, but had relented when his consultant decided to operate on Monday.

'I knew you would never forgive me if…if anything happened and I'd not told you,' whispered Millie in a voice hoarse from stress.

'I'll be home as soon as I can,' promised Anna. 'Tell him I love him, and I'm on my way.'

She put the phone down, turning to Izzy who had crept after her, and now stood shivering in her inadequate nightdress, her eyes brimming with tears.

'I need to get back. How do I change my ticket? Go to the airport and just hope I can get on a flight? Oh, God, I better ring Chris.'

She heard her voice rising to a discordant yowl. If she flew back today she would be able to spend Sunday with Hugh. She needed that quiet time to sit with him; to give him the bottle of grappa she had chosen. He would not be able to drink any, but the sight of the clear liquid in the delicate bottle would please him, she knew.

'Izzy, help Anna pack.' Will appeared. 'Anna, give me your passport and ticket. One of my students works in Thomas Cook's. With a bit of luck she'll be on duty and I can see about a flight. What's the maximum you can afford?'

'Anything…whatever it costs. What about paying them?'

Will waved a chequebook. 'I should have enough in my account. If not, I'll offer her my body. I've always suspected she fancies me.'

In just over an hour Will was back with a set of revised travel documents, and Anna began to feel less like a small rodent peddling on a wheel. Two hours later they boarded a bus at the Piazzale Roma and even in her distraught state she marvelled at the shocking transition from magical city to fume filled car park. As they sped along the causeway bridge, she did not turn to see Venice slip out of sight. When she remembered to look, it was too late; the city had vanished. She wondered if she would ever return; Venice, she felt, already belonged to another, carefree existence.

Waiting in the airport's sparse check in area for her flight to be called, Anna suddenly remembered Vittore Anzelieri. Now she would never meet the person to whom he so wanted to introduce her. 'You will let Vittore know what's happened?'

'Of course,' said Izzy. 'I'll pop round this evening. But you'll be back in no time. I'm sure your dad'll be fine, and everything'll be all right.'

But everything was not all right. The operation confirmed everyone's worse fears. The disease had triumphed, spreading so relentlessly that it would be only a matter of weeks before Hugh met that most unassailable of opponents. There was nothing medical science could do in the face of such a complete victory, but to try and keep pain at bay.

Hugh came home to the house in which he had been born, and knowing that he would probably die here seemed to give him comfort. It had surprised Anna and Millie that he did not rage against the dying of the light, but had met the news of his death sentence with a weary stoicism.

At first he was able to make short excursions. Anna would drive him to Richmond Park to see the deer flitting through the undergrowth, and sometimes he could manage a short walk by the Thames, watching rowers, in the full bloom of youth, pit themselves against the immutable river. But very soon his world was reduced to the confines of his house and then to the four walls of his bedroom. A room that had witnessed love and pleasure was now given over to the paraphernalia of dying. Nurses came in to supervise the inevitable process, three times a day, as regular as the breakfast, lunch and dinner that no one cared to eat.

During the final days, Hugh drifted into unconsciousness, borne aloft on a sea of morphine, but even so, his hands moved constantly, plucking at the bedclothes, intent on a task that only existed in the dark recesses of his mind, a mind that was now driven by the skewed bio-chemistry of his failing body.

Then, one wind-torn evening, towards the end of March, he opened his eyes and said in a delighted whisper, 'Guy,' focussing on Anna's face for the first time in days.

The breezy bright nurse swung round. 'No dear,' she chimed. 'It's not Guy, it's...'

But Anna held out a hand to silence her. 'No. If he thinks I'm Guy, that's fine. Let him think that.'

'Hello, Hugh,' she whispered and later it consoled her that the last words her father consciously heard her say were those of greeting rather than farewell, even if he did think they were uttered by a man long dead.

* * *

Hugh decides it is time to go home to his parents in Putney, but he is so tired he cannot move. He vaguely registers the presence of nurses and so assumes that he has been injured, but there is no pain, only a sense of great, great weariness.

Then he finds that he is flying, high above England. He is alone and wonders what has happened to the rest of the crew. And then Guy is beside him and he hears his brother's voice for the first time in over forty-five years.

'Time to bail out, old boy.'

He is so overcome with joy that he hardly hears the words. Guy was lost, years ago, so what is he doing here, and anyway there appears to be nothing wrong with the plane, so why bail out? He opens his mouth to explain but the next thing he knows, they are treading a path together through a limpid Fenland landscape. On either side there are reed beds, taller than he has ever seen. Everything is golden-bright, and he knows that they are walking towards a place that is safe and warm. Then he notices that Guy is not alone, but is holding the hand of a small girl, so like him that Hugh supposes the child is Guy's daughter. She smiles at Hugh and says very simply, 'Hello Daddy,' and he realises, with a lurch of his heart, that the child is his.

'We have to leave her but she'll be all right,' says Guy. 'We can still look out for her, even where we are going.'

Hugh opens his mouth to protest but knows that it is pointless. A higher power is at work here, and so the two brothers continue on their path. Hugh turns to look once again at the child's pale face. She seems a very long way away so he senses, rather than sees, that her cheeks are wet with tears, but she makes no attempt to follow them.

Once more he glances over his shoulder, but now she is lost from sight. For a moment he thinks of going back, but Guy takes his arm and together they walk towards a great, glimmering light.

* * *

The cold March dawn had yet to nudge the sleeping city into wakefulness when she heard it – or rather, ceased to hear it. The soft sound of Hugh's breath had become so much part of the geography of the sick room that it had faded into the background; a ticking clock, no longer consciously registered. Although its cessation was almost imperceptible, Anna, sitting by her father's bed, knew at once that he had gone.

51

She examined his face, so familiar but also strangely alien, and it occurred to her that he looked very young now that he wore death's mask, like his image in an old photograph. The lost child in her wanted to beseech him to waken, to use her fists to beat life back into his still chest, but the adult merely sat quietly, and taking his still warm hand, waited. Nothing happened: no voice from the heavens; no blinding lights; no sense of peace – just nothingness; silence, and the overwhelming sadness that never again would she feel the comfort of his arms around her.

Reluctantly, she broke the bubble of time and summoned Millie from a fitful sleep, leaving her, dry eyed and unbelieving beside the silent and still shell that had once been her husband.

Anna went out to the garden, surprised that her body was capable of registering the cold. Threads of wispy red had begun to streak the sky, and all around her was the murmur of London facing another new day. Planes flew into Heathrow; trains sped into Waterloo; traffic crawled down roads, and work bound commuters trailed along wet pavements. Somewhere a blackbird sang. She looked up to the room she had just left; a rosy glow filtered through the curtains – an obscene semblance of cosiness coming from a place where, for Hugh, there would be no new days.

She felt she ought to ring someone, but knew that reality would come beating on the door soon enough. And with the arrival of the morning nurse, the first day had to begin. Then the mundanities of death were set in motion – undertakers, forms and funeral arrangements, the clearing of cupboards and the shelving of memory.

Anna sat in the kitchen, hiding from the undignified taking away of "the body", while Millie flitted around like a moth, unable to settle, pretending not to hear the giveaway, heavy footsteps emanating from the stairs. That's not a body, Anna wanted to tell them – that's my Dad – the bravest and the best.

A few days after Hugh's death, Anna met with a young personnel officer at the headquarters of the bank at which Hugh, despite his long illness, had still been an employee.

'I'm so sorry for your loss,' the girl intoned, peering over owl like glasses, as she slipped the death certificate into Hugh's file. In return, she handed Anna various forms for Millie to complete.

Anna was familiar with the paperwork, having advised her own clients on the procedures following "a death in service". What surprised her was the form requesting information about her own bank account. At first she thought there had been a mistake, then the owlish girl explained that Hugh had not left everything to Millie; Anna also was a beneficiary. And there was something else in Hugh's file – an envelope on which was written her name and the instructions: "To be opened in the event of my death".

After the meeting concluded, Anna walked to Green Park. Even though it was not yet April, a profligate sun filtered through the trees, eager to share its glory before the onset of showers. The park was packed but eventually she found an unoccupied bench, where she settled herself, and after a few moments, tore open the envelope. The letter was typed, a formality that shocked her. Did he type it himself she wondered, or did his secretary? She thought she would ask him, and then remembered she could not. From the page, a slight scent of his usual aftershave tore at her composure. And she read her father's last words to her:

My dearest Anna,

I know that as you read this you will be sad. And I am so sorry, my dearest girl, to have left you. Please believe me, it will not have been without a fight.

I write this letter, now, in the hope that you will never see it, and that I will be with you for many years to come, but I fear that this will not be the case.

You are, I know, well aware of the financial arrangements in the event of my death. As the house is in our joint names it will belong solely to Mum and she will also inherit a modest sum from an old life assurance policy. Additionally, she will receive a pension, which should be more than adequate to keep her in comfort, if not luxury.

Dying before retirement means that a tax-free sum equal to four times my salary will be paid to my appointed beneficiaries. I have left instructions with the Bank that you should receive half of this amount, with the other half going to Mum.

What you choose to do with this windfall is entirely your decision but I hope that you do not mind too much if I take this opportunity (my only opportunity) to tell you what I would like you to do.

I am very, very proud of you, Anna. All your life you have worked hard and been so sensible, and now I see you forging a career in a field in which it is not easy for a woman to succeed. My only fear for you is that you have never allowed yourself much time for fun. I never told you at the time but it did seem, to me, a great shame that you didn't go to university. I do think you would have enjoyed it. However, it is not possible to turn the clock back, but looking to the future, would you not love to travel a little? I know you are not a jealous person but don't you rather envy Izzy and Tom? I know I do!

I don't mean trekking around India or the Far East for months. I don't think you would like that and Mum would be frantic with worry. But what about Europe?

Hartland should allow you a short sabbatical after all the years you have worked. With Izzy in Italy, you could make Venice your base. Anyway, my darling, think about it.

I hate to envisage you realising that it is too late to do all these things. Time does pass by so very, very quickly. I can't tell you what a shock it is suddenly to discover one is old.

Of course, I don't expect that you will be able to go away for a good few months. Mum will need your support at first. But I believe you will be surprised by how well she will cope. She is much stronger than most people think.

I've never been a religious man or believed in any sort of hereafter but if there is any way I can keep a watch over you from that "undiscovered country", believe me, I will, forever and always.

And as you sit on some sunlit terrace, raise a glass to your dear old Dad.

With more love than I can say.

And finally, handwritten, the one word

Daddy

The spotty office boy, sitting on the next bench, looked up from his sandwich. In another less cautious city he might have asked this white faced woman, who appeared to be sobbing, what was wrong, but you don't do that sort of thing in London; after all, she could be a nutter, so he turned his attention back to chewing, while Anna took a huge ragged breath and resumed what was to become the familiar process of pulling herself together.

* * *

Weeks and months passed. Shock and disbelief turned to a dull ache and an occasional seething rage that older or less worthy men should still be striding this world, kissed by health and happiness. A sympathetic colleague – most pretended nothing had happened and avoided the D word – gave her a book of reflective readings. Anna ploughed through well-intentioned poems about death being like slipping into the next room, and cynically wondered in what sort of house the poets lived. Chris attempted to cheer her up, arranging outings and weekends away, but his aggressive joviality unnerved her, and she sensed his irritation that she could not "snap out of it".

One morning, six months after Hugh's death, Anna opened the front door of her childhood home. Everything was as it had always been; the black and white tiled hall floor; the wooden staircase with its brightly patterned, but now faded carpet; the stained glass window on the landing spattering the walls with random patches of colour. But today there was something different about the house; an indefinable air of lightness that had been missing all through the summer. And she realised that the windows were open to the unseasonably warm day, and there was a smell of furniture polish and freshly brewed coffee. Millie disliked coffee; only Hugh had ever drunk it.

Seeing the light filtering through the open door of the kitchen, she followed it outside. Her mother was sitting under "Guy's tree", next to an exhausted flowerbed – this first year without Hugh, the garden had a weary look about it. An old photograph album rested on Millie's lap, and as Anna approached, she looked up. A tear oozed from the corner of one eye; a glistening snail's trail, laying waste to powder and paint.

'Look how happy we all were,' she said, indicating the photos of sepia children in big swimsuits, forever playing in the chill of an English seaside. There was Millie's nine-year old self, seated on a sand dune, wind-whipped curls framing a pixie face. On either side of her were two boys. One was still a child, perhaps eleven or twelve, his small neat features spread into a happy grin, but the other boy, the only one of the three who looked directly into the camera, was on the verge of manhood. In his dark hair, strong nose and jaw, Anna saw the familiar features of her Uncle Guy.

'So many memories in this house. Too many memories.' Millie slammed the album shut. 'Look, I'm sorry. There's no easy way to say this. I've decided to sell. An estate agent has just been round. That's why I made coffee.'

Anna said nothing, trying to process the information and all its implications.

'This place has never really been my home,' Millie continued. 'It's always been my husband's parents' house. You know, I had to fight for every little change we made. Your father wanted everything kept just how it was. Even this wretched tree.' She brushed away a couple of yellowing leaves that had fallen onto the album. 'It's kept the light out of my kitchen for the last forty years, but no one would ever chop the thing down because it was "Guy's tree". But, do you know, I think Guy would have been the first to say, "Get rid of it". You have to move on; life is for the living – however much we may love the dead.'

Anna took her mother's hand. 'I never knew. Never suspected,' she whispered, overcome by pity.

'Well, you don't like to complain do you? All my family and friends used to say, "Millie, you are so lucky. Only married a few years and you have this beautiful big house". But I loved our little flat in Chelsea. We only rented it of course, but it felt like ours, mine and your father's. And now I want somewhere of my own – really my own. Is that too much to ask?'

Anna gazed at the warm Edwardian bricks; the leaded panes winking in the sun; the last blowsy roses clambering to caress window frames. When had her grandparents moved in? The early 1920s? It was a hell of a long time for a property to be in the one family. And now the house was about to be handed over to strangers; abandoned like a puppy left at a lay-by.

'Look,' she reasoned, knowing reason had nothing to do with her motivation. 'It's very early days. Why don't you give it another six months or so?'

'No,' Millie retorted, the adamant set of her small mouth as hard as a ruby. 'There are too many ghosts here.' And Anna knew her mother was thinking of the lonely room upstairs, where remembered horrors seeped into the wallpaper, and in which she would never again sleep.

'OK,' conceded Anna. 'I understand.'

'You will help me, won't you? There'll be so much to do. I won't be able to manage – all on my own.'

'Of course, Mum. We should think about getting the old place painted. All over magnolia perhaps?'

* * *

Chris Webster sat, crumbling *grissini* onto the virgin whiteness of a starched tablecloth, gazing out onto the Fulham Road. It was Saturday evening and he had achieved game set and match so quickly at the Hurlingham Club that even after showering, enjoying a drink at the bar, and then driving through the heavy King's Road traffic, he was early. Anna was not due for another half hour and he was rather enjoying this unaccustomed time to himself, as he revelled in the memory of the day's sporting victory, and the even greater glory of yesterday's professional triumph.

The offer he had been made was better than anything he could have dreamt, and it changed everything. Until yesterday Chris had envisaged his life with the precision of chemical formulae. Salaried partner (he had ticked that box last year); equity partner; senior partner; a move to a more prestigious firm if necessary. He currently lived in a flat off Fulham Palace Road; it was on the small side, but the mortgage was virtually paid off, and now he aspired to a large, detached house towards the end of the Metropolitan Line; a place where it would be safe to bring up kids – and have a dog. Chris had only the vaguest mental picture of his children, but he could easily envisage the brown Labrador; Bertie would be its name.

Some of those plans would now have to be put on hold, but despite this, he was very glad for the opportunity to leave London. Brought up in the countryside, Chris had no particular affection for this city, but had assumed he would have to stay for the sake of the stellar career he planned. Whereas Anna, he knew, loved it, and had not left even to attend school or college; altogether a far too parochial existence in his opinion. This was one of the things about Anna that Chris found unsatisfactory: the fact that she did not want to expand her horizons.

It was ironic, but for the death of poor old Hugh, Anna might be Mrs Webster by now and her future set in stone. Chris had planned to propose during that abortive weekend in Venice, but Hugh's swift demise had scuppered that. Since then, another opportunity to broach the subject of marriage had not presented itself, as Anna was far too wrapped up in her own unhappiness. Perhaps it was just as well; over the past few weeks he had begun to doubt that she was an appropriate choice for the mother of his children. She had always been so level headed that he had assumed she would deal with grief as efficiently as she did everything else, so he was unprepared for this unconscionable sorrow. It was tiresome to watch the tears spring to her eyes at every passing reference to the grim reaper. He tried to be supportive but she was so much needier than he had ever imagined. Perhaps it indicated an emotional weakness in her. After all, it was what happened: your parents died. It was sad, but it was the natural way of things and it seemed, quite frankly, bad form to wallow in misery. Nearly six months had passed since Hugh kicked the bucket. Anna should be over it by now.

He saw her through the window as she approached the restaurant, and viewed her objectively, assessing her appearance so dispassionately that he surprised even himself. She had changed since her father's death, lost her sparkle. With some irritation, he noticed the way she walked. She had always held herself erect, but now there was a stoop to her shoulders. The weight loss did not suit her either. Chris liked slender women but at the moment he thought Anna a little on the bony side.

She disappeared from his line of vision, and a few minutes later was threading her way amongst the tables. Her shoulders had lifted and all that gorgeous dark hair was bouncing about her face. Despite his misgivings he really did find her very appealing. She gave him a huge smile and his body stirred with familiar desire. He imagined her stripped of the prim little dress: great legs, nice bum, a bit flat chested, but you can't have everything. And in that instant, he made a decision. He would let fate play its part. If she was enthusiastic and wanted to accompany him, so be it; he would marry her. But if she hesitated or prevaricated, that would signal the end of the line for them.

She sat down. The smile had vanished, and he registered the little line that had recently insinuated itself between her brows, making her look slightly bad tempered. He brushed her cheek with his lips, feeling his desire diminish. 'Had a good day?'

'Not really. I've been with Mum and she dropped rather a big bombshell. She…'

Chris had summoned the waiter as soon as Anna appeared, and the boy now hovered at their side, brandishing a distinctive green bottle enamelled with white flowers. Anna fell silent as her glass was filled. He could see her speculating as to the reason for this largesse. Perrier Jouet was extravagant, even for Chris.

'Are we celebrating something?'

'Most definitely, yes,' he paused. 'The firm is opening a new office in Hong Kong. Guess who they want to head it up?'

Anna stared at him. She opened her mouth to speak but no words came out. Her expression annoyed Chris. It reminded him of a fish.

'Well. Aren't you going to congratulate me? It's the most fantastic opportunity.'

'When do you go?'

'End of next month.'

'Congratulations. It's wonderful.'

As he watched her take a large gulp of champagne, he noticed her hand shaking. The waiter came and incanted the specials of the day. They chose with alacrity, neither really caring what they ate. Silence fell awkwardly around them.

'I'm likely to be there for five years at least. I have to do this, Anna. The whole package is…' He spread his arms in a gesture usually reserved for describing a fish that got away. 'It's a great life over there. Do you want to give it a try?'

He could not quite bring himself to say, 'Marry me.' For one thing, she might refuse, and for another, before committing himself he wanted to see how she would adapt to the role of an ex-pat wife. He needed to give it six months before he put a ring on her finger.

Anna was looking at him with a strange expression and when she spoke it was in the tone that an adult uses to a small child. 'Chris, I can't possibly go to Hong Kong. All my friends, my job, everything I've ever known, are here. And my mother was widowed only six months ago. I can't just walk out on her. And even if all…all that hadn't happened, I still wouldn't want to go. I'm sorry.'

'So you're content just to stay in your safe, boring little world? Not even give it a try. Well that's fine. Here's to you, Anna.' He raised his glass in a parody of a toast. 'I won't ask you again. I don't know why I did in the first place.'

They ate their meal mostly in silence, speaking when they did, about inconsequentialities. Just as they were leaving the restaurant, Chris remembered. 'Oh, didn't you say that Millie dropped a bombshell? What is it this time?'

'It was nothing. It doesn't matter.'

They usually spent Saturday night at Chris's flat but he had drunk far too much to drive, so they slept in Anna's bed where they made sad and perfunctory love. Despite their familiar physical intimacy, the air between them was as brittle as ice on a pond. Both could have ventured into the no man's land of compromise and looked for a way to salvage their relationship, but neither wanted to leave the safety of decisions already made, and words of truce were left unspoken.

'I don't think I can make it any evening this week,' Chris announced the next morning as he prepared to leave. 'It's going to be hectic, and next weekend I think I ought to go and see the parents. You know, break the news in person.'

'That's OK. I understand.' Anna stood behind him and hooking her arms around his ample stomach leant her face against his shoulder. 'In fact, I think it's best if we don't see each other anymore. I mean, we could meet for a goodbye lunch, or whatever, just as friends, but I'd find it easier if we made the break now. Wouldn't you?'

The words were not easily said, for Anna dreaded the prospect of being alone, but she was certain that to accompany Chris to Hong Kong would be an error of life blighting consequence.

Chris frowned, unsure of who was dumping who. 'Look, I'm sorry, Anna. I guess we just want different things out of life. I'll always...' He could not bring himself to say the word love. 'I'll always care for you.'

They hugged, like old chums, and he left, emerging on to the street so quickly that he must have run down the stairs two at a time. She watched him saunter down the road, swaggering like a ringmaster. Then he disappeared from view, and her life, without a backward glance.

Venice: March 1515

And so, I bided my time, and more importantly, also gave *papà* time, knowing that all I had to do was wait. It was about more than money; it was about him being able to follow the profession he loves. In the end it was this that changed his mind.

Throughout winter I continued to help him make potions and ointments, all the time knowing that the supplies of herbs from which they were made would soon have to be replenished. I even deliberately spoilt some of the preparations to hasten the time when he would have to gather more.

My father collects most of these leaves and flowers from the islands that dot the lagoon. He prefers to harvest them at night, so I guessed that even with a lantern and the brightest of moons, the illumination would be insufficient for him to manage alone. He really had no choice but to suggest that I accompany him.

The night appointed was mild for early spring, and I could hardly contain my excitement as we made our way past timber yards and workshops to the reedy banks of Cannaregio. There were many people still about, and the *calli* were alive with carousing, as men and women spilled out of taverns and hostelries. It was all wonderfully alive and so different from my usual existence that I was almost sad when we slipped away from the vibrant city, our small craft bobbing on the inky waters.

We Venetians are children of the sea, however, so I soon began to delight in the sensation of being on the open lagoon. These waters gave birth to us; they nurture us and protect us from our enemies, for only our native sailors know the channels where a boat may sail and not run aground. Without this narrow stretch of sea, the wars on the mainland would have certainly engulfed us in a frenzy of rape and butchery, such as that suffered by Ravenna and Brescia.

Venice has been at war for as long as I can remember; since the last Pope, intent upon destroying us, joined forces with France and the Holy Roman Emperor. When he died, no one in Venice mourned Julius II. Happily, his successor has shown himself more interested in annihilating the Turks and, unusually for a Pope, church affairs. So at last we have retrieved some territories on *terra firma* and have ceased to hear the pounding guns echoing over the waters. But even when faced with destruction, we never allowed ourselves to feel downhearted. Art and culture continued to flower, so it hardly seemed possible that the atrocities of war raged not so very far away. We Venetians possess the gift of self-deception, and if the end of the world came, I think we would still be merry-making in the Piazza, even as flood or flame engulfed us.

There are some, however, who may not feel such gratitude for the lagoon. It is here that criminals whose activities demand they die a secret death are brought. At dead of night they are rowed to one of its deepest channels, such as the Canale Orfano; then with bound hands and weighted bodies they meet a salty and silent end. I shivered with a delicious horror at the recollection of these stories and how our servant, Pasqualina, swore that she had heard the plaintive cries of ghosts shivering on the wind.

Mercifully, we encountered neither ghost nor storm, and only the cry of gulls disturbed the silence. Our boatman was a strong rower and we arrived at the island of La Certosa sooner than I thought possible. He helped us ashore, promising to return at the appointed hour. For a few moments we stood listening to the rhythmic splash of oars slicing through water, and then we commenced our task.

Even with a full moon, it was very dark, but we worked quickly, moving from one part of the island to another, as my father instructed what herbs and flowers to pick. Skipping through the long, wet grass, I made a great show of tripping over my skirts, and grumbling about the discomfort of damp fabric clinging to my legs, hoping that he would take heed of my complaints. Despite our industry, it took hours to gather all we needed, and when we finally dragged our booty back to the embarkation point, I was indeed shivering with cold. My back ached and my fingers were blistered from handling a knife, but I was proud and exhilarated to have done something so useful.

It was well after midnight when we returned, so the city was much quieter. Then, just as we were nearing home, a group of young men spilled out of a doorway and stood, shoulder-to-shoulder, blocking our path. By their clothes, especially the brightly coloured hose, I recognised them as members of the *compagnie delle calza* – young nobles who are responsible for staging our city's many celebrations. Very likely their evening had been spent in the planning of extravaganzas, and the drinking of wine, for they seemed very merry.

They were the type of men who are used to getting what they want, when they want, and the wine had, I believe, made them itch for feminine company. I had pulled my veil over my face, as befits a virtuous maid, but to no avail. They knew, as well as I, that a respectable woman would hardly be roaming the city at this hour, and whose wet and muddy clothes suggested she had been rolling on the ground with a man.

Their comments were ribald and although I think they meant us no harm, the insults made me blush, and my father rage. He lost no time in disabusing them of who we were and the reason for our nocturnal wanderings. But they were too far-gone in their cups to pay any heed. I had kept silent but when one grabbed my veil, declaring, 'The better to see your pretty face.' I knew I must speak.

'Shame on you, sirs,' I cried. 'If you doubt the honesty of our mission, look into these sacks and see the fruits of our labour. You should be thankful that the likes of us take the trouble. For if you, or those you love, are taken ill, you will be grateful that we have the means to make you well. Now let us pass.'

I do believe my protestation would have been sufficient for them to allow us to go unmolested, but just as they teetered on the verge of capitulation, another voice rang out.

'Leave them be!'

Its owner stood in a pool of light cast by a torch hanging from the tavern's wall. His clothes and voice proclaimed him to be of the nobility, but his shape, tall with wide strong shoulders, suggested a workingman. Here was someone not content to confine himself to effete pleasures. I could imagine him rising early to hunt wildfowl, rowing himself out to the lagoon islands, rather than relying upon his family's *gondoliere*. His face was strangely at odds with his body, round and golden skinned, with a small, straight nose, whilst his chin was as delicate as a child's. But it was the darting amber eyes that were his most arresting feature. Slanting and golden flecked, they danced with barely concealed amusement. For a second they made me think of the eyes of the stray cats that delight in taunting my poor Cesare. But unlike feline eyes there was nothing of cruelty in their gaze, only mischievousness. I was at once attracted to him, and also a little scared. Perhaps the other men were likewise in awe of his authority, for they had melted into the night.

'Is your house far?' he asked.

'No, we live near the Ponte de la Malvasia,' *papà* replied.

He nodded, satisfied that we would be safe for this short distance, and then went on to tell us that it was dangerous for a young woman to be abroad at night with a man who is no longer young and strong. Although he spoke gently, I thought this observation somewhat lacking in respect, but before I could respond he turned on his heels and strode away.

'Well, well. Enrico Sartorani soon put those young peacocks to flight,' my father chuckled.

'You know him, *papà*? Who is he?'

He did not tell me then, not in the open street where anyone might hear. It

62

was later, as we huddled before the fire, drinking hot, spiced wine, that he divulged some of young Sartorani's history (the rest, and baser part, I subsequently heard from Pasqualina).

Enrico is rightly regarded as one of the finest flowers of Venetian youth. Two years ago, our enemies, looking to invade, decamped themselves on the very shores of the lagoon. To aid our armies, Enrico led a band of young nobles who crossed the waters ready to hurl themselves at the foe. Faced with such valour, our opponents scattered and, as I now remembered, the name of Sartorani was lauded in the streets.

In the following weeks I could not forget the disquieting man, gallant, but muscled like a hunting dog. Oftentimes, I imagined how I would conduct myself should we meet once more. This was not so unlikely, for I gathered he had lately purchased a house near to ours. But, being a merchant, he was often absent from the city, so our paths did not cross again: for this, I confess, I was a little disappointed.

That evening's adventures, and our encounter with the boisterous youths, seemed to have also unsettled *papà,* for the next time we ventured abroad at night he suggested that perhaps, after all, it would be best if I did dress as a boy. Little did he know that I had already visited the second hand clothes dealers at the Rialto and purchased an appropriate set of garments.

I have never, I think, been a vain girl, but I longed to see myself trussed up as a boy. I have but a small looking glass in which it is impossible to see myself full length. I believe, however, that I cut a fine figure, or at least this is what I supposed from the admiring glances of womenfolk I passed.

Debra, my dearest friend, is the only person outside our household who knew my secret (although I cannot but think that some of our more nosy neighbours had their suspicions). We were born within days of each other and I have known her all my life. When I was a child, and knew nothing of the world, I thought she would always be there, but now I fear the day will come when we are parted. She is the daughter of my father's friend, Jakob, the Jewish physician. By now she should be married, but her prospective husband died. However, another will be found, and then what little freedom she currently enjoys will cease. Who knows if her husband will even permit her to see her Christian friend. And then again, they might leave Venice, for although *la Serenissima* does not persecute Jews as other peoples do, neither do we make life easy for them. The Venetians show more tolerance only because we need them for the good of the city. Despite this, there are rumours that change is afoot, and the Jews are fearful for their future.

But none of this concerned me on the day I first visited Debra, dressed in my hose, all puffed up with self-importance. Although she was shocked by my transformation, she pronounced me a "pretty youth", and perhaps *papà* was as impressed as she, for it was then he began taking me to see patients.

These visits are now part of my life. Together we lean over the afflicted person, my father asking what I observe about their medical condition. I tell him, and on this he can invariably make a diagnosis. He introduces me as his nephew who plans to enter the university at Padua (would that I were) when the city is liberated from enemy occupation. My "name" is Giovanni – not so very different from Ginevra.

I learn quickly, and think to the future. Perhaps if I become sufficiently knowledgeable I can establish myself in my own right as a physician. Who would ever know my secret? I plan and plot, and dream.

Screw Your Courage

The bus crawled down Sydney Place, then liberated by the traffic lights, swung onto the Fulham Road.

Whenever time permitted, Anna allowed herself the indulgence of this journey overground, in preference to the Tube, and today, although time was not on her side, she wanted to delay her arrival in Putney.

After months and many delays, Millie had exchanged contracts, and her departure was imminent. This weekend was earmarked for final packing, and would be the last Anna spent in her childhood home. She felt as though part of her life was about to be given away, forsaken on a skip or forgotten amongst the charity shop donations.

It was a Saturday morning, late in February, and for the first time that year she sensed spring in the air. From her vantage point on the upper deck she saw the promise of flowers in gardens and window boxes, brave buds burgeoning on scrawny trees, and the soft blue of an uncertain sky. Her mood lifted momentarily, only to sink as she remembered the reason for her journey. So instead of dwelling on the task ahead she concentrated on enjoying the ride. The road was flanked by fashionable squares and grandiose hospitals – the legacy of Victorian philanthropists. Occupying the smaller sites were antique and designer clothes shops, restaurants and bars, including the one where Chris had hosted a farewell lunch party a couple of Saturdays before his departure for Hong Kong. Anna watched its bright façade slip by and wondered what Chris was up to now. She missed him: not constantly, but his absence left a gap in her life.

The party itself had been a disquieting affair. Dispossessed of her role as girlfriend, she felt superfluous to the requirements of the occasion, especially as all Chris's friends pointedly ignored the fact that she was not accompanying him abroad. It reminded her of social gatherings shortly after Hugh's death, where no one mentioned that someone so close to her had died. She knew it was not indifference or callousness on anyone's part, just an inability to communicate with someone suffering loss; either the loss of a father, or the loss of a partner.

As everyone grew slightly tipsy, she had acknowledged that they were, after all, Chris's friends, not hers; men he knew from school, university and work. Like Chris, most of them were still unmarried, and their girlfriends came and went, as was now her fate. There was not one of them she would see again.

Watching Chris, Anna had felt a pang of desire for his robust and reliable body, regretting the oblivion that a vigorous coupling with her erstwhile lover might afford. She had half hoped he would ask her back for one last night, but a willowy redhead was flirting so outrageously with him that it seemed unlikely. The guests began to disperse, and as Chris's new friend showed no signs of relinquishing her prize, Anna had slipped away.

'I'll phone you before I leave,' he had promised. True to his word, he had, but his schedule proved too busy for them to meet. Perhaps it was for the best. They no longer had much to say to each other.

The bus drew to a halt outside St Stephen's Hospital, a bleak, red-brick building with a tower reminiscent of a fortress, a grim testimony to its origins as an infirmary for the poorest of souls. But despite this unprepossessing exterior, she had heard that a Veronese altarpiece illumed its chapel – a shining shard of Venice hidden within the Fulham Road. She was wondering if she would ever make the effort to view the painting when a female voice said, 'Excuse me, can I sit here, please?'

With a Londoner's instinctive desire for personal space, Anna had unconsciously spread her bags onto the adjacent seat.

'Oh, sorry,' she mumbled and turning to look at the girl, realised that she knew her face. There was no mistaking that sublime bone structure, emphasised by close-cropped hair; the dark skin and the deep intelligence of those wide apart eyes. She had been the surprise guest at Hugh's funeral, causing quite a stir.

'It's Anna isn't it?' beamed her travelling companion. 'Remember me? Zoë. I came to your dad's funeral with Dougie Forster.'

'Of course. I'm sorry we didn't get to speak, but you know how it is at these things…'

They were silent for a moment, remembering the chilly April day when Hugh's family, friends and colleagues had gathered together for that most sombre rite of passage, followed by the usual surreal party; the one where the guest of honour never makes an appearance.

Anna had been amazed by the number of people who had crammed into the chapel at Roehampton and later gathered in a local hotel. But what surprised her most was the presence of so many of Hugh's wartime comrades. She had almost not contacted them, knowing that it was only Dougie he saw regularly. However, on leafing through her father's address book she had found a section dedicated to these men, half of whom did not have normal first names but extraordinary monikers such as Tubby; Stuffy; Doc; Chips.

It was fortuitous that the first man she spoke to, blessed with the conventional name of Jimmy James (although it later transpired that his first name was actually Richard), displayed a talent for organisation. 'Tell you what, my dear, why don't I ring the rest of the boys. We can probably organise a spot of car sharing. I'll call you in a couple of days and let you know how many of us to expect. Would you like me to say a few words? You would? Excellent! Got to give the old boy a good send off.'

So they arrived; men in their sixties and seventies, who forty years ago had seen – and done – the unimaginable. They gathered outside the chapel, greeting each other in a way that suggested the years had fallen away and that they were united once more on a windswept airfield; boys doing a man's job and making history.

And it broke Anna's heart as, dry-eyed, she watched them, knowing how much Hugh would have loved to be part of the reunion.

At the same time she was elated that they were there and guided them to sit just behind Millie, Chris and herself, finding comfort in the soft murmur of their voices. A hush descended as those seated by the door saw that the pall-bearers and their load were about to enter. Then one of the company, who was presumably a little deaf because his not so *sotto voce* stage whisper resonated, 'Isn't that old Doc Forster. And who the hell is the dusky maiden?'

Those nearest the speaker swung round to look, and sure enough, there was Dougie, positively swaggering, with a beautiful black girl on his arm, as proud as any adoring father about to give away a blushing bride.

'You don't think she's his girlfriend do you?' another whispered.

'Lucky bastard!'

And then everyone was scrabbling to their feet, as the flower draped coffin made its entrance to a rousing organ accompaniment.

Later, "the boys" congregated around Dougie's friend, intrigued as to how "Doc" had acquired such a prize.

Tom, who had flown over from Paris, sidled up, having undertaken some subtle investigation of their exotic guest. 'Her name is Zoë. She's a medical student and sometimes works in one of the pubs that your Dad and Dougie drank in. Apparently Dougie was a bit apprehensive about coming on his own, so he asked Zoë to be his "date". She's rather gorgeous isn't she?'

Anna had intended to speak to Zoë as soon as possible, but had only managed to exchange a few words. Now, months later, it was Zoë driving the conversation.

'How are you? It must be nearly a year since Hugh died?'

'I'm fine, thanks.'

'Really?'

Perhaps it was the young woman's candour; her lack of reticence when referring to Hugh, or the simple fact that she used the word "died", rather than resorting to a coy euphemism.

Whatever it was, Anna's fragile carapace of self-defence began to crumble.

'No. I feel awful most of the time. Even worse than when Dad first died. Some mornings I don't know how I even manage to get up. But I do, of course; and I go to work, and in the evening I see friends, and sometimes I even find myself having a good time. And then I feel guilty about that. Things that used to matter – like my job – don't any more. I can be standing in front of a room full of people, talking about investments and think what a waste of time it all is. Everything is such an effort; I'm permanently exhausted and yet half the time I don't sleep properly.

'I mean, I know he's dead. For God's sake I saw him die, but there's a part of me that just can't believe it. Last night I was videoing some programme and I thought, Dad'll enjoy this when he gets back. Gets back from where? Perhaps I'm going loopy.'

'It all sounds like a perfectly normal response to losing someone you love,' said Zoë after a moment's hesitation. 'These things take time. Bereavement is sometimes one step forward and two back. At first, shock insulates us from the worst of grief. We come to terms with loss by degrees – it's the only way most of us can cope. He was a lovely, lovely man and you're sure to miss him horribly. I miss him, and I only used to see him for the occasional brief chat, but it was a privilege to know him the little I did.

'And you're not going loopy. In time you'll become accustomed to the fact that he'll never see those programmes, but you'll know that he would have enjoyed them. And when you watch them you'll be doing it partly for his sake, enjoying them partly for him. And don't feel guilty about having a good time yourself. You being miserable is the last thing Hugh would want.'

'I know,' said Anna, and then in an effort to lighten the mood. 'Just as long as I don't have to sit and watch hours of cricket for him. By the way, how's Dougie? My Dad used to take him to the Oval sometimes.'

'He's fine and guess what? One of his old comrades runs an import export business. They constantly have clients coming from abroad so they like to send a car to meet them at the airport; and also take them around London while they're here. Their current driver had just handed in his notice so Dougie was offered the job, there and then. He knows London like the back of his hand, and it also means he's had to cut down on the booze, which has done him the world of good. Anyway, he loves it.'

Anna felt a stab of jealousy that Dougie was enjoying a new lease of life, and as if aware of this, Zoë said, 'You see, your father is doing wonderful things for people even though he's dead.'

There was a short silence and then Zoë asked, 'Talking of wonderful things; did he ever do anything about giving you the means to travel?'

'He told you about that?'

'Well, yes. I can't remember how the subject came up. I think he just asked me would I want to travel if someone gave me the money. And then he said that he thought you'd really enjoy seeing a bit of the world and that perhaps he'd leave you enough to do it. He was laughing about it, all very light hearted, but I could tell he meant it. Look, it's none of my business and I don't mean to pry, but it sounds as though it might be just what you need. You know...a complete change.'

Anna made no response but stared out at the Saturday morning shoppers milling around the dusty red façade of Fulham Broadway station. She twisted the handle of her bag so tightly that it cut into her hands.

Undeterred by her silence, Zoë continued, 'And if you're that disenchanted with work, a few months away might well do you good. Is there anything else to keep you here? A man?'

'No. There was someone, but not anymore.'

'How's your mother doing?'

'Up and down, but all things considered, she's OK. In fact, she's moving next week, to a brand new flat in Weybridge; she's got cousins who live there. This is going to be her last weekend in Putney. You know, apart from my own flat, it's the only place I've ever lived. And my father was born there. It's where I feel close to him – sitting at his desk; going through his things. In a way, losing the house will be like losing him again.'

'That must be hard,' said Zoë. 'But perhaps it's one more reason to make a move yourself.' And she laid her hand on Anna's twisting fingers, stilling them.

Anna turned to face her. 'I know, but it just seems such a huge risk to take with my life, up-ing and leaving everything.'

'Well, sometimes you have to take risks to move on. Look at my father. He came over to England on the Windrush. Now that really was a risk. You see, my Dad, like yours was in the RAF during the war. I bet you didn't know that nearly 6,000 Caribbean men joined the RAF.'

'No, I didn't. Did my Dad know about your father?'

'Oh, yes. One day we had an RAF collecting box on the bar, and I saw your Dad put ten pounds into it. I must have looked surprised, and he explained that he'd been in the RAF, so I told him about my father. That was how we got talking. Dad joined up to help the "mother country" and was trained to be an engineer –

here in England. After the war he went back home, but apart from farming, there was no work. Then he saw an advert in the paper – twenty-eight pounds and ten shillings would buy a passage to Britain. During the war he'd felt very at home in England, so when he arrived at Tilbury, along with nearly 500 other Caribbeans, he was expecting to be welcomed with open arms…the reality was rather different. I suppose having black servicemen in your country helping to keep Hitler at bay is one thing; having them here for good, stealing your homes, your jobs, is another. The fact that most of the jobs on offer were those no one else wanted didn't seem to occur to people. Anyway, in spite of all his qualifications, the only work my father could find was as a porter.'

Anna imagined the succession of doors closing in the man's face. 'He must have felt so disillusioned – and betrayed. What did he do?'

'Joined up for another four years. Got more qualifications and eventually found a job with British Rail doing what he was trained to do. He's done very well for himself – for a black man, starting out in the fifties.' Zoë spoke without rancour or bitterness. 'Dad always taught us that we could be whatever we wanted. We just had to be brave and work hard. So when I was a little girl, and people used to ask me what I was going to be when I grew up, I'd tell them, "A doctor!" and they'd laugh. But they're not laughing now. And they won't laugh when Robert, my brother, qualifies as a barrister.

'The point is, Anna, to get what you want in life, you have to put your fear aside, or you'd never do anything. If my father hadn't taken a huge chance and left everything and everybody that was familiar to him, I'd almost certainly never have become a doctor. And it's all thanks to him, who was braver than I could ever be.'

Anna squinted out of the window, noticing that it had begun to rain, and said, 'You're right. Once I've got my mother settled in her flat, I'll go.'

'Brilliant. Where's the first stop going to be?'

'Venice,' said Anna, without hesitation.

They lapsed into a companionable silence, and as they crossed the khaki ribbon of the Thames, Zoë began to scrabble through her bags. She thrust a piece of paper into Anna's hand. 'I change buses next stop, but here's my number. Keep in touch, let me know how you're getting on.' She stood to go. 'You know, although your dad won't come back, he may still be watching you.'

'You, you believe…all that…that stuff?'

'Oh, I don't know. But the more I see of death and dying, the more I believe in the strength of the human spirit. That somehow, someway, death's not the end of everything. I could tell you things…but no time now, I'm afraid. Best of luck, Anna. Goodbye.' And finally, just before she disappeared down the stairs, 'Don't worry; I'll watch the cricket for him. But he'll have to accept that part of me will always be rooting for the West Indies!'

Seconds later, Anna saw her on the pavement, waving; a brave and beautiful woman, some of whose courage she knew had rubbed off onto her own cautious soul. And a little later, walking through the drizzle-damp streets of Edwardian terraces, she continued to feel wrapped in an unfamiliar euphoria that only subsided as she let herself into the house she still thought of as "home".

Millie had been busy during the past few days and much of the furniture had been sold or given away. Possessions were consigned to boxes stacked in precarious towers around the rooms, and pictures, stripped from the walls, lay orphaned, waiting to be wrapped.

Anna had watched her mother's elder sister descend into early onset Alzheimer's, and was reminded of this as she piled unwanted items into the car. Preparing a house for sale was a little like witnessing a beloved relative robbed of their personality by the thief of dementia; finally nothing was left but a shell – the same, but not the same as the person one loved.

The following evening, exhausted from trip after trip to the municipal tip, Anna picked at a supper comprising the remains of the freezer contents while Millie chatted about her cousin Ellen. 'As it's her sixtieth birthday in May, I thought it would be nice if I took her on holiday. So I've booked a three-week cruise!'

Anna almost choked with surprise and then, realising it was a heaven sent opportunity, rapidly outlined her own plans.

'So you'll only be gone for three months?' said Millie. 'Well, I'll hardly know you're not here, darling. Let's drink to us!' And she raised her glass, her smile brittle and brave.

The next day, after the removal company completed their job, and cousin Ellen drove Millie away to her new home, Anna walked around the house, thankful at last to be alone. It was unnaturally quiet, like one of the poems in her colleague's "comforting" book, with clocks stopped and telephones cut off.

Proceeding from room to room, she saw the scars time had made: the place on the carpet where, as a teenager, she had spilled a bottle of wine; the dents on the battered parquet floor where Hugh's desk had stood; how faded and worn the curtains were. It did not matter; soon everything would be discarded. But Hugh had walked on those surfaces; his hands had drawn those curtains. She did not like to think of it all dumped on a tip.

Upstairs, she went into what had been her parents' room, trying to recall chilly mornings when, as a child, she had bounced onto the bed, snuggling between their cosy bodies – secure and happy, and unknowing. Now, despite its total emptiness, the room twitched with memories of her father's last illness. She closed the door behind her, and coming down the stairs, there came a happier time-slip as she remembered her smaller self, sliding down the banister, crying, 'Catch me, Daddy. Catch me,' warm with the confidence that his strong arms would always be there.

And then it seemed that time shifted back even further and she saw, in her mind's eye, the two small boys who had once lived here. Rather than being confined to the house, they were larking about in the garden, playing among the first smiling daffodils. Feeling foolish, and yet compelled to look, she unlocked the back door and distinctly heard the chirp of childish laughter. For a second, the air buzzed with expectation before she realised that, after all, the noise came from the street, and the only sound in the garden was of wind teasing the withered leaves. The house was as empty as a discarded nutshell. But in a matter of hours, the children of the new owners would tumble in and out of these rooms, painting them with excitement. It was time to move on.

Anna locked the front door for the last time, put the key through the letterbox and walked to the car; away from the past and whatever invisible shades stirred the morning gloom with their airless breath.

The building blocks of her life lay scattered all about, as though a malevolent child had taken a petulant swipe at them. Gone was her father, her boyfriend, her childhood home. Even the job she had once loved was now reduced to a chore. And so, that evening, she phoned Izzy.

'Look, I've a favour to ask,' she said. 'I've decided I should do a bit of travelling, like Dad wanted. I thought I'd make Venice my base. Is there any chance you could find me a little place to rent for a few months?'

There was silence, and for an awful moment Anna thought Izzy might demur, perhaps not wanting someone who was so much part of her past to be such a fixture in her present. She was just about to assure Izzy that she would not encroach upon her life when her ear rang with an explosive whoop of joy.

'Oh my God, this is brilliant. I can't believe it. And do you realise that if you'd phoned tomorrow it might have been too late?'

'Too late for what? Izzy, slow down and tell me in words of one syllable.'

Anna heard Izzy take a deep breath. 'Well, a couple of weeks ago we decided we just had to move. I've had enough of this place. It's dark and damp, and worse of all...' she paused, '...we've been invaded by rodents.'

'Not the rat in the loo again?'

'No. Worse. At least we could keep him out. We've got mice, loads of them. It's like the plagues of Egypt.'

'I don't think they had mice. There were locusts and…'

'Then they got off bloody lightly. Do you know that mice don't have sphincter muscles on their bladders, so they pee all the time, over everything? We've tried traps, poison, asking them nicely to go, but nothing works. I've even lured in one of the local strays, but it's fuck all use; just lounges around all day, scoffing mountains of cat food. And to top it all, I think the little bugger's given us fleas! But the good news is, a friend's going abroad for a year, and he's offered us his apartment. It's gorgeous and the rent's very reasonable. But it's too big for just us, so we need to get someone else to share the cost. The trouble is, there's no one we really want to live with. We've been wracking our brains all week and tomorrow is the day Toni needs to know one way or other. But Anna, you'd be perfect.'

'Are you sure? What does Will think?'

'He's nodding like mad. Please say yes.'

'There's only one problem. I really can't see them giving me more than three months off work.'

'Toni would ideally like a year, but I suppose we could persuade him to accept six months, but that would be the absolute minimum. Anyway, three months isn't enough time for you either. That's not travelling. It'll be time for you to go home before you've even got here. God, I wish there was some way I could send you pictures of the apartment down the phone. You'd absolutely love it. It's just a short walk from Ca' Melisa, and there's a terrace overlooking the rio della Misericordia.' Then Izzy's voice grew fainter as she spoke to Will. 'She says she doesn't think work will let her have more than three months off. You talk to her. Tell her she's got to come.'

There was a rustling and then Will's husky drawl. 'It seems to me that your main consideration should be what *you* want, rather than how much time off you can wheedle. Ask for six months as if it's the most reasonable request in the world, and see what they say.'

'And if they say no?'

'If they'll only give you three months, agree to that, and when the three months is up, then ask for more time. By that stage they'll probably have no choice but to agree.'

'You're right, Will. Tell your friend you'll take the flat. I could be with you by mid-April, but I'll pay from whenever you need to move in.'

There was more rustling and muffled voices before Izzy came back on the line. 'You're sure about this, Anna? You won't back out? Because if we take Toni's flat, we need to hand our notice in on this place NOW, and I don't fancy having to camp out in the *Giardini Pubblici*.'

'Tell her to sleep on it and give us a call in the morning.' She heard Will say.

'No, no,' said Anna. 'I've made my decision. Wild horses won't keep me away.'

* * *

By Wednesday, Anna's high spirits had spiralled into near panic. She had passed two nights pursuing sleep down a corridor of half-dreams, and the lack of rest had left her frayed and exhausted. The morning after her conversation with Will and Izzy, she outlined her plans to her immediate boss, Trevor.

'Well, at a pinch I could cope without you,' he grumbled. 'It is the quieter half of the year, and I don't suppose it's any worse than someone buggering off to have a baby. But you do know the final decision won't be mine? And believe me, she won't like it one bit.'

He raised his eyes heavenwards, as if in deference to a higher power, although in reality he referred only to the incumbent of the office above. Though to be fair, Lettie Carne, the new Personnel Director – commonly known as Genghis – did terrify most staff more than the Almighty.

Just over a year ago Hartland Hyatt had merged with an American owned firm and its old-fashioned, paternalistic philosophy was being replaced by a tougher regime. Shell-shocked by her personal circumstances, Anna had initially barely noticed, but recently she had registered that when staff left they were often not replaced, and she had heard rumours of further cutbacks. So it was with some trepidation that she entered Lettie's palatial office to face the woman whose decision would determine her immediate future.

It was one o'clock, and Lettie was attacking a sandwich as though it were the enemy. As she looked up, a globule of mayonnaise escaped its confines of bread and lettuce, plopping onto what Anna assumed was her personnel file. It seemed an ill-omen somehow.

'So you want six months off?' said Lettie, scooping up the mayonnaise with a paper napkin. 'To travel?'

'Trevor doesn't think my being away will be a problem.'

Lettie smiled, the expression not reaching her eyes. 'I'm afraid it's not Trevor's decision. I've discussed it with Duncan.' She referred to the new chief executive. 'And he agrees that there should be no deviation from the company policy that sabbaticals are given only to those who have completed twenty years' service.'

Anna played her trump card of compromise. 'I appreciate that six months is rather a long time. What about three months? I've nearly clocked up ten years, so...'

Lettie's eyes flickered. Anna, sensing her impatience with this bazaar style bargaining, shut up.

Lettie made a little steeple of her hands, resting her chin on her fingertips. 'Six months…three months – it's immaterial.' She let the steeple fall and leaned back in her chair. 'If we conceded this to you, Anna, we'd have to concede to everyone. I'm sorry.'

Anna resisted the temptation to point out that most people could not afford to take three months unpaid leave. Sitting mutely, she saw the chimera of Venice slipping away; she imagined Izzy's disappointment; envisaged another ten years of work before she would have any real time to call her own. Above all, she thought how sad Hugh would be if she accepted Lettie's decision. She could hear him asking, 'Do you really want to work for these sods?'

She took a deep breath and not giving herself time to consider the consequences said, 'In that case, I'm afraid I'm going to have to give you my resignation.'

Lettie shrugged. 'Well, we'll be sorry to lose you, Anna. You can, of course, reapply for employment when you return from your jaunt. But I have to warn you; we're going to be running a much tighter ship. Whether there'll be any sort of opening for you, I really can't say.'

After that the interview wound up.

Back in her office, Anna sat behind the desk that she would soon begin to clear, hardly believing what she had done.

Trevor's head appeared around the door. He was wide-eyed with shock. 'She's told me. Are you sure about this? It's a very big decision, I do hope you won't regret it.'

Anna gazed out at the grey London rooftops. 'No…no, I don't think I will. I may look back and think that it wasn't exactly the most sensible thing I've ever done, but I'm sure I'll never regret it. Whereas if I don't go, I know I always will.'

Venice: Autumn 1515

Our nocturnal trips continued throughout summer and into autumn. And now, months later, I recognise what should be picked, and so my work is sooner completed. Even so, my father always takes provisions, for however mild the night, the weather can suddenly change and the vicious north wind we call the *bora* lash the sea, making it impossible for craft to be abroad. Our destinations vary: Malamocco, Santa' Erasmo, San Secondo and islands so tiny that only the fishermen know their names. After we have gathered what we need, we eat a small meal of bread, sausage and olives. Then we lie on our backs in the sweet grass and gaze at the wide hanging sky. Sometimes, above us, I see shooting stars, and below us feel the tender warmth of the earth, holding us in its arms like a mother.

It is on such a night as this, just as we have returned, that we receive the summons that changes my life. It is here that my story really begins.

When the call comes, I am in the *necessario*, (although I dress like a boy, I will never be able to piss like one, and my need is urgent) so although I hear the hammering, it is *papà* who goes to the door.

Hastily adjusting my clothing, I run to see who requires a physician, for I have no doubt that it is a professional summons. No one else would call at such an hour.

The man conversing with *papà* is, judging by his voice and clothes, a servant. I hear my father say, 'Corner Piscopia is some distance off. Is there no one nearer? Why me?'

'I would not know, sir. I was told to take my master's *sandolo* and find you, and that no other quack…sorry, sir,…doctor, would do. My master, Giovanni Battista Cima, says you are the very best, and what was the other word he used? Ah, yes…discreet.'

'What is the nature of the illness, and does it afflict a man or woman?'

The servant leans forward, his voice hushed. 'It's a young woman, sir. And she ain't ill. I think she's been hurt bad by someone. They didn't say nothing to me, but I heard a good deal of crying and there was a quantity of blood on my master's hands.' His voice drops even lower. 'I heard one of the womenfolk whisper of violation.'

Papà turns to me, and in the faint candlelight, I see the enthusiasm on his face; the desire not to let this adventure pass, and also the compulsion to help a fellow human.

'I must bring my assistant,' he says. 'Wait, whilst we pack some things.'

The man wanders back to his craft, and Cesare claws at my hose, somehow guessing that we are about to desert him again.

'Intriguing,' mutters *papà*. 'You do realise from whom this summons comes?'

I do indeed, having recognised the name. Cima hails from Conegliano – a day's journey away – but despite not being Venice born, he is one of our greatest painters. His work adorns countless churches and confraternities. A short distance from our home, in the church of Madonna dell'Orto, there is one of his finest altarpieces. It is of the Baptist, depicted against a background of mountains and fair countryside, peopled with exotic figures. I love it, for although I cherish my city, I do sometimes think it would be pleasant to live amongst hills and fields, for all that I have never seen them in reality.

Cima has a reputation for being a most Godly man, quite different from many artists, who, if gossip is to be believed, are a dissolute band of fellows. Some are not in the least abashed to use their latest mistress as a model for even the Holy Virgin, and the face of the purest saint may be that of a notorious courtesan, or even a common prostitute. (Perhaps I am jealous because with my long nose and sallow skin no one would ever desire to paint me.) But it is said that the face of the Virgin in Cima's paintings is always that of his first wife. Poor lady, she died young, and in his brushwork remains ever so, even though her body is consigned to the tomb. What his second wife, who remains in Conegliano, thinks of this, I cannot guess. However, as he keeps no mistress here in Venice, she is perhaps willing to forgive the tenderness he nurses for his first love, thinking that to worship a dead woman with paint is a smaller infidelity than to worship the flesh of one alive.

The artist's servant is waiting for us, and after I settle *papà* into a seat he casts off. I am thankful that we are not making the journey on foot. It is with good reason that so many of our *calli* bear the name Assassini. Although the patrolling *signori di notte* do their best to maintain order, there are many dark places where a man may be robbed of his purse, and his life.

We slip by the dark façade of Ca' Sartorani, the newly acquired home of Enrico, and I wonder if he is within. It occupies the whole of a little island on the Rio de la Sensa and is an old building, somewhat neglected, but he is beautifying it as only someone with no shortage of funds may. I suspect *papà* is watching me, so I turn my face away, not wanting him to guess my thoughts. I know I must banish these vainglorious notions. Enrico is a nobleman and could never be interested in the lanky daughter of a humble doctor. But then again, he does bear that single fault… a disgrace that may prevent him from making the most prestigious of matches, so perhaps…the remembrance of him makes my skin tingle; or perhaps it is just the cool breeze that whips around us as we pull into the wide Canale della Misericordia, past the *scuola* and the abbey church. But soon we are on the Canale Grande where the tall buildings on either side afford some shelter. The moon is high, and I gasp with delight, seeing how the Ca' d'Oro shimmers in the silvern light. During the day it is a wondrous enough sight with its adornments of gold leaf, ultramarine and vermillion glittering in the sunshine, but I think it even more beautiful when lit by the gentle moon. It is a place where the angels of Heaven might dwell.

I am musing on the notion that in Venice we have created a Paradise on earth, when we come to the Rialto, where the only bridge spanning the Canale stands, miraculously spared by last year's great fire. We must be approaching our destination, for our craft is bobbing towards the high bank of houses. Of late, I have visited some grand residences, but none as impressive as the one I am about to enter. The painter does not own it, but, as is the custom in Venice, rents part of it from the noble proprietors.

We slide through the open watergate. Torches hanging from the walls flicker into the basin of water, and as we scramble out of the boat, I see our shadows, huge and dark, dancing on the brickwork. A man appears who I assume must be the artist, the man who has summoned us, in the dead of night, to attend to his – his what? As yet we know nothing about our patient. I wonder what she is to him. He did, after all, specify a "discreet" physician. Maybe he is not so virtuous after all. The thought saddens me, for I do not like to think that the creator of such innocent beauty is profligate or violent.

I have no time to ponder further, for my father, who has been speaking to the artist in hushed tones, now introduces me. Cima gives a little smile. He is probably older than *papà*, but his light brown hair is thick and hardly touched with grey. I suppose for really quite an elderly man he is handsome, but above all, he has a kind face, and looking into his eyes, I am certain that he would harm no one.

Holding aloft an oil lamp, he then leads us up a staircase into a large space. The room is unlit, but I guess, as much by the smell, as from the little I can see, that this is his workshop. There is something about it both thrilling and intriguing, and I wish we could linger here. But he ushers us out, into a small bedchamber, where a fire is blazing; despite this, the young woman huddled before it is shivering. Her face, when she turns to us, is heart shaped, and her fair hair is streaked with something dark: blood, or mud – perhaps both. She is probably pretty but her eyes are swollen, and livid bruises mark her cheeks. Her lip has been split and blood trickles down her chin; she opens her mouth and I see that a tooth is missing. Then the screaming starts. It takes a moment for me to realise that I am the reason for her yelling. I am not used to being shouted at, and I think I am almost as frightened as she.

Papà approaches her, making soothing noises, as one would to a tiny child, explaining that we only want to ease her pain. She whispers something, and he nods in assent, saying, 'Please, will you all leave us. You too, Giovanni.' And then for my benefit only, 'I can manage alone, my boy.'

I know what my father is about. He has a gift, you see: a thing of marvel, something over and above his ordinary work-a-day skills. His very hands contain a healing power. When he places his palms near a place that hurts, warmth radiates from them, then the pain will fall away. It is a sort of magic, there is no other word for it. (I would say miracle, but that would surely be blasphemy; but for all that, it does put me in mind of the acts of our Lord.) However, he must take care how he uses this gift, for fear that some might cry, "witchcraft". And so he often gives a patient a cordial and they assume this cures their ills, rather than the healing power of his hands.

The painter takes me into a sitting room, not unlike ours, except it is larger, and has a fine decorated ceiling. A jug of spiced wine is warming in the hearth. He pours two measures, and hands me a cup. I sit, muttering my thanks as briefly as I can. When I am Giovanni, I avoid speaking over much, for fear I am discovered. But the painter, it seems, is more than willing to talk for both of us. All he requires is my attention as he tells me about the girl.

'Her name is Agnesina,' he begins. 'I knew her father…years ago when we were boys in Conegliano. We came to Venice at about the same time, but I was fortunate in having the ability to paint a little…' he spreads out his hands, well-shaped and paint-stained. 'My friend – Matteo – was not so blessed, but he was strong and intelligent, and found employment in the shipyards. So, our lives took very different directions, and our paths rarely crossed, but when I began to receive commissions I sought him out to model for me. With his ship builder's muscles and strong face he was the perfect John the Baptist, and as he had a growing family to support, he welcomed the extra income.'

Not for the first time I think what a fine thing it is to have one's likeness rendered in paint for future generations to look upon. Often I have wished that someone had used my *mamma* as a model, for then I would still see her sweet face. Forgetting my usual reticence I say as much, and by the way the painter looks at me I know he is assessing my suitability. Giovanni does not care to be scrutinised, so I change the subject. 'What happened to your friend, sir?'

'Do you remember the explosion at the shipyards six years ago? Matteo was killed, together with his two sons.'

There can be no one over the age of ten who does not recall the terror of that day. A spark ignited the powder magazine and within an instant the area around the Arsenale became an inferno. Even the councillors of the *Maggior Consiglio* cast aside their red robes and joined in the rescue mission, but despite everyone's best efforts, many *arsenalotti* met their deaths.

'Matteo left a widow, Veronica, and their only other surviving child – Agnesina.'

'Poor lady, was she provided for?' I ask, for in such cases, it is usual for the state to assist bereaved families.

'Yes, although hardly sufficient to compensate for the loss of husband and sons.'

I am sure this is true but at least they received something; in most cities they would have been left entirely destitute. I say nothing and let the painter continue.

'Veronica is strong and hard working and has established a laundry business. She has always shunned my offers of charity, but is happy to undertake modelling work for me and other artists in the city. You would recognise her face in many a Saint Helena or Anne.'

I still do not know how Agnesina came to be in such a sorry state but at last his story is leading to that.

'Veronica's greatest wish is to see her daughter well married. And it looked as though her prayer was to be answered, for the girl was fortunate in that the Scuola di San Marco have awarded her a dowry.'

She is indeed lucky, for this custom is one of the few ways by which poor maids may secure the financial means to make a good match

'The intended husband is a young man whose father owns a thriving business and the marriage will secure both mother and daughter's future. But Agnesina, rather than thanking Heaven for her good fortune, developed an infatuation for one of my apprentices – Alvise. It appears that after her poor mother falls asleep, exhausted from her daily labours, she sneaks out to meet him. It was on her way to such a tryst, this very night, that the attack occurred. When she did not arrive at the appointed meeting place, Alvise went in search of her. Miraculously, he found her, unconscious and badly beaten, bundled into a silted up canal. If he had not reached her when he did, the rising tide could have drowned her. Rather than take the girl to her own house, where all the neighbours would have witnessed her state, he brought her here and confessed the whole sorry tale to me. He is a good boy and totally distraught by what has happened. From the few words she uttered, we have ascertained that Agnesina had been forced against her will.'

I now understand the need for a "discreet" physician. If her betrothed discovers the nature of the abuse done to her person, he will almost certainly not want her for a wife.

'Did she recognise her assailant?' I ask.

My question is significant, for the violation of an unmarried woman is not considered so great a crime. If apprehended, the rapist will receive only a mild penalty, and if he is willing to marry his victim will escape punishment altogether. For my part, I would rather my attacker escape the rigour of the law than become my husband; he who would do such violence would not be a good mate.

'No, she did not,' says the painter. 'It seems...' but he stops, as a lean-faced woman bursts into the room. I at once recognise her from the painting of the Nativity in the Church of the Carmelites where she appears as St Helena. This must be Agnesina's mother. Following her is a tall young man who addresses the painter as "uncle".

The painter hurries the woman into the room where my father tends her daughter. Then the young man turns and looks at me. We regard each other for what seems a long time. If anyone else stared at me like that, I would think it most rude, but in those few moments something strange happens. I want, for the first time in my life, to know another person to the depths of their soul. I want to know everything about this man, to touch him to...I stop my thoughts for they lead towards matters that a virtuous maid should not consider.

His face is disconcertingly familiar, and he smiles at me; a funny lop-sided smile. I notice he has eyes like those of the painter and the same light brown hair. Then, to my horror, I feel myself blushing. Thankfully, at that moment, my father and Cima reappear.

'She should sleep for some hours,' *papà* says. 'I will make up a salve and send it round. Then I will let you know my decision.'

It seems our work is done and we are escorted out, but not before the painter's nephew gives me another of his heart-stopping smiles. I catch his name – Giacomo.

On our return journey we pass Enrico's house; I give it not a second glance. He has been quite supplanted in my fickle imaginings. Trying to sound as though it is a thing of little importance, I ask *papà* if Giacomo is also a painter.

'No, he is a woodcarver. He carves picture frames, so is affiliated to his uncle's workshop, though not actually part of it. But he does lodge with him.' *Papà* pauses, trying to recall everything he has heard. I do not know how, but he possesses a veritable knowledge of our fellow citizens. 'I believe that only one of *maestro* Cima's children has inherited his talent and he, rather than pursuing an artist's career, is a monk in Padua.'

I am about to ask more; if Giacomo is married or betrothed, but I see the boatman's beady eyes on me, and shut my mouth, turning my thoughts to the girl's condition. I am aware that she has been forced against her will, but unless she has conceived a child, all might still go well for her. If she plays the virgin on her wedding night, her husband may be none the wiser. Naturally, *papà* will divulge no information until we are safely in our own home but even then, he eschews my questions, telling me there is something he must consider overnight.

I go to bed, hugging Cesare for comfort, and my dreams are happily untroubled. Had I known the full story, I might not have slept so soundly.

The next day, when *papà* tells me everything, I understand the need for secrecy. This was no ordinary rape.

'The unfortunate young woman was also subjected to an ordeal that was,' he pauses for a second, 'unnatural; bestial.'

He refers to a crime that is so heinous it threatens our entire city. God's wrath against the miscreants who commit this most awful of perversions manifests itself in terrifying ways: plague and war; even earthquakes, such as the one that cracked the Campanile only four years ago. Consequently, to appease the Almighty, those who are convicted suffer the severest of punishments. Even noblemen have been beheaded between the pillars of justice and their bodies then burnt.

'You are aware,' he continues, 'that I am bound to report any cases of sodomy to the authorities?'

I do indeed know, and I guess that Cima has asked him to keep silent, for the girl's sake.

'I have turned it over in my mind. Agnesina said the man spoke like a noble and was young and tall, which is why the sight of you frightened her. But he threw a sack over her face, so she did not see his features. On such a scanty description, it is impossible that he will be apprehended. By reporting the crime she will suffer the ordeal of further questioning and her reputation will be ruined, all to no avail. So I have decided to keep silent. You must never breathe a word of this to anyone, Ginevra.'

I give him my promise, then say, 'You have a salve to deliver. Let me take it. And I will buy a nice fat duck from the Rialto.'

He agrees at once. *Papà* likes nothing better than the plump lagoon waterfowl. Also, I can see that the night's excursions have wearied him, and so, "Giovanni" sets off to Cima's workshop. There is no reason why it could not have been Ginevra running an errand for her father, but considering Agnesina's treatment, I feel safer as a boy.

Easter

'Nearly there, thank goodness! This next bit scares me stiff. I always think we're going to land in the sea!' twittered the elderly English gent who had been Anna's travelling companion since Heathrow. 'Looking at Venice from above you can see why they say it's like a fish, can't you? But, you know, to me, it looks more like a little dog snuffling along the ground. And I've an Australian chum who swears it's the shape of a kangaroo.'

Lionel was a nervous flyer, and to take his mind off their airborne state, as well as availing himself of the drinks trolley, had chattered almost incessantly. Not that Anna minded. He had been coming to Venice for over thirty years and had a wealth of anecdotes to share. Sadly, things were not quite as much fun now that he had to travel alone; his partner, Kenneth, could no longer manage all the walking, but the "dear boy" gallantly allowed Lionel to make solo visits, on the proviso he did not "get up to any mischief".

'Chance would be a fine thing,' he giggled. 'All those beautiful Italian boys! But at my age, one can merely dream. Our…my hotel is La Calcina – it's where John Ruskin stayed. I think I've probably had a lot more fun there than he ever did, poor fellow. And my absolute favourite time to visit is Easter, especially like now, when it falls so late. I do so adore the Saturday night vigil at San Marco. You really ought to go, my dear. It's a magnificent spectacle.'

'I'm afraid I'm not religious,' said Anna.

'Oh, but neither am I, not in the least. It's all mumbo-jumbo – but such exquisite mumbo-jumbo. I adore all those bells and smells, and it's heavenly just to enjoy that glorious building without all the hoi polloi pushing and shoving.'

He was still chattering as they came into the arrivals hall. 'Ah, there's my water taxi.' He pointed to a burly man holding up a notice bearing the name, "Signor Lionel". 'You know, the *only* way to approach Venice is by water. Being deposited at Piazzale Roma by a public bus is like entering a palace through a scruffy basement…Oh, but these must be your friends? Goodbye, my dear. Perhaps we'll bump into each other. And do go to the vigil.'

And with that, he rose onto his tiptoes and planted a kiss on Anna's cheek, before scuttling off towards the waiting taxi driver.

'Who's the boyfriend?' laughed Izzy as she and Will flung their arms around her.

'Boyfriend? Hardly!'

'OK, perhaps not,' said Izzy, watching Lionel trotting out of the airport. 'Well, it's nearly an hour before the next water bus, so let's sit on the *pontile* with a glass of wine and relax.'

It was a day of soft, milky whiteness; completely windless, and the lagoon, except where its surface was rippled by skidding boats, was as silvery smooth as a slick of mercury. Sky and water merged imperceptibly in the distance, and the towers and cupolas of the city were hidden in far off opacity.

For a while they just sat, sipping tepid white wine from plastic beakers. Although the day was by no means warm, it was noticeably milder than the breezy London Anna had left behind, and the lazy bobbing of the pontoon soon lulled them into quiescence. Will lounged back on the wooden bench, eyes closed, drawing on a cigarette. Izzy leaned against his shoulder, apparently oblivious to the smoke. Apart from the fretful call of water birds, it was strangely tranquil.

Izzy broke the silence. 'How do you do it? Make all these old men fall for you?'

'Fall for me? If you hadn't noticed, Lionel is the teeniest bit gay.'

'Well, I know one old man – well, old-ish – who certainly isn't gay, and who is over the moon you're here.'

'Oh, yes, who's that?' asked Anna.

'Vittore, of course. Who else? And guess what…we're all invited to a posh dinner at Ca' Melisa; next Wednesday.'

'It's the first night do for one of his art holidays,' said Will. 'Three of the guests can't make it till Friday, so when Izzy just happened to mention your arrival was imminent, he suggested we come along, "to make up numbers".'

'An excuse, of course,' Izzy added. 'There's no need to "make up numbers". It's a dinner, not a football match. He just can't wait to see you. I don't know what you did to enchant him, but it worked good and proper.'

'He wrote to me after Dad died. I meant to reply but never got round to it. He probably thinks I'm really bad-mannered.'

'Oh, I doubt it,' said Izzy. 'You know, I tried to find out who the person was he wanted you to meet…remember? But he shut up like a clam.'

A short silence fell. Then Izzy announced, 'Vittore made a special point of mentioning that Raffi would be at the dinner.'

'Oh, yes? And how is he?'

Izzy rolled her eyes. 'Oh, it's been one drama after another! Caterina, the girlfriend, has got herself some amazing job in Milan, at one of the fashion houses. Anyway, it's too far to commute everyday, so she lives there during the week and only comes back to Venice at weekends.'

'Raffi doesn't want to move to Milan?'

'No. Adamantly refuses to leave *la Serenissima*. So, to cut a long story short, they decided on a trial separation. Rumour has it she had her eye on someone else but it didn't work out, so she was soon back, all contrite. Then, within a couple of months it was all off again; this time she really had met someone else. Anyway, after a few weeks licking his wounds and nursing his male pride, Raffi started seeing a really nice woman; a visiting academic. She was from Denmark, so I don't suppose it would have lasted, but they seemed perfectly happy. And then wham! Caterina's back, like an avenging angel. Danish lady is given the old heave ho, and the Caterina and Raffi show is back on the road. There were even rumours of a spring wedding, but that appears to have died a death.'

'And they're still together?'

'Yeah – unfortunately. Patrizia, Raffi's cousin, you know, the one who had the party at Ca' Melisa…she was over the moon when they split up. Secretly everyone was. No one really cares for Caterina.'

'Why? She can't be that bad if Raffi's been with her all these years.'

'Actually, I hardly know her, but on the few occasions we have met, she's made absolutely no effort to be friendly. Apparently she hates not to get her own way; always has to be the centre of attention; says bitchy things etc, etc. If you want to get Freudian about it, I don't suppose it's all her fault. When she was just a little kid her mother ran off with an American bloke and then managed to get herself killed in a riding accident. So Caterina was brought up by her adoring father. He's something high-up in the *carabiniari* – bit of a brute, by all accounts, but he indulges his darling daughter unsparingly.'

'Well, we both know what it's like to be daddy's little darling, don't we,' said Anna.

'Admittedly she is very, very pretty,' continued Izzy. 'But that's not everything, even in Italy. I think what worries the family is that she'll hurt him. For some reason everyone's strangely protective of Raffi.'

'Perhaps because of losing his parents so young?'

'Possibly. But that was years ago and he's certainly landed on his feet with Vittore and Rosina as surrogate *mamma* and *papà*. And don't forget, one day he'll presumably inherit Ca' Melisa, which must be worth trillions and trillions of *lire*. Perhaps that's it; perhaps they think she's a gold-digger. Money could certainly be part of the attraction. Or perhaps she doesn't really want him anymore, but can't bear the thought of anyone else having him. It's like a *telenovela*, you know, a soap opera. Anyway, you're sure to see them before too long, so you can make your own judgement.'

'OK, you two, here's the waterbus,' announced Will. 'Stop gossiping and drink up.'

On her last visit, the furthest Anna had ventured was Murano. Now, as the boat churned its way between the gigantean wooden channel markers, she recalled how Venice had come into being. Fear of marauding barbarians had driven the earliest inhabitants of *terra firma* further and further from the land, and these brooding waters became their protector and ally. From a salty waste of mudflats and sandbanks, had sprung this most celestial of cities, an eternal testimony to the bravery and resilience of those long ago refugees. Now, centuries later, the sheer size of the lagoon surprised and disturbed her. This vast watery pool, studded by islands, was a strange, illusory place. Pallid in the afternoon's opaque light, a melancholic, slightly inhospitable air hovered over it. Possessing neither the calmness of a lake nor the vibrant boisterousness of the sea, it seemed chilled by incipient danger. As a sudden adrenalin rush of excitement and danger overwhelmed her, she had a vision of a tiny boat bobbing on this aquatic no man's land during the deepest of nights, with only a full, high moon for illumination.

The sensation was gone in an instant, and her attention switched to the city revealing itself on the vague horizon – no more than an indistinct greyish scrawl, as if an artist had dragged a brush across an off-white canvas. Then the skyline elaborated and a terracotta ribbon of buildings came into focus: hump-backed bridges; humble houses hob-nobbing with ornate *palazzi*; church towers claiming lofty precedence over their lowly neighbours. Colours quickened into life; gypsy smudges of blue and saffron blazing from awnings and parasols; coral roofs glaring against the marble sky; a flash of acid-yellow light from a passing speedboat – gone in an instant. And dominating the immediate view loomed an island, bulky and prosaic, its imposing red brick walls rising abruptly from the waters, like a ruddy cliff face.

'Is that the cemetery island?' asked Anna, thinking it a forbidding place, with its dark columns of cypress trees and bone-white buttresses.

'Yes,' replied Izzy. 'San Michele; well worth a visit: "The grave's a fine and private place", except in Venice where they dig you up after ten years or so, to make room for someone else.'

'And then what?'

Will picked up the conversation. 'Either a little niche in one of the cemetery walls, but that's very expensive, so usually a communal ossuary. In fact, there's an island not far from Torcello, Sant' Ariano, that's one big bone-pit. No longer used, but pretty unpleasant by all accounts, crunchy underfoot and supposedly infested with snakes. The whole thing's really bizarre, isn't it? Imagine, getting a letter one day. "Dear *signor*, we are writing to inform you that next Monday we are going to exhume your granny. What shall we do with her?"'

'Will, for God's sake, shut up,' Izzy hissed. 'I'm sorry, Anna. He can be a tactless bastard at times.'

'Shit! I'm sorry,' Will's hands flew to his mouth, as if trying to shovel back the words.

'It's OK,' Anna reassured them. 'Please don't think you can't mention death, or my dad, or make jokes that might upset me. I can deal with those things. I'm fine now…really.'

And it occurred to her that, perhaps for the first time in months, she spoke the truth; that she was fine, or certainly better than she had been for a long time.

* * *

Anna's new home was on the top floor of a renovated nineteenth century building and was everything she could have hoped for. It had an immediate, easy familiarity as she instantly recognised many of Izzy's possessions amongst the eclectic mix of antique and modern furnishings. The main living space was large and airy, leading onto a terrace overlooking the rio della Misericordia. Izzy and Will had already established themselves in the larger of the two bedrooms, having correctly predicted that Anna would be happy with the smaller room as this possessed the canal view. Simple wooden furniture, whitewashed walls and a bright bedspread and rug combined to create a harmonious mix of warmth and freshness.

Directly opposite, on the other side of the canal, was a building that may have once been a convent but was now a care home. The part of the edifice most visible from the flat was a windowless, crumbling wall, but beyond it lay a large, somewhat neglected, but beautiful garden, filled with blossom-laden trees.

That evening Izzy made a special effort with dinner. After a bottle of *prosecco*, they ate a salad of bitter little leaves, nestling under slivers of sharp blue cheese and juicy slices of ripe pear, followed by a creamy risotto studded with tiny prawns, pink and sea-scented.

After Will had cleared their plates, Izzy twirled out of the kitchen, bearing a platter of tiny pastries. Resembling a benign Salome, she announced, 'Didovich's best!'

'Not a Russian ballet dancer,' said Will, 'but the best *pasticerria* in town.'

They demolished tiny chocolate filled horns; dainty choux kisses bursting with zabaglione cream; layered wafer thin pastry sandwiches oozing zingy lemon custard. Afterwards they sprawled on the squidgy sofas and polished off another bottle of *prosecco*. Eventually, Izzy's chatter degenerated into a gentle snoring, and Will whispered, 'I think I'd better put this one to bed. See you in the morning.'

A little later, when the apartment was quite silent, Anna slipped out onto the terrace, hugging herself against the chill.

'Well, I made it, Dad. Hope you're proud of me,' she whispered, gazing up at the starry Venetian sky, feeling not at all foolish; after all, where else do you look when speaking to the dead? And it seemed that, for an instant, the dancing stars twinkled a little brighter. But probably it was just her imagination.

* * *

Only as she settled into the rhythm of her new life, did she succumb to exhaustion, the consequence of endless months of holding herself together. She did very little, retiring early and waking late. For long hours she curled up with a book, or sat on the terrace, watching the comings and goings in the garden opposite. The staff, who were mostly nuns, often helped their patients outdoors to catch a little spring sunshine. When an old lady waved a greeting from her wheelchair, Anna was strangely touched, feeling she had been given permission to share their secret world. She bought herself a thick pad of drawing parchment and began to sketch the scene. Soothed by this peaceful occupation, that great healer, time, at last began to dispense its medicine. The dark mantle of sadness began to slip from her shoulders; her step became lighter, and the world a brighter place.

She felt a little guilty that she was not immediately visiting museums or galleries, but reasoned that there was no need to snatch and tear at Venice like a child with a Christmas stocking. Time was on her side, she could savour and relish the city; allow it to woo her as it slowly revealed its secrets. Long, delicious months lay ahead; there was no hurry.

But, on Lionel's recommendation, she was determined to attend the Easter Vigil at San Marco.

Initially, Izzy was deeply suspicious. 'Oh, please don't tell me you're going all religious!' Then she relented. 'Well, we might as well, I suppose. We've nothing else planned for Saturday night, and it has to be cheaper than the cinema.'

Her happy, atheist cynicism was counter-balanced by Will's muted enthusiasm.

'Well, he is a cradle Catholic,' Izzy confided. 'Packed off to some grim public school with a load of sadistic monks for teachers. But old habits – if you'll forgive the pun – die hard; he says he finds something strangely comforting about the familiar rituals. Personally, I think all that incense is just a substitute for drugs. But I'm willing to give it a try, as long as we don't have to stay the full three hours, because even God'll be bored by then. What time's curtain up?'

They arrived at the Basilica well before nine o'clock, and were each handed a skinny white candle. The ancient church was already packed, and judging from the plethora of languages, the devout, or curious, of many nations were represented. Only after other worshippers had accommodatingly shifted and shuffled along the rickety wooden chairs did they find three places together.

'These are good seats,' said Izzy, gazing up at the glowing inside of a great, golden orb shining above them that splintered light like a fractured sun. Then the gentle luminescence was replaced by an echoey darkness. 'They really should have paid the electricity bill,' she giggled. 'What's all that about?'

'They've lit a fire out in the narthex,' whispered Will. 'It represents the risen Christ bringing light back into the world, dispelling darkness and death. The Easter Candle is lit from it and gradually the flame will be passed to everyone else's candle.'

As he spoke, the congregation began to rise, and above a sea of bobbing heads, Anna saw the flickering flame of a huge candle being borne slowly down the nave. A procession of priests appeared and a loud chant commenced, echoed by the assembled masses.

'They're saying, "The light of Christ", and we're all responding, "Thanks be to God",' Will translated. Then the basilica was bathed in a growing radiance, as the dancing glow-worms of candlelight passed from person to person. It gilded the side chapels, the vaulted apse and each of the succession of arches, vaults and domes, displaying, in glorious abundance, not just gold but a multitude of colours, shimmering from every surface.

'Look,' squeaked Izzy, indicating the high altar, which was dominated by a great, glittering screen. 'They've turned the *pala d'oro* round. It was worth coming just for that. Do you know, some parts of it are nearly a thousand years old, and it's studded with hundreds of gem stones?'

The wonders of the sumptuous Byzantine treasure were not, however, sufficient to hold Izzy's attention for long. Despite the exultant organ playing and the ethereal strains of a perfect choir, after less than an hour, bored by the readings and psalms, she hissed, 'I don't think I can take much more of this. You don't really want to stay till the end do you, Anna?'

'Actually, yes. I'm never likely to experience this again. You two go if you like.'

'No, I'll stay too,' said Will.

'OK. I'm sure some of the gang will be in Paradiso Perduto,' said Izzy, naming one of Venice's few late night drinking spots. 'I'll see you back at the flat.' And with that, she slunk away in search of more earthly pleasures.

Anna knew that "bells and smells" featured in the Mass, but nothing could have quite prepared her for the moment, just before the Gloria was sung, when it seemed that every bell, in not just the Basilica, but the whole city, rang out. The giddy carillon reverberated and bounced from the walls, as insistent and energetic as a horde of jubilant children, leaving not a corner of that revered space untouched. And she realised she was weeping – not so much for the sacred mysteries or the ancient rite, which she ill-understood, but for all the countless thousands of people who had participated in this same ceremony, on this same spot down the clouded centuries; and also for all those who would be embraced by the sacred continuum in the years to come, long after she was gone. The daunting continuity of it was like life itself, and she felt a warm sense of belonging, even as a bright face a few rows ahead turned and smiled ecstatically at them. Lionel, her companion from the plane, who appeared as transported by joy as a medieval pilgrim, blew her a kiss.

Shortly after, the service came to an end, and arm in arm, Anna and Will walked out onto the moon-drenched Piazza – blue, dim and dark. Another jubilant crash of bells was marking the midnight hour. It was now officially Easter Day; a time to greet the happy morn; celebrate and give thanks for all that life had to offer.

There was no need to venture down the Piazza, as it would have been quicker for them to turn right and cut through under the Torre dell' Orologio, but with unspoken agreement they walked straight ahead, amongst the small groups of people dotted about the wide space, many of them greeting each other with wishes for, '*Buona Pasqua.*'

They passed by the Caffè Florian, its orchestra, together with that of its rival at Quadri, now departed, whether in deference to the hour, or the solemnity of the day, Anna did not know. It was then she caught sight of half a dozen young men and women laughing and joking together. One of their number appeared to be relating a story, speaking rapidly to the accompaniment of wide gesticulations, and although Anna only saw him in profile, she at once recognised the speaker. He was wearing glasses and his hair was a little shorter than she remembered, but it was undoubtedly Raffaele Anzelieri. On seeing him, she felt a sherbet-sweet fizz of delight.

In the moments before she was about to alert Will, she saw that hanging on Raffi's arm was a young woman, whose corona of bright hair seemed plucked from the gold of the San Marco mosaics – presumably Caterina. She was indeed very fair of face, but as she caught sight of Anna looking at Raffi, her benign expression changed. The pretty features were marred by a hostility designed to warn off impertinent onlookers, and her arms tightened around her companion in a gesture of possessiveness that said, 'He's mine.'

Will had clearly not noticed the little group, and eager not to initiate a meeting in the face of such blatant animosity, Anna swung him around, saying, 'I'd like to look at San Giorgio Maggiore in the moonlight.' And so they walked back towards the Basilica, leaving Raffi and his friends unaware of their presence.

As they meandered home, Anna tried to put Raffi, and the girl, out of her mind, but for the first time since arriving in Venice, her sleep was troubled. She dreamt of being trapped in an unknown, alien place where the walls breathed a quiet menace. Catatonic with fear, she waited for someone who would take her to safety, but her unknown rescuer did not materialise. Only as she struggled towards the surface of sleep did she realise that the person she awaited was Raffi. She awoke, troubled and embarrassed, angry at her subconscious mind for disturbing her equilibrium. However, she had little time to flounder in her discomfiture, for the morning air was punctuated by wild squeals of, '*Cioccolato! Cioccolato!*'

A few days ago, Izzy had commenced a belated Lenten observance and given up chocolate, though more in deference to her waistline than the Almighty. Now she awoke in ecstasy, having discovered the cornucopia of goodies that Will had piled on the end of their bed. Seconds later she burst into Anna's room, clutching a chocolate rabbit, and Easter day began, as it so often does, with a feast fit for Montezuma.

Venice: Autumn 1515

A servant grants me admittance and I swagger upstairs. I later discover that compared to those of other artists, Cima's workshop is a small affair, but it is still a thing of wonder. The artist himself is working on a large altarpiece. It shows an enthroned St Peter flanked by two figures. One is clearly John the Baptist, but a very young John. In his gentle features I see Giacomo, and realise why the face of the artist's nephew is so familiar. Only weeks ago a very similar altarpiece was installed in the nearby church of Santa Maria dei Crociferi. In this too, there appears the figure of a youthful Baptist. When *papà* and I first looked upon it I had thought how handsome was the saint. And now, with a guilty thrill, my eyes creep down to his legs: they are bare and well-shaped, and I wonder if they are modelled on Giacomo's own limbs.

I know that the painter senses my presence but is too engrossed to move, so I turn my attention to the four other men in the room. One, a handsome young man, is labouring with a mortar and pestle. I suppose that he is grinding something that will be transformed into paint. Two others are busy at their easels, working on unfinished Madonnas: the faces and hands of the Virgin and Child are complete, but the rest of their bodies are heavy blocks of uniform colour on which they pick out the folds of garments with a darker paint. Another, a very pretty youth, is painting small panels, possibly the altarpiece's predella. He looks up from his work, giving me an appraising look. That he should regard me thus when I am dressed as Giovanni is not, I am sure, proper. But I have heard that many men following an artist's life are disposed to such inclinations, although why it should be, I cannot fathom.

Banishing such unmaidenly conjectures, it occurs to me that this place is not so dissimilar to *papà's* workshop – perhaps even more thrilling. For although I have never had the opportunity to handle brushes and paint, I can draw, and capture a person's likeness very well. Paper and drawing implements are costly, but sometimes *papà* has bought me small supplies, and when I was a child he would make charcoal in the embers of the fire, so I could draw upon a slab of white stone. I find myself wishing that I had been born into an artistic family, for in such cases, if a daughter shows talent she may assist, all be it in a small way.

I stop these thoughts and chide myself for not being content with what the

Heavenly Father has sent me. Why must I always be yearning for what cannot be? And indeed, what is it I do want? My eyes turn again to the youthful Baptist in the altarpiece. At that moment, the painter straightens and stretches, rubbing the small of his back under his long, paint smeared robe. Wordlessly, I hold out the jar containing the salve.

'Come with me,' he says, and I follow him out of the workshop. After ascending several flights of stairs, he shows me into a small room that must be at the very top of the house. Sitting by an open window is the girl, Agnesina. I am afraid she may start screaming again, but she is quite calm and regards me with expressionless eyes. Less than twelve hours have elapsed since we saw her but she looks much improved. Someone has washed her hair and I can see that *papà* has stitched her lip. I do not know how he managed: I believe he is learning to do such things by touch.

'I have brought you some salve,' I say. 'Smear it on the…the place where the hurt is.'

I can only imagine the pain the assault must have caused her. She blushes, and I sense my colour also rising. I go to her, bending down so my face is on a level with her own. 'I promise that neither the doctor nor I will ever speak of what happened to you. Your secret is safe.'

She smiles, her relief obvious, and I notice her missing tooth. The loss spoils her mouth but no doubt she and her mother will invent some story to explain her damaged face.

As the painter leads me from the room, she whispers, 'Thank you, doctor.'

I realise that she is the first patient I have seen unaccompanied. This makes me feel exceedingly important, giving me the courage to speak. 'Might I see the altarpiece you are working on, sir? I hardly had a chance to look at it. It is very like the one you painted for the Crociferi, is it not?'

He nods, pleased: even the greatest of craftsmen can be sweetened by a little flattery.

'So you like paintings, do you?' he says as we return to the workshop. I am thankful to see that the apprentices have vanished, apart from the eldest man who is still diligently working.

'Oh, yes,' I reply. 'For where is this one destined?'

'The convent of Santa Maria Mater Domini in Conegliano.'

We look at it for some moments and then I ask, 'Is that your nephew, sir?'

'Indeed it is. Giacomo is a fine model. You may think it an easy task, but I assure you not everyone can do it. It takes a certain aptitude, as well as the appropriate physical requirements.'

93

I sense him looking at me, and I feel as though the feet of a hundred tiny animals are scampering over my flesh; it is not an altogether unpleasant sensation. Somehow I know what he is about to ask.

'I have been commissioned to paint an Annunciation by a man whose eldest son is named Gabriele. It is consequently essential that the depiction of the archangel is particularly fine. If you are willing, I think you would be a most suitable model. Do you not agree, Marco?'

To my delight, the other man responds in the affirmative.

'The payment is not large,' Cima continues, 'but...'

'Yes,' I interrupt. 'Yes, I would be very willing. It would be an honour.'

'Could you come the day after tomorrow?'

'Certainly.' Then I ask a question that I think must surprise him. 'What will I wear?'

(I do not suppose that boys are generally so particular about their attire.) In answer, he walks over to a large chest in the corner of the room and throwing open the lid, pulls out a long, loose robe. It is the colour of the early morning sky when the sun is still sleepy. Thankfully, it is also so voluminous that it will conceal my secret.

'The same shade as your eyes,' he says. 'And I shall paint you a fine pair of wings – all the colours of the rainbow and more.'

Apart from my work with *papà*, this is the most exciting thing I have ever known, and I stand like a zany person, staring at the blue robe. At that moment, the door of the workshop opens. I expect the apprentices to appear, but it is Giacomo. I cannot look at him for fear he will see something in my eyes – well, in Giovanni's eyes – that will horrify him, for I am sure he is not of the inclination of the pretty apprentice.

'This young man, the nephew of Doctor Vannitelli, is to be the archangel for my Annunciation,' Cima explains.

Giacomo smiles in approval, and I find myself regretting my doublet and hose. It is a cruel irony that I will only meet this man whilst dressed as one of his own sex. I am indeed a poor monster.

But the thrill of being painted soon lifts my spirits, and that afternoon, with Cesare trotting at my side, I visit Debra. I tell her everything, even the awful fate of Agnesina, although I omit some of the more intimate details. She would not say, of course, but I can tell she is envious of my adventures. Although she enjoys more freedom than most Hebrew women, her movements are greatly curtailed and she rarely leaves her home. Like me, she is her father's only child and is also motherless. Her aunt, who used to keep house, married two years ago, so it is a lonely life for Debra. Sometimes, when her father is attending his patients, or is busy in his workshop, she sneaks out with me, but she is always frightened of being recognised, even when heavily veiled. Fortunately, she lives in an area where there are few Jewish families, for otherwise busybodies would be tattling to her *papà*. Christian or Jew, old wives like to gossip and cause trouble for their younger, prettier sisters.

'There is something I want you to do,' I say. 'Fetch your father's instruments and cut my hair.'

I am a little vain about my hair and have not, so far, felt obliged to cut it, for I hide it under a *bareta*. But I know that it is too long, even for the prettiest of boys, and so it must be sacrificed. Debra hacks and chops at my curls, her small hands struggling with the unwieldy scissors, until the floor is littered with dark tresses. Cesare thinks this a fine game and chases after them, pretending they are mice, gagging and sneezing as the hair gets into his mouth and up his nose. Debra shows me the result in her mirror. It will do; and will grow soon enough when need be. I have only the smallest regret at its loss.

Later, as I leave, she embraces me, saying, 'Take care, Gina.'

I laugh off her concern. 'There is nothing to be careful of. I am only having my picture painted.'

But I know, as does she, that I am venturing into the unknown, and such actions always sniff of danger. And so, two days later, when I arrive at the workshop of Giovanni Battista Cima, known as Cima da Conegliano, I am undeniably nervous.

Thankfully, he is alone. I take off my cap and shake out my newly shorn locks, hoping he will approve. Propped on an easel is a large wooden panel that has been prepared with layers of what I now know is gesso, ready to receive my image. Next to it, on the floor, is a gnarled piece of wood and a coil of rope. He sees me looking at the things, and explains. The man who commissioned the painting has been angered by the misdemeanours of his son, Gabriele, who is consequently now out of favour. He no longer requires an Annunciation; instead he wants a Madonna and child, flanked by two plague saints – San Rocco and the saint after whom his second son is named, Sebastiano. I realise, with mounting horror, the implication of this as, in place of the decorous blue robe, the artist hands me a bundle of white fabric that has been fashioned into a loincloth. Mother of God: this is what he expects me to wear. I stare at him, open mouthed.

'Do not look so scared, I will paint the arrows in afterwards,' he jokes. And when I still do not move, he continues, 'Is anything amiss? Is the room too cold?'

'I am sorry,' I stutter. 'I cannot do this. It is too…I cannot wear this, this… thing.'

He does not attempt to press me but is clearly surprised by my embarrassment. Maybe he supposes I have some awful birthmark or skin affliction.

'I am also sorry, Giovanni,' he says. 'You would have made a fine Sebastiano. I intended to show the saint in his very early youth, so that his suffering and sacrifice are particularly poignant.'

The wooden panel stares back at us, white and blank: it should have held my image, which, God willing, countless men and women would gaze at for more years than I can imagine. I know it would not be me; that it is the saint to whom they would whisper their prayers, but preserved in paint, I would not disappear from this world, like *mamma*, whose features I can no longer recall. The disappointment is too much for me, and I am unable to prevent my self-pitying tears. I can tell by his face that he is shocked by my unmanly behaviour. Despite admiring this man so deeply, I am making a great baby of myself in front of him. This makes me feel even worse, and before I know it, rather than earn his contempt, I blurt out the truth.

I am prepared for any number of reactions, apart from the one that follows. He begins to shake a little and then, unable to disguise his mirth, he laughs. He laughs until his eyes water and his cheeks become rosy. I can hardly credit it: this quiet, circumspect man is chortling like a Rialto fishwife. Whilst I am grateful not to have incurred his wrath, I am shocked by his amusement.

'I shall never forget your face when I gave you this,' he at last manages, holding up the loincloth. 'You poor child.' And then, suddenly serious. 'But why?'

It seems I have no choice but to tell him about *papà's* poor eyes. I conclude by pleading, 'You must never speak of this to anyone. It would ruin his reputation.'

'Ginevra, as I think I must now call you, rest assured I will hold my tongue. It seems that we both are keepers of each other's secrets. But now, you must go home.'

I nod in miserable agreement, averting my eyes, which come to rest on Giacomo's image in the guise of the Baptist. Perhaps it is this that gives me the courage to say, 'Please, may I visit again. Apart from knowing the secrets of my father's profession, there is nothing I should like more than to be able to paint. If I were only shown, I do believe I could be of some use. I can draw, a little,' I add.

The painter says nothing, but presents me with a piece of reddish chalk. He then fixes a sheet of blue tinged paper onto a board.

'This is *carta azzura*,' he says. 'A speciality of Venice.'

I run my fingers over its slightly rough texture, breathing in its unfamiliar smell. I sense the importance of what is to follow.

'Draw me,' he commands.

My hands shake so much that I doubt I can even scrawl my name. But perhaps an angel lends my fingers skill, because although I work slowly, I know that I have captured his likeness. I step back and he examines my efforts.

'You have much to learn,' he says, and I feel my heart sink, and then soar, as he adds, 'But you have ability. You do realise there are religious houses in the city where your talent would be nurtured?'

'I have no vocation,' I say flatly.

He seems to accept this and continues, 'It would be different if you were my daughter, or niece, but for you to work here with me, and the apprentices, would be unseemly. Does your father know of your aspirations?'

I shake my head. Perhaps I look so woebegone that he takes pity on me, for he says, 'Your father must be a very busy man, but if he could spare the time to accompany you, then I would be willing to give you lessons. The daughters of noble households have drawing masters, so why not you too?'

I can hardly believe my good fortune, and hurtle back to our house like a whirligig. On the way, I buy some of the marzipan biscuits that *papà* loves so much. But there is no need to sweeten him, for the dearest man agrees at once. He takes my hands and whispers, 'That's my clever girl.'

Then Cesare, jealous of the attention *papà* pays me, pretends to growl, but is easily appeased with a nibble of biscuit and a cuddle.

That night I cannot sleep. The image of Giacomo's bare legs disturbs my peace and for the first time I think about the joys of the marriage bed, and though I have seen him only the once, I am sure I love the painter's nephew. What else explains the fact that I think of him almost every minute of every hour of every day? Fate smiles on me, for surely he and I will henceforth meet often?

And so, Cima has transformed my life. I have now been twice to his workshop, and he is a patient and kind teacher. He shows me how to hold a pen, made from a sharpened goose feather. The ink is produced from gallnuts and is black when first applied but then turns brown. Mixed with water it is used as a wash, and my fingers are permanently stained with it. Then he sets me to copy the images contained in model books. These are made of vellum, a paper produced from animal skins; it is exceedingly expensive but is smooth and very strong. One day, he demonstrates how to create light and shade by cross-hatching with different sized pen-strokes. Soon he will let me watch paint being produced from raw pigments and will teach me to make brushes, from the largest, to the tiniest ones that are fashioned from the finest miniver.

So far I have not seen Giacomo again, but it can only be a matter of time…

Pride and Paint

After Easter Sunday the weather changed; cool, marshmallowy softness was replaced by hard spring sunshine, bringing warmth and soaring temperatures. It was as if Venice had sloughed off her dull winter garb and in honour of approaching summer had decked herself in vibrant clothes and sparkling jewels, ready to greet her growing entourage of admirers.

Fortunate were the guests due to lodge at Ca' Melisa for their ten day holiday. April can indeed be the cruellest month, bringing rain and squally winds, but these lucky pilgrims were to be blessed with sun and the lightest of breezes. They hailed from towns large and small; from Brighton and Boston; London and New York. They arrived by plane and train; one couple by car en route from the Lakes. For some, it was the holiday of a lifetime, a luxury for which they had long saved; for others, it was just another trip in a life crammed with such delights. The less affluent hauled their baggage from the waterbus stop at the Fondamente Nuove; others took a taxi from the airport and were deposited at the watery threshold of Ca'Melisa, as guests had arrived in previous centuries, although by *gondola* rather than motorboat.

One such couple were Graham and Edie Singelmann, who were celebrating their first wedding anniversary.

'I'd like to do something a bit different,' Edie had said when they were planning the trip. 'What about one of Vittore's art vacations?'

'That's a splendid idea, darling. And look, I know how fond you are of the old boy, but let's stay at the Danieli again rather than Ca' Melisa,' Graham had wheedled. 'I admit, it's a beautiful house, but at the end of the day, it is just a glorified B&B.'

'Oh, come on, Ca' Melisa is still a *real* Venetian *palazzo*,' Edie had retorted; and Graham knew any further discussion would be pointless.

Edie was a millionaire several times over but her father, a formidable New York businessman, never let her forget how extremely privileged she was. So sometimes she enjoyed doing the "ordinary" things that "ordinary" people did. Graham, on the other hand, having spent nearly thirty years of his life below the firmament, was only too pleased not to be ordinary. But if Edie wanted to rough it in a crumbling *palazzo*, with no room service, so be it: this was a small price to pay, for there were moments when he could hardly believe how lucky he was.

It had not always been the case. For as long as he could remember, Graham had wanted to paint, but had been persuaded to forgo art school and study chemistry at Imperial College. Brought up in a remote part of Somerset, London had presented itself as a vast pleasure ground. Unable to abandon his fixation with art, he spent hours in galleries and museums, even attending evening classes, where he painted nudes and landscapes; flowers and fruit.

With his razor sharp mind, Graham should have easily attained a first, but he had spent so much time pursuing his hobby that he graduated with a distinctly lack lustre degree. If he was dejected by this, it was nothing compared to the sadness he experienced upon finally realising he did not have the artist's eye. Although he was technically accomplished, he would never be more than a gifted amateur. He simply did not have that indefinable something to lift him out of the ordinary.

Then a fellow student at his life drawing class suggested that he consider a career as an art restorer; his attention to detail and technical ability were the ideal prerequisites. To his amazement he won a coveted place on the Courtauld's conservation course, his science degree giving him an advantage over arts graduate applicants. From the first day, he loved it and knew that, at last, he had found his vocation.

After the Courtauld, he was employed by the National Gallery, where his undoubted ability meant that he was soon entrusted with Old Masters. His days were spent working on pictures that had gasped for years under layers of dirty varnish. He restored colour and warmth, uncovering the bright glint of an eye, or the moist curve of a lip. Because of his skill the public saw these paintings as though new born from the artist's studio – fresh and vibrant. He felt very powerful, like a magician. And he relished making his small mark on the paintings. Someone seeing these masterpieces hundreds of years from now would look upon his work, even though they would never know that it was he who had made those brushstrokes. He would never be a great painter, but this was a sort of immortality – a little consolation prize. And his life was now crammed with so many prizes, Edie being the greatest prize of all. Yet they might so easily have never met.

She had been over from New York and, as always, visited the National Gallery, where her arrival had coincided with a talk being given by Graham. One look at his floppy golden hair and film star smile, and Edie was lost. He was, she decided, quite the most beautiful boy she had ever seen – boy being the appropriate word. With regret, she estimated that he was probably still in his twenties, whereas she had just celebrated her fortieth birthday. Nevertheless, after his talk, she approached him and related, quite truthfully, that she owned a small publishing company in New York specialising in the production of high quality art books. Some of the Gallery's collection was to be included in a forthcoming publication, and she wondered if he would write a few lines about the chosen paintings.

They met at The Ivy, to discuss the project over lunch, and talked for nearly four hours. Graham was particularly interested to learn that Edie was active in the American charity, Save Venice, although she failed to mention her significant personal donations to the cause. Nor did she tell him that her publishing company ran as a tax loss, providing her with amusement rather than income. Before they went their separate ways Graham had asked her out to dinner. Then he took her to lunch again, and then to the theatre, and then to bed.

Edie was head over heels in love, but continued to be evasive about her considerable personal fortune. She wanted to be loved for herself, not her money. Graham was no fool, however, and a hundred little things gave Edie away, from her designer clothes to her unintentional name-dropping.

Neither of them would ever be quite sure of who proposed to whom, but just weeks after their transatlantic romance began, they decided to get married. Edie's father was, at first unenthusiastic, but when Graham suggested that he took Edie's name, the old man was completely won over. Although he had two sons, it was Edie he loved best.

Faced with the stunning reality of his new financial situation, Graham was adamant about one thing: he had no intention of giving up his work. Edie's solution was simple: he should come to New York. With his talent (and well connected wife) he would surely be offered a place in the Metropolitan's conservation department. But Graham was determined to be his own boss – and to choose his own projects. Edie's influence meant that the world was now his oyster, and he wanted not just prestigious commissions, but ones that would stir his heart and quicken his pulse. And, most significantly, to determine the methods used. Liberated from the constraints of Gallery policy, he had been experimenting with pigments and solvent formulae, and was now longing to try out his new findings.

Graham was musing on these things during their first evening at Ca' Melisa as, still damp from his shower, he lay on the bed and watched Edie emerge from the bathroom. Droplets of water glistened on her broad shoulders, and he experienced a sudden and irresistible urge to lick them from her flesh. When he grabbed her towel, she made only a token gesture at retrieving it and, yielding to his greater strength, landed next to him.

'No, honey,' she protested, as the bed creaked under their weight. 'We're supposed to be down in the *sala* for drinks at six, and I've still got to do my makeup.'

'You're beautiful just as you are,' murmured Graham, burying his face in the warm hollow of her neck, as his hand strayed downwards, insistent fingers nuzzling into the damp knot of her pubic hair.

'Well, we better be quick,' she whispered, pushing aside his bathrobe to reveal the all too obvious evidence that he could surely be nothing else. Less than five minutes later Edie was stifling gasps of pleasure as Graham took a swift and sure possession of her dewy body.

Three floors below, the *sala* was brushed gold with evening sunshine as small groups of people, basking in its warmth, tentatively made each other's acquaintance. The *prosecco* was flowing; birdsong drifted in from the garden, along with a faint perfume of early flowering lilac, and dinner promised to be excellent. Everyone was at ease and happy.

And yet one of the company was distinctly nervous. Ever since she had seen Raffi in St Mark's Square, Anna had faced the prospect of dinner at Ca' Melisa with trepidation. She knew the reason – the possibility of again encountering Caterina. Consequently, she was relieved to find that the girl with the bright hair and hostile eyes was not there; but then neither was Raffi. Just as she faced the possibility that he also may not be coming, she heard someone call her name and saw Vittore striding towards them, his arms held wide.

'Anna, I am so pleased that at long last I can welcome you back to Ca' Melisa.' He kissed her warmly on both cheeks, and his hands tightened around her upper arms in a gesture of support. 'My deepest commiserations for your loss.'

'I'm sorry I never replied to your letter, but...'

'Oh, my dear girl, I did not expect a reply. We just wanted you to know that we were thinking of you. But now you are here, and you look marvellous. Will, you are a lucky man to be accompanying two such beautiful women.'

Beside her, Izzy glowed, feeding greedily on the compliment, while Anna also felt a prickle of pleasure at such appreciation. Will, ever the reticent Englishman, grunted in agreement, having not really noticed the care they had taken.

In contrast to the skimpy outfit Izzy had lent her on her last visit to Ca' Melisa, Anna was wearing a sleeveless dress in the palest of grey silk. Cut on the bias, it was of a modest length and while clinging closely to her hips, fell in soft folds across the bosom.

Vittore continued chatting and then Anna saw his eyes fix on something behind her.

'Ah, here's Raffi,' he announced. 'Better late than never.'

'*Ciao*,' a voice said, a little breathlessly, and she sensed the air stir as its owner approached; the scent of cologne, a shiver of lime and sandalwood, indicating his proximity. She turned; he was so close that when he spoke she felt the soft expulsion of his breath on her face.

'Anna!' As he kissed her she registered the slight roughness of his cheek. 'It's so good to see you.'

Imperceptibly, and within a matter of moments, Vittore, Izzy and Will had drifted away. They were talking to a fair-haired man blessed with the looks of a 1950s matinee idol whose face Anna found vaguely familiar. However, the only man in the room who held her attention was the one standing before her: the high cheekbones, wide apart hazel eyes and soft spill of light brown hair were all as she remembered.

'So, what have you been doing since you arrived back in Venice?' he asked.

'Shamefully little. But we did go to the Easter Vigil at the Basilica. I thought I saw you in the Piazza.'

'Oh, when?'

'Around midnight.'

'Why didn't you say hello?'

'I wasn't sure it was you,' she said untruthfully, adding by way of excuse, 'You were wearing glasses.'

'Ah, yes, I'd lost a contact lens. Sometimes I think they're more trouble than they're worth. But I got used to them when I was doing my national service – it was easier on manoeuvres.'

'You had to do national service!' echoed Anna. 'In England it stopped years ago.'

'Well, I'm afraid it's still compulsory here. If you really don't like the idea of the armed forces you can do some sort of community work instead. But to tell you the truth, I rather enjoyed it. For a boy brought up in the city, even a city as beautiful as Venice, it was good to spend so much time outdoors. And there was lots of weekend leave. All the *mammas* of Italy would rise in revolt if the government deprived them of their adored sons for too long. The worst thing is, it delays your graduation, so if you study architecture, like I did, you're quite ancient before you even start your career.'

'Hardly ancient,' laughed Anna.

'I'm twenty-nine next birthday. After that, thirty, and then it's all downhill. Caterina, that's my girlfriend, is threatening to buy me a pipe and slippers.'

"Girlfriend". As soon as he uttered the word, Anna felt as though the room had dimmed a little. Even as she experienced the disappointment the casual reference brought, she chided herself. He was not single – she knew that; it would be ridiculous to develop any sort of attachment.

She forced her mouth into a bright smile, hoping that her features had not given her away. If they had, Raffi showed no sign of noticing.

'She stays in Milan during the week,' he added somewhat superfluously, as Anna had made no comment about Caterina's absence. Then he lowered his voice, glancing around to make sure no one could hear. 'She doesn't really like these dinners. Says she hates having to make small talk with fat old men who don't give a damn about art, but are only here to indulge their wives.'

'And you?' she asked. 'Do you mind them?'

'No, not really. I'm more tolerant of people's motives than Caterina. And it is my uncle's – what's the expression – bread and butter. You see, he likes me to chat up the elderly single ladies; makes me sound like a gigolo, doesn't it? But I think, tonight, I have the evening off. Apparently there are no unaccompanied lady guests.'

'Apart from me.'

'Hardly elderly. Though I am surprised that you are unaccompanied. But then I suppose you've had to leave your boyfriend in England?'

'Actually, right now, there is no boyfriend.'

He smiled, and said blandly, 'I suspect that will soon change.'

'That's not why I came to Venice,' said Anna, with a defensive primness that appalled her, and then, trying to retrieve the situation, 'Holiday romances never last, do they?'

'Well, sometimes they do, but you're right, they're probably best avoided. But you'll have to put up a strong resistance; Italian men are such flirts. I'm allowed to say that with complete impunity, being only half Italian.'

Ah, Raffi's mysterious parentage, she thought, but before the subject could be pursued, a gentle ringing rose above the room's muted conversation. Everyone looked towards the sound's direction. Vittore, holding a small bell, stood next to a screen and a cloth-draped easel.

'My uncle is about to shower you with words of wisdom. You'll enjoy it, but I've heard it many, many times, so if you'll excuse me, I'm going to find my aunt. I'll see you at dinner.' He gave her that unnervingly appealing lop-sided grin, and added, 'I've taken a look at the seating plan; Vittore has placed me next to you. Can you bear that?'

Oh, I think so, thought Anna, as she watched him weave his way towards the door.

'Hello, a hundred *lire* for your thoughts.' Izzy appeared at her side, and with linked arms they made their way to a cluster of seats placed in two curved rows. 'How's Raffi? You two were very deep in conversation. I hope he's coming back.'

'Oh, yes, he'll be back. Turns out I'm sitting next to him at dinner.'

'Lucky you!'

A hush then descended, as the shutters were closed, and Vittore took his place. Urbane and immaculate in a beautifully tailored suit, he surveyed his guests with a paternalistic smile.

'Ladies and gentlemen, may I start by thanking you all for choosing to spend your vacation at Ca' Melisa.' He paused, his wise grey eyes warm and animated, obviously enjoying himself. 'The next ten days will, I hope, provide memories that you will long treasure, whether you are first time, or seasoned, visitors to Venice. Either way, I intend to share some of its magic with you, and show you places and sights usually denied the casual tourist. It will be a busy holiday, but rest assured, I do not expect anyone to hand in essays – unless they really want to! Above all, you must enjoy yourselves, and tonight my talk will be brief because this evening is for you to relax and to get to know one another.'

The lights were dimmed and the first slide shone onto the screen. It comprised two separate photos, placed side-by-side, showing very different buildings. One was an impressively solid edifice, its lower storey made of rough-hewn stone, and although it possessed windows, they were neither large nor elegant. It resembled a medieval fortress and certainly did not look as though it belonged in Venice. The other building, with its airy balconies and fairy-tale crenulations, Anna recognised. It was the Ca' d'Oro, that phantasmagorical jewel of the Grand Canal.

'Venice,' began Vittore, 'is unique for many different reasons, some of which we will explore over the next few days. But perhaps most obvious to the visitor, is the particular nature of its architecture. You will see here, two palaces. Both were built for wealthy noble families within a decade of each other. But how different they are. And why is that? The reason is quite simple – and all around us. Ladies and gentlemen, it is this.'

He paused and picking up his drinking glass, held it high. There was a flash as, for an instant, the projector's light transformed the content to liquid gold.

'Yes, the reason is – water! The building you see here is the Palazzo Medici-Riccardi in Florence, and even if we Venetians had wanted to build such a palace it would have been impossible to do so in most of the city. The majority of our *palazzi* are built upon land stolen from the lagoon, erected upon thousands of wooden piles sunk into sand and silt. For those early architects, then, as now, the weight of a building was a major consideration. But we had no need to erect such fortress-like homes. Our main defence already surrounded us – the lagoon. Its protection allowed us to create this beautiful building – the Ca' d'Oro. Let me show you more.' And he flicked onto the next slide.

Even without looking, Anna could tell that the audience was rapt. It was not just the content of his talk, but the delivery. He spoke with the graceful, easy authority of the true expert, interspersing facts with small jokes and anecdotes, demonstrating how the Venetian architects and painters had, down the centuries, made their mark on the culture of many other countries.

'Finally,' he concluded, 'after all these grand masterpieces and noble buildings, I am going to show you something very plain, very old, and quite humble, but which to me, also demonstrates the indisputable influence of Venice and her artists. But first, look at this altarpiece.'

Onto the screen burst a painting immediately familiar to Anna.

'This,' continued Vittore, 'is the Adoration of the Shepherds by the Venetian artist, Cima da Conegliano. It still hangs in its original position in the Church of the Carmini. Although it is undated we are almost certain that it was painted between 1509 and 1511. We know this because it was commissioned by the wealthy merchant, Giovanni Calvo, who was preparing his sepulchre at that time. The shepherd kneeling in the foreground may well be Giovanni; donors' portraits frequently appear in the works they commissioned. But what about the inclusion of the other figures?'

Silence. No one, it seemed, wanted to speak. However, after a few seconds a female voice, clearly American, said, 'Well, I guess that the woman with the cross is St Helena. She was often associated with the Nativity because she founded a church in Bethlehem. Right?'

'That is quite correct. Thank you, Edie. St Helena was also a particular favourite of the Carmelite order. Any idea about the others?'

Anna stole a glance at the woman; she was seated next to the handsome, fair-haired man who had been chatting to Vittore. She had wonderful auburn hair but ordinary, rather bland features. However, upon receiving Vittore's praise, she smiled and her face was brushed with radiance, as she continued, 'The woman on the far left must be Saint Catherine. A part of the wheel on which she was tortured is at her feet. Then on the right there is little Tobias with the angel Raphael. All I can think of is that Calvo had family with those names?'

'Correct, but only partly so. His wife was indeed named Catherine. But the angel Raphael is included because Calvo lived in the parish of San Raphael. We do not know why he chose the Carmini for his final resting place rather than his own parish church. However, not many years later San Raphael was demolished and rebuilt, suggesting that perhaps it was somewhat dilapidated. So, as I am sure you will agree, this painting shows a unique configuration of subjects, totally determined by time and place. Now, please may I have some light and I will show you something from my own modest collection.'

He turned to the draped easel, and even before he whipped away the cloth, Anna knew exactly what it would reveal – the cradle-end she had first seen so many months ago.

Vittore's words faded into the background as she again felt the painting exert its strange fascination, pulling her into a private world where she felt overwhelming joy, tempered by heart quickening trepidation. With an effort she forced herself to listen to Vittore.

'...it was painted many miles from Venice, and ten years after the Carmini altarpiece. The artist has omitted Helena, Catherine and even Joseph. The Virgin is placed on the other side of the manger and there is only the single shepherd, but Raphael and Tobias, even the dog – although a rather different little hound, I admit – remain very prominent. Moreover, if you compare the placement and gestures of the figures in the two paintings, you will find them almost identical. This, I am sure, is more than coincidence. I do believe that whoever decorated this piece of furniture must have been familiar with the Cima Adoration. Perhaps he carried its mental image all the way from Venice to far off Bruges. Why he – or possibly she – because there were a number of female artists in the North, chose the Cima as their model, I am afraid we will never know.' As he said this, Vittore caught Anna's eye and a complicit smile played around the corners of his mouth, and she remembered her certainty that the painter had been a woman. He seemed about to say more, when something in his peripheral vision distracted him.

'My apologies, ladies and gentlemen. As usual, I have over run and I am being alerted to the fact that unless we immediately take our seats for dinner your *risi e bisi* will be quite ruined, and if that happens my dear wife will never forgive me. Thank you so much for listening. *Buon appetito.*'

To the accompaniment of enthusiastic applause Vittore strode towards a beaming Rosina who was sentinelled by the dining room doors. Everyone followed, eager to discover where they were sitting. To her surprise, Anna found that she was next to Vittore, who, predictably, was at the head of the table. Izzy and Will were a few seats down and, true to his word, the place card on her left bore the name, "Raffaele Anzelieri". Opposite her was the knowledgeable American lady, and the matinee idol. They stood, leaning against their chairs, deep in conversation, but fell silent when Anna approached.

'Hi,' said the woman. 'You must be Anna. I'm Edie Singelmann, and this is my husband, Graham. We're having a huge argument about Vittore's lecture.'

Their cosy body language suggested that "amicable discussion" would be a more appropriate description.

'Oh, yes. About any particular aspect?'

'It's a charming notion,' said Graham, 'but it doesn't remotely prove that the artist who painted the cradle knew the Cima. He probably included Tobias and Raphael because it was intended for a child with one of those names.'

'Oh, you are so unromantic,' protested his wife. 'And you heard Vittore; it could have been a woman. There are all sorts of fascinating reasons why some unknown, rookie – female – painter from Bruges was familiar with the Carmini altarpiece. What do you think, Anna?'

'Well, I've no knowledge on which to base my opinion, apart from Vittore's talk, but yes, I agree, the painter could well have known the Cima. That's just my gut feeling.'

'Two against one, honey.' Edie gave her husband a peck on the cheek, before turning her attention to Anna.

'Vittore tells me you're taking a career break and spending six months in Venice. How splendid. It's something Graham and I hope to be able to do in the fall if…' She stopped mid-sentence. Her husband's handsome features remained unruffled but something made Anna suspect that Edie had received the smallest of kicks from his no doubt elegantly shod foot. She glanced sidewards, gave an enigmatic little smile and continued, '…if things work out. Oh, here comes Vittore at last. And, oh, Raffi – I haven't seen him in an age.'

Anna felt a hand on her shoulder a second before Raffi whispered in her ear, 'I'm sorry to have abandoned you for so long. I couldn't get away; everyone wants to chat tonight.'

Present company it seemed was no exception, for Edie also was clearly eager to talk. By the time Raffi extricated himself and took his seat next to Anna the first course had been served. On a large white plate three silver fishes glinted from a sea of onions, pine nuts and raisins, topped with a verdant sprinkling of parsley.

'*Sardele in soar*,' said Raffi, offering her the breadbasket. 'Lightly fried sardines marinated for at least forty-eight hours. Best in the city. The secret is Rosina's marinade, a recipe handed down from mother to daughter, and now me! It's one of Venice's oldest dishes; a very good way of preserving the fish, and the onions used to protect people from scurvy. But now we eat it just because it's delicious.'

Anna tentatively teased a morsel of tender flesh onto her fork. She had never cared for sardines and remembered that Millie had sometimes served them up on soggy toast for tea. But these bore no resemblance to that flaccid boniness. The piquant combination of sweet and sour took her by surprise, as the tartness of the sauce cut through the oiliness of the fish. The pine nuts added crunch, the raisins a beguiling exoticism, and the parsley a springy freshness. Silence fell as everyone turned their attention to the serious business of eating.

'Those were absolutely wonderful,' she at last said. 'Believe it or not, I've only ever eaten sardines out of a tin.'

'What an ignominious way to treat such a jewel of the sea,' said Raffi, pouring her another glass of wine. 'We Venetians have a great respect for sardines. On Pellestrina there's a church known as San Pietro delle Sardelle. I don't know what is more revered, the saint, or the fish. Promise me you'll never eat sardines out of a tin again.'

'I promise,' she said, and found that they were giggling like children.

'Hey, you two,' Edie's voice chimed. 'What's the joke? Let me in on it, please. These guys,' and she indicated Vittore and her husband, 'are being way too serious. Just listen to them.'

'What is the point of restoring paintings unless you're going to make a real difference?' Graham was demanding of his host. 'We've just been to the Louvre… seen a Titian altarpiece, supposedly restored. I don't know why they bothered. To me it still looks muddy…dull.'

'Well, my dear boy,' replied Vittore. 'The French are famously cautious with their treasures, rather like ourselves who…'

'You're telling me. At least in Britain and the States, we…'

'Stop it!' Edie's voice was low, but firm. 'I like paintings as much as anyone, but arguing about the minutiae of different types of varnish, or whatever you're getting so het up about, at the dinner table is just too much.'

'I do apologise, my dear,' said Vittore. 'We are being abominably rude.'

'Yes, I'm sorry too, darling,' said Graham. 'But you know how carried away I get. And,' he added deferentially, 'it's just so difficult not to discuss technicalities when faced with such an expert.'

There was an awkward silence, broken by Anna asking, 'So, are you a conservationist, Graham?'

'He is indeed,' declared Edie. 'He gives back to the world what time has stolen.' And then, as a steaming bowl was placed in front of her, 'Oh, my goodness – risotto! My poor waistline.'

'No talk of diets, please, Edie,' Vittore scolded. 'You can live on lettuce leaves when you get back to New York but while you are here, you must eat, eat, eat. And this is not risotto, my dear, but *risi e bisi*. Rice cooked with the first of the season's peas. A humble concoction you may think, but traditionally always served to the Doge on 25 April, which is, of course, St Mark's day, so we are eating it three days early. But as the sweetest of spring peas have just appeared in the market, Rosina could not resist serving it. Now please, don't stand on ceremony. You must eat whilst it is hot.'

Raffi leaned towards Anna and indicated the creamy mixture, studded with emerald bright peas and rosy niblets of bacon.

'It's very important to get the consistency just right. It has to be *all' onda* which means "with waves". If you tilt your bowl, like so, you should see the liquid making a little wave.' He demonstrated, and a heady, parmesan-laden cloud drifted up to tickle their nostrils. '*Perfetto*. I hope you're not going to tell me you've only ever eaten peas from a tin?'

'I shall ignore that remark. We have beautiful fresh peas in England, although I admit most of them do end up frozen,' said Anna, between spoonfuls of the fragrant broth, which for something comprising such simple ingredients was unexpectedly delightful; both aromatic and comforting. 'You're obviously a very knowledgeable cook.'

'Well, I was rather a greedy little boy and I soon discovered that the best place to be was the kitchen, but Rosina wouldn't let me get away with simply sitting there with my mouth open, like a baby bird, waiting for tasty morsels. She made me tear basil leaves, grate *parmigiano*, mould *gnocchi*, anything that didn't involve hot liquids or knives, and all the time she would tell me what she was doing, and why. Some of it couldn't help but sink in.'

'A man who can cook! You are going to make an ideal husband,' said Edie who was unashamedly listening in to their conversation. 'When I next speak to Lucia, I'll tell her how much I approve. It's a shame I'm already spoken for.'

Everyone laughed before Graham asked, 'From what sort of career are you taking a break, Anna?'

'Oh, boring financial stuff.'

'My dear, there is nothing boring about finance,' said Edie. 'Blessed are the moneymakers, that's what I say. After all, if it weren't for them, we'd have none of this.' And she threw out her arm in an extravagant gesture that Anna supposed was meant to encompass all of Venice. 'And worst of all, there would be no wonderful paintings for you to look after,' she added, turning to her husband.

'What sort of paintings do you work on?' asked Anna.

'I was with the National Gallery, so the very best.' And Graham proceeded to mention some pictures, none of which Anna knew, although she attempted to look impressed. Then, as he spoke, she realised why his face was so familiar.

In the dark days after her father's death, she had often abandoned her desk at lunchtime and slipped into the Gallery. Here she could be anonymous, and if anyone caught the tears in her eyes, they would presume that it was a Rembrandt or Titian that so moved her. Then one afternoon, she had been confronted with a huge altarpiece she had never before seen. It represented the Incredulity of Thomas, and a very handsome young man was talking in animated tones about it. Drawn by his enthusiasm, she crept nearer, and heard that the artist was none other than Cima da Conegliano, and that the painting was on display for the first time since 1947, having newly emerged from the Gallery's conservation department.

At its centre stood a pale-skinned, titian-haired Christ. Draped in a silver-grey winding sheet, he displayed nail pierced hands, his expression both sad and serene. Next to him, resplendent in red and green, was Thomas, a forefinger insinuated into the wound in his master's side, forever frozen in the moment when he ceased to doubt the resurrection. The other apostles were assembled in various attitudes of prayer or devout acceptance: good, wholesome men, their attention fixed on the drama enacted before them. However, the second figure on the left stared out beyond the painting's confines. Seconds ago, it seemed, he too would have been intent upon the sight of man, made God, but at the exact moment the artist chose to portray, he had moved his eyes to interact with the viewer, inviting them to share the sacred revelation. His expression was passive, with no hint of confrontation, as though he were saying, 'Here I am, an ordinary man, but I am witnessing the greatest miracle the world has ever known. You too, can share my faith – if you wish.'

Even when she moved away from the painting and looked at other works in the room, Anna found herself constantly turning back to it and noticed that wherever she stood, his gaze followed her. Meeting his clear eyes, she had known, without a shadow of a doubt, that she looked upon the features of the artist; this was a self-portrait of the man who had created the work. Standing in the National Gallery, the certainty had unnerved her, but months later, on a balmy Venetian night, her mind freed by wine and the warm exoticism of her surroundings, the conviction did not seem so outlandish.

'I once listened to you talking about Cima's Incredulity,' she said. 'Just after it was put back on display. Were you involved in its restoration?'

'No,' replied Graham. 'The Incredulity was very much my boss's baby. He spent nearly four years chipping away all the wood from the back of it before he could even begin to transfer the painting to a new panel.'

'That first time I saw it,' said Anna, 'I had the strangest feeling that one of the disciples – the one almost totally obscured by Thomas – was a self-portrait. Is that possible?'

Graham shrugged and resumed eating. 'Oh, I don't think there's any evidence for it.'

Then Vittore spoke, very softly. 'Actually, I believe that it is possible. I think it could well be the case, Anna.'

Graham visibly bristled as Vittore continued, 'The painting was in a terrible condition. In the nineteenth century, long before it came to London, it was submerged under floodwater for several hours, which resulted in significant paint loss. What the National Gallery has achieved is quite remarkable.' He paused. 'However, I do question why it was transferred to a synthetic panel.'

Although he was smiling, his words hung in the air like a challenge.

Graham turned towards him, his face a little flushed; his expression and body language undoubtedly adversarial. 'Oh, Vittore, surely you, of all people, appreciate that wooden panels are no longer...'

Edie raised both hands in a gesture that managed to be both conciliatory and authoritative, quashing the threatened verbal skirmish.

'Now boys, please, not again! I am on vacation and all I want to do is look at beautiful things and not worry about why or how we are going to save them for posterity. You two can argue about panels and resins and gesso another time, but now let's just enjoy our dinner. Please.'

The two men smiled at one another, although their eyes remained steely. Peace was, for the moment, restored, and Graham planted an apologetic kiss on his wife's cheek. But on this warm spring evening a palpable frisson of coolness unsettled the mood, as though autumn had made an early and unheralded visitation.

Then the dining room doors flew open and Rosina appeared, as bright as a diva stepping onto the stage, kingfisher blue dress shimmering in the candlelight. Behind her, two teenage boys, with the bearing of Renaissance princes, held aloft a huge platter, on which reposed a vast, silver fish. Everyone burst into spontaneous applause.

'*Branzino al finocchio*,' said Raffi. 'Sea bass with braised fennel.'

At the sight of this treasure of the sea, discord was banished and all thoughts, other than the anticipation of the next course, were quite dispelled.

Venice: Winter 1515

Shortly after my lessons commence, *papà* falls ill. Praise God, his ailment is not serious and he soon recovers. But for a few days he suffers a slight fever, and a quantity of catarrh on his chest causes him to cough a good deal, so he keeps to his bed. Although I tend him diligently, I am loath to miss my lesson and beg his permission to go alone. After much cajoling he agrees, on the condition that if Cima objects, I am at once to return.

When I arrive, Cima is intent upon the altarpiece and is apparently oblivious to my solitary state. I now know the painter better and realise that whilst immersed in his art he hardly notices the time of day, or the food on his plate, and certainly not whether I am accompanied or no. Only when he tears himself away from his work does he turn his attention to me.

'No Francesco today?' he says, looking about the room, as if expecting *papà* to suddenly materialise.

I explain, expecting to be dismissed, but thankfully he seems unconcerned and sets about showing me how to make objects appear distant by the use of perspective.

Now, more often than not, I come alone, and providing I am safely home before dark, neither *papà* nor Cima minds. Well, I am not totally alone as Cesare usually accompanies me. He is fascinated by all the new smells, and dashes about the workshop like a mad creature, his shiny little nose twitching with excitement. Then tired out, he curls up in the warmest corner he can find, whilst keeping a watchful eye upon me.

Even the apprentices now accept me. I am fortunate that Cima does not allow ribald talk, for otherwise I should hear things unfit for my ears. I would not mind this so much, but I do not wish them to feel inhibited by my presence. They are good boys, respectful and hardworking, even Bernardo, the one who leered at young Giovanni. In Ginevra he shows scant interest, although I do sometimes catch him staring at me, but with curiosity rather than lust. I do believe he has guessed, but dare not voice his suspicions.

In fact, it seems that it is only Giacomo who is party to my secret. He too, having seen me dressed as Giovanni was intrigued by how alike this youth was to Ginevra. But being family, and therefore allowed greater liberty, said as much to his uncle. Giambattista, as I have come to call him, being too honest to lie on my behalf, told him the whole truth. To my amazement, Giacomo, far from disapproving, is impressed by my subterfuge. He tells me how he admires all that I am doing to help *papà*. When he says this, I see sadness in his eyes, for he lost both his parents when he was but eight years old. After their deaths, his uncle took him into his household, and later found him an apprenticeship with the best woodcarvers in the city.

It is now winter and with the shortening days there is less time for us to paint. I am sorry for this, but there are compensations, for I am more likely to meet Giacomo when he returns from his work. He has taken to walking me home, for which I am most grateful, because in addition to the usual nocturnal perils of our city there is a new terror lurking. It is rumoured that two young women have been attacked by a monster, who has inflicted the most unnatural and bestial acts upon them.

Papà and I look at each other under lowered lids. I cannot help thinking that had we spoken out, the brute may have been apprehended long ago, for surely he is the same man who hurt Agnesina. The apprentice, Alvise, who was sweet on her, is also very quiet, as is the painter. We are all joined in a guilty and silent conspiracy. It is, however, too late for regrets, and at least Agnesina is now safely married to her prosperous husband. I wonder what her wedding night was like. (Of late, I find myself thinking of such things more frequently than I believe I should.) Did she cry out when he took her, feigning the loss of her virginity, even as her body remembered those earlier, violent penetrations?

For my part, when I am with Giacomo I feel quite safe, although sometimes I counterfeit fear, so that he will draw closer. We walk through the crowded city, keeping to the well-lit byways and one night, with the sound of the angelus bells falling all around us, he tells me about his parents. He misses them still, especially his mother. She was Giambattista's youngest sister whom he often painted. It is a small consolation for Giacomo that her face lives on in these images. He tells me there is a Saint Catherine in the church of San Rocco in Mestre that is a wondrously good likeness of her. I have never seen it – why should I cross the lagoon to *terra firma* in such troubled times? When I say that I should like to look at it, he promises that one day he will take me. This greatly heartens me, for it must mean that he likes me.

I cannot believe that I, who until a few weeks ago, abhorred the idea of marriage, am now so sure that here is the man I wish for a husband. It would be perfect: he could move into our house whilst I continue to help *papà*. I know men do not usually marry until they are much older than Giacomo, and his uncle would undoubtedly wish him to complete his apprenticeship before taking a wife, but I am sure I could win him round. Some day, when the time is right, I will tell *papà* everything, and he will speak to Giambattista. In the meantime, I just have to be patient.

* * *

It is late November. I am at the workshop, intent on the task of stirring oil into a powder made from charred grape vines. This makes an intense black paint, some of which I later discover is smudged across my forehead. I am in my oldest clothes (many layers of them too, for it is mightily cold) and I suspect that my nose is red from the chill. It is one of those sharp winter days when the light is so merciless that it shows up every imperfection in a woman's face, so when we receive an unexpected visitor, I certainly do not look my best.

He is so bundled in furs that at first I do not recognize him; then I realise that it is Enrico Sartorani. Indoors he exerts a power even greater than when I first met him on the street all those months ago. It is as though a wild animal has invaded the workshop – even the smell of him, though in fairness, that probably emanates from his apparel. His eyes scan the room, but he seems not to notice me.

'I should like to present my father with a painting. And…and I mean no disrespect by this…' he gives us – the apprentices – a conciliatory smile. 'I require the entire work to be executed by the master. I want a Madonna for personal, devotional use, to hang in the bedchamber. But something a little different…' he stops, as though embarrassed, 'not one of your…your usual milk-sop virgins.'

I suspect that he is trying to humour us, but if I were Giambattista, I would find his choice of words most insulting, and would be tempted to tell him to go hang himself in his fancy hose, especially as the "usual milk-sops" are, of course, the artist's beloved first wife, Corona. But Giambattista merely gives a little smile – and waits.

'Give me a Madonna like those women Giorgione da Castelfranco used to paint,' says Enrico.

He speaks about an artist who died in the same outbreak of plague that carried off my uncle Carlo. It is said that Giorgione's mistress contracted the pestilence but rather than shun her, as most would have done, he rushed to her side and shared her bed – and inevitably her death. Some believe that had he lived, he would have been as great an artist as Giovanni Bellini. Certainly, his frescoes adorning the Fondaco dei Tedeschi are a marvel to see, although already they are beginning to fade, I think.

'My father is to remarry,' continues Enrico, 'and his new wife is particularly devoted to Saint Catherine. Therefore, I should like you to make me a representation of the Mystic Marriage. But my father's bride is a nut-brown little thing and may not want her tawniness compared to a golden girl, so be sure to use dark haired models. This will kill two birds with one stone. My father will have a brace of pretty virgins to look at, whilst his wife can gaze on her favourite saint. So their minds, no doubt, will be concentrating on very different things, even as their bodies strive towards the one end.'

His words shock me a little. I know full well that paintings of a lewd nature are sometimes hung in bedchambers so as to encourage a couple to a greater mutual pleasure, which in turn aids the conception of a child. But his veiled implication that the image of the Virgin and a saint will be used for such a purpose is unseemly. Saint Catherine's vision of wedding herself to the Christ child had nothing to do with what we humans get up to in bed.

Next to me, Bernardo sniggers. Enrico turns, laughing, and looks at us. I see, at once, that he realises he is in the presence of a woman.

'Forgive my blunt words, lady. I hope that I have not offended you?'

The shock of his attention steals the breath from my throat, rendering me speechless, but Giambattista comes to my rescue.

'I give Ginevra drawing lessons. Her father, Doctor Vannitelli, usually accompanies her.'

'Ah, yes. I do believe we have met before? Yes – I remember now. The good doctor and his plucky assistant!'

His amber eyes take in my stained hands and paint-smeared clothes. He must think these lessons very different to the ones that his noble sisters receive in their grand house. As he looks at me I feel that, despite my layers of clothes, he can see right down to my pale, goose pimpled flesh. I know that I am blushing; this too, does not go unnoticed.

'What a pretty thing you are when your cheeks have a bit of colour,' he says. 'I think I have found the model for my Madonna.'

'I doubt Doctor Vannitelli would approve,' Giambattista retorts.

I can sense the protectiveness in his voice and I bless him for it, but then I say, with so little decorum that I surprise even myself, 'Oh, but he would.'

Both men are looking at me. Enrico's cat eyes are dancing in amusement and his hand moves towards me. Cesare growls; he does not like strangers to touch me.

'Be quiet, you naughty dog,' I say, scooping him up. The interruption gives me time to think. 'Please, I should so like to be painted, and I am sure *papà* would be honoured.'

115

I turn my most pleading look on Giambattista. He knows, better than any, how man seeks a little immortality in having his likeness made, for those who commission a grand painting will, more often than not, choose to have their faces incorporated into it, whether as saint, angel or shepherd. And most artists, also, cannot resist making their own portrait. Even Giambattista, who is little given to vanity, told me that he once donated his face to a disciple witnessing the incredulity of St Thomas. He says I would not recognise him, for the altarpiece was completed many years ago – and he gave himself a beard!

'Please,' I say again, and to my delight, Giambattista agrees.

Then the discussion turns to who will suffice for Saint Catherine. Before my courage fails me I interrupt again, 'I have a friend who will be perfect. She is exceeding pretty with dark hair and the most beautiful eyes and,' I glance at Enrico, 'mouth.'

As I speak, I realise I have darted my tongue over my lower lip. He looks away, clearing his throat. 'Well, bring her here and we may both see if she is an appropriate choice.'

After this, they lose interest in me and discuss the financial aspects of the commission. I make an excuse and leave early, for before returning home, I have a call to make.

Old Scandals

Following the dinner at Ca' Melisa, Anna slept fitfully and late. It was hardly surprising. After the *branzino* they ate local cheeses with homemade *grissini* and a honeyed mustard concoction that Raffi told her was *mostarda*. A supposedly "light" dessert turned out to be a generous portion of *semifreddo*; voluptuously creamy and chocolate-oozing. Finally, they staggered into the *sala* for coffee and grappa.

That next morning, she would have snoozed for longer, but the light filtering through the shutters was too insistent to ignore and was accompanied by a noisy chanting and a sharp, savoury smell. In deference to the morning chill, she pulled on a dressing gown and found Izzy on the terrace. Clad in a jumper and pyjama bottoms, with shower damp hair, she was pottering about the tubs of infant flowers, singing tunelessly. In one hand she held a watering can and in the other, a piece of toast and Marmite. The pungent scent of geraniums mingled with her breakfast. As always, Anna marvelled at Izzy's ability to shake off the effects of inebriation; for someone who last night could hardly stand, there was not a trace of a hangover. She looked at Anna with a woebegone expression.

'I haven't watered the things for ages. Toni nearly gave himself a hernia lugging them up here. He'll never forgive me if they're all dead when he comes back.'

She wilted onto a chair amongst the hapless flowers and picked up another piece of toast. 'So, how are you this morning?'

Her tone was light, but Anna detected a wicked glint in her eyes.

'Fine. I don't think I'll ever eat again.'

'You'll be ravenous by lunchtime,' said Izzy.

'The food was amazing, wasn't it? Raffi was telling me; there's one old boy who comes over every autumn, in the game and mushroom season. But he doesn't bother with the art talks anymore. If the weather's fine, he simply sits in the garden, reading; goes out for the occasional walk, and just waits for Rosina to feed him.'

'Sweet. So what else did you and Raffi talk about? Every time I looked, you were so deep in conversation I thought we'd need a crowbar to prise you apart.'

'I'm surprised you can remember anything about last night.'

'Oh, however pissed I am, I always remember the important things,' replied Izzy, her good humour not in the least dented. 'So when are you seeing him again?'

'I'm not, as far as I'm aware.'

Anna remembered their goodbyes. She had not expected Raffi to suggest they meet but had still felt crestfallen when he did not. Although he had said, most definitely had said, 'See you soon.' But perhaps that was just one of those things that people say.

'Well, you will, of course, because you both live in Venice and unless you stay locked in the flat your paths are sure to cross, I guarantee. But he didn't make any definite date? That's a bummer.'

'Why should he? He's got a girlfriend. Last night he was just being nice. I'm sure he's not remotely interested in me.'

'That's not what it looked like from where I was sitting. And I think you are very interested in him.'

'No, I'm not.'

'Don't believe you,' chanted Izzy, breaking into song. '"I'm not in lu-u-u-v-e, so don't you forget it. It's just a..."'

'Oh, fuck off, Izzy.'

'Sorry.'

'OK, I admit it. I fancy the pants off him. But as you so pointedly informed me the night I met him, he's taken.'

'Yes, but that was then. Now, Caterina's in Milan. Well, for most of the time.'

'Yes, but not all of the time. I don't want to be his bit on the side. And fighting over men really isn't my style.'

Izzy was quiet for a moment and then said, 'But you might win. Faint heart never won fair bloke.'

'And even if I did, what's the point? Come October I'll be back in London.'

'So? You have six wonderful months of unbridled passion with Raffi.'

'Look, I know it sounds wet, but I can't risk getting emotionally involved... getting hurt. What with everything else that's happened over the last year or so, I don't feel strong enough to put myself through all that.'

Izzy dropped her head down into her cupped hands. Looking up between her fingers, she said, 'I'm sorry. I wasn't thinking. You really like him, don't you?'

'Oh, I don't know,' Anna replied as briskly as she could. 'I hardly know him. It's probably just lust.'

'Oh, never underestimate lust. Empires have toppled because of it.'

'Exactly. It causes nothing but grief. Honestly, I think the best thing I can do is steer clear of the whole Anzelieri clan.'

She squinted up at the sky. A small flock of birds swooped past, squabbling and chattering as they pursued their breakfast – or a mate.

'It's much easier for them, isn't it?' she said.

'Not in Italy it isn't,' replied Izzy. 'They trap little birdies and serve them up with polenta.'

At that moment the telephone rang. Izzy sprang to her feet and ran indoors. Within moments she was back.

'Talk of the devil; it's for you.'

'Raffi?'

'No, 'fraid not. The old devil, Vittore. Shall I tell him you're on the plane back to London?'

'No, of course not.' And Anna went inside to take the call, both relieved and disappointed that it was the elder, rather than the younger man.

The conversation took less than three minutes. When she returned to the terrace, Izzy had resumed the desultory watering.

'Well? What did he want?'

'He started by saying that I must think him a, a…what was it? A very foolish, fond old man and…'

'A quote from King Lear. He loves his Shakespeare, does Vittore.'

'Then, he went on to say that he clean forgot, what with all the excitement of last night, that he still has to introduce me to this mystery person. He's got some free time tomorrow, because the guests have part of the day off for shopping or whatever. So he suggested we meet at Ca' Melisa, then visit whoever it is, and after that he'll take me to lunch.'

'But you won't be going, because you're steering clear of the Anzelieri. Right?'

'Of course I'm going. Anyway, it's only Vittore I'm meeting. I'll be safe with him.'

'I don't suppose he extended the invitation to me?'

'Sorry, no. I didn't think to…'

'Don't worry. Anyway, I'm working. And I'm sure you'll manage without a chaperone. Oh, well, can't sit around any longer. I've got to go and sort out some things at the Post Office, so I may be some time. People have been known to grow old and die in those queues.'

And with that Izzy abandoned the watering can and went to finish dressing.

Much of Anna's day was spent shopping, as it had now become imperative that she acquired something new to wear for her meeting with Vittore. First, however, she headed to the *Pescheria*, intent on buying some fish for supper. But as the morning was almost over, the vendors were already packing up to leave. She tiptoed through puddles surrounding crates of shiny silver and pink sea creatures, some still writhing, and approached a stall that was not yet empty.

Unfortunately, the labels had been removed, so she had no idea what to ask for.

The fishmonger paused from the task of piling his slippery wares into containers. '*Si, signorina?*'

Anna pointed at a pile of flat fish she supposed were sole. '*Tre, per favore.*'

But he seized one of their neighbours, more than twice their size. '*Rombo, si?*' he said, holding up the huge creature.

Before waiting for Anna to reply, he piled three of the monsters onto his scales, shouting out a price that, although incomprehensible, she guessed was vast.

'No, no,' she stammered. 'Smaller, please. *Piccolo, piccolo.*' And she made little pincer movements with her hands in demonstration.

But he didn't seem to understand, intent, it appeared, on selling her the three leviathans. They stared at each other; he, impatient to complete a sale and get home for his lunch; she, lost as to how to extricate herself from purchasing sufficient fish to feed ten people.

'It's OK. *Non, grazie,*' she muttered, making an embarrassed and hasty retreat. She would call at the supermarket where the checkout girls were brusque but proficient in English. The *Pescheria* would have to wait until Izzy or Will could accompany her.

By this time, other shops were also closing for lunch, so she continued walking. Eventually, she came to a lively *campo* where small boys, pursued by ecstatically yapping dogs, were playing football. Elderly residents, sitting on benches under a few spindly trees, laughed and gossiped. Facing the back of the ubiquitous church was an unassuming little bar. She went inside and ordered two *tramezzini* – the gorgeous, stuffed to the point of bursting, little sandwiches to which she was becoming addicted. The selection here was particularly good. She chose artichoke and ham, asparagus and egg, and then, realising she was, as Izzy had predicted, ravenous, also a *gamberoni piccante*, which she guessed was prawn.

'And to drink?' asked the barman in English.

'*Un ombra – bianco, per favore,*' she said, recalling that in Venice this was how one ordered a glass of wine. Something to do with stallholders selling wine in the Piazza under the shadow of the Campanile. Izzy had reliably informed her that *ombra* meant shade. She should know: a *giro d'ombra*, the Venetian equivalent of a pub-crawl was one of her favourite recreations.

'You sit outside?' asked the waiter.

Anna nodded. She wanted to bask in the sun and watch the world go by, so the extra *lire* were a small price to pay. The sandwiches were very good and she ordered another *ombra*; the glasses were, after all, very small.

After finishing her lunch, she wandered through the *sestiere* of Santa Croce.

Its higgledy-piggledy maze of *calli* were so different from Cannaregio's wide *fondamente* that within minutes she had lost all sense of direction. Refusing to consult her guidebook she went where her feet took her, although twice her path led precipitously to the murky waters of a canal, and once into a malodorous little courtyard inhabited by cats and a washing line of robust underwear. Undeterred, she continued walking until she found herself approaching the familiar territory of the railway station.

She had no idea where to commence her clothes buying mission, but guessed that the area around San Marco would be the best starting point. Rather than walk, she took the *vaporetto*. It was packed with people newly disgorged from a train, so she made her way to the open-air stern. Here she sat and watched the kaleidoscope of *palazzi* slip by, day-dreaming of what lay behind their crumbling facades.

At the Ca' d'Oro stop, a man pushed open the cabin doors. Probably in his forties, he was strikingly handsome and beautifully dressed. As he spoke he glanced at the empty seat next to her so she assumed he was asking if he could sit down. When she nodded, his smile could have melted ice.

My God, she thought, *I've no idea what he asked, but I'm happily agreeing. He may have said: "Ah, beautiful and mysterious English woman, my wife is away* (his left hand sported a thick, gold wedding band); *come back to my lonely palazzo, and let us make love in its gilded rooms".* As he was now engrossed in his newspaper, this did seem unlikely, but she realised, with delighted shock, that had he spoken the words, she may well have assented. She had never experienced such erotic flights of fancy while sardined into an Underground compartment, so perhaps it was simply the heady effect of such gorgeous surroundings. But surely there was something more. Venice was, as Izzy constantly affirmed, an incredibly sexy place.

It was traditionally regarded as one of the world's most romantic cities, but in reality it possessed an earthiness that underlay its reputation as the perfect honeymoon destination. After all, according to Will, it was once the biggest knocking shop in Europe with a vast population of courtesans, famed for their beauty and inventiveness. Izzy reckoned that all those centuries-old sex pheromones still lingered in the ether, waiting to enwrap and seduce the unsuspecting visitor. For the past five hundred years Venice had been a place where you came to get laid, and, in her opinion, at the end of the twentieth century nothing much had changed.

Anna had observed that surely the majority of visitors came to look at the city's artistic treasures, which were primarily inspired by Christianity.

'Yes, but it's still all about sex,' Izzy had said. 'Think about it: all those peachy Madonnas; well, what man doesn't want to screw a virgin? And then there's the half-dressed saints; the penitent Mary Magdalene in the desert…just an excuse to paint a woman with her tits out. And that's even before we move onto the Venuses. But it's not just the blokes who are catered for; we girls get our share. As soon as the Renaissance gets in full swing there's no more scrawny Jesus. He acquires the physique of an athlete, positively hunky in some cases. Even Job looks as though he's been down the gym, and there's a Saint Sebastian in the Salute you could eat for breakfast. Where else could people look at sexy pictures? If you don't believe me, check out what Mark Twain said about Titian's *Venus of Urbino*. He thought it was the obscenest thing he'd ever seen, because,' and her voice dropped to a mischievous whisper, 'the naughty girl seems to be…touching herself. You know, a bit of DIY.'

And she went on to confide that Venice was still the easiest place in the world to pick up, or be picked up by a handsome man. 'Take a stroll through the Piazza and along the Riva degli Schiavoni any evening, and you'll see what I mean. And it's not just the natives to choose from.' She still remembered, with great affection, the Russian sailor she had taken back to her flat one cold winter night. He had spoken hardly a word of English but had been so beautiful, and so energetic. When her supply of condoms was exhausted, they extricated themselves from the tangled bed sheets, and she had made him scrambled eggs, before he slipped into the still dark morning, bound for his waiting ship.

Perhaps that was the answer, uncomplicated, brief liaisons, preferably with visitors to the city, so there was no chance of running into them again; no chance of an involvement; no chance of being hurt. Leave well alone someone like Raffi who could rob her of her heart.

The *vaporetto* was approaching the Accademia, and Anna's handsome neighbour looked up, folded his paper and rose to leave, but not before gracing her with that smile again, and once more saying something that, despite its incomprehensibility, sounded gently seductive.

It gratified her that people so often spoke to her in Italian, assuming, at least until she opened her mouth, that she was not a foreigner. She would look even more like a Venetian when she bought some new clothes; something in linen perhaps – smart casual that she could wear to the office. Then, with a delicious thrill of guilt, she remembered that, for the moment at least, she did not have an office.

Leaving the boat at San Marco, she eventually found a department store where a particularly pleasant sales assistant helped her choose a linen shift dress in pale ice blue and a cotton knit jacket in a dusky air force shade.

That evening she modelled her purchases for the benefit of Izzy. 'Will I do?'

'Oh, yes, you'll do all right. You look lovely. Quite the *bella figura*.'

And for the first time in her life Anna detected the slightest note of jealously in her friend's voice, which both surprised and pleased her. Izzy was the pretty one. Next to her she had always felt gawky and dull, but perhaps now it was her turn to blossom a little.

The next day, Izzy waved her off, saying, 'If you're not back by midnight we'll send out a search party.'

The morning air was fragrant with perfume from hidden gardens; sunlight danced happily on the *rio* and wisps of music drifted from open windows. When she reached Ca' Melisa the *portone* was open. Stepping into the garden, she stood for a moment, appreciating its tender greenness. The plants were newly watered and an earthy dampness mingled with the scent of brewing coffee. Then a cheerful voice cut through the quiet and Rosina appeared on the balcony.

On the previous occasions they had met, Rosina had been too busy to exchange more than a few words, but Anna had immediately liked her. She now beckoned her to come up, saying that Vittore was on the telephone, but he would not be long. Rosina, by her own admission, understood English better than she spoke it. She tapped her head in a gesture of exasperation, saying that she was a stupid old woman who could not remember the words anymore. However, her English was a great deal better than Anna's Italian, so it was in this language they conversed.

'My husband is in his study. Come and sit in the *sala*, and wait. I will have you the coffee sent.' And with that she hurried off.

Seeing the *sala* empty, Anna could fully appreciate its fine proportions and intricately patterned floor, where the terrazzo chips had been laid out to create a border and a central motif of flowers. Above her, on the painted ceiling, young men and women cavorted in a pastoral idyll; a maelstrom of rosy limbs and half-naked bottoms and breasts. *Perhaps Izzy's right about sex and art*, she thought, peering up at an especially provocative nymph.

'Eighteenth century,' came Vittore's voice. 'Much later than the house. Reputedly the workshop of Tiepolo. Do you like it? I prefer next door. Come see.' And he led the way into the dining room, but not before he had kissed her warmly on both cheeks and made complimentary noises about her appearance.

She had not noticed the ceiling before, but now saw why it won his preference. Thick wooden beams spanned its entirety, every one exquisitely and identically painted.

'Sixteenth century, in the style of Sansovino. After so many years the colours have faded and much of the gold leaf has flaked away, but that gives it the subtle beauty that only time can endow. Have you been to the Scuola di San Giorgio degli Schiavoni to see the Carpaccios? The ceiling is virtually identical to this. I am convinced that the same hand was at work.'

At that moment, a sparrow-tiny woman entered the room, bearing a tray. She wore a wraparound floral apron, straight out of the 1950s, and chirruped happily in quick fire Italian as she set down cups, coffee pot and sugar, before scurrying out of the room, twittering with laughter at something Vittore said.

'That was Magda. She has worked with Rosina for years; an artist in the kitchen.' And returning his attention to the artistry above their heads, he continued, 'The *sala* is the same underneath all those amorous nymphs and shepherds. I imagine that once that first room was finished the money ran out, so they could not continue the project. We are very fortunate that Venice became increasingly impoverished and there was no alternative but to shore up what was already here. If we had been richer, many ancient buildings would have been pulled down and replaced.'

He handed Anna a small cup of the strong black coffee to which she was becoming accustomed. As it was after eleven, no Venetian would drink *cappuccino*.

'We were lucky to keep the nymphs. During the war Germans were stationed in the house and the commanding officer intended to dismantle the ceiling and pack it off to the Fatherland. My grandmother, Dorothea, managed to hide or disguise many of our smaller treasures but even she was not capable of concealing a ceiling. There she is, *nonna* Dotty.'

He indicated a picture hanging on the wall behind the head of the table. Anna had noticed it on the night she dined at Ca' Melisa, but only now, seeing it bathed in glorious morning light, did she appreciate its magnificence. Against a foliage-ribboned wall stood a woman, wearing clothes so deep a purple as to appear almost black. Her life size figure was subsumed into this primal background so only her face and white-gloved arms stood out in bold relief. A wine red mouth was fixed in a little crescent smile and she scrutinised the beholder with large eyes, one brow ever so slightly raised. Her gown was suggested by bold sweeps and swirling contours, but with paint so expertly applied that one could imagine the rustle of taffeta, or suppose that the feathers in her wide-brimmed hat would stir in a breeze. A large dog, her adoring guard for all eternity, rested its head against her thigh so that just the single aureate eye winked at the viewer, a vivid helix of colour.

'She's beautiful. Who's the artist?'

'John Singer Sargent. Painted in the garden here, in 1903. He used to stay with his distant cousins – the Curtis family, Anglo-Americans, who owned the Palazzo Barbaro. *Nonna* knew them well. They were all part of the same set; Henry James too. He wrote *The Wings of a Dove* whilst at Barbaro.'

'Dorothea was American?'

'Oh, yes, very much so. I seem to remember promising to tell you something of my family's colourful past. Dorothea was born in 1873, the eldest daughter of a wealthy New Yorker. Her father was what we would now call a robber baron, one of those ruthless men whose fortunes had been amassed by somewhat questionable means. It was common practice for such families to seek a sort of respectability by allying themselves to European aristocracy: a perfect combination – new world money and old world breeding.'

'Like Churchill's mother?'

'Exactly. So at the age of twenty, Dorothea was taken to London and married to an English lord, impeccably bred, but comparatively impoverished. And who saw matrimony as no impediment to retaining his mistress, an actress of some renown, by whom he had a daughter. The liaison was common knowledge, but kept secret from Dorothea.'

'You know, you're actually making it sound rather like a Henry James story.'

'Yes, I suppose I am. Well, by her own account Dorothea adapted well to English society and initially was very content. The couple did not take a proper honeymoon for some time because Dorothea's mother-in-law was ailing. However, when the old lady died, Dorothea's husband agreed to take his wife on a grand tour of Europe, and top on her list was Venice. Nothing unusual in that; then, as now, it was a prime tourist destination. But what subsequently occurred was distinctly out of the ordinary.'

'I'm presuming she didn't stay married to the English lord. Did she meet someone else? An Anzelieri?'

'She did indeed. Whilst she was here, Dorothea decided to purchase two matching chandeliers for their house in Belgravia, so she met with my grandfather, Luciano Anzelieri, who owned a glass factory on Murano. The chandeliers are those still hanging in our *sala*. They were designed for Dorothea by Luciano, and are totally unique.'

'So she didn't take them back to London?'

'No, simply because she herself did not return there. I never knew exactly why her marriage failed, but after my mother died I was clearing her things and came across letters to Dorothea written by her sister, Mabel. From these it was evident that *nonna* was deeply disillusioned with her husband. Nothing is explicit but there are dark hints about "unreasonable demands". Also it transpired that his little actress was carrying another child by him. That appears to have been the last straw, and Dorothea refused to accompany him back to England. I am sure that by now she was in love with my grandfather. He was still a bachelor, but despite this, they wisely maintained absolute discretion. So, she returned to New York, and citing her husband's persistent infidelity, persuaded her robber baron father that a divorce was essential. Surprisingly, he agreed. From being a dutiful daughter she had grown into a formidable woman and was livid that her parents had as good as sold her to such a man. She held them to ransom, ordering them to settle a very substantial sum on her husband. If they did so, he would agree to a divorce, in which he would appear the guilty party. But if they refused, she intended to give her husband ample reason to divorce her, and create such a scandal that her parents would never again be able to hold up their heads in New York society.'

'What would she have done?'

'Probably nothing so very dreadful by today's standards. But whatever she threatened, her father obviously did not think she was bluffing, because he did as she requested, and also provided her with her own small fortune. It was then she bought this house and, after a suitable interval, married my grandfather. Their son – my father – was born eighteen months later.'

'There's not much of a family resemblance,' said Anna, perusing the sumptuous Dorothea.

'No, I take after my mother's family. But Fabrizio, my brother, is very similar, or he was when he was young. And his daughters are just like her. She was an amazing woman and lived to be well over ninety. I adored her, we all did. Raffi was only seven when she died, but he still remembers her. She is the reason why I speak with the best Fifth Avenue accent, and also the reason for my modest art collection. She was a great patron of the arts, even providing bed and board for some of the more impecunious painters.' And Vittore reeled off a list of names, most of whom Anna did not recognise.

'Walter Sickert was a great favourite. He was really quite impoverished at one stage, you know. Come into my study and I'll show you three particularly lovely studies of Chioggian fisher girls.'

Anna obediently began to follow him, when he glanced down at his watch and exclaimed, 'Oh, what am I thinking of? Look at the time. If we don't leave at once we will make Angelo late for his lunch, and that will never do. Are you ready? It is only five minutes away.'

She nodded; as ready as she would ever be for this long planned meeting.

Together they walked along the Fondamenta della Sensa, past the Campo dei

Mori with its mysterious statues of turbaned men, one sporting a metal clip in place of a long lost nose; past Tintoretto's house, and over a diagonal wooden bridge overlooking a boatyard. Finally they passed under a wooden beamed *sotoportego*, before stepping into a *campo* with a distinctive herringbone brick pavement. Facing them, the wide Canale de la Misericordia, busy with traffic, sparkled in the sunlight; to their right loomed the huge bulk of the Scuola Nuova Misericordia.

'I noticed a sign outside saying "*palasport*". Is it really?' asked Anna, looking over to the imposing building.

'Oh, yes…or it was. Particularly famous for the *urlo della Misericordia*…'

'*Urlo?*'

'Literally, scream, but in reality just the cheering of basketball fans watching their home team. We called it the frescoed gymnasium because of its sixteenth century artwork; school of Veronese – now sadly decayed.'

Then to her surprise, rather than heading past the *scuola* in the direction of the Strada Nuova, Vittore turned and walked towards the church that stood to their left.

'Here we are,' he said cheerfully. 'Santa Maria Abbazia della Misericordia, but everyone just calls it the Misericordia. It has a most colourful history, you know. One of its priors was murdered whilst saying Mass.'

'Oh, so we're meeting someone in a church?'

Vittore only smiled enigmatically as they approached the ornate but crumbling façade. Two huge figures with sturdy legs stood atop plinths on either side of the doorway, begging *putti* clawing at their robes. It was not, Anna had to admit, the most attractive church in Venice, but there was something about it that she found particularly appealing. She had walked by a few times, but it had always been closed. Now, however, the door stood ajar, a dusky red curtain hiding whatever lay inside. Vittore smiled, pushing the door wide, and she stepped over the threshold. The curtain brushed the side of her face with its dusty caress and she breathed age and incense. The interior was dark, as all the windows were covered by heavy drapes faded to a dirty pink. Blinking, in an attempt to acclimatise her eyes, she knew that when she could see, this place would be disturbingly familiar and that, in some deep recess of her mind, she would recognize it. Then she heard a rustling. The noise made her jump, but it was only a man, a jovial, plump little man, with round spectacles and a red face. He scuttled towards them on inadequate legs, like a mechanical toy, his arms outstretched in greeting.

Vittore, she could tell, was apologising for their lateness but the man, whom she gathered was Angelo, the church sacristan, evidently dismissed this as unimportant. He grabbed her hands, only occasionally breaking his hold to gesticulate widely about him. The one word she understood was *"si"*, which he kept repeating with increased excitement.

Eventually, Angelo retreated to the shadowy depths, leaving behind a faint smell of cigarettes and mothballs. A few seconds later a weak light flooded the area immediately behind them. Turning, Anna saw that over the main door was a choir loft supported on pillars. Under it, to the right of the door, there hung a solitary painting. Quite a small painting in an ornate frame; a painting commonplace in Venice; a painting of a solemn-eyed Madonna and her child; a painting she knew as well as her own face, but a painting she had never before seen. She walked towards it, turning once to meet Vittore's eyes.

'This is who, or what, I wanted to introduce you to, Anna. I am sorry that I gave the impression that it was to someone made of flesh and blood, but to me, she is almost corporal.'

As she stood before the picture, a long finger of sunlight triumphed in penetrating one of the curtained windows, stroking her face – warm and reassuringly real. Outside, a motorboat roared, the canal lapping in its noisy wake; sparrows chirped in the *campo* and pigeons cooed. And Anna looked, long and hard, and as she did so, it seemed there was a time-slip: she heard sounds not of this century, and sensed an almost imperceptible shifting of the air around her. Then, in this city of water, the stone beneath her feet took on an aquatic quality; it rippled and moved, and she felt herself sinking into its cool, swirling depths.

A Madonna

But they were strangely merciful waters, for rather than dragging her down, they held her up, carrying her to a place of safety where she could take great gulps of cool air.

The thunderous noise in her ears subsided; she heard familiar voices and found she was sitting on a wooden chair. Its cold solidity penetrated the linen of her dress, contrasting with the warmth of an arm around her shoulders. Someone had forced her head downwards between her knees and for one awful moment she thought she was going to vomit. *Oh, God,* she prayed, *please don't let me be sick – not in a church.* With a huge effort she breathed deeply and as her churning stomach began to still, she raised her head to encounter the wide-eyed gaze of a woman she supposed she knew, but could not place.

'Hi there, honey. How are you feeling?'

Of course: it was that nice American lady, Edie. Her handsome husband hovered several steps away, the picture of sartorial elegance in cream linen, a panama clasped to his chest. She turned her head and met Vittore's concerned eyes. It was he who held her.

'What happened?'

'I think you fainted,' said Edie. 'We walked into the church just as you fell. Luckily Vittore was here to catch you, otherwise you'd have hit the floor with one hell of a bang.'

Anna was flabbergasted; modern women did not swoon. It was, surely, an affliction confined to Victorian ladies with over-tight corsets. Never before had she fainted, however great a shock she had received. And seeing the painting had been a shock, certainly, but it was, after all, just a painting. She badly wanted to look at it again, but the area beneath the choir loft was once more in deep shadow.

At that moment Angelo appeared, proffering a glass.

'Drink,' he said. 'Is good.'

Anna did as commanded. The fiery liquid burnt her throat but had an undoubted restorative effect.

'Feeling better?' asked Vittore. 'I am so sorry, Anna. Me and my dramatic little games. I didn't realise it would be such a shock for you. Forgive me. I should have warned you before we…'

'What have you been doing to this poor girl?' interrupted Edie. 'And what can be so shocking in a church?' Her suspicious eyes came to rest on poor Angelo, who grabbed the glass and shuffled back to the gloom.

'There's nothing to forgive. I've not eaten today and probably felt a bit faint because of that.' Anna was reluctant to mention the painting, but then Angelo, somewhere, flicked a switch.

Edie jumped with surprise at the sudden illumination and then said, 'Look, Graham, that's the painting. The Cima that may or may not be a Cima.'

She bounded over to it, and after a few seconds turned around with slow motion smoothness, her mouth forming an O of surprise. She stared at Anna and whispered, 'Oh, my goodness. I see it now. No wonder you were shocked, Anna. It's you, isn't it? The Madonna is the spitting image of you.'

Anna wished they would go. It was embarrassing, the way they kept looking at her. She stood up, and supported by Vittore, went to join the Singelmanns, trying to regard the painting dispassionately.

A young woman sat, as though in a darkened room, her face bathed in a soft golden light that emanated, not from a window or a lamp, but from the child on her lap. She was dressed in a high-waisted gown of dusky red, over which was thrown a mantle of deep blue. Although she wore a veil of a white gauzy fabric, it was positioned so far back on her head that much of her abundant dark hair was visible; a loose ringlet caressed her neck and would have fallen over her breast had not her baby held it in his dimpled fist. She sat facing forward but with her head turned towards the left so that her face was shown three-quarters. While the first impression was of pensiveness there was something in her eyes that hinted at merriment, as though she were looking at someone beyond the confines of the picture, and was about to smile at them. The infant Jesus was also intent on something, or someone, not visible to the viewer. His free arm reached out, his chubby fingers curving around something. Anna thought she had never seen a child so realistically rendered in paint. She wanted to rest her hand on his small torso, to feel the baby warmth of his rounded tummy, and catch the butterfly beat of his tiny heart.

In the end she said, 'She's a lot younger than me.'

It was true – the Virgin still had the soft rounded cheeks of a woman hardly out of girlhood. But Anna knew that in one of her mother's photo albums there was a picture of herself, taken ten years ago, holding a friend's baby, in which her eighteen year old face was the mirror image of the girl at whom she now gazed.

'That's immaterial,' said Edie. 'You're just a bit thinner than she is.'

'And her eyes are brown. Mine are blue.'

'Discolouration of the varnish,' declared Graham. 'Give her a good clean and those ol' blue eyes would be back.' He appeared to be on the verge of elaborating when a muffled cough reminded them of Angelo, now lurking by the church's open door.

'We should leave,' said Vittore. 'Angelo's wife will be on the warpath if his lunch is burnt.'

Anna was relieved to be out in the sunshine, and even more pleased when Graham and Edie excused themselves and strolled across the wooden bridge in the direction of the Strada Nuova. Before doing so, Edie hugged her, whispering something that made Anna laugh out loud.

'No, Edie, no, definitely not,' she said, while the two men looked on, excluded from this mysterious female badinage.

'I will walk you back to your apartment,' said Vittore.

He must have registered the look on her face, because he continued, 'I am presuming that you do not feel like eating, but if you are hungry...'

'Actually,' said Anna, 'I'm starving.'

'Good, I am glad.' Vittore took her arm, leading the way back towards the direction of Ca' Melisa, retracing their steps, past the house and along the Fondamenta della Sensa.

'What did Edie say to make you laugh?' he asked after a while.

Anna smiled at the memory. 'She asked if I was in the family way.'

For a second Vittore looked confused and then laughed, 'Ah, I understand. She was asking if you were pregnant.'

'Exactly. I'm not of course,' she added. 'But what an archaic expression. I don't think I've ever heard anyone actually use it before.'

'Dear Edie. She probably thought it sounded very English. She is a great Anglophile.'

'Hence the English husband?'

'Well, I daresay that was part of his attraction. What do you think of him?'

Anna considered the question for a moment. 'He seems rather self-satisfied and a bit arrogant. But he is spectacularly handsome. I can see why women would fall for him. Perhaps I'm speaking out of turn, but I don't think you like him very much.'

'Oh, I hardly know him. I've only met him once before, a year ago, when they were here on honeymoon, but I have known Edie for years; she has published three of my books. I know she is a little over-whelming; very up-front; very New York, but she is the kindest of women and has great integrity. I am very fond of her. She plays it down but she is also extremely wealthy, whereas Graham has no money of his own. But he is exceedingly ambitious. I am not saying he married her for her fortune, but her wealth will allow him the sort of professional freedom that others could only dream of. I only hope he uses that privilege wisely rather than to cause harm.'

Anna was about to ask what sort of harm Graham could possibly do, when Vittore drew to a halt outside a small, canal-side bar.

'I hope you were not expecting anything too grand, but I thought you would appreciate somewhere authentically Venetian and relatively untouristy. It may not look much, but you will not find better food anywhere in Venice than here at Martinàso's.'

It was the sort of establishment that Anna would never have dared enter alone, its leprous walls and flaking name sign imbuing a run down and faintly intimidating appearance. There was no sign of a menu, only a scruffy notice stuck to the window listing the cost of various beverages. The front bar possessed three small tables and bore no evidence of anyone having ever given any thought to its decoration, the only adornment of its walls being framed photos of rowing teams. It smelt of fish and garlic, smoke and coffee, but was packed with a varied and happy clientele, clutching glasses of wine and nibbling *cicchetti* – the bite sized appetizers that were served in most bars.

Vittore was evidently well known, as a number of people greeted him by name and after only a few moments a frazzled but cheerful man appeared. He enthusiastically shook Vittore's hand before leading them to an airy backroom containing a number of scrubbed wooden tables, most of which were already occupied. Whereas no effort had been expended on the bar, here a loving hand had used brushes and paint to transform the space into a fantastic lagoon-scape. On the walls, a mirage of grassy islands hovered, as on a spring morning when the day is warmed by the first rays of sunlight. In the distance, the bell-towers and domes of Venice rose mistily from the waters, and above them, the ceiling swarmed with swallows and swifts skitting across a pale blue sky.

'Enzo – the owner, he has a brother who is a fisherman and, as you can see, quite a painter. This is a celebration of his livelihood: the lagoon, and all that lives in it, fish and fowl, not to mention the wonderful vegetables from San Erasmo. Apparently, he completed it in just the single weekend.'

'It's fantastic. He should come to London. He could make a fortune painting murals for kids' bedrooms.'

'Oh, you would never tempt Mario away from the Venetian lagoon. His family have been fishermen here for generations.'

At that moment a young waiter appeared, and placed before them a basket of bread and two large glasses containing a deep coral liquid in which floated a twist of orange and an olive pierced by a cocktail stick. He reeled off the list of dishes on offer and left them to make their decision.

Vittore raised his glass. '*Saluté*. To you, Anna, and to your stay in Venice. May we be everything you could hope for.'

Anna took the drink, thinking that it rather resembled Tizer. Whatever it was, it was good; both bitter and sweet and, she suspected, deceptively alcoholic.

'This is a *spritz*,' said Vittore. 'A generous measure of campari, white wine and a dash of sparkling mineral water. The name is derived from the German word for splash, and we have drunk it here in the Veneto for nearly two hundred years. It is one of the better legacies of the Austrian occupation. Now what would you like to eat? I am assured the *moeche* – soft-shelled crabs – are excellent today. Have you ever tried them?'

'I've never even heard of crabs with a soft-shell, let alone eaten them!'

'Ah, let me explain, but I warn you, if you are squeamish you may not approve. In the mudflats of the lagoon lives a species of small crab. Each spring and autumn, they shed their shells, at which point they are harvested and sold, *vive* – that is alive. A few hours before being eaten they are tipped into a large bowl of beaten eggs. Naturally they gorge themselves on this feast and then,' he paused dramatically, 'and then, like Christian martyrs, they are thrown into hot oil and cooked till golden brown.'

'Alive?'

'Apart from the ones that drown in the egg. Is it too barbaric for you?'

'I'd love to try them,' she said, feigning more enthusiasm than she felt and reasoning that it made no difference to the crabs whether they died in boiling oil or water, and at least these little creatures enjoyed a hearty last meal.

'Excellent. And before the crabs, I suggest the *cape sante* – scallops. Enzo serves them in a fresh tomato sauce.'

The hovering waiter, sensing a decision made, was immediately by their side, taking the order. With his departure, the air between them squirmed with unspoken questions. At last Anna spoke. 'So, tell me all about her.'

'The Madonna? Was seeing her such a shock?'

'Well, yes…yes it was; the thought that all those years ago there was someone, here, in this tiny city, hundreds of miles from where I live, who looked just like me. It's spooky – me somehow inheriting her face.'

Vittore smiled knowingly, pausing to taste the wine. 'It happens, you know. My doctor is the image of Bellini's portrait of Doge Loredan. And in England there is a Titian in the collection of the Earl of Halifax that bears more than a passing resemblance to my Raffi.'

'Yes, but they're both Venetian. The occasional doppelganger's not that surprising. But me – what am I doing here? If it had been a painting of someone

English, I don't suppose I'd find it nearly so weird.'

'I remember the night we met, Anna. You said something about feeling that you had been here before. Do you still feel that?'

Anna shrugged. 'Yes, but it doesn't mean anything.'

Vittore was not letting the subject drop. 'Does it not? Tell me, what do you believe in, Anna? Do you think there is any credence in the transmutation of souls – reincarnation?'

'No, although I suppose it's no more outlandish than any other belief system. I once used to vaguely believe in…in something.'

'Used to? So not anymore?'

Anna met his eyes. The conversation was becoming uncomfortably serious. She just wanted to know the history of the painting, not discuss theology.

'No, not anymore. Not since my father died.' And as always she felt the sour taste of treachery, as if speaking the words, yet again condemned him to nothingness. 'What about you?'

'No. Not since the war.'

Anna waited, hoping he would elaborate, but it was now Vittore's turn to be evasive. His discomfort was palpable, and then an unwelcome thought, as sinister as a snake, slithered into her mind. 'Is that why you befriended me? Because you think I'm the reincarnation of the woman in the painting?' And she felt a curdle of disappointment; to be liked because she resembled someone long dead was faintly repugnant.

Vittore was visibly shocked and touched her arm in reassurance. 'No, not at all. I no more believe in reincarnation than you. I admit that your appearance was the reason I first spoke to you, but believe me, Anna, my affection for you is based on something deeper than that. You know how it is when you meet someone and within minutes feel that indefinable something – that connection? So if I did believe in reincarnation, perhaps I would say we had been close in another life.' He laughed, trying to lighten the conversation.

At that moment the scallops arrived – tangy, steaming and sweet. It was a relief to take refuge in the prosaic diversion of food. Equilibrium was restored, with trust back in their midst.

'So tell me about the woman in the painting.'

'I am afraid I know nothing about her. But it is extraordinary how different she is from every other Madonna Cima painted, who are all, without exception, fair haired, delicate featured creatures and remarkably similar, as though he were painting the same woman throughout his career. But a woman who never aged.' Vittore was warming to his subject. 'I cannot help but be fascinated why this representation should be so very different. I feel sure that it is a late work, perhaps one of the last things he painted, and one of the finest. Was this unknown girl his final muse? If he had lived longer would he have painted her again?'

'What sort of women were artists' models in those days?' asked Anna.

'Wives, daughters, mistresses. Sometimes, especially if the subject matter was a little racy, prostitutes. Occasionally, artists even used boys, softening their features to make them appear more feminine.'

Into Anna's mind came a picture of a young man: a teenage uncle Guy, but with Renaissance curls rather than a short back and sides. She instantly dismissed the idea, convinced that "her Madonna" was certainly female.

Swallowing the last tiny scallop, she wiped the shells with a hunk of bread. 'What did Edie mean by, "the Cima that may or may not be a Cima"?'

Vittore expelled his breath, making a small dismissive sound. He waited till their plates were cleared and then continued, 'There is some uncertainty because the painting is not signed. However, when you examine it without the frame, which is nineteenth century, it is evident that it has been cut vertically down the middle. The frame hides the fingertips of another person, which explains why the Virgin seems to be looking at someone. Also, although some of the paint has flaked away, the baby appears to be holding something. The original painting was probably a depiction of the mystic marriage of Saint Catherine, which was a popular subject at the time. In all likelihood the signature was on the other half.'

'But why would anyone cut it in half?'

'Money. It was easier to sell smaller paintings. Many altarpieces were split into ten or more parts and sold piecemeal. You find them today, scattered between galleries and private collections, usually with one or two pieces lost forever. But the odd feature about this painting is that it seems to have been crudely hacked, rather than neatly cut. It is as though it fell into the hands of someone who had no respect for it whatsoever.'

'And where is the other half?'

'Lost. I suspect that it perished centuries ago. Perhaps in a fire. They were very common in Venice. The area around the Rialto was devastated by one in 1514, and in 1577 irreplaceable works by Carpaccio, Bellini and many others were lost in a conflagration at the Doge's Palace. There would have been countless other losses in private homes. I would guess that about a quarter of Cima's work has not survived.'

'But what makes you certain that it is a Cima, especially as the Virgin is so different from how he usually painted her?'

'When you have spent as long as I have studying Venetian painting you acquire an instinct for these things. I won't bore you with technical details but one thing, above all, convinces me, and that is the depiction of the Christ child. No one, Giovanni Bellini included, painted such lifelike *bambini* as Cima. Other artists created serious, pallid children, many of them looking half dead, which, to be fair, was intentional as this prefigured the crucifixion. But Cima's are full of life and fun, as though they are innocent of the Passion. I feel that his love for children, especially babies, shines out from his work. But whatever my convictions, without the other half, we will never know for certain if he truly was the hand behind it.'

'You know,' said Anna, 'I had a feeling that you were going to introduce me to an old lady.'

'Well, I suppose she is. I cannot think it was painted before 1510, and if our model was, say, twenty at most, her birth date would be around 1490. So she is a very old lady indeed – nearly five hundred.'

'Perhaps that's why seeing her made me feel so uncomfortable. Whoever she was, however vibrant and hopeful, now she'll be nothing but, but…dust. It's rather a stark reminder of one's own mortality.'

'Or a symbol of the continuity of life…and talking of life and death, here comes the rest of our lunch.' He picked up his glass. 'Another toast, I think. To life! "Golden lads and girls all must, as chimney sweepers come to dust", but for today, let us enjoy the "heat of the sun".'

'To life,' echoed Anna, as a platter, bearing a battalion of tiny crabs, touchingly vulnerable in their inadequate armour, was placed on the table. She watched as Vittore took one of the pathetic army, hearing the slight crunch as he bit into it. Following his example, she was pleasantly surprised.

'These are SO good. Can you buy them in the shops?'

'Certainly. At the *Pescheria*.'

'Ah, I don't think my Italian is quite up to the *Pescheria* yet,' she said, and related her ill-fated attempt to buy fish.

'I will ask Rosina to arrange a time to take you shopping. She will introduce you to some of the stallholders, and in future, when they know you are our friend, they will look after you.'

Anna smiled, happily dismembering a crustacean. She had an irresistible urge to hum a silly tune and make the creature "dance" across the table.

'Once, when my little sister, Lucia, Raffi's mother, was about thirteen, Fabrizio raided the kitchen and put some of the crabs in her bed. I'll never forget her screaming. I don't think she has ever forgiven him – even now, after so many years.'

'I thought Raffi's parents were dead,' said Anna, before she could stop herself.

'Good Lord, no. Well, I do not know about his father, but Lucia is alive and well and living in New York. She is great friends with Edie. My darling sister is another of our scandals. Well, not really scandalous by today's standards, but she caused quite a stir in the 1950s. It is really Raffi's story, but I am sure he would not mind my telling you. So, going back to the late 1950s, did you know it was the golden age of Italian cinema? Rome was known as the Hollywood of the Tiber.'

'Really? *La Dolce Vita* and all that, I suppose?'

'Indeed. And Lucia decided she was going to be a film star. She envisaged herself as the new Sophia Loren. Unfortunately for her, the film industry was very happy with the Sophia Loren they already had. But she was a very determined young lady and ran away to Rome. Somehow, she did manage to secure a small, non-speaking role in a film, the name of which escapes me, but alas, her brief appearance ended up on the cutting room floor. But she did take away one lasting memento of her short career as an actress – Raffi. She came back to Venice, four months pregnant, quite unrepentant, and, as she confided to me, not at all sure who the father was. There was more than one candidate, none of whom she had any intention of sharing her life with.'

'What did your parents think?'

'They were scandalised. Like many people whose own parents were a little renegade, my father was the epitome of respectability. But they supported Lucia's wish to keep the baby, obviously hoping that she would find a suitable young man to look after her and the child. However, Lucia had no wish to settle down, and shortly after Raffi was born, she decided that her next step was Hollywood.'

'Hollywood! What did she do about Raffi?'

'To everyone's horror she took him with her. Fortunately, we have relatives in New York, descendants of Dorothea's robber baron father. Incidentally, the family fortune was mostly lost in the Depression, so we don't have a Frick or a Guggenheim collection in the family, I am sad to say. Anyway, New York was as close to Hollywood as she got. But she found some modelling work and with this, and help from various boyfriends, she earned enough to get by. When Raffi was coming up to five, I visited her and found her living like Holly Golightly…you know, *Breakfast at Tiffany's*? Well, it was no life for a child. Half the time he was cared for by neighbours or babysitters. She loved him, I don't doubt that for a moment, but her lifestyle simply did not allow her to look after him properly. As it happened, I arrived at a crisis point in her life. Her latest boyfriend had proposed marriage, but although he wanted Lucia he did not want a child, or more to the point, the child of another man. She had to choose. Him, or Raffi.'

'What an awful thing to ask. He can't have been a very nice man.'

'Oh, he wasn't, but he was charming, powerful and extremely rich. And Lucia thought she could get the better of him. She asked me to take Raffi back with me, just for a few months. She was sure that after they were married she would be able to make him change his mind. I was not so sure. I had met this man, and I did not think him the type to be manipulated. So, I took a gamble and agreed. You see, we had lost our only child, also a little boy, who had been stillborn, and Rosina had been told that she would bear no more children. I telephoned her from New York and told her: "Rosina, there is a little boy here who needs loving, will you do that? But, it may be for only a few months, so do not love him too much". My Rosina has never been a religious woman; she'll go to Mass on Sundays, but that is more to see her friends than anything else, but I could hear her sobbing and thanking God for sending us a child. So Raffi came back to Venice, and despite my warnings, Rosina loved him at once, completely and utterly, without reservation.'

Anna had a sudden vision of a small boy, fair hair falling over tear filled eyes – Raffi would have been fair as a child, she supposed – eyes that are wide and hurting with abandonment as his mother deserts him.

'But wasn't he devastated to leave his mother?'

'Well, Lucia lied and told him that he was here on holiday and that she would be joining us in two weeks. When this time passed he began to ask if *mamma* was coming, and sometimes we heard him crying in the night. But Rosina would cuddle him, tell him a story, give him freshly baked *biscotti* and he was fine. In fact, I think Rosina's cooking was the main thing that won him over. I'm sure my sister did not mean for him to go hungry, but I do think that she sometimes forgot to feed him. The poor little thing was very thin when he came to us.'

Anna remembered how Raffi had told her he was a greedy child who loved to spend time in the kitchen snaffling tit-bits; no wonder – he had been half starved. She felt a pang of tenderness for the child he had once been.

'And after six months he completely ceased to ask after her. He began to call us *mamma* and *papà*, even though we always reminded him that we were his *zia* and *zio*, and made sure that he did not forget his real *mamma*.'

'Life in Venice must have been very different to New York?'

'He loved it here, from the first, even though he hardly spoke Italian. I will always remember, a few months after he came to live with us, we were on a *vaporetto*, sailing up the Grand Canal. It was a glorious day and the city was as beautiful as you could ever hope to see it. He looked up at me, linked his arm through mine and said, "I love you, *zio*. And I love it here. I don't ever want to live anywhere else in the whole world". I thought my heart would burst, and I too found myself praying that Lucia would never try to get him back. Because if she did…' He stopped mid-sentence and looked down, intent on tidying a scattering of crumbs into a neat little pile, but not before Anna had glimpsed the moist glint in his eyes.

'And did she?'

'Not for some years. I was quite right. She was never able to persuade her husband to change his mind, and after a few months she was pregnant with his daughter. A second child quickly followed, another little girl, and by then, I suppose she did not need Raffi in quite the same way. Then about four years after they married she discovered her husband was having an affair with one of her so-called best friends. They divorced and she was awarded a good settlement. So for the first time in her life, she was financially independent. It was then she asked if Raffi could come back to her. In those four years she had visited us twice, and although we always told him she was his real *mamma* she was no more to him than a pretty lady who brought him lovely presents. As soon as she left he quite forgot her.'

'My God. You must have been devastated.'

'We were. It was foolish of us not to adopt Raffi, but I always feared that if we tried, it would make Lucia realise what she was giving up, and that she would take him away. I reckoned that when Raffi got to be older his opinions would count for more. You see, I never had any doubt that he would wish to stay with us, and indeed in Venice. Perhaps because he had been away from the city for those few, but very formative years, he seemed to appreciate it more than other children; he was constantly enchanted by his surroundings, and his favourite bedtime stories were of the city's history.'

'And Raffi was how old now?'

'Not even nine. I told her that he would not want to return, but she said, "I don't want my child brought up in a decaying museum of a place that only exists because of tourists. In a few years it'll sink, and all its precious treasure will end up in America anyway". On the evening she arrived, I suggested we take a stroll around the Piazza. It was the hour of *passegatia* and I can still remember how she made such an effort not to show what a hold the city still had on her. I had no idea how I was going to persuade her to let Raffi stay, but then we passed Bartolomeo Bon's carving of the judgement of Solomon, next to the Porta della Carita. Do you know the story?'

'Something about a baby?'

'That is right. Two women approach Solomon, asking him to decide who is the true mother of a child they both assert is their own. As neither will give up their claim, Solomon commands that the little boy be cut in half. The sculptor captures the moment when a soldier grabs the child by its wrist and prepares to strike. The false mother makes no objection, but the true mother, rather than see her baby killed, agrees to give up her claim. We see her, dumbstruck with horror, attempting to stay the executioner's hand. Solomon concludes, quite rightly, that the child is hers because she loves him sufficiently to give him up. I showed this to Lucia and said, "Let Raffi decide whom he wants to live with. If you love him as much as you say, then you'll let him choose".

'Did she agree?'

'Yes, to my surprise, she did. I'll never know why. She may have been tired after the long flight, or felt guilty; or perhaps the power of the carving somehow affected her. Whatever it was, I can never walk by it without saying a little thank you to Solomon, and to Bartolomeo Bon. So the next day, when Raffi came home from school, we asked him.'

'Just like that?'

'The plan was to broach the subject gently, but that was never Lucia's style. She had spent the day buying presents for him. There was one particular toy, it was very modern; you pressed buttons and it spoke to you. It captivated Raffi. He was quietly playing with it and out of the blue she said, "If you like that, we have even better ones in New York. Come back and live with me and you can have lots more".'

'And what was his response?'

'Raffi was a very placid child. Apart from those few tears when he first came to us he was always happy, never demanding; never had tantrums. But when Lucia said that, his little face went stark white. He turned to me and said, "But I live here with you". I replied that indeed he did, and we hoped that he would stay, because we loved him very much, but that if he wanted to go back and live with his *mamma* again, he could do so. And then the floodgates opened. I have never seen such a change in a child, such devastation. He threw down the toy, which smashed into bits, and screamed, "But she's not my *mamma*! *Zia* is my *mamma*". He was howling, it's the only word for it. At one stage he looked at me and yelled, "Why do you want to send me away, *zio?* I thought you loved me. What have I done wrong?"' Vittore took a deep breath and with a forefinger dabbed at the corner of one eye. Anna sat very quietly, imagining the child's trauma. 'He would not let any of us touch him. In the end it was Lucia who quietened him. She just grabbed him and yelled that he would never have to leave us; that she would never try to make him leave Venice. When we all gave him our word, he gradually calmed down. Rosina took him up to bed and sat with him, reading him stories, until he fell asleep. Lucia and I sat and drank too much. In the end she was sobbing almost as much as her son. She did – does – love him very much – enough to let him go.'

'And she never tried to get him back again?'

'No, she left the next day, and we did not see her for another three years. She kept in touch of course, wrote letters, telephoned. Raffi was very cautious about speaking to her at first, but eventually he settled down. By the time she again visited he was twelve, and even though he was still a child, I think he understood some of the difficult emotional issues. Anyway, by then Lucia's situation had changed yet again. This time her future husband accompanied her. At long last, she had met a decent man. Patrick had been widowed and had two small boys – twins – who had only been two when their mother died. They clearly adored Lucia, and her own daughters were very fond of Pat. Together they made, and still do, a splendid family. Lucia is a lucky girl to have fallen on her feet.'

'And what's their relationship now?'

'Raffi and his mother? It's very good. Ever since she married Pat, she visits us every year or so, sometimes with the family, sometimes alone. We have visited them twice, and since he was sixteen Raffi has gone over by himself. He even spent a semester at Columbia University. Lucia is the reason he has his own apartment. Property is so expensive in Venice that young people like Raffi starting their career, after years of study, cannot usually afford to buy, but Lucia insisted on giving him the money. We miss him of course, since he moved out. But it is better that he has his independence, and he visits once or twice a week.'

'Don't tell me,' said Anna. 'He brings his laundry?'

'Only occasionally,' laughed Vittore, and then leaning back in his chair said. 'So, my dear, you now know all about us. Are we far too scandalous a family for a respectable English girl to mix with?'

'I think I'm very lucky, and honoured, that you do want to mix with me.'

Their plates, with the mangled remains of the crabs, had been removed and now their waiter appeared with two glasses of deep red liquid and a plate of S shaped biscuits. Another toast was inevitable.

'To us.' And Vittore raised his glass.

Anna did likewise, and took a sip, presuming that it was port. It was, however, like nothing she had ever tasted. Sweet and rich with a slight pétillance and an unmistakable aroma and taste of, of…ripe strawberries.

'It's *fragolino*,' said Vittore, seeing her surprise. 'Made from the *fragola* grape, which tastes of strawberries. We drink it with these *buranei biscotti*, as an alternative to dessert.'

'I can't think why Izzy hasn't introduced me to this,' said Anna. Then she remembered; Izzy was allergic to strawberries and consequently avoided anything remotely connected with the fruit.

'Anna, you are so fortunate to be here for six months – sufficient time for you to be introduced to, and appreciate, so many wonderful things in our city. I am sure Izzy will prove to be a…an interesting guide, but perhaps you will allow me, and Rosina, occasionally to take you under our wing.'

Before Anna could assent, he glanced at his watch. 'But today, I must return to Ca' Melisa and my guests. Excuse me for a moment while I pay the bill.'

He was gone for only the briefest time. In his absence Anna sat in a happy, woozy bubble of contentment, supping the blood red wine, scrambling to her feet when he returned.

'Stay and finish your drink,' he said. 'Goodbye, and thank you again for your company. When our current guests leave, I will telephone you and we can arrange a time for Rosina to take you shopping.'

With that he kissed her goodbye and left. Anna drained her glass and feeling slightly unsteady, strolled back to the apartment. For the first time since arriving in the city, she paid scant attention to her surroundings, but lost in thought, gazed down at her feet. (Izzy asserted there was a sure way of distinguishing Venetians from tourists – the Venetians walked with eyes glued to the ground, avoiding the odorous little piles left by the city's canine inhabitants.)

It was amazing, she decided, that someone as extraordinary as Vittore should be interested in her. All intentions to distance herself from the Anzelieri family had long since faded. They held her quite in thrall and there would be no escape. Vittore had wound a thread around her as strong as spider's silk. She briefly saw herself as a small, fluttering insect caught in a web, and then dispelled the image. There was no danger…none at all. It was the third time they had met, but she knew there was between them an affection and trust that usually comes only after a far lengthier acquaintance. She felt safe, even cherished, in his company, but at the same time a little suspicious of her own motives. Although no one could ever replace her father, there was something about Vittore that, whilst not exactly paternal, was comfortingly avuncular.

'*Zio* Vittore,' she mouthed, wishing, with a little tightening of her heart, that she could have introduced him to Hugh; they would, she was sure, have liked one another. And she realised that she had appropriated Raffi's father/uncle for herself. If Vittore was her surrogate uncle, what did that make Raffi? A brother? A cousin? The expression, "kissing cousins", capered into her mind.

'Stop it,' she whispered, reassuring herself that no harm lay ahead. After all, by October she would be back in London. Whatever happened, however deep her involvement with this charismatic family, it was only for a few months – not for a lifetime. She would embrace it for what it was: a glittering interlude in a sensible life; a taste of Arcadia.

Venice: Winter 1515

Debra lives not far off my route home, so I am at her door in minutes. Most Christians never enter a Jewish dwelling and even I, who have been here many times, still feel the difference between it and our own house. It is devoid of the things that ornament the meanest of Christian homes, so neither crucifix nor Madonna adorn its walls. There are no paintings, which is hardly surprising, for the Church will not permit Jews to take part in the creation of art, and its rooms are always very dark, as they look onto a small *campiello,* unlike our house which fronts a wide canal. Jews may not own property and their Christian landlords have no qualms about extracting as high a rent as possible. I daresay Jakob pays handsomely for what is quite a humble abode.

For all that, there are many books and other beautiful objects, such as an ornate silver goblet called a Kiddush cup. And on the right hand side of every door hangs a silver case. Inside is a sacred parchment text, the mezuzah. This reminds them that God is always present in their lives. Certainly, even though Debra and her father are, I suppose, infidels, their house always seems a place of peace and Godliness. It is I, who on this winter afternoon shatter the harmony.

As I tell her my plan, I scrutinize her face, trying to see it as the painter would, for if anyone should have her likeness made, it is she. Her skin is as pale as ivory, except for a subtle brush of pink, skimmed over high cheekbones, and her jaw is so fine that you really cannot imagine it accommodating all her teeth. But, believe me, she has a full set – tiny, very white and perfectly shaped. When she shows them, her smile lights up her face; it is then that her eyes, slanting and dark as sloes, sparkle. I suppose her nose could be better shaped, perhaps completely straight, or slightly upturned, in accordance with the ideals of beauty, for it is, rather, a tiny, delicate beak. Finally, there is her mouth, which gives her otherwise restrained loveliness a sort of wildness; her lower lip is particularly full and rounded, glistening like a peeled fruit and, even to my female eyes, seems to ask for a kiss to be placed upon it.

As I could have foretold, she raises objection after objection. The painter, as a good Christian, will not want a Jewess representing Saint Catherine: he will not know, I assure her. Her clothes will give her away, she says: wear some of mine, I retort. How can she be in the company of men, without a chaperone? I will be her chaperone. And finally: her father will not allow it. This is difficult for me to counter. Do not tell him, I say. You need not lie, just do not tell him. It is as simple as that.

'Why is this so important to you?' she asks, weary from my bombardment.

It is all so complicated, and being no scholar, I am not even sure myself. We ceased to discuss our different faiths long ago, for our beliefs will never be reconciled. But from what I understand, the Jews also have a heaven – Gan Eden; and a Hell, a fiery place called Gehinnom, where all souls, even virtuous ones, must spend eleven months. It does not sound so very different from our Purgatory, except that we Christians are condemned to spend a great deal longer in expiatory fires. If Gan Eden does exist, I am confident of Debra's admittance, for she is a good person. Surely though, it is not the same place as our Christian paradise? I hate to think of us being in different Heavens for all eternity, so I have a notion that if our images appear together, bonded permanently onto a wooden panel, we will somehow remain forever united. For unless it has the misfortune to reside in a building that is consumed by fire this picture will certainly be more durable than our weak flesh.

I cannot possibly explain all this, so I say, 'To have one's image rendered in paint by so great a master is no small thing, and I should like to share this with you.'

She scowls, a slight puckering of her brow and a little pursing of her mouth. She knows there is more and that I am not sharing my deeper concerns. Nevertheless, she agrees, as I knew she would, to please me. And having elicited her agreement, I leave. She stands in the doorway, and when I turn back to wave farewell, I see her face, luminous in the dark, and I wonder what I have started.

My visit to Debra has made me late, so I hurry home as fast as possible, keeping to the busiest routes; ones with *cesendoli* – little votive shrines to the Virgin, which help illuminate the city. Giacomo, when he accompanies me, often shares a glass of wine with my father, a habit I naturally encourage. *Papà* enjoys his company, so I am surprised when he does not comment on the fact that I am alone. However, he appears unusually distracted tonight, and I soon discover why. Another girl has been attacked in the same loathsome way.

Already, many women are reluctant to venture abroad, and this latest assault will increase their terror. I cannot countenance being imprisoned in my home by fear, but nor do I intend to suffer Agnesina's fate. Consequently, I decide that, from now, I will secrete a small knife about my person.

Trying to forget the unfortunate girls, we settle down to a dinner of stewed goat, prepared by Pasqualina. We eat in silent appreciation, mopping up the fragrant sauce with hunks of bread, fresh from the baker's oven. It tastes all the better for knowing that it will soon be Advent when, as in the Lenten season, we must abstain from meat.

It is now, whilst he is warm and well fed, with some good wine coursing through his veins, that I tell *papà* about the painting. He takes a seat by the fire and Cesare jumps onto his lap. *Papà* pretends to be indifferent to him, but I know how the little poppet has wormed his way into his heart.

They say that dogs do not possess souls but I believe they have the gift of memory, for I am sure that Cesare recalls the day that *papà* saved his life. It was my thirteenth winter, so I was still a child…but only just. *Papà* came into the house, holding what I thought was a fur hood. It was white and pale gold, and I ran towards him, knowing it was a present for me. And then my present moved, making me squeal with surprise, and in the "hood" appeared a darting pink tongue and two black pebble eyes, as shiny as *zecchini*.

'There was a sack floating in the canal,' *papà* said, and only then did I notice that the bottom of his robe dripped water. 'There were four others, all dead. This one must have clambered onto their backs to keep his nose out of the water. I should have left him. He is only a few days old and without his mother will certainly die.'

Half dead puppies are a common enough sight in Venice, and I am not usually so tender hearted, but there was something about this plucky little creature that made my eyes smart with tears and my arms long to hold him.

'I'll look after him. Give him to me, *papà*,' I pleaded.

And so he did and the dog immediately vomited canal water and the last of its mother's milk down my bodice. But I did not mind, and with *papà's* help, Cesare flourished and is now the heartiest of animals, although inconveniently for a Venetian dog, he hates water and abhors being on any sort of boat.

Painters use the dog as a symbol of faithfulness, but I think they must know dogs with nobler hearts than my Cesare. I watch him lick *papà's* fingers and suspect that, although this may be prompted by affection, it is because the taste of stewed goat lingers on them. I pick a bit of meat, too gristly for my taste, and make a small gesture with my hand. In an instant Cesare bounds from my father's lap and onto mine: such is his fidelity!

Although *papà* cannot really see us in the dim light, I register the affection on his face. This is the moment.

'*Maestro* Cima received a new commission today,' I say. 'For a Madonna. It has been suggested that I should be the model. Do I have your consent, sir?'

'A Madonna without the face of his beloved Corona?'

'The patron said he wanted, wanted…a different look,' I mumble.

'You met the patron? Who is he?'

'Enrico Sartorani. It is for his father who is remarrying.'

'Ah yes, I had heard as much,' says *papa*. 'The Sartorani are a family both blessed and cursed.'

This is most certainly true; you will find their name in the Golden Book – although they are not one of our most ancient families. In fact, they bought their way into the nobility when the state coffers were in need of replenishment. They possess vast wealth, and in addition to Enrico's home, their house on the Canale Grande is one of the largest and most beautiful in the city. Also, they own many other dwellings that generate thousands of ducats in rent. The Sartorani are, and have always been, supremely successful merchants. God seems to favour their endeavours, for whilst other families lose ships and cargoes, those of the Sartorani never flounder. Sixteen years ago when the Portuguese sailed around the tip of Africa and thus reached India, this so threatened our control of the old trade routes that there was widespread consternation at the Rialto. But the Sartorani remained undaunted, for they had already turned their attentions westwards, to the great trading cities of Europe. Never afraid to take risks, their gambles always pay off.

But there is one area in which their luck withers – engendering the next generation.

Enrico is strong, bold and intelligent. But he, and this is his great misfortune, is not of legitimate birth. For all that his father dotes on him, he is a bastard.

The only son of his father's marriage is Alphonso Sartorani, and he is the bitterest disappointment to his family. I have never seen Enrico's pathetic half-brother, but apparently he is a piteous sight. His limbs are puny and weak and his scrawny neck unfit to support his oversize head, which is dominated by a large mouth from which a copious amount of spittle dribbles, together with words quite incoherent. It is a wonder that he has survived so long.

Following Alphonso's birth, the old man's wife squeezed out baby after baby – all girls…and the last one killed her.

'I had thought,' says *papà*, 'that when his poor wife died, Sartorani might marry Enrico's mother and declare Enrico his legitimate heir.'

His words surprise me, for although it is not unheard of for nobles to marry their concubines it is frowned upon. I say as much, adding, 'Also, surely she must be quite aged by now?'

Papà makes a mental calculation. 'Nearing fifty. But she was a great beauty in her youth, and is still a handsome woman.'

But however comely she is, it is well known that old Sartorani has been feasting on firmer flesh of late, and no doubt simply hankers after a virgin bride.

'Not as handsome as his little betrothed…aged all of sixteen,' I say. 'Veronica Mocenigo.'

'True,' concedes *papà*. 'She is a younger daughter, so her dowry will not be great, but the Sartorani have wealth enough not to worry about the size of her marriage portion.'

This is true; her physical charms and powerful family, who can count three doges amongst their forefathers, will more than make up for any shortage of ducats. Moreover, her elder sister, already married, is a prolific breeder of sons and this, probably more than anything, has recommended her as a Sartorani bride. Within a year she may produce a legitimate heir, strong in mind and body, to replace Alphonso – and Enrico.

'I wonder what Enrico thinks of it all,' muses *papà*. 'Is he angry?'

'Why should he be?' I reply. 'You yourself told me that his father showers him with gifts. And his trading ventures have made him wealthy in his own right. He has no need of money.'

'Ah, but think, Ginevra, he will forever be regarded as a bastard and an outsider. The direct bloodline of the Sartorani will not slip down the centuries through his offspring. It is this, I suspect, that will cause him the most perturbation.'

'He said very little about the marriage,' I say, thinking it best not to repeat Enrico's ribald remarks.

'And the painting?' asks *papà*. 'Will it represent anything other than the Virgin and Child?'

I hear the sharp intake of my breath and Cesare, disturbed by the sudden movement of my body, opens a bleary eye.

'It is to be a mystic marriage,' I say.

'A very beautiful subject. And who will sit for Catherine?'

I cannot possibly reveal that Debra is to be the model. *Papà* would certainly tell Jakob, who would as certainly prohibit her involvement.

'Oh, that is still to be decided,' I say. And this is true, for both the painter and his patron have yet to give their approval. Though not for a second do I believe either will be anything but entranced by my lovely friend.

St Mark's Day

In Venice, the twenty-fifth of April is a propitious day and has been so for centuries, as it marks the *festa di San Marco*. But since 1945 it has acquired even greater importance, being the day when all of Italy celebrates the final annihilation of Mussolini's Fascist regime and the country's liberation by Allied forces.

The two events meant little to Anna: neither the death of the Evangelist, who met his end when a pagan mob in Alexandria threw a rope around his neck and dragged him through the streets, nor of the dictator, shot and then hung upside down, also at the end of a rope, as another angry mob, no doubt with more justification, vented their anger on his broken corpse. However, she was eager to witness the pomp and ceremony taking place in the Piazza, and persuaded Izzy to join her. Will refused, on the grounds of being anti anything that remotely glorified war.

It seemed to Anna that Venice had been untouched by the hostilities. There was no evidence of damage, unlike in London, where, even if the scars left by bombs had been built over, it was still obvious where they had fallen.

'It was lucky that both the Axis powers and the Allies wanted the city left unscathed,' explained Will, as he and Anna sat over breakfast, waiting for Izzy to get mascara-ed up.

'I can't imagine it having much strategic importance,' said Anna.

'Well, not at first, but eventually the road and rail networks were so damaged that the Germans shipped goods into Venice and moved them on by any means they could. So the Allies decided that the Bacino Marittima – the harbour and docks area beyond Piazzale Roma – had to be destroyed.'

'How could they do that without damaging the rest of the city?'

'Only by very skilful and precise bombing,' said Will. 'The operation was code named, "Operation Bowler," because...'

'Bowler?'

'Yeah...as in bowler hat. It was assumed that if Venice suffered any significant damage those responsible would be sent back to civvie street, ie: bowler hatted. The pilots dive-bombed the docks, almost vertically, making sure they hit the exact targets and nothing else. I can't remember the details of what was destroyed, but I think it included a stockpile of mines that could have killed thousands. In the end, the only damage to the city was a few broken windows. Apparently people climbed up on their roofs to cheer the RAF pilots.'

'Did you know that there were Germans billeted at Ca' Melisa?' said Anna. 'I wonder what Vittore got up to in the war? He started talking about it and then suddenly went all cagey.'

Just then Izzy appeared. 'Well, Patrizia once told me that he was in the Resistance, but he never talks about it. You know, I once saw some amazing photographs of Venice when it was occupied. There was one, I'll never forget it, of the Grand Canal, and hanging out of half the *palazzo* windows were huge banners with swastikas on them. It was like one of those Nuremburg rally things, but here – in a place I thought of as home. And it made me realise how easily it could have happened in the place that really is my home, England. And how much we owe to men like your dad, Anna.' Izzy looked as though she was about to burst into tears. 'You know, I only vaguely knew what he did in the war, but now it's too late, I wish I'd thanked him.' Sitting down, she sniffed loudly. 'Sorry. I'm a bit PMT-ish today.'

Anna was quiet for a couple of moments and then said, as if she could hardly believe it, 'If it's any consolation, I never thanked him either. Not for that…for plenty of other things, but not for that.'

Izzy rallied and took a huge bite of brioche. Like a baby with a dummy, it seemed to comfort her. 'Yeah, well, let's get down to the Piazza and when they're all strutting their stuff and eulogising, we'll think of your dad and your uncle Guy…our fallen heroes.'

Although it was only a little after nine, the Piazza was packed. To the accompaniment of piped music, *carabiniari* were herding the crowds behind flimsy barriers. Then silence fell as attention was focused on the three lofty standards towering before the Basilica, each tipped by a sword-bearing lion. With a great show of ceremony the flags were raised: the great gaudy lion of Venice, boasting six gold and red streamers; the bold but simple Italian flag; and finally, optimistic with stars, the symbol of European unity. For a few seconds they hung, limp and sullen, until enlivened by a sudden gust of wind, they danced in the air.

'Just over forty years ago, everyone in Europe was killing each other, and now they share a flag,' said Izzy. 'I suppose that's progress.'

After much saluting and speech making, the celebrations began in earnest with parades and marching bands. Most of the participants were painfully young, and there was incessant camera flashing as they marched around the Piazza.

'This lot are mostly lads doing their national service,' said Izzy. 'I really don't think I can stand much more. It's like a bellicose version of the Scouts. Let's go and find a coffee while it's still not a *brutta figura* to have a cappuccino.'

'OK,' said Anna, realising she also found the sight of little boys playing war-games rather depressing. 'Is there a bookshop near here? I'd like to buy Vittore's book on Cima?'

'Yes, on Campo di Santa Marina. It's more or less on our way home. We can call in at Didovich and buy something scrumptious for lunch.'

Izzy, brightening at the thought of food, began to giggle. 'Will was so pissed off that he hadn't spotted the resemblance between you and that painting. He won't rest till he's gone to look at it again…actually, I bet he's already been. Oh, you'd better check that it's in the book before you buy it.'

She need not have worried. When they located the book, "Anna's Madonna", as Izzy had christened it, was honoured with a full page.

Izzy looked at it, long and hard, before pronouncing, 'Yep, that's you all right. Circa 1977, I'd say. Ten years ago. God, do you remember that summer?'

As they came out of the bookshop and crossed the *campo*, Anna suddenly registered that every other man she saw was carrying one, or more, cellophane wrapped roses.

'What's with the red rose thing?'

'Yet another reason why today's so special,' replied Izzy. 'It's the Festa del Boccolo – festival of the blooming rose, when it's virtually obligatory for men to give a red rose to the women in their life. And not just their *inamorata*; but their mum, their sister, cousin, secretary; anyone they hold dear. And if Will hasn't got one for both of us, his life won't be worth living.'

'What's the story behind it?'

'Don't know. Probably something to do with star-crossed lovers. Usually is, isn't it?'

And then she froze on the spot, grabbing Anna's arm. 'And talking of lovers. Look.'

Anna followed the direction of Izzy's gaze. Outside the café next to Didovich, basking in a little suntrap, was Raffi. At his side sat Caterina, a loose beige coat hitched up over her knees so that her legs, already summer brown and prettily crossed, were on show. She sat very upright, looking about the *campo*, her face partly hidden by huge sunglasses, so the most noticeable feature was a cherry red mouth. The tip of one gold trimmed shoe tapped her ankle. By contrast, Raffi lounged in a pose of complete relaxation, one long leg thrust out, the other crooked under his chair. His head was tilted back, in a salute to the sun, and he too wore dark glasses. One arm rested on a table to his right, while the other was draped across the back of Caterina's chair. Although not visible, Anna supposed that his fingers teased a tress of that bright hair.

They looked like any other smart young couple enjoying the spring weather, but Anna found something faintly disturbing in their body language, or at least, in Caterina's. For while one hand played with her chunky gold necklace, the other rested proprietarily on Raffi's inner thigh, the long red nails vivid against the dove grey of his trousers. There was something disarmingly erotic about the insouciance of that hand, as though, despite the public place, it might, at any moment, drift towards his groin.

They've not long been out of bed, thought Anna, envious of their easy intimacy. 'Quick, let's go,' she said, about to turn her back on them.

But then Raffi looked down, pushed his sunglasses onto his forehead, and their eyes met.

'Good morning. Come and join us,' he called, as Caterina's hand retreated to the decorum of her own lap.

Anna and Izzy settled themselves at the table next to the couple, but not before the usual round of kissing, although Caterina merely extended her hand. When, Anna wondered, did it become acceptable to kiss as a way of greeting? On one's second meeting perhaps? Or the third? Presumably with some people it was a stage never reached. Like switching from the formal *lei* to the familiar *tu*, it was a social minefield.

'So, Caterina, are you back for just the weekend?' Izzy asked, after they had ordered coffees.

'Oh, yes,' Caterina replied. 'I will return to Milan on Sunday afternoon as I have a very important meeting on Monday.' She spoke fluently but with a pronounced accent.

Izzy turned her attention to Raffi. 'Your uncle's a dark horse isn't he? All this time, we're thinking he's going to introduce Anna to a person, and it turns out to be a painting!'

'Yes, he told me when we spoke last night. So, Anna, at long last you've seen her. What do you think?'

Before Anna had time to reply, he turned to Caterina. 'You remember? The painting I told you about? The one in the Misericordia that looks so much like Anna? Vittore showed it to her yesterday.'

If Caterina remotely cared about a little known sixteenth century painting resembling the English woman sitting before her, she gave no sign of any interest, but merely said, 'Oh, yes, you did mention it.'

Raffi soldiered on, suggesting that they visit the church later that day. Caterina could not have looked less enthusiastic had he proposed an afternoon dredging a canal.

Almost feeling sorry for the girl, Anna came to her rescue. 'No need. It's here in Vittore's book.'

She heaved the book out of its bag and handed it to Raffi.

'You bought *zio's* tome. He'll be so flattered. But you should have waited. Edie's planning to publish it, so you could have had it in English.'

'I don't suppose that will happen for months. Anyway, reading it – or trying to read it – will help me learn Italian.'

'I should not bother,' said Caterina. 'You are here for a short time only? Everyone speaks English in Venice. Well, the sort of English tourists need.'

Raffi was too busy leafing through the book to notice her dismissive tone.

'Here she is.' He held the book out to Caterina, who examined the painting for a few moments, peering over the rims of her sunglasses with amber flecked eyes.

She looked up and pushing the shades up her retroussé little nose, pronounced, 'Yes, yes. I see a resemblance. But you are, I think, older than the model.'

Anna had said as much herself; so had Izzy, but coming from Caterina, the observation somehow sounded insulting.

'Oh, I don't think that's the case,' said Raffi.

'It's not a question of age,' said Izzy. 'Anna's been through a lot lately; she's lost weight, so she's thinner in the face than usual. A month or two of good Venetian food and she'll put on a few pounds and be as plump cheeked as the Virgin.'

'Especially as Rosina's going to teach her how to cook,' said Raffi.

Anna gaped. 'Is she?'

Izzy clapped her hands. 'You didn't tell me this. Well, if it's true and you end up cooking half as well as Rosina, then I'll take you prisoner and never let you return to England.'

'All Vittore said was that he would ask Rosina to introduce me to some of the people she buys food from.'

'Ah,' said Raffi. 'She probably thinks that if she's going to suggest buying certain products then you should know the best way to prepare them. If you don't want to, I'm sure she won't mind.'

'Oh, she'll want to! Won't you, Anna?' said Izzy.

'I don't know if she'll find me a very able pupil,' said Anna, imagining the gory preparation of crabs and squid and other squirming creatures. 'But if she's willing to teach me, then I'm very willing to learn.'

Caterina was smiling sweetly. 'Well, don't get too fat,' she said.

'Anna couldn't get fat if she tried,' said Izzy. 'Unlike the rest of us poor mortals, who have a constant battle to stay in shape, eh?' And she looked at Caterina, her face as innocent as a flower.

Caterina ignored the remark but turning to Raffi, said, 'We should go. I need to do some things at home before we go to Ca' Melisa. We are having lunch with Vittore and Rosina,' she added.

Raffi agreed that it was indeed time to depart, but not before scrabbling under his chair and producing two of the ubiquitous roses.

Presenting one to both Izzy and Anna, he said, almost shyly, 'These were for Rosina and Magda, but I think you should have them.'

While Izzy accepted her rose with effusive thanks, Anna stammered, 'Oh, I can't possibly. What about Rosina and Magda?'

'I can easily buy two more. Please take them. From Vittore – if not from me.'

'On one condition,' said Izzy. 'Tell us the story behind the Festa del Boccolo. I'm sure Will knows it, but it'll be so much nicer hearing it from a real Venetian. You do know it, I presume?'

'Oh yes, backwards,' said Raffi. 'When I was little, every year Vittore bought me a rose to give to Rosina. And every year, when I presented it to her, she would feign amazement as though it were the biggest surprise of her life, and then sit me down and tell me the story. I soon knew it better than she did.'

He took a sip of water and began, 'Well, many years ago, in Alexandria, there was a red rose growing by St Mark's grave, and when the Saint's body was smuggled back to Venice, one of the sailors was given a cutting. He planted it, here in the city, where years later, long after his death, it still flourished. Unfortunately, by this time, his descendants had argued with each other and the rose marked the border between their respective properties. Then, one twenty-fifth of April, a boy and a girl from the two branches of the family saw each other and fell instantly in love. *Colpo di fulmine.*'

'Like a thunderbolt,' Izzy translated.

'Exactly. Love at first sight; the most powerful of all loves, and the most dangerous.' Raffi paused for a moment, catching Anna's eye, before continuing, 'They, of course, began a secret courtship, meeting by the rose beds.'

'Oh, it's all going to end in tears,' Izzy wailed. 'Romeo and Juliet all over again.'

'Actually, no,' said Raffi. 'When they were – inevitably – discovered, their families were so touched by their love that they decided to bury their differences, and instead of a stage strewn with bodies, everyone lived happily ever after. Since then it's been the custom for Venetian men to give rose buds to the women in their lives.'

'Aaahhh!' purred Izzy. 'A happy ending for once – how nice.'

153

'But there is another story,' said Caterina, 'in which a musician falls in love with a noble lady, and to impress her goes to war. He is wounded, and dies next to a rose bush. Then on St Mark's day, someone tells the lady he is dead and sends her one of the roses. So she also dies: I suppose of a broken heart. That is the version I was always told. And now, *tesoro*, we really must go.'

'I don't suppose either are true,' said Raffi, getting to his feet. 'Just enterprising florists making money.' And he planted a kiss on Caterina's expertly blushed cheek.

'Now, I think that may be true,' she responded. 'Especially as there are some men, like you, who buy their beloved twenty red roses, rather than just the one.' And she cast a disparaging and slightly triumphant glance at the two single roses, an apologetic duo; mere crumbs, falling from the rich man's table.

Having said their goodbyes, this time Caterina deigning to join in the round of kissing, Anna and Izzy watched the couple saunter across the *campo*, arm-in-arm.

'Trust Caterina to know the Leonard Cohen version of the rose story,' said Izzy. 'Now call me over sensitive but I don't think she likes you much.'

'She didn't actually say anything unpleasant.'

'Well, she wouldn't, would she? Not in front of Raffi. But come on, her whole attitude was so… so dismissive.'

'She certainly made no attempt to be friendly,' agreed Anna. 'I can't think what I've done to offend her.'

'You've done nothing. It's what other people have done. She's jealous.'

'What of?'

'Of Vittore and Rosina taking such an interest in you. I'm damn sure she wouldn't want to go trailing round churches with Vittore, and she'd probably rather eat dirt than slave over a hot stove with Rosina, but that's not the point. She doesn't want to do it, but she doesn't want anyone else to. The Anzelieri are her territory, and she doesn't like trespassers.'

'In that case, she's worrying over nothing. Whatever interest Vittore and Rosina have in me it's not going to alter her relationship with Raffi, is it? And from what I've just seen, they look as close as two peas in a pod.'

Izzy wiped a finger around her empty coffee cup, scooping up the remaining foam. 'Mmmm…you're right. She certainly had that well rogered look. The big romance is obviously back on.' She stood up, sucking a frothy digit. 'More fool Raffi. Come on, let's go and buy our lunch.'

That afternoon Izzy and Will were rehearsing with a disparate group of other British ex-pats who were endeavouring to stage a production of A Midsummer Night's Dream. Izzy was, predictably, Titania, and Will, not a natural thespian, was struggling to breathe life into one of the lovers.

Anna pottered about in the kitchen, making a lasagne for dinner. As the meat sauce bubbled, she took the opportunity to look through Vittore's book. Despite understanding hardly a word of the text, she felt, having scoured the reproductions of works attributed to Cima, that she understood something of his appeal. Will possessed a huge book, which covered all the Renaissance masters and she could see that compared to Titian and Giorgione, Cima's paintings lacked a certain drama and probably displayed little that was innovative. Despite this, however, they possessed a graceful innocence that was all their own. Looking at the gentle Madonnas, perfect babies and grave Christs, she was sure that this artist totally believed in God made man. There was about them a transcendent luminosity that spoke of utter faith and a serene goodness.

Vittore was right. "Her Madonna" was startlingly different, and not just because the central figure bore no resemblance to her pale sisters in other paintings, but also because of its background. This Mary sat against what appeared to be a plain wall, devoid of any detail to relieve its dark uniformity. Nearly every other Virgin, Saint and Christ was placed in front of a backdrop comprising fairy tale castles, hill towns and mountains scattered with shepherds and soldiers, rabbits and deer.

She turned the page and saw that Vittore had written an unusually large amount about this particular picture and she supposed he was expounding his theory about the missing half. In the midst of the text appeared a small black and white photo of the Madonna. Next to it was an economical line drawing of identical dimensions. It was of a woman – presumably an artist's impression of the long lost Saint Catherine. There had been no attempt to delineate her features and only two small dots, representing her eyes, appeared in the oval of her face.

'Who were you?' Anna whispered to her tiny black and white self, and then to the sparse little drawing. 'And who the hell were you?'

The images stared back at her, unwilling to reveal any secrets, when into her mind came, with astounding clarity, the features of a young woman, familiar and yet unknown: dark, slanting eyes; a full sensuous mouth; the palest of skins. For a second, they imposed themselves onto the linear sketch and then were gone, like a face glimpsed through the rain-splashed window of a passing train.

By the time Izzy and Will returned, it was late afternoon and the hitherto flirtatious sun had, at last, decided to show itself in earnest. The temperature had soared, so Anna opened a bottle of *prosecco*, and they took themselves, and the book, onto the terrace.

'Just translate the bit about Cima's life,' said Anna.

'OK.' Izzy cleared her throat, skimming the introduction. 'Lots of waffle about his place in the canon of Renaissance artists; that his work, although quite distinct from the acclaimed Giovanni Bellini, has nevertheless been constantly compared to this more famous artist. Consequently, he is not fully appreciated in his own right etc, etc.' She turned a couple of pages. 'Ah, here we are – biographical note. Hmm – it's not very long. Right, here goes: "Giovanni Battista Cima was a native of Conegliano, which lies approximately 60 kilometres north of Venice. A prosperous market town, it stands above the Venetian plain in a fertile, gently rising landscape, amidst vine-clad foothills, and will be familiar to art-lovers from the paintings of its most illustrious son".' She broke off. 'We must go some time. I think you can visit his house.'

'Yes, I'd like that,' murmured Anna.

'"His family name was derived from the trade pursued by both his father and grandfather who were *cimatori di panni*".' She paused for a moment, trying to find the right words. '"Craftsmen employed in the local wool industry, specialising in trimming and finishing newly woven cloth". Doesn't sound very arty does it? I wonder what they thought when young Giambattista announced he wanted to be a painter. "His exact date of birth is unknown, but it must have been sometime in either 1459 or 1460 because his name first appears in his father's tax returns in 1473, which indicates that by then he would have attained the age of 14. When his father died in 1483 he inherited the family home in Conegliano. It's not conclusive when he became a resident of Venice. Certainly he was by 1492 and possibly as early as 1486 when he received a payment from the *Scuola dei Calegheri*. Cobblers!"'

'What is?'

Will laughed. 'The *calegheri*; they were cobblers. The *scuola* was their guild.'

'"During the 1490s Giovanni Bellini was permanently occupied with commissions at the Doge's Palace which meant that Cima became the leading painter of altarpieces. He established his workshop in rented space in the Palazzo Corner Piscopia".'

'Where's that?'

'On the Grand Canal, near the Rialto. He may also have lived there. "Unlike many Venetian painters his workshop was not a family affair. We know that his eldest son, Pietro, reverted to the family business because he's recorded as holding office in the Conegliano wool guild. His second son, Fra Niccolo, took holy orders and was a Benedictine monk at Santa Giustina in Padua. He must have had some artistic talent as he reputedly undertook an early restoration of Cima's altarpiece in the Duomo in Conegliano. Despite living in Venice, Cima owned two houses in Conegliano, plus a number of smallholdings that were rented out to farmers. It's likely that he spent the summer months in his home town, escaping a Venice that, being more densely populated than it is now, would have been very hot and crowded". Ah, here's a bit about his personal life. "He was married twice; first to Corona with whom he had two sons, and then to Maria, who bore him three more sons and three daughters. He died in Conegliano, but the date's not recorded. A document which refers to Masses said in November 1518 for his soul mentions that he was interred in the family sepulchre in the church of San Francesco on 3 September. It's unclear whether the burial was in 1517 or 1518. Vittore thinks it more likely to have been the earlier date.

"As there were no family members involved in his workshop, it appears to have been immediately closed and its contents dispersed, many of them undoubtedly lost, with possibly all his preparatory drawings being destroyed as they would have been considered of little value".

Izzy pushed the book away and speared an olive with a cocktail stick.

'Is that it?' asked Anna, surprised at the paucity of detail.

'Yes, more or less.' Izzy wiped her hands on a paper napkin and leafed through the next few pages. 'There's a list of citations and a separate section about where he may have learnt his craft, but that's mostly erudite stuff about technique. And there's a bit about each picture, of course, but nothing else about him, as far as I can see.'

'What does it say about my Madonna?'

Izzy found the relevant page, once more applying herself to the task. '"Unusually for Cima, it's painted on canvas, rather than wood. It's been in the church since at least 1620, as it's mentioned in an inventory of that date and..."'

She continued, but her translation provided nothing in addition to what they already knew.

'You think there'd be more,' Anna said, aware of how peevish she sounded.

'It was an awfully long time ago,' said Izzy. 'Vittore appears to be quoting from a work first published in 1893. Most of the original documents were destroyed during the two World Wars, so it's unlikely anyone will discover anything new.'

Will refilled their glasses. 'You know, it's probably just as well you don't know anything about who she was. Like as not you'd find it upsetting. For most people then, life was short and brutal.'

'Especially for women,' added Izzy. 'Think how many died in childbirth – Titian's wife for one. I'd swap all that romance and swishing silk for our anaesthetics and antibiotics, not to mention the pill.'

'You're right, of course,' said Anna. But even as she spoke she knew that the next morning, when the church opened, she would once again visit her Madonna – the pull of the past too strong to be ignored.

157

Venice: November 1515

The first sitting falls at a time when Venice is beset by cold and damp. Many people are afflicted with agues, and Jakob is much occupied with house calls. And so, Debra is at liberty to steal away.

I call for her and find that she is almost sick with anticipation. What, for me is now commonplace, is for her a great adventure, all the more exciting for its illicit nature. Her cheeks are flushed to a becoming pink and her eyes glitter. As promised, I have brought her some clothes, for her own betray her origin.

Papà has always been generous, and I possess a fine collection of garments, suitable for all occasions and seasons. I am now eighteen, and believe that I have ceased to grow. (I do hope so, for I would not wish to outstrip Giacomo.) I should already have lengthened skirts that two years ago brushed the ground, but now show a deal of leg. However, I have been too occupied elsewhere to find time for needlework, which is fortuitous, for they are the perfect length for Debra. The bodices likewise will fit her, for though she is smaller in stature, she possesses the womanly curves I lack.

In her little bedroom we shiver by the inadequate fire, as she fiddles with the ties of her plain pinafore dress – the customary attire for a young Hebrew woman. It is not a flattering style, for as well as being a dull grey, it disguises her pretty shape. At my command she steps out of it and into the russet dress I hold. The fire splutters and flares, bathing the room, and Debra, in colour. It is a good sign; she is moving out of darkness into light, and any guilt I feel at our subterfuge disappears. We are about to create art; or perhaps it is art that is about to create us.

She thrusts her arms into the bodice and I lace it tightly, so that her breasts lift and swell above the white fabric of her shift. Then I attach the sleeves, fashioning the laces into bows.

'There. 'Tis done,' I say, and she squints into her little mirror.

Her hair is loosely braided, coiled at the back of her neck, and she looks so beautiful that I feel an unaccustomed tweak of jealousy.

'What if he does not like me?' she says, her hands flying up to cover the full white throat and bosom.

She means Giambattista, for I have not told her that she will also have to earn Enrico's approval.

'Oh, he will,' I reply. 'Any man would.'

At this, she smiles so broadly that little dimples appear in her cheeks. I do not think I have ever seen her so happy. As we step out into the biting air she links arms with me. 'Thank you,' she whispers.

It is mid-morning, so the city's byways are teeming with citizens going about their daily business of buying and selling. Even on this desolate winter day the open-fronted shops are piled high with brightly coloured produce, and everywhere there is the sweet, nutty smell of roasting chestnuts. We move swiftly through the bustle, and no one takes any notice of the two young women in mouse coloured cloaks, walking in close unison, their heads modestly bowed.

Although I have described the artist's workshop to Debra as best I can, I see that it amazes her. Like most of her race she regards the creation of devotional images with suspicion, even revulsion. She once told me that to fashion the face of God is akin to making a graven image. But now she stands before a Madonna and Child – transfixed.

'It is beautiful,' she whispers. 'The baby looks so real.'

To be honest, it is a work hardly touched by the master's hand, having been wrought almost entirely by the apprentices. To my mind, the colours are over bright – the face of the Virgin bland, without character, and the baby stiff, like a wooden doll. The workshop produces many such paintings and they, of course, sell for far less than a work by Cima himself. But Debra has never been into a church. She has never seen the perfect saints; the ethereal angels with wings as bright as butterflies, nor the gold and marble frames that encompass these glorious images. She has never watched as ancient mosaics glitter and wink in the candlelight, so that one may imagine the figures dance in a mist of incense. She is as unfamiliar with our Christian images of devotion as a monkey. It is now that a small worm of cunning squirms in my mind.

There is an old belief that a person responsible for converting a Jew is assured of a place in Heaven. Occasionally, those who are fearful for their immortal souls kidnap Jewish children and forcibly baptise them (an action more likely to guarantee damnation than salvation, in my opinion). I honestly do not think such self-interest motivates me; rather, I wish that if Debra and I are to be forced apart in this world, that we could be reunited in the next. But whilst she is a Jew this is impossible. So I resolve to show her some of the city's finest paintings, even if they do hang in churches. These works are intended to reinforce piety in the already faithful, so why should they not encourage devotion in the non-believer? Intellectual argument would never convert Debra, but beauty may.

Bernardo is looking at us; curiosity etched into his sharp little face. Predictably,

159

he is unmoved by her beauty but bemused by her astonishment. I mutter that she should hold her tongue. He is good-natured enough, but gossips like an old woman, and I would trust him no more than a sparrow trusts a fanged cat.

At that moment Giambattista arrives and I make introductions. As he scans Debra's face his expression is of a man seeing something precious and sublime – a holy relic perhaps. He is profoundly moved in the way that only an artist can be. I sense that this commission will become more than a simple depiction of Virgin and Saint; it is a challenge for him to capture her loveliness, her very essence. I at once feel ordinary, like a battered pewter mug skulking next to an exquisite drinking glass. It is not a sensation I relish and I am aware of my face settling into sulky folds, not at all appropriate for Our Lady.

No one notices, however, for Giambattista is hurrying us into a small room off the workshop. Piled on a wooden chest is a motley collection of garments. Seeing them, my good humour is immediately restored, for I have never dressed up before. I imagine that this is what it must be like for the participants in masques and plays. Whilst costumes are often wildly extravagant, however, the clothes that we struggle into are rather more sedate.

My garb consists of a reddish-coloured gown. With its high-waist and full loose sleeves it is not of the current fashion, and judging by its faded colour, I suspect that it is quite aged; certainly it smells musty. As Debra laces me into it, I wonder if Giambattista's first wife ever wore it, and my flesh creeps. There is also a long white veil, embroidered along the edges, that I assume will be draped over my head. I think this a shame, as my hair has grown since Debra hacked at it with her father's scissors, and now it falls into shiny fat ringlets, of which I am rather proud. Finally, I have a cloak of deep blue. Like the dress, it has seen better days and its brightness has, in parts, been stolen by time. Despite this, I know that the artist will restore and even better its original hue, for I heard Enrico instructing him to use a paint derived from lapis lazuli. We call this pigment ultramarine because one has to cross the sea to obtain the stone from which it is derived. Not even azurite can match its vibrancy, and it is so costly that it is reserved for the robes of the Virgin.

Debra will not receive the honour of lapis lazuli, but nevertheless her clothes are splendid. The gown has a bodice of gold brocade with long tight sleeves, slashed so that the white of her shift peeks through. It resembles a breastplate, and confers a bellicosity at odds with her delicate appearance. The skirt is of a dark mossy green, and a length of heavy silk fabric, in a deep rose pink, serves for a mantle. Finally, there is a small golden crown for her head.

In this hotchpotch of ill-fitting garments Debra and I trail into the workshop, like two embarrassed children. And this is how we are recorded for posterity. It does not matter that her skirts trail on the ground and the gown gapes at the back, or that half my shins are on display. None of this will old Sartorani and his bride, or anyone else, ever see.

The corner of the room in which we are to sit is curtained off; this means we are kept warm and afforded some privacy. I am glad of it, for the apprentices are grinning at us, and Bernardo makes what I suspect is a lewd gesture at my display of leg. I ignore him as Giambattista guides us towards two chairs. He is intent upon perfecting our poses, and with unabashed hands he arranges our limbs, and the fold and drape of our clothing. I see this disturbs Debra but I know that he has ceased to see us as women; we have become the instruments of his art; merely the bare bones of what he creates.

I am given a hard wooden doll to stand for the Holy Infant, while Debra is told to lean one arm on a spiked wheel. A large palm is propped by her side. She regards these things with curiosity. As Giambattista fixes the crown, she silently mouths, 'What are these?'

Why should she understand their significance? Of course, she does not realise that the martyr's palm is the symbol of victory over death. Neither does she know that the wheel is the instrument on which they intended to torture Catherine, but that when they bound her to it, it broke in two. (I do not divulge that they then beheaded the maid.)

'I will tell you later,' I also mouth, just at the moment when the white veil is draped over my head and shoulders.

At last, satisfied with our appearance, Giambattista moves to the easel, on which a large piece of *carta azzura* is attached. The paper is criss-crossed with lines, dividing it into fifty squares. These will enable him to accurately copy his preliminary drawing onto a wooden panel.

I remember him telling me that not everyone is suited to being an artist's model, and I soon understand why. Every few minutes I am compelled to shift my position or scratch my nose. The wooden doll becomes intolerably heavy, with its hard little limbs biting into my thighs. I catch Giambattista's look of annoyance, but he is too kind to reprimand me. Debra, in contrast, is a paragon and hardly moves a muscle. We have been instructed not to smile but the corners of our mouths cannot help but upturn, and our eyes, that remain fixed on one another, flicker with mirth.

At long last we are granted a break and Alvise brings us food and drink. We stretch our arms and legs, jumping up and down on feet that have become numb with cold. While we eat and warm ourselves before the fire, Giambattista continues working. And then something changes in his expression. I see that he is satisfied with the drawing. He takes a glass of wine, his face beaming, and once again regards us as fellow humans, rather than merely the ciphers of his art.

Encouraged by his smile, Debra asks, 'May we see?'

'You may,' he says, and we trot round to examine the fruit of his labour. The drawing is really a painting, for he uses the very tip of a brush dipped into a grey-brown wash, adding highlights with white paint. Despite its simplicity it captures our likenesses so perfectly that Debra stares in amazement.

'It is us,' she giggles, linking arms with me.

We are not allowed much of a break, for Giambattista wishes to execute another study, in which we sit in slightly different positions. After this, he makes some likenesses of Debra's hands, for these will be a focal point of the finished work.

Whilst he works, I settle myself in front of the fire and sketch the artist drawing my friend. Then I hear a door open, followed by a cold shiver of air. There is the sound of footsteps, the curtain is thrust aside and Enrico is looking down at me.

'I have come to see your little friend,' he whispers. 'She is here?'

I scramble to my feet, wanting to witness whatever is to take place. The painter has his back to us, but at the sound of Enrico's voice, he lays down his brush. The room is suddenly very quiet. I no longer hear the apprentices working, and even the seabirds' squawks are hushed. Debra has not moved. She looks at Enrico with eyes as open and innocent as a child's seeing the Doge for the first time. And overlaying her guileless expression is wonderment and admiration, for he is an impressive figure, with his mane of dark hair and strangely animated face. He has discarded his cloak and is dressed in purple and black, but only a blind woman could fail to miss the powerful body under the rich cloth.

When he speaks his voice is very soft. 'So, you are my Saint Catherine? Such beauty will make my father forget his God.'

Instantly her cheeks become like roses. She lowers her eyes so that her lashes lay in black crescent moons on the white skin. No one moves: it is as though they are the only two people present. For all his gentle tone, I sense danger. I would like to grab Debra by the hand and drag her away, but it is too late – he has seen her. For the first time I am glad she is of the faith she is, for I know that nothing would induce her to consort with a Gentile. This, I am sure, will keep her safe.

'Come and see the drawings,' I blab, for Enrico has not even glanced at the easel.

At my words, the spell, for I know no other word to describe it, is broken and Giambattista and his patron turn their attention to the painting.

Enrico leaves soon after this, but not before turning his attention to me. He takes hold of the veil that covers not only my hair but also half my forehead, and teases it back. 'Wear it like this,' he says, 'so that it shows your hair.' He looks at the painter, conveying the instruction to him also. And then he is gone, leaving an atmosphere that is like the unease before a summer storm.

A Knight in Shining Armour

Days passed and April tripped towards May. Venetian matrons abandoned tweed suits for linen; men relegated green loden coats to the back of wardrobes, and the skies were full of chattering swallows, and the *calli* and *campi* full of chattering tourists. Spring had arrived and winter was consigned to mothballs.

Taking advantage of the break from classes, Izzy and Will arranged daytrips to the mainland. The three of them made the tortuous journey to the hill town of Asolo, in the foothills of the Dolomites, and climbed up to its medieval fortress, while Will related tales of those who had lived nearby: Caterina Cornaro, the exiled queen of Cyprus; Robert Browning; the libidinous actress, Eleonara Duse. When it began to rain they stumbled into a *trattoria* where they feasted on spatchcocked poussins, char-grilled over an open fire, and drank local wine, served icy cold from earthenware pitchers.

Another day they took the train to Padua, and meandered under its picturesque arcades, before viewing Giotto's frescoes, commissioned by a dutiful son in the hope of saving the usurious soul of his dead father. They visited Verona, touring the Roman amphitheatre, once the home of gladiatorial fights, but now the venue for a summer opera season. And then onto the *Casa di Giulietta* with its pretty, but graffiti scrawled courtyard, presided over by a graceful bronze statue of the eponymous heroine, her right breast burnished to a shiny gold from the hands of those who hoped their caress would bring luck in love.

'Go on, Anna, you know you want to,' urged Izzy. And Anna had done as bid, hoping, but not believing in the old magic.

On the first day of May they walked past Ca' Melisa, just as dusk was falling. Light and laughter drifted from its open windows, and Anna realised that this must be the night of the farewell dinner. Tomorrow the guests would return to their various homes, and for a short time, normality would return to the house. Now, she thought, Vittore would ring to arrange her rendezvous with Rosina.

It was not, however, until the following Tuesday, when she was beginning to think that he had forgotten, that the summons came.

'I am so sorry not to have called earlier. Our guests left us on Saturday but Edie and Graham stayed on till yesterday. We needed to finalise the details of my book's publication. Also they had some other secret mission in the city.'

'That sounds thrilling,' said Anna. 'What was it? Or was it so secret you never found out.'

'She said she was not at liberty to tell me – yet. But she did promise that it would greatly please me. I have an awful feeling that she is buying an apartment.'

'Why's that awful? I thought you liked her.'

'Oh, I do, very much. But I do not like the idea of yet another property being bought by someone who may live in it for only three or four weeks a year. I am afraid that because of people like Edie this city is slowly dying. Venetians can no longer afford to live here, yet holiday homes sit empty for months at a time.'

As a tourist, although one who could never dream of buying property in the city, she felt there was little she could say. Perhaps sensing her discomfiture, Vittore hurriedly continued, 'But I did not ring to lament the fate of Venice. Rosina, at long last, has some time to herself and would love to take you shopping. Is Thursday convenient?'

'Yes, absolutely.'

'Excellent. Be here a little before eight. And she will also teach you how to cook some classic Venetian dishes – if you want to that is? You can make lunch together and we will sample the results.'

'I can't think of anything nicer,' said Anna.

Two days later at the Rialto markets, Rosina was greeted by name at each stall she approached. It was soon obvious she had carefully chosen which traders she would introduce to Anna. Foremost, it was essential they speak English, as a pleasure, rather than a chore; their produce had to be excellent and as an added bonus they should be eager to advise and guide her protégé.

Anna was soon on first name terms with Marcello, who sold a dazzling array of cheese and salami; Beppe, who presided over a riot of fruit and vegetables; and Sergio, whose kingdom was a butcher's shop selling everything from heartbreakingly tiny birds to huge cuts of beef, plus all sorts of dubious looking offal. At the *Pescheria*, Rosina introduced her to Giuseppe. Tall and pale, the only colour on his face was bequeathed by reflections from the scarlet awnings, and his down tilted eyes were rainwater grey and so heavily baggaged that he rather resembled one of his wares. He promised Anna, in excellent but archaic English, to "serve her faithfully".

Finally, they visited Antica Drogheri Mascari, where Rosina had shopped since it opened in the late 1940s. Appropriately located in the Calle degli Spezieri – the street of the spice merchants – it was an Aladdin's cave. Here one could buy sweets and spices; teas and truffles; oils and vinegars; grappa and liquors of every conceivable colour; and even Marmite and tomato ketchup.

Anna's first lesson was how to transform spider crabs into a sauce to accompany homemade gnocchi.

'Steam the potatoes rather than boil them,' advised Rosina, 'and use as little flour as possible.'

Then, with a fork, she demonstrated how to mould the mixture into little shapes that, when tossed into boiling water, cooked in moments. The crabs presented a greater challenge and Anna had to suppress her natural squeamishness upon hearing the creatures clamouring inside the cooking pot. After this, extracting the meat and making the sauce posed no problem. At lunch Vittore declared the end result superb, and little Magda twittered superlative after superlative, '*Bellisima, perfetto, delizia*.'

On Saturday she visited her new friends at the Rialto, and duplicated the meal for Izzy and Will. In place of dessert, she allowed Marcello to persuade her to buy a slab of artery blocking cheese comprising layers of *dolcelatte* and *mascarpone*. They ate it with crisp-baked biscuits and the season's first cherries, dark and bittersweet.

Later, as she stretched, replete and woozy on the sofa, Izzy muttered, 'Promise me you'll never go home. Stay and be our personal chef forever.' She drained a glass of grappa which she had declared a medical necessity and asked, 'So, when's your next lesson?'

'Wednesday. Stuffed zucchini flowers and some sort of veal dish.'

'Bliss,' said Izzy, reaching for another draught of medicine.

And so it became a weekly ritual for Anna to accompany Rosina to market, and to cook and eat lunch at Ca' Melisa in the company of Vittore and Magda. As June approached, the produce grew increasingly tempting: asparagus, slender and green, or fat and white from the foothills of Bassano, best eaten hot and dipped into the yolk of a softly boiled egg. There were artichokes, spiky and purple-tipped from Palermo, or plump and round from Rome. And *fondi* – the creamy flat discs revealed after the stallholders, with a few deft swipes of a knife, had hacked away the stem and leaves. But best of all was the seasonal delicacy, *castraure*; tiny buds that were the very first artichokes, picked in their infancy to encourage the rest of the plant to grow, so tender that they were eaten whole in a single mouthful.

Vying for space with boxes of crimson blood oranges were infant summer fruits: apricots and cherries; punnets of fragrant wild strawberries, each tiny scarlet jewel bursting with flavour. Also making their debut were early salad vegetables; perky green leaves; vibrant bunches of rosy, white tipped radishes and the first tomatoes in all sizes, shapes and colours.

Their lunches were fun and informal. They chatted about the food; what was happening in the city; the weather; friends and relatives. Magda did not appear in the least perturbed that the majority of the conversation was in English. She ate in contented silence, but would occasionally interject and wait for Vittore to translate. It was usually some snippet of gossip concerning the neighbours, but she was also particularly partial to discussing Raffi's life. Anna found that listening to these family discussions was the next best thing to seeing him. Disappointingly, their paths had not crossed since St Mark's day. Despite Izzy's assurance that one always bumped into people in Venice, Raffi was proving surprisingly elusive.

Then she saw him three times in the space of five days.

* * *

Friday evening

She had spent a long, hot day in Vicenza, and had just spilled off the train at Santa Lucia, longing for a shower and a cold drink, when she saw him. He was leaning against one of the fluted pillars comprising part of a hefty colonnade that the architect had perhaps hoped would give the station the air of a classical temple. The sight of him, dressed in pristine cream linen, stopped her in her tracks. He looked up from his newspaper and their eyes met.

'Hello, Anna. Where did you spring from?' he called.

She ambled over, conscious of her creased clothes and smeared make up.

'I've been to Vicenza,' she said, and leaning forward for the obligatory kiss, was painfully aware of the prickle of sweat between her shoulder blades.

'Ah…on the Palladio trail? And I hear things are going really well with the cookery lessons. Rosina says you're a model pupil. I must try and join you for lunch one day.'

'Oh, yes, please do,' said Anna, showing more enthusiasm than she intended, and then quickly changing the subject in the hope that he had not noticed. 'Are you off somewhere?'

'No, I'm meeting Caterina. She should be on the 18.32 from Milano.'

Anna glanced at the clock. It was 18.30. She had no desire to encounter Caterina, no doubt immaculately coiffured and cucumber cool.

'Well, she should be here any minute. Have a lovely weekend. Bye bye.'

'You too,' he said, his gaze shifting to the far distance, where the *rapido* train had just appeared. And when he turned back to Anna, she had already scuttled off.

* * *

Jonathan, a friend of Will's, was in Venice for a long weekend. He was staying at a cheap hotel near the station; not the best choice as he hated crowds.

'Show me a part of Venice where the tourists don't go,' he challenged. And so, minus Izzy, who could not be bothered to get out of bed, they headed westwards, cutting through the hospital grounds, before skirting by incongruous gasometers onto the blustery openness of the Fondamente Nuove. They crossed a bridge and continued along a sun drenched concrete pathway that hugged the side of the Arsenale, where the occasional heavily grilled window afforded a glimpse of the derelict and abandoned shipyards. The formidable walls eventually gave way to rows of cottages, from which the tinny sound of radios and crying babies drifted – workers' residences with vegetable plots and neat gardens.

Side stepping silent men holding slumbering fishing rods, they passed a ramshackle sports stadium and continued walking until the path ended at a barred and shuttered military zone, leaving them no option but to retrace their steps. On their right, the lagoon sparkled, wide and open in the late morning sun; the cemetery island shimmering hotly, a mirage in terracotta and bone white.

'We'll cut down past the Arsenale and then head into St Elena,' said Will. 'For lunch there's a place I know where the *vaporetto* drivers eat. No tourists there, I promise.'

Anna's skin prickled at the mention of the Arsenale. It was, of course, where Raffi lived.

She had recently caught the number 5 *vaporetto* that chugged through the inner canal of the Arsenale where huge red walls loomed on either side of an urban lake. In the absence of all other traffic, it was eerily quiet for a place that had once reverberated with noise and industry. After disembarking she had lingered over an *ombra* and *panino* at the bar on the corner of the *campo*, before making the acquaintance of the quartet of enigmatic stone lions that guarded the great gates of the Arsenale. Her favourite was the lanky, hairless beast on the left, with what Will assured her were ancient runes carved on its haunches.

On that particular day she had gleaned from Magda that Raffi was out of the city, and had passed front doors, trying to look casual, as she studied the names. She soon found it, "Anzelieri", engraved on a small brass plate by a bell push. It was ridiculous, she knew, to try and work out which were his windows. Judging by the bell's placement, probably the ones on the third floor. She felt like that character in *My Fair Lady* who sings *On the Street Where You Live*, except she was secure in the knowledge that Raffi would not suddenly appear.

But now it was Sunday. Raffi was in Venice, with Caterina, very possibly in his apartment, and could certainly appear any moment. As they approached the Arsenale, her nerves crackled with anticipation. And there they were, sitting at a table outside the *campo's* only restaurant. Will hailed a cheerful greeting and strode towards them. Anna followed, reluctant in his wake. It soon became obvious that all was not well. Beneath the make up, Caterina's face was like a bruised flower, her lids red and swollen. Raffi's eyes were darkly circled and a little frown line was etched between his brows. Before them, two plates of untouched food congealed in the noontime warmth; a solitary fly crawled over Caterina's *antipasto*.

It was one of those palpably awkward moments. Will introduced Jonathan but there was none of the usual kissing and handshaking. Everyone clearly wanted to extricate themselves, with the exception of Raffi, who was oddly inclined to chat. Anna sensed that he hoped their presence might diffuse a difficult situation. He was wrong. After he suggested, with a brittle enthusiasm so different from his usual relaxed manner, that they join them for a glass of wine, Caternia sprang to her feet. The sudden movement sent her glass spinning. Not that it mattered; it was empty and so was the bottle from which it had come. The couple may not have eaten much, but they had clearly polished off at least a bottle, on empty stomachs. She fired a verbal shot at Raffi, and with a swing of her bag that threatened more carnage, swept towards his flat.

For a few seconds no one moved. Then Raffi stood and deposited a bundle of notes on the table. With an embarrassed shrug he said, 'I'm sorry. She's not feeling well. Please excuse me.'

He caught up with Caterina just as she won her struggle to open the door, and the couple disappeared from view.

Jonathan let his breath out in a long, low whistle. 'What was all that about?'

'God knows,' said Will. 'All she said was, that if she was going to get the 15.30 back to Milano, she ought to start packing. Looked suspiciously like a lovers' tiff to me. By all accounts she is a bit of a prima donna.'

'Hell of a looker, though,' observed Jonathan, as they made their way towards the wooden bridge that crossed the *rio* and led them out of the *campo*. Trailing behind her companions, Anna cast a furtive glance back at Raffi's windows. For a second, she thought she saw a figure looking out at them, and then it was gone – perhaps just a figment of her imagination. And with a frisson of guilt, she realised that whatever sympathy she may feel for Raffi, it was dwarfed by an ignoble delight that all was not well between him and Caterina.

* * *

Anna sat at a table outside a canal-side restaurant on the Fondamenta di San Lorenzo, gently fanning herself with a menu. The previous day she had realised that, despite having been in Venice for some weeks, she had visited hardly any museums or galleries. Although, as she spent much of her days walking around the city, she had taken in many of its churches: from the homely places of parochial worship such as San Martino, boasting a surprising *trompe l'oeil* ceiling, to the vast meringuey whiteness of the Salute, with its iconic wedding cake silhouette.

She had also fallen into the habit of visiting the Misericordia church on an almost daily basis, where she would sit for fifteen minutes or so, before moving on. However, time spent here did not count as real sightseeing, so she had decided that it was time to do more than aimlessly wander. Leafing through her guidebook she had chosen the Scuola di San Giorgio degli Schiavoni, a little confraternity building erected by Dalmatian merchants in the mid fifteenth century. It apparently boasted, "an irresistibly appealing sequence of pictures, executed by Vittore Carpaccio".

Unfortunately, the guidebook had failed to mention that it closed for three hours over lunchtime, and she had arrived just as the taciturn guardian was about to lock up. Returning home, the restaurant where she now sat, had caught her eye and she could not resist lunching at one of its outside tables. Across the canal, a Gothic palace rubbed shoulders with its Renaissance neighbour, facing her was the leaning bell tower of the Greek church, and from the nearby bridge she could hear gondoliers touting for business. Nothing, she thought, could be more quintessentially Venetian.

Even though there was no reason why he should be in this part of the city, when a shadow fell across the table, she somehow knew it was Raffi.

'Hello,' he said. 'We seem to keep bumping into each other.'

She looked up from the menu, hardly daring to believe it was indeed he.

He was wearing a coffee coloured linen suit and a cream shirt, open at the neck. A brightly coloured tie peeked out of his breast pocket, and in the little hollow of his throat, light beads of perspiration glistened. When he planted the obligatory kiss on her cheek, his face felt slightly damp.

'That looks good,' he said, eyeing the *spritz* that she was drinking.

'It is. Why don't you join me and have one yourself?' she said, surprised at her boldness.

'Good idea. I could do with a cool drink. It's too hot to be charging across the city. Are you meeting anyone?'

'No, I'm all alone,' she said, watching as he thrust a hand into his hair, pushing it back from his forehead in a gesture that she now recognised as habitual.

'I've never eaten here,' he said, collapsing into the empty chair opposite her, and calling out his order to a passing waiter. 'Bit of a tourist trap, but it doesn't look too bad.'

'Aren't you working today?'

'I was supposed to meet a prospective client from New York. They like to send me to meet the Americans. He's negotiating to buy a property here and wanted an idea of what alterations he could make. While I was on the way to his hotel some emergency came up and he cancelled. So, no meeting, no lunch and no great loss. He wanted to eat at Harry's Bar!'

His nose crinkled at the idea. Anna had read about the establishment once patronised by Ernest Hemingway, Noel Coward and the like, and rather fancied splashing out on one of their famous Bellinis, but Izzy had dismissed the suggestion. She had been, but only once: the barman had been surly, the place half-empty and her Bellini made with tinned peach juice, even though fresh ones were in season; and the price had been astronomical. These days, Venetians rarely went to Harry's, unless they bowed to the whims of guests.

Raffi's drink arrived and he and the waiter discussed the menu. Today's "special" was monkfish, roasted with *pancetta*, accompanied by the lightest of cream sauces. And to start, there was freshly prepared *carpaccio* – slices of raw beef, beaten to a papery thinness, served with a mustard dressing, shaved *parmigiano* and a rocket salad.

'Sounds good to me,' said Anna. 'I've never eaten *carpaccio*, but it's rather appropriate as I'm killing time before going to see them.'

Having informed the waiter of their choice, Raffi leant back in his chair, looking into the middle distance, as if trying to remember something.

'I haven't been to the Scuola di San Giorgio for years. The paintings are beautiful, you'll love them – the English always do. I adored them when I was a kid. You know, I think I may come with you, if, that is, I wouldn't be intruding?'

'No, of course not.' Anna struggled to sound casual. 'You can tell me all about them, but don't you have to be back at work?'

'Theoretically yes, but my client has asked that we reschedule for Thursday evening. So as I'll be giving up my time then, I think, as a quid pro quo, I can spend a few hours today looking at beautiful paintings with a beautiful woman.'

Embarrassed, and yet delighted, Anna found a loose thread on her napkin inexplicably fascinating. She looked up and caught his eye. *Please don't flirt with me,* she thought, *not unless you mean it.*

Their drinks winked naughtily in the sunlight and from nowhere she heard herself say, 'Did you have a good weekend?'

Now it was his turn to be discomfited; the smile vanished and his gaze drifted away.

Silence: and then. 'No, not really. You saw…on Sunday, didn't you?' His voice trailed off and he grabbed a packet of grissini, tearing the paper wrapper.

'I'm sorry,' she stammered. 'I don't know why I said that. Just making conversation.'

He snapped the bread stick in half, but with such force, that part of it ricocheted across the table and improbably flew past Anna's cheek and caught in her hair. Neither of them said anything for a second and then she began to laugh.

'*Mio Dio*, I'm sorry.' He leant over to extricate it; in doing so, his cuff caught the edge of a glass, which went flying, the contents spilling across the table, staining the white tablecloth a deep pink.

'Oh, God!' He buried his head in his hands, shaking with laughter. 'Shall I just go now, and leave you in peace before I do any more damage?'

'No, please don't.' And she caught hold of his wrist, pulling it from his face.

He looked up, twisting his hand so that his held hers. 'Believe me, I'm not usually this clumsy.'

He did not, she realised, relinquish his grip until their waiter arrived, balancing two plates in one hand and holding a bottle of wine in the other. With no more than a nonchalant lift of the eyebrows he indicated another table, and they decamped to drier territory.

To her surprise Raffi made no attempt to change the subject. 'As weekends go, it was not a success. I've known Caterina since we were teenagers and I thought I knew her through and through, but she's changed since going to Milan. I wish to God she'd come back to Venice.'

'You miss her?'

'Well, yes, of course. But it's more than that. It's what the place is doing to her.'

'So you don't like Milan?'

'It's a big city, brittle and hard and full of ambitious people too busy trying to get on in life to really enjoy living. Too busy trying to look beautiful to appreciate all the beauty around them. It's not everything, this…' He searched for the right expression, and not finding anything appropriate in English, switched to Italian.'… this need for *la bella figura*. Tell me, Anna, surely there's more to life than shopping for designer clothes?'

Anna made a show of thinking deeply. 'Yes, of course there is…there's shopping for designer shoes!'

Raffi laughed. 'Sorry, I'm being far too philosophical. The trouble is, Caterina loves it…loves it so much she won't be content until I go and live there too. That was the cause of all the trouble over the weekend. A friend of a friend of a friend, who's an architect there, wants someone to join his practice. Caterina's convinced herself that it's the perfect opportunity for me.'

'But you don't want to go?'

'No…no, I really don't. Venice isn't just where I live. It's what I am…a major part of how I define myself. You probably feel the same way about London?'

'Well, yes. I certainly think I'd find it difficult living anywhere else – permanently that is.'

Raffi smiled. 'Apart from Venice, of course?'

Their eyes met.

'Oh, I've never really thought about that,' she lied, turning her attention to the *carpaccio*.

And then they talked of multifarious things and ate fragrant monkfish, followed by trembling *pannacotta*, drizzled with strawberry sauce, and drank coffee and grappa and hardly noticed the church bells telling them that it was three o'clock which meant that the *scuola* would now be open. When the bill came, they squabbled about it and, because Raffi was a man, and a Venetian, and undoubtedly in league with the waiter, it was his money that was taken.

'You must come to dinner,' she said, and when he said he would love to, she wondered whether he was interpreting "you" as singular or plural, and silently thanked the English language for its ambiguity.

When they reached the *scuola*, a chattering flock of early birders were already departing, pushing their way between the heavy red curtains that guarded the half open door. As the last one hopped out, Anna stepped into the small space. She was vaguely aware of Raffi offering payment, but he was recognised and they were waved through gratis.

Apart from the custodian they were alone. After the dazzling afternoon light the interior seemed very dark but then, behind them, the breeze caught a curtain; sun filtered in through grilled windows, casting patterns on the floor and catching the golden picture frames. It smelt of age and dust, of beeswax and old, old knowledge. Above them, the intricately painted ceiling, so like the one at Ca' Melisa, contributed to the sensation of being trapped inside some sort of ornate box – a jewellery or musical box brimming with treasures, playing old tunes. She could see no books, but felt as though she stood in a library, for although the room was quite still, it hummed with ancient tales. But surely no library boasted such brilliant, colourful, inventive and stomach churning decoration. It unfolded, as her eyes grew accustomed to the dimmed light, like a bright patchwork. The lower part of the room was wood panelled, and furnished with simple pews, but above these on the left, right and facing walls was a series of paintings, the like of which she had never before seen.

'Do they tell a story?' she whispered.

'Absolutely.' He linked his arm through hers. 'Let me talk you through them. This first one was my favourite when I was a kid.'

He pointed to a dragon, frozen forever at the moment when St George's spear smashed into its gaping mouth; all around, a scattered gallimaufry of detached limbs and body parts testify to its insatiable greed. On the ground, with a face as peaceful as though she slept, lay a young girl, her small pointed breasts peeking through the thin stuff of her dress, the lower part of her body completely gnawed away. Nearby, the mutilated corpse of a naked man, perhaps her lover and failed rescuer, is stretched, his flaccid genitals a reminder of his impotence against such evil. The landscape is parched and inhabited by toads and vipers. Stumps of trees cower, scorched to blackness by the creature's fiery breath, yet in the background there are castles, graceful ships and leafy forests.

'When I was a bit older,' said Raffi, bending his head so close that Anna felt his breath on her cheek, 'I used to imagine I was St George rescuing the maiden.' And he pointed to the virgin princess, who watches as her life and virtue are saved by the thrust of a penetrative spear.

He talked her through the rest of the paintings. The dragon, still alive, but pathetically shrunken, is presented to the king and queen. And the princess, George's prize, whether or not she wants to be, walks alongside her parents, holding her father's hand, a touch John Ruskin found particularly moving. Next, a wholesale baptism; Christianity triumphs and the old heathen religion is discarded as carelessly as the turban abandoned on the palace steps. Then the paintings switched to another saint, St Tryphone, who has managed to exorcize an innocuously gawky basilisk from another pagan princess.

Finally, on the right hand wall were three paintings, telling the story of St Jerome, a saint particularly venerated in Venice because of his association with a lion. The holy man, venerably bearded and leaning on his stick, is followed by his leonine friend, who displays his healed paw in a gesture of feline winsomeness, guaranteed to charm the viewer; not so, however, the timid monks who scatter in terror like a flock of magpies. In the second picture the saint is newly deceased; his fellow monks weep and the lion yowls in brute sorrow for the only thing it has ever loved. The last painting, it seemed to Anna, was a non sequitur. A middle-aged man, pen in hand, sits at a book-laden table in a room flooded with light.

He gazes out of a window, in a state of obvious amazement.

'That's St Augustine hearing a divine voice telling him that Jerome has died,' said Raffi. 'It's full of symbolism but what everyone remembers now is the dog. It's the reason the *scuola* is so popular with all you English dog lovers.'

Certainly, the small animal basking in a warm sunbeam was undeniably appealing. Indeterminate of breed, white and tousle haired, it sat back on its haunches, eyes fixed on the saint. For all its cuteness, it had strangely un-canine front legs ending in large flat feet, like a toddler in a sleep-suit.

'He's a funny little thing isn't he,' said Raffi. 'There's a preparatory drawing of the painting in the British Museum and in that he's a cat. I think he must be suffering from an identity crisis. Apparently he's also transfixed by the holy voice.'

Anna looked at the adorable scruff; bright eyed and blackberry-nosed: seemingly quite unconcerned with the spiritual, he looked as though he were about to leap up and tug on the saint's robe for solely doggy reasons.

'I think he just wants to go for a walk,' she said.

'Either that, or Augustine's forgotten his dinner.'

At that moment a group of tourists arrived. Although they spoke in whispers, their presence robbed the place of its intimacy, so after a brief visit to the ornate, but rather disappointing upper room, they left.

Only then did Raffi say, 'I'm sorry. Had you seen enough? I didn't want to drag you away. We can go back if you like.'

'No,' she said, not wanting to risk spoiling what had been so perfect. 'It was wonderful. I'm sure I'll go again.'

They stood blinking in the bright sunlight, neither wanting to make the first move. Then he said, 'Are you going home now? I'll walk with you and call in at Ca' Melisa.'

It seemed perfectly natural that he should take her arm as they strolled, their steps falling into the same easy rhythm. The mood between them was relaxed, so it was a slight shock when, out of the blue, he asked, 'Don't you get lonely, sightseeing all by yourself?'

'No, not really. Anyway, Izzy and Will are around a lot of the time, so it's not like being completely alone.'

Raffi stopped mid-stride and turned to her. 'I've just had an idea. I think you could help with Vittore's tours.'

'Me? How?'

'Sometimes there are minor problems. For instance, on the last tour there was a couple, well into their seventies. She was really quite frail and kept feeling so tired she insisted on returning to Ca' Melisa. So her husband had to take her back and he kept missing Vittore's talks. Now, if Vittore were accompanied by, say, you, then you could have helped her back home, or just sat with her for five minutes until she felt better. What do you think? I don't suppose he would be able to pay much.'

'I wouldn't want paying.'

'But you'd visit places that you wouldn't normally be able to see,' Raffi continued, 'and be able to listen to his lectures, which, as you know, are really rather good. And you wouldn't have to trail around by yourself. I don't know why none of us thought of it before. I'll mention it to Vittore right away. Do say yes.'

Found and Lost

When Anna recalled those days working with Vittore, she did not so much remember people or places, but a heady mix of sun splintered-light and colour. Always colour. Colour drenched her days, dripping from the city's mercurial palette like thick drops of the finest olive oil – warm and rich and yellow. Every morning, as she threw back the shutters, she was seduced by the sight that unfolded: the canal, its waters the colour of ancient jade; the crystalline flashes of magnesium white perforating its surface; a gaudy daub on the wet *fondamenta* – not, after all, a smear of paint, but the reflection of garish mooring poles. Hours later, as she drew the shutters on night, the same canal bewitched her anew, its espresso-black waters drizzled by reflections from lollipop-bright street lamps and a creamy moon.

Buildings that had once been merely shades of brown were now ochre, peach, russet red, terracotta and sienna. Blue was no longer simply blue, but the shifting hue of the Venetian sky, limpid and dreamy in the early hours; unrelentingly intense at noon; softening at sundown, when it was streaked with buttery yellow. It was the radiant lapis lazuli of the Virgin's robe, or the deep turquoise of the Bacino.

There were golds and reds: the scintillating brilliance of the mosaics in San Marco; the outrageous scarlet of Titian's Assumption in the Frari that had so shocked the conservative friars; the astonishing blaze of the setting sun on the Grand Canal, and the blush of geraniums tumbling from window boxes.

Equally enchanting were the shy and subtle shades: a sliver of waning moon hanging in a velvet-heavy sky; the grey lagoon, skimmed pink by a rising sun; the colours of dawn, when the morning was swirled with the same pearly tones that graced the marble pillars of the Basilica, its light as translucent as bottle glass.

One afternoon, in the jewel box of La Fenice, Venice's opera house, surrounded by rose madder and mellowed gold, Anna lifted her eyes to its opalescent ceiling of soft green, and for a second, felt her head swim. She sat down, a little dizzy, knowing that for the first time in her life she was seeing, really seeing, the unfathomable beauty and texture of colour. She looked at Vittore, who was waxing lyrical about the graceful figures painted above their heads, and silently thanked him for this gift, a gift that she would treasure for the rest of her days.

But all that was still to come on the Sunday afternoon when she and Izzy lunched at a somewhat humbler venue; a two bedroom flat in Santa Marta, near the docks that had once been bombed by the British.

'I can't make any more excuses,' Izzy had said, putting down the phone. 'When I first came to Venice, Bettina was in my adult class. And she was terrible; couldn't get to grips with English at all, but for some reason was desperate to learn. Anyway, as she was getting left behind, I suggested she had private lessons. Well, she's still having them. Her English has hardly improved but she loves it and, bless her, every now and again insists I come for lunch. I told her you were living with me and she's adamant that you come too.'

'And what about me?' demanded Will. 'I'm living with you too. Aren't I invited?'

'No, 'fraid not. I don't think she likes men…dirty, smelly things. Can you bear it, Anna? It'll be really boring but she's ever so sweet.'

'I'd like to, honestly.' Anna said, eager to be allowed into any genuine Venetian home.

Bettina's flat, although by no means small, was intimidated by furniture of monstrous proportions, testimony to when she, her parents and two sisters had lived in more palatial surroundings. Her father had died twenty-odd years ago and when both her sisters had married and left home, Bettina and her mother were re-housed in their present dwelling. Now, *mamma* too had left, the stairs having become too much for her, and lived with Bettina's youngest sister in Belluno.

Bettina was in her mid-fifties and professed to remember wartime Venice well: the occupation, the air attack carried out by the British, and the long awaited liberation by Allied troops. Her English was not up to making coherent conversation, but because Anna showed interest in her past, she produced a number of photo albums, sticky with age, and bearing the musty scent of a charity shop.

They squeezed onto an uncomfortable horsehair sofa, Bettina providing a running and incomprehensible commentary, which Izzy translated as best she could. Here were her family, her life, her past. There were first communions, christenings and weddings posed outside various churches. Staid studio portraits were interspersed with beach shots of bathers squinting into the Lido sun. And finally, a very few photos from the war years.

'Ah, *i tedeschi*,' gasped Bettina, as though the picture still surprised her. It showed a group of young German soldiers sitting outside a bar, looking amiable and inoffensive: apparently they were, most of the time. Bettina remembered food shortages, but no one starved, and most people were unharmed, unless they caused trouble – or were Jewish. She had known a Jewish girl; not a friend exactly, just someone who had attended the same school. In 1943 the girl had disappeared, along with all her family; taken not by the Germans, but the Italian Fascists.

Bettina shook her head, tutting sadly and closing the album, smiled brightly, as if trying to dispel all the sadness and shame of those times.

'*Café*?' she asked, and without waiting for a reply bustled into the kitchen, leaving the albums in the place she had vacated on the sofa.

There was one they had not looked at, and Anna began to flick through it. The photos it contained appeared to be of an art collection, a meticulous pictorial catalogue of an eclectic hotch-potch, with annotations in a language that was not Italian: a tiny and ancient sculpture of an earth goddess; a small canvas by Corot; two icons; a tapestry depicting a hunting scene; a painting by – Cima da Conegliano.

At that moment Bettina pottered back in. For a second she looked confused and then began to apologise. She had not meant them to see that album; it was dull stuff belonging to her mother.

'Will you ask Bettina if I could borrow it, just until tomorrow. There's something I'd really like to show to Vittore.'

'What?' Izzy shuffled over to look. 'Oh, I see…a Cima.' She squinted at the writing and translated, '"Picture of Saint Catherine. Oil on canvas. Signed and dated 1516. Evidently part of a larger work. Purchased 1847 in Brussels from a private collector". Good to know I can still remember my German. Why would Vittore be interested? He must have seen it before.'

'I don't think so. I reckon this is THE Saint Catherine – the missing half of my Madonna. He's convinced it was destroyed hundreds of years ago, but this proves that it still exists – or at least it did till quite recently. Ask Bettina if she knows where these photos were taken.'

It transpired that Bettina had no idea, but she certainly did not object to Anna borrowing the album.

'Why are you so sure about the painting?' Izzy asked, as they strolled home. 'That it's the missing half?'

'Just a feeling,' said Anna. 'But I can tell you one thing, it's definitely not reproduced in Vittore's book.'

What she did not tell Izzy was that she had instantly recognised the face of the unknown saint: the pale skin and fine jawline; the delicate beak of a nose; the slightly slanting eyes and high cheekbones; her full wide mouth, so different from the tiny rosebud fashionable in the Renaissance. These were the exact features that her imagination had superimposed onto the line drawing in Vittore's book. She did not tell Izzy because it was too bizarre; too strange to comprehend or believe.

Neither did she tell Vittore, later that evening when she arrived at Ca' Melisa and presented him with the evidence. There were no guests at the house and he and Rosina were in the garden enjoying an aperitif.

Rosina puffed on a cigarette. 'My only vice,' she laughed, as the smoke mingled with the scent of flowers, ambrosial from a recent watering.

'So what is this mysterious object you must show me so urgently?' Vittore asked, as he poured her a glass of chilled *pinot grigio*.

Wordlessly, Anna handed him the album. She had marked the relevant page but with his habitual meticulousness, Vittore started at the beginning, peering intently at each photo through half-moon spectacles.

'Interesting,' he murmured, examining a seventeenth century portrait. 'I am no expert on Rubens, and his output was prodigious, but I do not recollect having ever seen this. Do you have any idea where these were taken?'

Anna shook her head and told him the little she knew.

'I would imagine,' Vittore continued, 'that they date from the thirties. And it appears the collection was in a private residence rather than a gallery. The notes are written in German, but that does not necessarily mean the location was in Germany.'

When he came to the place Anna had marked, nothing, apart from a slight tremor of his hand, belied his feelings. After a few moments he looked up and ran his fingers through his silver hair, reminding her of Raffi's habitual gesture.

'Please excuse me for a moment,' he said, rising from his chair and moving towards the house. He was gone for less than five minutes and when he returned she noticed that his cheeks were flushed. He was holding something – a black and white postcard of her Madonna. Without saying a word he placed it next to the photo in the album.

Even to someone with no knowledge of the paintings' history, it would have been obvious that, although now sundered, they were two halves of a whole. The women held each other's gaze, warm and animated, as though in the midst of a conversation. Replace their Renaissance clothing with modern garments and they could have been women of today, revelling in the joys of new motherhood. The baby Jesus smiled at the saint as rapturously as any child would at a favourite aunt about to hand him a soft toy and, indeed, although the frame obscured her fingers, Saint Catherine was clearly holding out her hand as though to give – or receive.

'This is unbelievable, Anna,' Vittore said at last. 'I must speak to this lady. You say her mother is still alive?'

'Very much so.' And she handed him a piece of paper. 'Here's Bettina's number. I told her you might call. She's in all this evening.'

Vittore made a little saluting gesture with the paper and went back into the house. When he returned he was smiling broadly. 'Bettina will telephone her mother and hopefully I can meet her next Tuesday. The old lady is very deaf, but as bright as a button.'

Less than a quarter of an hour had passed when Bettina rang to confirm that her mother would be delighted to receive Vittore. After this Rosina bustled off to prepare supper and Vittore grew quiet and increasingly preoccupied, so Anna excused herself. As they said their goodbyes, she noticed that his high colour had faded and his face had acquired an uncharacteristic pallor.

'We must not hope too much, Anna. None of this means we will find St Catherine,' were his last words as they parted. And it seemed, from the way he spoke, that he was preparing for disappointment, elation having given way to doubt and disbelief.

His sudden mood change was contagious, and rather than going directly home, Anna turned in the opposite direction and took the circuitous route to the Fondamente Nuove. She walked to the first bridge and leaning against its parapet, gazed out onto the lagoon – transformed now to a shimmering palette of silver and peach. The early evening had a strangely pellucid quality, the light as limpid as water held in a glass. In the far distance she could make out the craggy outlines of mountains and caught a flash of light as a plane came to land at Marco Polo. Overhead, screaming swifts scythed the sky, plundering the heavens of the mosquitoes that feasted on the city's inhabitants. To her left loomed the dilapidated sixteenth century house known as the Casinò degli Spiriti. Isolated on its lonely promontory, it was reputedly haunted by a pair of lovers who refused to let even death part them, and whose adulterous passions continued beyond the grave. Or, less sensationally, it might have derived its name from the intellectuals who once gathered there. The thought of these long ago literati brought to mind Vittore. Tonight she had glimpsed a side of his character that troubled her. His interest in the painting was, she suspected, bordering on the obsessive. Here was a man whose hopes were pinned on a chimera and who, she feared, would be deeply disappointed should the missing half be unobtainable.

Gnawed by a sudden melancholy, she turned to retrace her steps back towards home, and in the distance saw a figure, the sight of whose easy stride threatened to make her knees buckle. But as the man drew nearer, she realised that he bore little resemblance to Raffi. The kick of disappointment she felt was now commonplace: recently she imagined she saw him at least ten times a day; thought about him constantly; sought his face out in a crowd; heard his voice in the mouths of strangers and had to stop herself from peppering her conversation with

181

references to him. Obsession was, she knew, a dangerous companion; both Vittore's preoccupation with a five hundred year old painting, and her own hopeless fixation for his nephew.

* * *

Two days later, at Vittore's suggestion, Anna called at Ca' Melisa, to hear the outcome of his meeting with Bettina's mother. Magda showed her to his study, a book lined room off the *sala*, and whispered, '*È infelice*.'

He sat at his desk in a pool of golden light, his battered swivel chair moving slightly, as one hand idly played with a pile of paperclips. His disappointment was palpable, but he managed a wan smile. The album lay opened at the photo of Saint Catherine, and he regarded it with the sadness of a lover, contemplating the likeness of one who has long since left.

'This, I fear, is all that remains of her. I believe she is truly lost.'

He reached for a decanter and poured Anna a glass of *vernaccia*, a sherry like wine from Sardinia. She sipped the sweet, slightly bitter liquid, waiting for the story. He was so long silent that she almost thought he had forgotten her.

Eventually he began, 'Bettina's mother, Marta, is an extraordinary lady. Very frail but,' he tapped his temple with a forefinger, 'totally with it. The album belonged to her cousin, Annuziata, who passed away nearly twenty years ago. Annuziata never married, so when she died it fell to Marta to deal with her possessions. Annuziata had once told her the story behind the album, so Marta kept it rather than see it thrown away. During the 1930s Annuziata had worked as a housekeeper for a wealthy German industrialist, Raimund Thalberg, who lived near Domodossola on the Italian-German border. He was a collector of paintings and objects d'art, as were both his father and grandfather. But they were what the English would call "cagey", so despite owning such an impressive collection, they were reluctant to let anyone outside the family see it.'

'Which explains why you didn't know about their Cima?'

'Exactly. The couple had no children so Thalberg intended to leave both the house and its contents to the state as a permanent museum, named after him. The album was compiled in the early 1930s as a detailed record of his treasures. Unfortunately, with the rise of Fascism, Thalberg's world was increasingly under threat. Both he and his wife, Jutte, had Jewish blood. In his case, he had only the one Jewish grandmother who had converted to Catholicism on her marriage, so he was what was known as a Mischling of the second degree.'

'Mischling?'

'Yes, it's German for cross-breed. Like the English word, mongrel.'

'Deliberately insulting,' murmured Anna.

'Exactly. But being only a quarter Jewish, he would not have been under any serious threat from the Nazi racial laws.'

'What about his wife?'

'That was a different matter. Jutte was fully Jewish – both her parents, and all four grandparents. Even then, being married to Thalberg may have saved her from the worst of fates, but it seems she was an outspoken woman, who vociferously opposed Fascism. They should have left the country when they had the chance, but like many people they refused to believe the full extent of the threat. They had their wealth, their art collection, powerful friends, all of which they presumably imagined would protect them. Of course, in the end they lost everything; they were herded away with the poorest of the poor; the same destination; the same obscene end.'

'A concentration camp?'

Vittore nodded.

'But you said that he would have been safe. Why was he taken too?'

'I guess because he loved Jutte so much he wanted to share her fate – however grim. Annuziata did not know exactly what happened, but she heard that he physically resisted when they took his wife; that he insulted the commanding officer, the Führer, the Reich. He probably thought that wherever they were destined he would be able to protect her. He wouldn't, of course; the first thing they did in the camps was to segregate the sexes. Dear God, I keep imagining if that had happened to Rosina and me.' Vittore took a deep breath and continued, 'Thalberg might have had some delusions about his own fate, but he was a realist when it came to the future of his collection. He knew that it would be seized by the Germans; probably broken up and dispersed. So he gave the pictorial record contained in this album to Annuziata and asked her, in the event of an Allied victory, to pass it to the appropriate authorities. He hoped that someone, someday, would be able to reunite the works of art, and his ambition of a Thalberg Museum would be realised.'

'I don't suppose that ever happened?'

'No. After the Thalbergs were taken, the Nazis requisitioned their house. Some months later there was an uprising in the area; a free partisan republic was declared and the incumbent commander fled. It was all in vain of course. German rule was quickly re-established. But in those chaotic few weeks there was some looting at Thalberg's house, so as soon as the Nazis returned they began moving the most prestigious works of art to Germany, no doubt in an attempt to curry favour – Hitler was planning to build a collection of Aryan art in Linz, the Austrian town where he spent his childhood. Then in 1945 a final attempt was made to save the remains of the collection from the advancing Allies. Everything was put on a train, with the intention of it being safely stowed at Hitler's mountain retreat in Bavaria.'

'Did it get there?'

'No. It was intercepted, just ten or twelve kilometres along the line, by a pack of locals. Apparently, they thought it contained food supplies. They were hungry and had no interest in art. Why should they? Annuziata heard that paintings were trampled into the mud; tapestries cut into bits and used as chair covers; statues and porcelain smashed.'

'Was anything ever found?'

'Not that I am aware of; although I will check. The Allies did establish a post-war art commission, which operated for ten years or so. They catalogued all recovered artworks with a view to returning them to the owners, if the owners could be located that is. But there has never been any mention of a Cima. Occasionally, lost works will appear in auction houses, but only very rarely.'

'So, there's some hope it could be found one day?' Anna attempted to sound optimistic.

'Ah, hope; that most treacherous of emotions.' He followed this by something in Italian, quickly translating, 'What is born each night and dies each dawn?' And when Anna gave no sign of comprehending, he continued, 'The answer is "hope". It is a riddle from *Turandot* – the opera.'

She watched as he touched the faded photograph, before closing the album, softly, reluctantly, like a parent shutting the door to the room of his sleeping child.

'I am sorry not to give you better news. But,' and he rose from his chair, 'we must not dwell on the loss. I will see you tomorrow? All our guests should be here by five o'clock, so I suggest you come around then.'

His tone was unusually cursory and Anna, sensing she was being dismissed, felt saddened that he chose not to let her share his disappointment. Just as she left the room she heard him say, in an off-hand tone, 'Edie and Graham are joining us for dinner. Edie is ready to reveal her big secret. They are staying at the Cipriani this time, so that Graham does not miss his pre-breakfast swim.' The look he gave Anna suggested that this was the silliest thing in the world.

* * *

The guests, as Vittore had predicted, arrived throughout the day. By late afternoon everyone, apart from one unfortunate couple, who had missed their connecting flight at Frankfurt, was safely ensconced, and when Anna arrived, the majority of them, being British, were enjoying cups of tea in the garden. They promised to be an easy-going group, rather less highbrow than usual. This was perhaps explained by the theme of the tour. In an attempt to attract a wider clientele, Vittore had departed from his usual Renaissance based themes and was focussing solely on the eighteenth and nineteenth centuries, with particular emphasis given to the lives of Casanova and Byron.

Surprisingly, he was nowhere to be seen, and Rosina was doing her gallant best to make introductions and ensure everyone felt comfortable. She was clearly relieved when Anna arrived, telling her that Vittore was with Edie and Graham. They had been closeted together in his study for ages, and whatever they were discussing it was presumably very important to make Vittore ignore his guests. She made no attempt to hide her annoyance at this dereliction, scurrying back to the safe haven of her kitchen at the first opportunity.

Anna mingled as best she could, hoping that no one discovered how superficial was her knowledge of Venice – let alone of the libidinous writers. So it was with some relief that she saw Vittore, Edie and Graham appear on the balcony. In the seconds before they assumed their public persona it was obvious something was amiss. Edie was glancing from man to man, her face a mask of worried concern. And there was something in the hard set of her companions' faces that spoke of conflict; well mannered, gentlemanly conflict to be sure, but nevertheless heartfelt. Anna remembered their altercation of a few weeks ago and knew instinctively that whatever dispute had occurred, it must concern their opposing views on the conservation of paintings. Even as she registered their discomfiture, Vittore, the consummate professional, visibly rallied. His stance straightened, his face lifted into a beaming smile, and his mellifluous voice conjured the already enthralled guests.

'My dear ladies and gentlemen. Dear friends, as I am sure we soon will be, a thousand apologies for my tardiness. I beg your forgiveness for not being here to greet you earlier.'

Glancing around, Anna guessed that few amongst the predominantly female assemblage would be capable of denying him anything. Within seconds he had exerted a charm as potent as that of Byron himself. She watched in amused admiration as he bounded down the steps to meet his adoring public.

Anyone who did not know Vittore would have suspected nothing amiss. Indeed, his lecture was more animated than usual, as he warmed to its slightly risqué content. He appeared as bright as the slides of sumptuous interiors, and as carefree as the extravagantly painted Tiepolo ceilings that flashed onto the screen.

Anna, however, could sense the stress beneath his calm exterior. A few minutes into the lecture she heard a door open, and glancing round saw Raffi slip into the room. He mouthed a "hello", before finding himself a vacant chair.

She hoped that they would be seated within speaking distance at dinner, but in deference to the large number of single women, Raffi was placed between two middle-aged ladies who were clearly delighted to have such a charming companion. Edie and Graham were at the far end of the table and, Anna noticed, slipped away before coffee was served. Only when they moved into the *sala* did she have a chance to speak to Raffi.

'Do you think Vittore is all right? I know it's not my place to speculate, but I think he may have had a few words with Graham.'

Raffi glanced at his uncle. 'I thought he was a bit more animated than usual but I put it down to this being a new subject for him. You know, first night nerves.'

Anna shrugged. 'I'm sure it's nothing. I was just a bit worried about him. You've heard about the Cima Saint Catherine? That it was probably destroyed in the war.'

Raffi nodded. 'Tell you what; most of the guests are exhausted. When they've all disappeared off to bed, he and Rosina will sit and drink some herbal tea to wind down. Stay, and we'll join them. Now, I better get back to my girlfriends.'

'You heartbreaker!' she hissed.

Contrary to Raffi's prediction, however, some of the guests showed no signs of flagging, and it was nearing midnight when the last couple stumbled up to bed. As soon as they made their exit, Rosina, who had long since decamped to the kitchen, reappeared, bearing a large silver teapot. Free at last to relax, the weary quartet adjourned to a comfortable little sitting room off the *sala*.

'I think this group is going to quite wear me out,' said Vittore, lowering himself into an easy chair.

'Well, don't overdo it,' advised Raffi, pouring the camomile tea into elegant china cups. And then, as nonchalantly as he could manage, which was not very. 'Talking of overdoing it, are you all right?'

Vittore squinted at them through tired eyes, as Anna placed a hand on his arm, saying, 'Please tell us. It's something to do with Graham and Edie isn't it? Is it her great secret? Have they bought a holiday home?'

Nudged into animation by her touch, Vittore leant forward, elbows resting on his knees. 'Yes, yes they have. But the "great secret" is something rather more alarming.'

Although so late, it was still very warm. Through the open window drifted the sound of footsteps and the put-put of a boat. In the distance a dog barked. Everyone waited.

'As you all know, Edie is a major contributor to the Save Venice fund. As such, she has some influence over the choice of restoration projects. On her specific recommendation, the fund proposes to commence a total renovation of the Misericordia.'

Anna was the first to speak. 'But surely that's good news? It does need it, doesn't it? You can still see water marks from the 1966 floods.'

'Oh, indeed,' conceded Vittore. 'And I am sure an excellent job will be done. However, it is further proposed that all the art works in the church be restored, including,' and he fixed his gaze on Anna, 'the Cima. Graham will be in charge of their restoration.'

Anna thought of the Madonna's eyes, dull and brown, rather than the light blue they should be. 'Is that necessarily a bad thing?'

'No, no. I have no doubt that in the right hands the painting could benefit from the attention of a conservationist. Unfortunately, I do not believe that person is Graham Singelmann. He has been well trained; he is talented, but the restorations for which he has been solely responsible are eighteenth century works. He has little experience of five hundred year old pictures. That in itself would not be an insurmountable problem but I sincerely believe that, in his desire to impress, Graham uses techniques that I can only think of as irresponsibly innovative.'

'But he worked for the National Gallery, surely they...'

Vittore made a little sound, somewhere between a snort and a laugh. 'Oh, Anna, my dear, you have no idea of the battles raging in art galleries all over the world, have you.'

'Battles?'

'Perhaps that is overstating it, but I am afraid that there are those of us who are deeply suspicious of what has happened at your National Gallery. Next time you are there, take a look at Tiziano's Bacchus and Ariadne. After it was restored they fixed it to composition board, so now it looks flat and two-dimensional. Then there's that garish blue sky and, I'm sorry, but since the restoration, the expressions on the faces, well, they have, quite simply, lost something indefinable.'

He paused, as if waiting for a challenge that never came, and then continued, 'One has to be so very careful. It is all too easy for a restorer to imbue a painting with the tastes and fashions of his own age.'

'I don't understand,' Anna said. 'How?'

'I can cite countless examples: cinquecento works, restored in the nineteenth century, where the faces are now pure Victoriana...cloying, over sweet, or...'

'But present day restorers don't do that, surely?' interrupted Raffi.

'Not so obviously. But now there are more insidious dangers. I really do not think that I am a Luddite, as Graham implied, but there has to be a middle way by which the effects of time may be reversed. I know about Graham's experiments with solvents. I do not pretend to have a deep scientific knowledge of his work; but I have friends who do have that expertise. The fierce chemicals he uses have an immediate and impressive effect, but because a painting is not a piece of impermeable plastic, those chemicals can continue to seep into its core, causing continual damage over the years. The paint could become dry and brittle; some pigments will react more than others, unbalancing the entire composition. Edie has bought her husband a very expensive and precious toy, and I fear that in playing with it, he will ruin it beyond repair.'

Silence fell. Vittore opened his mouth to continue but at that moment a strangled, guttural breath escaped Rosina's lips. She sat bolt upright, wide-eyed and obviously shocked not to be curled up in bed.

Hearing the midnight peal of San Marco, Anna took her cue, making apologies for staying so late. Vittore ordered Raffi to escort her back to her flat – an old worldly gesture she found rather charming, since it was less than a five minute walk in one of the safest cities in the world. As they strolled along the *fondamenta* she thought of all the times she had wandered through dubious parts of London, unaccompanied, in the early hours of the morning. That life, and that city, seemed a long way off. When Raffi left her at the front door, brushing her cheek with his lips, she imagined, or hoped, that they lingered there for just a moment longer than necessary.

Although Anna did not fall asleep until nearly two o'clock she woke early. Nervous and excited by the prospect of the day ahead, she was showered and dressed by eight. It was two hours before she was due at Ca' Melisa, so unable to settle, and mulling over the previous evening's conversation, she hurried to the Misericordia. Vittore had not said when work would commence and it occurred to her that the doors could be barred and shuttered at any moment. It may be many years before she could enjoy its quiet peace again. The thought filled her with a sort of panic, and she felt it imperative that she visit the church as a matter of urgency, before it became a bright and shiny travesty of itself.

Certainly, despite its extravagant façade, it was clearly in need of repair, especially internally, where the damage caused by repeated flooding was evident. The water-stained walls were painted to resemble patterned brickwork, perhaps inspired by the Doge's Palace, but this had faded and in some places the plaster had fallen away to expose crumbling bricks. Apart from the Madonna, the valuable

188

art works had been removed in the nineteenth century and replaced by poor quality paintings of a cloying sentimentality in pastel but garish colours. The greatest treasure, an altarpiece by the young Titian, resided in a far-off gallery, its original marble frame, now reduced to an unseeing eye. But the church retained its original choir loft and had a fine ship's keel ceiling, coffered into blue painted squares, emblazoned with golden stars. Angelo had once shown her through a side door to the cloister, a place of quiet greenness, overlooked by a sturdy red brick *campanile* whose bells no longer sounded. He had managed to convey that, should the door be open, she was welcome to rest there. But not wishing to disturb the few monks who still pottered about, she had never ventured into its peaceful environs.

Most of all though, she liked to sit and look at her Madonna, whom she had almost come to think of as a friend. To her, she told all her fears, past pain and future hopes.

It was here that Vittore found her.

'When will it start?' she asked, as he settled himself next to her.

'The restoration? Not till after the summer.'

Anna felt the calm wash of relief. Hopefully, the church and its paintings would be left undisturbed until she returned to London.

'Couldn't you speak to Graham? He must respect your opinion.'

'I'm sure he does, but only in my capacity as an historian. Regarding our ideas on restoration we are, unfortunately, poles apart. Just to give you one example; glazes. The Renaissance painters used a glaze not just to protect their work; it was a way of making those most delicate of final touches – the blush on a cheek; the almost imperceptible blueness of a vein. But it is very, very difficult to remove discoloured varnish and still retain the glaze. So there are those, and Graham is amongst them, who, in the interest of restoring intensity of colour, advocate sacrificing the glaze. To me, that is madness, sacrilege. Do you know, Titian travelled from here to Ferrara – over a hundred kilometres – to adjust the final glaze on his Bacchus and Ariadne. A glaze is not just an afterthought; it is the last loving touch of the painter's hand – an integral part of his masterpiece, and to remove it is to destroy the integrity of his work.

'Perhaps it is because I am very nearly an old man that I find myself respecting time more and more. You see, I am convinced that the Old Masters knew exactly what time would do to their work, and they chose specific pigments and glazes accordingly.'

He turned in his chair to face Anna and lifting his hand to her face, traced the line of her jaw with his index finger.

'Look at you – as yet hardly touched by time, even though it is waiting to make its mark on you. But there is no need to fear it; the man who truly loves you will always love you, despite your changing face. Just as I still find Rosina as beautiful as the twenty-year-old girl I first knew, although I can see she is, of course, different. This desire for perfection and everlasting youth is a product of our modern age. It is why beautiful women needlessly subject themselves to the surgeon's knife. And why we deface perfect paintings in a fruitless attempt to make them appear as they did when still wet from the artist's studio.'

'But isn't it natural to want to turn back time? Is it so wrong to try?'

'Not wrong perhaps, but misguided. Let me tell you a story. I do not suppose you have heard of Joseph Addison?'

'No, I'm afraid not.'

'He was an English poet and dramatist, and early in the eighteenth century he described a dream in which he found himself in a gallery. One wall was hung with paintings by living artists, and the other with those of the dead. He was surprised to see a very old man moving along the wall of Old Masters, and who seemed to be re-touching those paintings. His brush and pencil strokes were so light as to be imperceptible, but then Addison realised that in repeating his touch again and again, the old man was adding shades and mellowness of colour to the paintings so that they appeared even more perfect. He was intrigued by who this artist could be and then, looking at the man's ancient visage and long hair, he knew that it was none other than Time himself.

'The work of Time, Anna; we cannot stop it and we cannot reverse it, so we may as well make it our friend and appreciate what it brings to us, and never, ever take it for granted. But enough philosophy!' He stood and offered Anna his arm. 'Let us have coffee; then face the day and our guests before we turn our attention to bad Lord Byron.'

Venice: Advent 1515

Work in earnest starts on a bitterly cold morning when the light, although clear, is thin and grey. Giambattista has already transferred our outlines, copied from his drawings, onto the prepared canvas. Rather than the usual creamy white gesso, he has applied a thin wash of rose-tinted brown, which will imbue the final colours with subtle warmth.

I am surprised that the painting is not to be on a wooden panel, but Enrico has demanded canvas. Old Sartorani has purchased a house on *terra firma* and now that hostilities are much reduced, he means to divide his time between it and the city. Enrico is desirous that his gift may travel with his father, and canvas, being light, is easily transportable.

The original concept was for the Virgin and Saint to be seated against hills and fields, but Enrico is determined that the painting be finished by late April. As pastoral backgrounds are time consuming, Debra and I are now to appear as though in a darkened chamber, with the only light emanating from the Christ child. I am sorry for this, for I should prefer us to be basking in a warm meadow where rabbits and deer cavort, rather than a room as murky as the grave, even if the heavenly babe does illuminate it.

One thing I am grateful for is Enrico's insistence that my veil should not be worn like that of an old nun. I suspect that Giambattista thinks it a little immodest but if so, he holds his tongue. I mention this to Giacomo and he tells me that his uncle is eager to leave Venice and spend all his time in Conegliano. Consequently, he is accepting any work offered, however demanding the patron. The revelation of his impending departure saddens me, for not only do I enjoy my lessons, I have come to love him. But he is no longer young, and I can well understand the wish to spend his last years in his native town, amongst his children and their little ones, whom he dotes upon. The pull of one's birthplace is indeed strong, and had I to leave Venice, my heart should be very heavy.

I have not seen Giacomo for days, and am longing for Debra to meet him, although she has, in a fashion, already seen him. The figure of the young Baptist in the altarpiece is all but complete and is a perfect likeness of Giacomo. Over the weeks, as layer after layer of thin paint is applied, I have watched it become increasingly life-like, and in that time my love for its flesh and blood original has deepened. Even his inanimate image makes me dizzy with joy, and yet I am also sad when I look at it, for in the summer Giambattista will take the painting to Conegliano. Here, he will supervise its installation and apply the final glazes. Then he will settle in his hometown, content in the bosom of his family.

I fear that Giacomo may accompany him, for without his uncle he will be alone in Venice. But in the next instant I rejoice, for if he stays to complete his apprenticeship, which surely he must, he will be in need of companionship, and who better to provide it but *papà* and me. Then, before I have had time to enjoy the elation this prospect brings, I am fretting that he may go somewhere altogether different and that I may never see him again. I sink into despair, for if I cannot have him, I will have none at all. I would join the nuns at Conegliano, for then I could at least see his image. However, I think like this only when I am particularly despondent; most of the time I giggle to myself as I imagine what those poor sisters will make of my Giacomo. Will the picture help them in their devotions or will they, like me, look at those shapely legs and wonder…?

When he walks into the workshop, I allow him only the briefest smile before settling my face back into the demure countenance of the Virgin. But I watch him all the while, noting his expression as he sees Debra. Within seconds, I realise that she has tangled his eyes too. And when we take a break, he talks to her, and not to me. Today I have brought Cesare, and I retreat to a corner sulking, hugging my little dog. At least he still loves me best.

Later, we all walk home together, Cesare and I trailing behind. Giacomo is much taller than Debra, so he must bend his head to catch her words. Occasionally she laughs – a sweet tinkling sound – and by the time we reach her home and part company, I am bubbling with anger. She kisses me goodnight and whispers, 'He is an excellent young man, Gina.' But even that does not mollify me, and I am obstinate in my sullenness.

Giacomo and I trudge on silently, until he asks, 'Why so quiet tonight?'

'You and Debra were talking for all three of us,' I retort.

When he says nothing, I cannot resist twisting the knife deeper into my self-inflicted wound. 'So, what think you of Debra?'

We have left the main thoroughfare by this time and are crossing a deserted *campiello*. Noises echo from nearby *calli* but this small space feels strangely cut off from the everyday bustle.

'I think,' says Giacomo, 'that she is the most beautiful woman I have ever seen. But she is so shy. She would tell me very little about herself.'

Then I, who have been so mindful of her secret, spit out the words, 'Her reticence is not to be wondered at. She is a Jew. Do you still think her so fair, now?'

192

I do not know who is more shocked; Giacomo, at this unexpected revelation or I. The vehemence with which I utter the words horrifies me. I sound like a Jew baiting preacher, making denouncements from the pulpit; or the ignorant rabble accusing Jews of stealing and killing Christian babies so their blood may be used in some hateful ritual.

I fancy that Giacomo looks sad as he says, 'Perhaps a handsome Christian will fall in love with her and she will convert. It does sometimes happen, so I am told.' And then he gives me that love potion smile, and I am sure that he means himself.

I want to hit him but instead I gather up my skirts and stride away, hurtling the words over my shoulder, hoping that they hurt, 'Perhaps it does. But Debra would want a bigger fish than an apprentice woodcarver, however handsome he may be.'

Even though it does not lead me home, I escape down the nearest *calli*, running until I find a dark corner where I may hide my shame. Here, I lean against the wall, letting the tears pour down my face. I am as ugly and as bad-tempered as a bear. It is no wonder that Giacomo prefers my friend.

When he finds me, his footfall is so soft that I hear it only seconds before he speaks. 'Is a poor woodcarver to be so despised?'

'No, of course not,' I sniffle. 'I am so sorry. You fashion such wonderful things with these…' I grab his hands, feeling the rough palms and calloused fingers. Then, realising how forward this is, I try to pull away, but he holds me fast. I blunder on, 'But if you care for Debra, you must tell her.'

His face is very white in the darkness, and his eyes open wide, catching the moonlight. 'Care for Debra? What makes you think that?'

'You said she is the most beautiful woman you have ever seen.'

'She is, but I hardly know her. And she is a Hebrew. I have no objection to the Jews living here, but I cannot imagine allying myself with them. They are different from we Christians: their beliefs, background…all their customs. Anyway, she is so delicate, so fragile. One could imagine a gust of wind from the lagoon blowing her away, but…'

I remain silent, sensing that if I hold my peace, he will continue speaking. When he does, his words are the most wondrous I have ever heard.

'…but none of this is of any matter. My affections lay elsewhere.' He swallows hard and his grip on my wrists is so strong it hurts. I hardly dare breathe. 'Ginevra, you must have realised that it is you I care for.'

And then he kisses me – properly, on the mouth. It is my first kiss and it is the sweetest thing I have ever known. Sweeter than honey; more thrilling than being on the open lagoon at night; warmer than the sun, and as tender as a songbird's flesh. My insides feel as though they are turning to warm oil.

Cesare, piqued at his exclusion, whines and claws at my ankles. His protestations remind me that I must show some modesty. I pull away.

'Dare I hope that you feel the same?' he asks, as if my greedy mouth was not indication enough.

I nod my head in happy agreement, as he continues, 'Can I speak to your father? I am young, I know, and cannot offer much until I complete my apprenticeship, but then, I do believe that I will be able to support you, and…'

I stop his words by placing my finger on his mouth. 'We need not wait so long. You and I will live with *papà*. He will need my help more and more. I cannot possibly leave him. You realise that?'

In reply he kisses me again and, hand-in-hand, we make our way through the loud and joyous city until we reach home, and tell my father the great, good news.

Papà is overjoyed. He embraces Giacomo and already, I know, is thinking of him as a son. Then they begin to discuss my dowry. Giacomo looks embarrassed – nearly as embarrassed as me, so I scuttle away to find Pasqualina in the kitchen, to organise cakes and wine.

* * *

It is strange how things turn out. My betrothal means I no longer accompany *papà* to visit patients, but this perturbs me little. Anyway, the frequency of these excursions has reduced of late, for we have discovered something quite extraordinary. *Papà* believed we could conceal his fading sight, but people are not so easily deceived. Moreover, he was wrong to think they would eschew his services when they discovered his affliction. On the contrary, his expertise overcomes the inadequacy of his eyes, and if anything this enhances his reputation. So shortly before Giacomo's proposal, we had decided that my father should hire a qualified – male – assistant. This would have once aggrieved me, but since becoming Giambattista's pupil I realise that all I wish to be is an artist. I know my work will never adorn great churches and public places – for who would commission a woman? But I can decorate the furniture and picture frames my Giacomo carves. *Papà's* workshop at the top of our house benefits from abundant light and will more than suffice for my needs. Thus, everyone will be content and prosperous.

The future glows as rosy as the dawn – not just for me, but for our whole city, where there is widespread rejoicing. This jubilation springs from a recent victory on the battlefield of Marignano, after which our enemies cede many stolen territories back to us. And so we live in hope of a speedy and glorious end to the long wars.

We are to be married in May, and I count the days until the time when I will no longer sleep alone.

Redentore

Vittore Anzeliere was a popular man, held in such high esteem that many of the great and the good of Venice consented to throw open their homes and workplaces to his guests. Because of their generosity Anna found herself invited into an extraordinary range of hidden places, such as the rooms of an elderly *contessa* where Byron had once lodged, or an erstwhile *ridotto* – one of the gaming dens that had proliferated in eighteenth century Venice. It now housed a private institution, but still retained its original décor, complete with spy holes and camouflaged cupboards. She breathed in its air of dusty decadence, imagining shady business deals and liaisons between masked lovers.

And then there was the visit to the stunning Palazzo Labia, the headquarters of a radio and television company. On the walls of the ballroom Maria Labia had commissioned Giambattista Tiepolo to paint frescoes that could now be viewed by the fortunate few.

I will probably never see these again, thought Anna, as she contemplated an elegant and bare breasted Cleopatra dropping a priceless pearl into her wine glass. Vittore assured them, however, that Cleopatra's gesture was all for show – pearls do not dissolve in wine. The conceit was an illusion, like so much else in Venice.

But it was the less grandiose experiences that Anna valued more: a visit to an elderly man's home – just a ground floor flat, in what had once been a patrician residence, but on whose garden wall there were a few surviving remnants of sixteenth century fresco; or a side chapel, unlocked by a normally taciturn sacristan, that housed a rarely seen painting; or being allowed a peek into a shallow crypt, permanently flooded with murky water.

And best of all, were the sights evident for anyone with stamina and a pair of keen eyes, but which few did see, simply because they were under their very noses. In the tangle of Castello they walked under a *sotoportego* and came to an abrupt halt. Huddled together in a narrow *calle,* Vittore directed their attention upwards to where a crumbling stone angel presided, one arm held aloft as if blessing those who passed under the archway. On either side of him were reliefs, depicting scurrying creatures that, on closer inspection, turned out to be hedgehogs.

After everyone had stopped exclaiming at their cuteness, Vittore explained that they were probably porcupines and had been placed there by a family with the name of Rizzo, whose crest included this animal. When Napoleon's armies conquered the city and began plundering or destroying its art, the family hid the hedgehogs by bricking them over, but then presumably had quite forgotten them. It was only when repair work, at the beginning of the present century, was carried out, that they were discovered and liberated from their long hibernation. Since then they had become a beloved feature of the Venetian townscape.

Such anecdotes made Anna yearn to know all the secrets of the city's watery soul, and she found herself reluctant to leave its confines. When she had first arrived in Venice, she envisaged visits to other parts of Italy – Rome and Florence; perhaps even Sicily or the Lakes, but as time wore on she reasoned that there were years ahead for those trips. Now she had no inclination to leave Venice. Her tenure here would be over all too soon.

Certainly, as midsummer approached, she became increasingly aware of time's swift passage. Whereas her days in Venice had once stretched out as a seemingly endless patchwork of delight, she now felt them slipping through her fingers like silk. Then in mid-July, the moment arrived that marked the halfway point of her stay – the festival of *Redentore.* These celebrations commemorated the deliverance of Venice from an outbreak of plague that in two years had killed 50,000 of its inhabitants. When the sickness finally abated, the Venetians had built a huge votive church to the Redeemer, whose Palladian whiteness still dominated the Giudecca skyline. At its consecration, the people, led by the Doge, had made their way from the Zattere to celebrate Mass in the new church, processing via a temporary bridge constructed of boats and barges. Now, over four hundred years later, the citizens of Venice maintained the tradition, after which there was partying and a huge firework display.

As usual, Izzy came up trumps and secured, for all three of them, an invitation to a street party on the Zattere. They sat at long tables, under strings of coloured lanterns, opposite the glimmering church, eating and drinking throughout the summer night. On the other side of the city, Rosina and Vittore were spending the festival quietly at home. '*Redentore* is not what it used to be,' Rosina had declared. 'Too noisy and too many people.' She did not say it but Anna knew what she meant. The festival was just one more thing the tourists had hijacked.

Their party broke up only when some of the revellers decided to cram into a friend's motorboat and go to the Lido for a midnight swim. Anna, Will and Izzy meandered home to Cannaregio, together with half a dozen young Venetians. Back at the apartment, they dragged cushions outside, and scattered themselves about the terrace. One of the boys had brought his guitar and sang soft and haunting

Venetian songs. Izzy lit candles and they lay back and gazed up into the star-spiked night, watching small bats flit around the moth-laden lamplight.

'Look,' squealed Izzy. 'A shooting star. Make a wish everyone.'

But no one else had seen it, so they assumed that it was the *prosecco* lighting up her sky rather than a meteor shower. She soon fell asleep in Will's arms; then the boy with the guitar decided it was time to go and departed with two of his friends.

This left one couple, who had slipped indoors and were now deep in conversation, and a young man called Giorgio. Anna guessed his age at perhaps twenty-one or two, and he had clearly taken a great shine to her. He was tall and slim with skin so smooth she suspected it hardly needed the attention of a razor; his eyes were large, and round and a deep liquid brown; his hands when he touched her, and his mouth, when he found the courage to kiss, were as soft as a puppy's.

Feeling his lips on hers, she experienced a tempting flutter of desire. He was far too young, of course, but that was part of the attraction. It would be a liaison uncomplicated by any possibility of a future. What was the harm? Encouraged by her response to his advances, his hand strayed to cup her breast. Perhaps it was this sudden boldness, but in that instant she realised that if they spent the night together it would not be Giorgio she thought of, but someone altogether different. Ridiculous though she knew it to be, the prospect of taking this young man into her bed seemed an infidelity. Her concupiscence melted away and she pulled away from him, apologising and inventing a boyfriend back in England.

The petulant look on his boyish face made her glad that she had called a halt to their amours, and avoiding his attempts to fondle her again, she asked him what he was planning for *Ferragosto*. This was, strictly speaking, a day's holiday in the middle of August, which coincided with the feast of the Assumption, but many people took the whole month off, fleeing the sweltering city for cooler, sweeter smelling destinations.

'I go to the Lakes,' replied Giorgio, and then added, with no shame whatsoever and a distinct air of one-upmanship, 'My girlfriend's parents are renting a villa there.'

Hoping that Giorgio had not mistaken her momentary shock for disappointment, Anna told him her own plans. 'Izzy and Will are off to Corfu for a fortnight, so I'm popping back to London, just to check up on my mum.'

'Here, it is very hot,' said Giorgio, attempting to kiss her again.

'I know, but it's not as if I have to battle my way to work and sit in a stifling office all day. I'll do what you Venetians do, stay out of the mid-day sun, sleep if I can, and...'

'*Andare per lo fodere*,' yawned Giorgio. 'Go by small alleyway where there is no sun.'

'I'll live on salad and ice cream and pant like a dog,' she laughed, attempting a joke, but Giorgio, now that the adrenalin fuelled by lust had subsided, was surrendering to sleepiness…or boredom. So she took pity on him and suggested that as she was inclined to retire, he might wish to leave. He had the good grace to look disappointed, but there was no mistaking the alacrity with which he left.

Leaning over the terrace wall, she watched him bound along the *fondamenta*, not giving her a backward glance, and she was reminded of watching Chris, all those months ago, leaving her life. Another man, strutting along another street. In retrospect that parting had hurt hardly more than this one, but they both reinforced the sense of what was missing from her life. Love – that old black magic.

For the first time since coming to Venice she felt lonely, and self-pity, no doubt engendered by the large amount of wine she had consumed, welled up inside her. In a few days she would be twenty-eight, not exactly ancient, but no longer a young girl. Where would she be in five years? Still alone in her little flat? The thought of returning to a life less glorious filled her with a dread as dull as lard.

She feared that these months would become the yardstick by which she would measure everything else. Venice had shown her so much beauty, teased her with so many possibilities, and yet everything it offered was unattainable. It was a life filled with things, and people, that would always be just out of reach – as illusionary as the myriad reflections in one of its canals. The city had seduced her and she would be forever under its spell. She had a sudden vision of Raffi and Caterina, their long limbs entangled together in a moonlit room overlooking the Arsenale, and felt such a surge of sexual longing that she almost called Giorgio back. Instead she crept away and fell into bed, and immediate oblivion.

She awoke with a blazing headache, and a blazing resolve not to succumb to such negativity again. Her time in Venice – this summer romance – would soon be over, but unlike an erstwhile lover, Venice would always be there for her. And if ever she made love here, the man would have to be as special as the city, because even though their affair may not last forever, she would remember it for the rest of her life, and hopefully he would too.

So, on that hot Venetian morning, to the sound of scolding Sabbath bells, she raised her face to a sky that seemed astonished by its own blueness, and looked forward to the future. Whatever autumn may bring, here in Venice there was another tour starting next week; then there was her birthday to celebrate; and soon she was going home to London. To her city; the place of her birth; a place she knew and loved; a place not to be taken for granted: Soho and King's Road; Covent Garden and Kensington. In friendly and familiar pubs, she would meet old friends; go to the theatre and cinema, understanding every word that was said; eat fish and chips; say hallo to Landseer's lions, and from the South Bank, watch the Thames roll by.

Nevertheless, three weeks later, as her plane rose into the air and she watched Venice disappear, Anna was sorry to be going. Izzy and Will were now sunning themselves in Corfu, and leaving the shuttered and darkened flat had felt horribly like a rehearsal for her final departure in October.

But they had had a happy time since *Redentore*. She had been determined to make her birthday celebration special and had booked a table at Corte Sconta. This unassuming little *trattoria*, hidden in the maze of *calli* near the Arsenale, was regarded as one of the best restaurants in the city. As well as Will and Izzy, she had invited Vittore, Rosina and Magda and then, with feigned casualness, as though it were an afterthought, wondered if Raffi would like to join them.

'Why don't you ask him?' Vittore had said, scribbling some figures on a piece of paper, a mischievous glint in his eye.

It took some time to summon the courage to phone Raffi and on hearing his voice she nearly slammed down the receiver. But when she explained the reason for her call he accepted the invitation with enthusiasm.

The restaurant deserved its reputation. It was plain to the point of austerity but the food was sensational. The first course consisted of plate after plate of antipasti, each delivered with theatrical aplomb: *carpcaccio* of sea bream scattered with ruby pomegranate seeds; tiny *vongole* in a white wine sauce spiked with ginger; a huge platter of *canocchie* – the strange mantis shrimps that thrived in the Adriatic Sea – their salty sweetness requiring only lemon, parsley and a dribble of olive oil. Then there were spider crabs; tiny pink shrimps served with polenta, and rubbery, fishy octopus eggs. The pasta courses consisted of gnocchi in a lobster sauce, which Magda gallantly declared were not as fine as Rosina's (although in fact they were); spaghetti with squid ink, and sea bass ravioli. So they ordered one of each and shared them in a messy orgy of gluttony. Finally, after a suitable interval, they demolished three huge *rombo* – the exact species of fish that had so alarmed Anna on her first visit to the *Pescheria*.

She was determined to pay the bill and in anticipation of attempts to thwart this, had, upon her arrival, surreptitiously slipped three hundred thousand *lire* to the manageress, hoping that this would cover the cost. To her amazement, when the bill arrived it was presented with a number of refunded bank notes, representing a substantial reduction to the actual price. No, no, they assured her: it was not an error; they had simply applied *lo sconto* – a discount. When the *signorina* had made the advance payment they had not realised that Vittore was amongst the diners. They could not possibly charge a Venetian, and such an eminent Venetian, and one of their favourite customers, the price shown on the menu. Moreover, they had noticed it was *il compleanno della signorina*, so there was complimentary *sgroppino* for everyone, an alcoholic sludge made from *prosecco* and lemon sorbet, with just a touch of cream to alleviate its tartness.

She had not said that it was her birthday, just that she wanted to host the meal as a thank you to everyone. But Izzy had bumped into Rosina and told her, and Rosina had told Magda, and Vittore had told Raffi. So she was given earrings and perfume and books, including the Italian cookery "bible", *Il Cucchiaio d'Argento*. And from Raffi, an embroidered silk scarf. After she unwrapped it, he looked into her eyes and said that it matched their very colour.

When they left the restaurant they saw that it had been raining – one of those sudden, summer Venetian downpours that appear from nowhere, and the air, for the first time in weeks, was cool and fresh.

'Let's walk to the Piazza,' Izzy suggested, linking arms with both Will and Raffi. 'I could murder a chocolate ice cream.'

But Vittore and Rosina, accompanied by Magda, went straight home, pleading tiredness. They too were soon fleeing the city and escaping to the foothills of the Dolomites, where Vittore's brother, Fabrizio, lived. Even little Magda was bound for her sister's farm near Stra.

'But, Anna, do join us for supper on the night before we leave,' said Vittore. 'Because by that time, you will be here alone.'

'Come too, *caro*,' Rosina whispered, kissing her nephew goodnight, who, accompanied by Caterina was soon departing for a two-week holiday at a fashionable Italian beach resort.

As her plane soared over the Alps, Anna remembered the evening. Raffi had indeed joined them and they had eaten a simple meal, sitting in the garden. The air was heavy with the heartbreaking sweetness of summer flowers and dreamy with birdsong. They chatted and laughed and touched each other in the way that Italian families do, and she had experienced a sense of belonging as warm as a sleeping cat.

Vittore, she noticed, appeared to have regained his old equilibrium and was more relaxed than she had seen him in weeks. He even brought up the subject, which everyone else had assiduously avoided, of the Misericordia's restoration. There had been further telephone conversations with Graham regarding the Madonna and whatever had been discussed seemed to have allayed some of Vittore's concerns. Edie wanted him to be involved in the project and he now appeared to be looking forward to its commencement.

'Once Graham has finished work on the painting it will be displayed at the

Correr, because work on the church will take several years. The anticipated date for completion is spring, 1990, but that is no doubt an optimistic estimate.'

'I'll have to make sure that I visit as soon as it's all finished,' said Anna. 'You will let me know how everything progresses, won't you?'

Three pairs of eyes fixed themselves on her, all with an expression that suggested she had said something very wrong.

Vittore was the first to speak. 'I am sorry, my dear. It is just that we have all grown so accustomed to you being here; it is a shock to realise that you will be leaving us so soon.'

'I know it's not the same, but I'll come back as often as I can,' she said.

Rosina leapt up and, standing behind Anna's chair, encircled her in a pillow-soft hug. She smelt of rosewater and, very faintly, of perspiration and cigarettes.

'We have to try and make you stay,' she said, and kissed the top of Anna's head in a gesture that almost brought tears to the younger woman's eyes.

Their little party broke up at about ten as, apart from Anna, everyone had an early start the next day. As usual, Raffi walked her home, and as usual they lingered outside her front door. She almost asked if he would like to come in for coffee, but stopped herself…they had already drunk more than enough espresso. So they simply wished each other well for their respective holidays and then Raffi said, 'You know, if you could stay for longer, Vittore and Rosina would be so pleased. I think they have almost come to think of you as a daughter.'

'I have to go back,' she said. 'I've financial commitments – a mortgage, a career. I can't just throw it all away. And anyway, however much I love it here, London's my home, and I've my own family there. It's like you with Venice: it's where I belong.'

'I understand. I'm sorry, we shouldn't try and pressurise you.'

And then, instead of the usual formal kiss on the cheek, he put his arms around her and held her close, their thin summer clothes a flimsy hindrance to the sweetness of flesh on flesh. Her head rested on his shoulder, and his hair tickled the tip of her nose. She was tempted to ever so gently take the lobe of his ear between her teeth. Her own arms hung loose; she did not dare move. They stood so, locked together, for just a few moments before he released his grip, taking a step backwards. The movement was so unexpected that she felt herself sway slightly. He gripped her arms, steadying her.

'Take care of yourself in London. I'll see you when we all get back.' And taking the scarf she wore – the one he had given her as a birthday present – between his finger and thumb, he said, 'It really does match your eyes.' And then he was gone, striding down the *fondamenta*.

'Bye,' her voice trailed after him, as thin and pathetic as a wraith. She assumed that he had not heard her, but as he crossed the bridge he turned and waved, blowing a kiss that evaporated into the night.

* * *

The London that Anna flew into was overcast, the sky pale and sickly; the sun, a reluctant visitor. With temperatures well below the seasonal norm, she stood shivering at Waterloo Station, waiting for the train to take her to her mother's new home. Her flight had been delayed and this, coupled with signalling problems on the Piccadilly Line, meant she hit the full vehemence of the rush hour. This daily phenomenon to which she had once been immune was now an unexpected affront. Although there were crowds in Venice and crushed *vaporetto* rides, most people, even the long-suffering Venetians, were good-humoured. But here, in this grey station, grey faced people wearing grey suits and bad-tempers forced themselves onto grey trains, and stood like penned animals as they were shunted through a grey townscape. It began to drizzle.

Putney, a place that had once been home, came and went, as cluttered houses, hugging the railway embankment, gave way to the leafier suburbs of Barnes and Kew. At Brentford she acquired a seat and watched London merge into Surrey.

Millie's flat was a short walk from the station: a redbrick block at the end of a cul-de-sac, set within a garden of regimented saplings and struggling rose bushes. Anna saw her mother standing on the small balcony, scanning the street. Unaccountably, she seemed to be expecting her daughter to approach from the opposite direction, so Anna had the opportunity to observe her covertly. Even from this distance, she could appreciate that her hair, lately faded to an apologetic straw, was now newly styled and shone golden-bright. She had gained a little weight and, wearing a clingy white dress, looked almost voluptuous. At last, catching sight of Anna, her face broke into a radiant smile and she waved madly.

'Cooee, darling. I'll go and press the entry-phone thingy. Third floor, remember.'

Anna stepped out of the lift and into her mother's arms. After they hugged each other, Millie scuttled into the kitchen and produced a bottle of champagne. As she poured the wine, Anna realised how much she had missed her mother but even as they chatted and giggled she found her eyes constantly drawn to the sitting room door, half expecting her father to walk in, wearing the frozen smile borrowed from a black and white 1950s photo that graced the mantelpiece. While she was in Venice part of her had half-believed he was still here, with her mother in a London suburb, but now she was forced to face, once again, the fact that he had gone. The knowledge crept around her like a mist, despondent and chill, and she had to make an effort to keep smiling as she ate supper: salad vegetables laying in wilted attendance to a hard-boiled egg and two slices of damp ham rolled around pallid grated cheese. For pudding there was shop bought tart with cream from an aerosol. After the vibrancy of Italian food it was tasteless and anaemic.

Anna phoned Millie from Venice at least once a week, so there was little new to say, but as her mother chattered, it was impossible to miss her animation. Anna initially flattered herself that it was due to the excitement of a visit from her only child, but as the evening progressed it was evident that Millie was enjoying her new life. She had joined a local bridge club, which was clearly the source of many new friendships. Before long, Anna realised that her conversation was invaded by constant references to a widower called Leslie. When she spoke his name it was with a softness that left her daughter in no doubt as to the nature of her fledgling hopes. Anna recognised them all too well and realised, with a small shock, that no one is ever too old to be kidnapped by infatuation.

Then Millie made an announcement, with such studied casualness it was evident she had been working up to it. 'Will you be in Thursday night? It would be nice if you could be. I've invited a few people from the bridge club – just for drinks and nibbles.'

Millie's cousin Ellen, whom Anna had always called, "auntie", would be there and although he was not mentioned by name, Anna assumed that Leslie would also be among the guests. And indeed he was. Tall and slender with a receding hairline he did not seek to disguise, he wore beige cavalry twill trousers, a jolly bow tie and an air of such affability that Anna found it impossible not to warm to him. Even though she suspected that Leslie was destined to supplant Hugh's place in her mother's heart, she could not find it in herself to resent their blossoming relationship – only slightly envy it. Leslie clearly adored Millie, and they flirted with each other like teenagers.

After the guests had departed, Millie was washing glasses, and asked, out of the blue, 'What are you planning for Christmas, darling?'

Startled by the question, Anna remembered last Christmas, the first one without Hugh. She and Millie had spent it together in un-splendid isolation, not wishing to inflict their grief on anyone else. They had not even pretended to enjoy themselves, and had been thankful when it was over.

Before Anna had time to respond, Millie continued, 'Both Leslie's daughters live in Scotland. They went to Edinburgh University and married local boys, so since his wife died, he stays with one or other of them over Christmas and New Year. And this year – well, he's asked me if I'd like to come too.' She paused for a second to let Anna appreciate the implications of this. 'Of course, I said I would have to see what you were doing…that I couldn't possibly leave you alone at Christmas. So Leslie suggested you join us. Apparently there's plenty of room. It'll be such fun – a real Scottish Hogmanay. What do you think?'

Anna had no idea what she thought. It certainly sounded a better prospect than last year's glum festivities, but she was not at all sure she wanted to commit herself to a week in the company of strangers, so far from home. Then she heard herself say, 'Well, actually, I thought I might stay in Venice a bit longer – till early January. I doubt there'll be much going on in the job market till next year, and my tenant has asked to extend his lease till the end of December. I would have come back for Christmas, of course, but if you'll be away it would be rather nice to spend it in Venice. Izzy and Will are going to be there, so it should be fun.'

Although it was true that her tenant had asked for an extension, she had no idea of Izzy's plans. But now she imagined the three of them, warm and cosy in the apartment. She and Will would go to midnight Mass at the Basilica. They would walk home through the bell-loud night under a star-pricked sky, and the slumbering city would be covered with a sugar frosting of snow. The next day, after a sumptuous lunch, they would take a walk through a Venice deserted by tourists, and as a misty darkness fell, would call at Ca' Melisa, where gathered around a huge Christmas tree, they would drink mulled wine and exchange gifts and kisses. She envisaged shopping at the Christmas market on the Riva dei Schiavoni, eating chestnuts from a paper bag, and visiting churches glowing with Christmas cribs, as carols trembled in the winter air. She saw Raffi, wrapped up against the cold, standing outside the little bar in the Campo Arsenale, laughing and toasting in the New Year, while the quartet of lugubrious lions looked on – unimpressed by the celebration of such a paltry passage of time. She would stay until the feast of *Epifania*, the day on which she first saw Venice. Only then would she return to England and ordinariness.

She was brought back to earth by the sound of Millie sniffing into a sheet of kitchen-roll. 'But Anna, it'll be our first ever Christmas apart. Are you sure you don't want to come?'

'No, Mum, I think it's best you go by yourself. Things…life…have to move on, don't they? Perhaps next year.'

In the morning, Anna advised the letting agents that her tenant could have the flat till the end of the year.

Her visit turned out to be an anti-climax. Many of the friends she planned to see were away on holiday, and although she met Trevor, her old boss, he spent much of their lunch date complaining about the effects of new legislation. Two of the shows she had hoped to catch were fully booked, and the one she did see was disappointing. Even Millie, after their first couple of days together, became a little distant, distracted by her own affairs. She found herself longing to be back "home" in Venice.

On her last day, she lunched with a school friend who lived in Wandsworth and, on a whim, rather than take the train straight back to Weybridge, walked to her parents' old house.

Almost six months had passed since the day she had closed the door on her childhood home, but an indelible image of it was engraved upon her mind. So, standing before the house, she examined it for changes: the window-frames had been painted a startling white; the door, that had been natural wood, was now a jaunty green, and the front garden had been revamped to a military tidiness with colour co-ordinated flowerbeds. But everything else was as it had been, and she half expected to see the silhouette of one of her parents waving from a window. Battling against churning emotions, she passed the front of the house and walked around the corner, alongside the back garden wall. Then she saw it – or rather did not see it. Outrage hijacked her footsteps, bringing her to an abrupt halt as she stared in disbelief. It was gone: they had cut it down. The new owners had had the effrontery to get rid of Guy's tree.

Even worse, something stood in its place; something garish and blue. It took her a few seconds to realise that it was a child's swing. Then a door banged, and she heard the bright peal of children's voices as the ropes suspended from the frame moved. A little girl soared into view, her sturdy brown legs stuck out straight, in an attempt to gain as much height as possible. She wore a pink dress with a gathered skirt that billowed up, revealing a flash of white knickers. To and fro she went, her face a happy blur, auburn air streaming out behind her. And Anna watched the little sprite with mounting warmth.

'Phobë. Let me have a go! It's *my* birthday present,' squeaked another voice.

Almost immediately, the swing lost momentum and she was gone. A few moments later a small boy took her place. He was darker than Phobë, with something about him that reminded Anna of photos of Guy at the same age. And she remembered her father saying that, before its branches grew fragile with age, a swing had hung from the tree. Then an unbidden thought skipped into her non-believing mind. That if ever the spirits of Hugh and Guy were to return to the house, they would be heartened that small children should fly through the air on the very spot where their childhood selves had soared, happy and carefree, and unknowing of the oh-so-different flights awaiting them in a world torn by war. She stayed for a few more moments, lost in her own happy memories, and then turned back towards the station.

Venice: Spring 1516

By rights, *papà* would have discovered Debra's secret sooner, but with so much illness in the city he is too busy to visit Giambattista. Even when the two men meet to discuss our forthcoming nuptials, the artist comes to our home. But inevitably the day arrives when *papa* makes the observation that the painting must be nearing completion. It is a sunny, albeit cold morning, and he proposes we walk to Corner Piscopia to view it. I do everything I can to dissuade him, but to no avail.

Giambattista greets us warmly and enthuses about the painting. He was, at first, unsure about it, but now he feels it is one of his finest works. Without further ado he leads *papà* to the curtained-off section of the room and with a flourish that is at odds with his usual modesty, presents his masterpiece.

The light is so clear that even with his failing sight, I know *papà* can discern some of the features of the two young women who shimmer from the canvas. His shock is palpable, although he is too diplomatic to say anything, and the artist interprets his awestruck expression as one of admiration. Only I detect his displeasure. He refuses offers of refreshment and we take our leave.

Walking home, he is ominously silent and sensing that he will not talk in the street, I wait until we are indoors before I say the only thing I can think of, 'I am sorry, *papà*. Please do not be angry with Debra.'

'Debra? I believe it is you, Ginevra, who has transgressed. You persuaded her to this enterprise, did you not?'

'Yes, sir,' I confess.

'You must know that Jakob would never have given his consent. And also that I am honour-bound, as his friend, to tell him.'

'Please, no,' I plead. 'You've seen how fine the painting is, and there is so little more that needs to be done, at least on Debra's portrait.'

This is true. Whilst my face remains roughly sketched, Debra's is all but finished. Perhaps some presentiment that she will be stolen away has urged the artist to work quickly, or possibly he just cannot hold back from the delight of committing her likeness to canvas, like a child devouring a favourite sweetmeat.

'It will break Giambattista's heart if Debra cannot be there for the final sittings,' I say, although I am not altogether sure this is true. He is quite capable of completing Saint Catherine without her. After all, he paints his dead wife from memory. What really troubles me is the likelihood of incurring his anger, for whilst he remains in Venice I mean to garner as much knowledge as possible. I cannot risk being banished from his workshop.

I continue to cajole *papà*. What good will come of telling Jakob? He will be angered and Debra will be the innocent victim of his wrath, and yet the painting will still hang in old Sartorani's bedchamber, nothing can stop that. And it is not as if Debra will be on public display; no one else will see it. If he, my father, holds his tongue, no one need be any the wiser. No one need be hurt.

Eventually, he relents, on the condition that Debra's involvement ceases by Palm Sunday. He stipulates this date because feelings against the Jews are always heightened at Easter tide, when most do not venture abroad for fear of attack. He wants to ensure Debra stays safely at home. As for me, the only further reprimand I receive are his words, 'You disappoint me, Ginevra, you really do.'

And after that he says very little to me for several days, which is punishment enough, for I would rather be whipped than suffer his silent disapprobation.

When I tell Debra that in less than three weeks she may no longer visit the workshop, she visibly pales, but rallies when I assure her that her father will remain ignorant of our escapade. Even so, melancholy now surrounds her. I believe I know the reason why.

Of late, Enrico has been a frequent visitor to the workshop, where he silently watches his commission take shape. He professes to be interested in the artistic process. I suspect, however, his true fascination is for flesh rather than paint. I can see the power Debra's beauty exerts over him and once or twice I have caught her returning his looks. They remind me of cats circling each other in a *campo*, but the next moment she lowers her eyes, all modesty, and I conclude I am mistaken. Then I fancy they touch palms as a note is passed from one hand to the other. And one evening when she scuttles towards her home, I think I see a dark figure emerge from the shadows and wrap an arm around her shoulders.

When I broach my concern, she changes the subject and will not be drawn. Lately she has become secretive, and I feel she is distancing herself from me. Maybe these fears spring from my imaginings. I am so ensnared by my own amorous thoughts that perhaps I suppose everyone else is similarly addled. But I am glad that she will soon be out of Enrico's sphere, for no good could come from such a liaison, however much he may love her. I had thought her Jewishness would keep her safe, but now I am not so sure. Spring is upon us and it is not just the birds that wish to couple.

Moreover, there are other reasons for Debra to feel uneasy. Less than a year ago the Senate suggested that all the Venetian Jews should be forced to live on the island of the Guidecca. However, their community, led by Anselmo del Banco, vehemently objected and nothing came of the proposal. But this Easter, trouble once again erupts. It seems that synagogues have been secretly established, in contravention of our city's laws. People scream that this has incurred God's disapprobation and explains why hostilities on the mainland do not completely cease. Powerful men join the clamour: they publicly state that Christian neighbourhoods are being contaminated, and that the Jews must be segregated.

A week after Easter their fate is sealed: it is decreed that they leave their homes. I know the place to which they must transfer themselves. It is only minutes from our house, although I seldom venture there for it has no beauty. It is an island within the city, accessed by two bridges. A hundred years ago the municipal copper foundry stood here, so high walls were built around its perimeter. When the foundry moved to *terra firma* the area became waste ground until, at the beginning of our current century, houses were built against the walls. There is a large central area where it was once thought a church may be erected. It is named after the Venetian word for foundry – Ghetto.

I cannot believe that into this small space all the city's Jews are to be crammed. People say all manner of things: that gates are to be installed; that these will be locked at night so no one may come and go after sundown; that the canals will be patrolled by Christian boatmen who will report any infringement of rules.

All this, *Papà* and I hear at the Rialto. We walk home, trying to ignore the high spirits of those around us, who think that peace and prosperity will now triumph. It is a warm day and we sit in the little courtyard at the back of our house, willing the sun to dispel our gloom. I listen to Cesare growling at the sparrows, and think of Debra, soon to be imprisoned in that grim place. It will be like putting a lark in a cage.

Papà has lately softened towards me, and the sight of my distress finally melts his heart. I have told him that Debra's part in the painting is finished, and that she has bid farewell to Giambattista. On her final visit to the workshop, she made her excuses, pleading a sick relative. I am sure that the painter believed her. He has so little personal guile that he does not recognise it in others. I do not suppose he will ever know that the Saint Catherine, of which he is so proud, is a Hebrew.

Like me, Debra has refused all payment, so he gave her a little silver comb for her hair. He does not say, but I think it may have belonged to his first wife.

Remembering her delight in the pretty thing, tears begin to run down my face. *Papà* puts his arm around me. I am once again his little girl, and for this I am grateful.

'These measures against the Jews may seem harsh,' he says. 'But it is also for their protection. If people do not have to live in such close proximity they will, I am sure, feel more charitable towards them, so the insults and violence will lessen. Many other people form their own communities – the Albanians, the Greeks, the...'

'But no one compels them, it is their choice,' I interrupt.

He makes no reply. Like me, he recognises the iniquity of what is happening.

'Can we go and see them before they move?' I ask.

'I think it best if we leave them be. I will send a note to Jakob, asking him to let us know when they are ready to receive guests.'

When we do visit, a few days later, their house is in turmoil. Piles of books and cooking utensils scatter the floor. There are mounds of clothes and linen, ready to be loaded onto carts. At least they are prepared. Some families have refused to believe that the decree will be enforced and do nothing. Anselmo del Banco has appealed to the Senate but they are obdurate. The decision has passed into law. The Jews have three days to move to the Ghetto. The families currently living there moan and blame the Jews for their dispossession. The only happy ones are the Ghetto landlords, for they have been allowed to increase the rents by a third.

We have heard that, as a doctor, Jakob will be exempt from the nightly curfew, but is now prohibited from donning the physician's gown with its wide sleeves and silk trimmings. Even worse, the requirement for the hated yellow hat, marking him out as a Jew, will be newly enforced. But despite these insults he appears in reasonable spirits. Debra's face, however, is pinched and white with misery. As soon as possible, we go to her room, leaving the old men to talk. Usually we sit together on her bed, but today she does not join me and goes instead to stare out of the tiny window into the permanently dark courtyard.

'In all likelihood it will not be so very bad,' I say.

'Do you know how many of us will be in that place?'

'I hear some families are planning to leave the city, and risk whatever should befall them on *terra firma*, so perhaps there will not be so many and...'

'Seven hundred,' she interrupts. 'We will not even be able to throw the contents of our chamber pots into the canal because they are blocking up the windows looking outwards. They talk about providing a cesspool, but will they? Summer is coming. Can you imagine the stink? What else are they planning? Perhaps they will dismantle the bridges and burn us alive in there?'

'Debra, no. They would never do that.'

'You are right. The sparks might spread to the rest of their precious city. Likely, they will just slit all our throats, like your St Ursula and her virgins.'

210

'We are a civilised people, not pagan Huns. No harm will come to you.'

'Civilisation soon melts in the face of hatred,' she replies.

'I am sure it will come to nothing. After a few months everyone will start sneaking back to their old homes and this whole enterprise will be quite forgotten.'

'I think not. Once we are imprisoned they will never grant our freedom. But even if they do, it will be too late for me.'

'What do you mean?'

'Few of us will have any privacy. Families must, perforce, live together, so my father has spoken to the marriage-broker and accepted a proposal of marriage for me. I have no choice but to agree.'

'Who is he?'

She names the man; he is a del Banco.

'Be assured, if any can extricate themselves from the Ghetto, it will be those of that family,' I say.

'That is what my father thinks. He tells me that is why he has agreed to the match. I have begged him to change his mind but he is adamant. So, by marrying into the del Bancos, even if we are not forced to live in the Ghetto, I will have simply exchanged one prison for another.'

'You do not like him then?'

'No, I do not like him. I do not like to think of...' Her voice trails off. I know to what she refers; the intimacy between a man and wife. I long for the night when I shall give myself to Giacomo, but if I did not love him, how very different I would feel.

'His mother will be my jailer,' she continues. 'She will watch me like a hawk, day and night. My life is over.'

She speaks with such quiet conviction that I fear she may intend some self-harm. I embrace her, and she begins to sob. There is nothing I can say to provide comfort. She must suffer what so many women have to endure. Parents often choose our mates with scant regard for our sensibilities. That is life. Jakob is a good man and I am sure he loves Debra, but he is not so tenderhearted as *papà* who, I know, would never make me wed against my wishes.

She pulls away from me and says, 'You are so very blessed. Be happy, Gina. Be happy for both of us. Pray for me to your God.'

And then I hear *papà* calling for me to come away.

'Send word when you are ready. I will visit, as soon as you are settled in your new...home.'

For, like it or not, that is how she must think of it.

Ghosts

The Venice to which Anna returned throbbed under a relentless sun. Heat reverberated from the walls as the soaring temperatures seeped into the city's ancient buildings. Every stone of every *calle* and *campo* became a brick-oven, baking those who were foolish enough to linger. Geraniums wilted from dusty window boxes, and listless dogs stretched themselves out in the shade – heaps of panting fur, too hot to growl or tail-wag. Even the pigeons, permanently stationed by drinking fountains, seemed too exhausted to strut or squabble, and the only creatures that thrived were mosquitoes, gorging on any Achilles' heel of flesh missed by insect repellent. Many of her favourite shops and restaurants displayed notices stating they were closed "*per ferie*". Apart from weary tourists, jaded by the heat, the city emptied.

Even with all the shutters closed, the apartment was hot before the sun rose. Occasionally, she ventured onto the terrace but the humidity soon forced her inside, where she padded barefoot on the terrazzo floors, dressed in her underwear. She lived off salads bought from a depleted *erberia,* and drank too much ice-cold *prosecco.*

The only buildings that afforded respite, apart from air-conditioned shops and restaurants, were churches. So she would take a book and read for hours at a time in their shady and hallowed spaces. Because of its proximity she frequented the Misericordia more than most. Looking at the Madonna, she doubted whether the woman it depicted had ever felt so hot and sticky.

One morning she ventured to the public beach on the Lido, where the sand scorched her feet and the air burnt her lungs. She quickly fled, and the antics of the perfectly tanned boys and girls only made her think of Raffi, newly returned from his own beach holiday. With Vittore and Rosina away, there was little reason for his usual visits to Cannaregio, and although she looked out for him on her disconsolate walks around the city, she never did spy his loping gait. She tried not to feel disappointed that he had not phoned – why should he? And yet she hoped he might, knowing she was alone.

This period of seclusion lasted less than a week, but those days, and nights, passed very slowly. While she was not exactly lonely, she felt at a permanent loose end, listless and strangely weary. She found herself once again assailed by disquieting flashes that seemed to be plucked from a past that did not quite belong within her own store of memories. These feelings, that had disturbed her peace when she first arrived in Venice, had largely disappeared, but now she was again beset by the uncanny sensation of something exerting its will over her. It was as though an alien part of the city sought to pull her down to a darker place in its history, sucking her through the swirling waters of its slimy past. She would wake in the middle of stifling nights, gasping for breath, terrified of something that she sensed, rather than remembered – the muffled echo of experience. In those dreams, something threatened her safety, but also there was someone who could protect her – Raffi perhaps? Her father? But whoever her saviour was, they never appeared and it was only a sweat-soaked tumble from sleep that saved her.

She reasoned that it was due to the heat; to lack of sleep; to an excess of wine; to a vulnerability occasioned by so much time alone. Whatever the cause, it was with delight and relief that, late one afternoon, she heard a clattering and banging on the stairs, accompanied by Izzy's soprano squeal. Like the call of a baby bird, it was impossible to believe that such a tiny creature could make so much noise.

Izzy bounded into the flat, having left Will to struggle with the luggage. The sun had kissed her curls with white-blonde streaks, and transformed her skin to the colour of warm honey. As they hugged, it seemed to Anna that she carried with her the scent of the Ionian Sea, of lemon groves and wild thyme. But even sweeter, she brought normality and an immutable sense of the present.

'So, are you glad to see us? Has it been horribly lonely all by yourself?'

'Not horrible,' said Anna. 'But, yeah, a bit lonely.'

'Oh, you poor thing. Never mind. We're back now. And so are Vittore and Rosina. We've just bumped into them on the *vaporetto*.' Izzy had collapsed onto the floor, and was retrieving her holiday souvenirs from a tapestry shoulder bag. 'We're all invited to an impromptu party at Ca' Melisa, the day after tomorrow, to celebrate the fact that everyone has returned safe and sound to the bosom of *la Serenissima*. Anybody would think we'd all come back from the wars. So what's been happening here? What news on the Rialto?'

'Well…I've decided to stay until January. Is that OK?'

'OK? It's fantastic,' whooped Izzy. 'Everyone will be SO pleased.'

'You think so?'

'Absolutely.'

Izzy was right, and at his drinks party, Vittore even insisted on making an announcement that was greeted by gentle applause. Embarrassed by the attention, Anna snuck a sly glance at Raffi and, with relief, witnessed his undisguised pleasure. Even Caterina, who was at his side, managed a smile.

The couple had arrived only minutes before, and Anna had not, as yet, had an opportunity to speak to them. They stood slightly separate from everyone else, and around them, Anna detected an aura of contentment she had not seen before. Their relaxed demeanour was as visible as their suntans, suggesting that the problems previously disturbing their relationship had melted in the warmth of holiday sunshine.

Caterina wore a simple dress of dazzling yellow, and was as golden-skinned as a warm peach. She oozed the quiet confidence of a woman secure in the knowledge that she is easily the most attractive person in the room, and as she smiled, Anna saw something unexpected in those amber eyes. Her expression was one of magnanimity and seemed to say, 'I thought, fleetingly, you might be a rival for my lover's affection, but now I see how foolish I was.' Then the moment passed. Caterina whispered something to Raffi and raising her hand to his face, brushed back the hair from his forehead. As she did so, Anna found herself surprised not to catch the teasing flash of a diamond on her ring finger. Surely it could only be a matter of time. She turned away, a pang of jealousy twisting her guts.

A few glasses of wine soothed her ragged edges, and after an hour or so, Raffi and Caterina slipped away. When they left, they did so without saying goodbye, and it was only by chance that she noticed them go. Raffi gave her a small wave just before he closed the door, depriving her of even the shallow air-kisses of farewell. She wondered what insanity had prompted her to prolong her stay in the city and more particularly what had happened to the man who had held her so close under a dark sky, beside the Misericordia canal. Perhaps their embrace had been no more than a symptom of *Ferragosto*, when the cloying heat, a radiant moon and a young man missing his girlfriend had conjoined to produce a little summer madness. But with the approach of level-headed autumn the moment was now quite forgotten.

The month of September also marked the arrival of the next group of Ca' Melisa guests, eager to immerse themselves in the delights of, "Byzantine Venice and the Dawn of the Renaissance". As always, the first night dinner would be an extravagant affair, and Anna was at Ca' Melisa by mid-day. Her presence meant that she was on hand to welcome early arrivals, and in the meantime there was sure to be something for her to chop or stir.

Normally, Rosina's kitchen was the epitome of calm, but today it teetered on the verge of pandemonium and Rosina was conspicuous by her absence. Magda and a teenage assistant, Giulietta, were attempting to prepare the meal, and clearly there was something seriously amiss. Rosina had, Giulietta explained, *il mal di denti*. Vittore had taken her to the *dentista*, who was based in Mestre, but because she did not have an appointment, no one knew how long they would be. In the meantime, nothing was going right. Anna could not understand the complete litany of mishaps but the latest disaster appeared to be a broken food processor. Normally this would not be a catastrophe, but the *secondo* tonight was *fegato alla veneziana*, a dish that called for a very large quantity of onions. Giulietta had to leave in a few minutes and Magda did not have the time required for all the necessary chopping. Anna viewed the pile of vegetables without enthusiasm. It was not the most appealing of tasks, but it was one she was quite able to manage.

'Io farò. Può darmi un cottello,' she said, settling herself at the kitchen table. With an audible sigh of relief, Magda handed her a knife.

Anna had cooked the dish a few weeks before under Rosina's supervision and remembered how crucial it was that the slices were thin to the point of translucency, otherwise their flavour would overpower the liver. Unfortunately, despite the tutelage she had received, her knife-skills remained basic and she lacked the dexterity to complete the job speedily. *I could be here for some time*, she thought, blinking away the first tears, suspecting that her cheeks were already smeared with mascara.

After dealing with six onions, she stepped outside for a break. As she stood in the garden, dabbing her eyes, she heard the key turn in the lock of the *portone*. Rosina, followed by Raffi, appeared, both regarding her with an expression that could only be described as horror-stricken. She immediately realised why; with her tear-drenched face, she must look like a soul who has received terrible news.

Raffi was by her side in a moment. 'Anna, what is it?'

'Onions,' she said, laughing. 'I've been slicing onions. The food processor isn't working.'

Rosina muttered a string of expletives in Veneziano, then scuttled into the kitchen.

'How is she?'

Raffi made the universal so-so gesture. 'They extracted the tooth – there was an abscess under it. Vittore had an appointment he couldn't miss, so he phoned me to see if I could come home with her. So here I am. And not a second too late by the sound of it. You may not know this, but I am an expert onion chopper.'

In the kitchen, Magda and Rosina were poking and hitting the silent food processor. They turned hopeful faces to Raffi, their expressions saying that surely he, a man, would be able to perform a miracle and breathe life into the moribund machine. Under their anxious gaze, he too poked and hit the thing; he fiddled with the plug, and teased off a panel and poked about a bit more, then he shrugged his shoulders and admitted he had no idea, but would guess that the problem was the motor.

'I think you'll need a new one. But in the meantime, you have me.' And he grabbed the knife. 'Find something for Anna to do that won't spoil her pretty eyes.'

'I must look like a panda,' she said. 'Anyway, what about your pretty eyes?'

Raffi was already attacking an onion. 'Ah, but I have a secret weapon. Contact lenses! They protect the eyes. I never cry. Well, not from peeling onions. The trick is…' He continued chopping, but glanced up, '…to…ah, *porco Madonna!*'

'Raffi!' exclaimed Rosina, at this sudden profanity, and then, 'Oh, *poverino.*'

The three women saw his smile replaced by shock, and watched as a rosary of red drops fell onto the glistening onions.

After a few moments, during which everyone was transfixed by the carnage, Magda and Rosina leapt into action. The stricken chef was dragged to the sink and the blood rinsed from the wound. A first-aid box appeared. Then, with a drying up cloth wrapped around his hand, he was made to sit down. They were all chattering in Veneziano, but from the odd word that Anna picked up she guessed that the cut was not too bad. Raffi was intent upon laughing off his injury but the two women fussed over him like wartime nurses around a soldier fresh from the battlefield. Antiseptic was produced. Raffi cursed again in response to its application, and was told off again. Finally, a hefty plaster was wound around the injured digit, and the ministering angels stepped back, satisfied that their patient would survive intact.

Confident that he would not bleed to death, or lose his finger, Rosina proceeded to scold Raffi once more. Switching to English, presumably for Anna's benefit, she berated him with the fact that the onions already prepared would have to be discarded. Because of his carelessness they were covered in blood so he had only added to their problems. She concluded with an exasperated, 'Men!' accompanied by an extravagant gesture to the heavens, as if asking for the agreement of the almighty that His first attempt at humanity was an abject failure. But a second later she had scurried to her nephew's side and taking his injured hand in hers, raised it to her lips. Like any mother with her baby, she was kissing it better. On his other side, Magda bent her sparrow-brown face and pecked his cheek, chirruping Venetian endearments.

Anna had been a spectator, rather than a participant, of this little drama and watching its conclusion thought of the Italian phenomenon of *mammismo,* the excessively close attachment between mother and son, and wondered whether this was what she was witnessing. And then Raffi caught her eye and raised his own heavenwards, giving her a self-deprecating grin, and she knew that here was no *figli per sempre.* He tolerated the scoldings and cluckings because of an innate kindness and generosity of spirit.

It was this, more than any other thing that made her so sure. Standing in an untidy kitchen, with the air zinging from the smell of onions, was the time she would always remember as the hour and the place when she knew she loved him. It was as simple – and as complex – as that. She loved him: deeper than liking; truer than infatuation; gentler than lust; saner than obsession and as passionate as birdsong in spring. All previous loves were nothing in comparison. For the first time, she understood why women let hopeless years drift by, wasting their youth on affairs with married men. Given the opportunity, she would share Raffi, rather than never have him. All the warm lustre and wonderment of life, all its meaning and worth were encapsulated in the fact of his existence.

She loved him; loved him for traits as yet undiscovered; for the small boy he had once been; for the old man he would become; the father, perhaps, and the grandfather. It seemed she had loved him long before they met; long before their births; loved him in a far off place only accessible by imagination. She marvelled how she had managed to exist in this world without the knowledge that he too inhabited it. And if the time came when he was no longer part of it, she would love his memory, and that to be parted from him would be like an expulsion from Paradise.

Time shivered; her heart was going to be broken and she was powerless to prevent it. *What I feel is as merciless as death*, she thought, *and as permanent*. The realisation knocked the breath out of her like an unseen hand hitting her in the stomach, and she exhaled with a little gasp.

Raffi looked at her, frowning. 'Anna, what's wrong?'

She did not, could not, answer.

'*Il sangue*,' said Magda in a knowing voice.

'Oh, the blood, of course.'

'Yes,' she replied, immediately regretting it. Now he would think she was a complete wimp. 'Well, no, not really,' she backtracked. 'I mean, I was a girl guide... I got my first-aid badge...'

They stared at her, uncomprehending.

Rosina broke the silence. 'Both of you, go. Shoo, shoo, shoo. Anna, take him away from my kitchen before he do more harm. If you want to help, go and prepare the table in the dining room. And put that away for me, please.' She indicated the first-aid box.

Anna picked it up, and with Raffi in her wake they trailed out of the kitchen, like chastened infants.

As in all ancient Venetian homes comprising more than a single storey, the original kitchen at Ca' Melisa would not have been on the ground floor. In a city

217

particularly vulnerable to fire, the flames required for cooking were less of a hazard if confined to an upper storey. After *nonna* Dotty purchased the house, a ground floor kitchen was installed in what had been the *androne*, the place where the original merchant owners had kept their wares. A large part of it had been water filled and here the family's *gondola* had lurked. When it became too costly for any but the most wealthy – and eccentric – to maintain their own *gondola*, much of it had been reclaimed, leaving only a small basin of water. Where fishes and crabs had once swarmed, there was a large indoor courtyard; where green waters had once lapped, there were hefty paving stones, tons of mud and wooden piles.

'I'm just going to make sure that boat's secure,' said Raffi, walking over to where a motorboat bobbed, knocking at the watergate, as if trying to escape.

While he checked the craft, Anna made her way to the one feature of the *androne* that remained unchanged – the original storerooms on the opposite side of the house from the kitchen. It was in one of these that the first-aid box was kept, together with wine and oil, condiments and bottled preserves; spare china, cooking utensils and anything else that could survive high-water occasionally reclaiming its territory. Unlike the kitchen, where the floors had been raised to thwart *acqua alta*, here the original flagstones had not been built over. As she opened the storeroom door, the immediate drop in temperature engulfed her. She flicked on the light, her feet groping for the two uneven steps. The neon bulb flickered light onto the walls, and she registered that the first two feet were stained a bilious green from repeated flooding.

But it was not just the sudden chill that made her shiver. Ca' Melisa was the happiest and warmest of houses. Vittore had shown her each and every room, and it was as if all its many inhabitants had left their small mark of peace and contentment. But this place was different; here something lurked, evil and old, as though venom seeped from the walls; as though the very stones were unwilling to forgive a violation long since forgotten by man. And there was that smell; something she could not identify; something primeval and repugnant.

As she shoved the first aid box into its place, the door banged shut and then, without warning, the room was plunged into darkness. The shock made her cry out. She turned, hands clawing the empty air, when the door flew open. Raffi stood silhouetted in the narrow doorway. Behind him, the canal's reflected light filtered through grille-covered windows, trembling on the ochre walls and ceiling. Seeing that she was unhurt, his initial expression of alarm turned to amusement and then to something she could not read.

'I think the bulb must have gone,' she said, feeling foolish.

'Possibly. I'll look at it later.' He held out his hand. She took it, thankful for the reassuring sensation of his skin on hers. And then he said, 'You feel it don't you? I should have guessed you would.'

'Feel what?'

'Whatever it is that those susceptible to it, do feel. You're not the only one you know.'

'And what about you?'

'No,' he replied. 'Men never do. But apart from that, it's quite arbitrary. Neither Rosina or Magda have ever detected anything. But some of the girls who help with the catering have. And Caterina.'

Anna asked no more until they reached the warm normality of the dining room. Laid out on the sideboard, beneath the painting of Dorothea, were shiny battalions of knives, forks, spoons. Picking up a handful, she looked at the image of Raffi's grandmother; brave and beautiful, eternally smiling down at them.

'I bet it didn't worry Dotty.'

'On the contrary,' said Raffi. 'Apparently, she was acutely aware of it. That's the reason she didn't touch those rooms, and left the floors at their original level. Ca' Melisa may be haunted but as long as it was confined to one small room on the *androne* she could live with it. But she certainly wasn't going to risk disturbing anything that might invade the rest of the house. She used to say it was some long-dead Sartorani incensed that the place now belonged to an upstart American and a humble Anzelieri.'

Anna had once asked who Melisa was, only to be told that the house had not been named after a person. Melisa was simply Italian for lemon verbena, which, in the sheltered garden, had once grown in abundance. It was after this perfumed profusion that Dorothea had named her new home. But until then it had always been Ca' Sartorani, after the Venetian family who had owned it. *Nonna* Dotty had bought the house from the only surviving member, an old lady who died childless. As the last of a noble but now impoverished line, she was glad to sell the crumbling edifice, and live her last days being pampered in a kinder climate than that afforded by her native city.

'Haunted! That's putting it a bit strongly, isn't it?' said Anna. 'It's just that there's not a very pleasant atmosphere down there.'

'Emilia, she was one of my school friends, said it smelt. And not just damp or the usual sort of smells you would expect in a store-room.'

Anna silently acknowledged that this was true, but could not place the elusive odour.

'Did she say what it was?'

Raffi paused from his task of placing glasses on the table and said, 'Fear. She said it smelt of fear.'

Anna felt the hair prickle at the nape of her neck. Emilia was right; nothing else could describe that feral and desperate rankness.

'Are you trying to frighten me?'

Raffi resumed laying the glasses. There was a tiny tinging sound as one just touched another. He was concentrating on lining them up and as he did so, his hair fell over his eyes. She watched, wanting nothing so much in the world but to brush it back and lay her lips on the warmth of his forehead.

'No,' he said, straightening and shaking back the stray lock. 'I'm just fascinated why some people feel it and others don't.'

'Well, I'm not usually susceptible to that sort of thing,' she said. 'Like most people, I've been to places that are supposed to be haunted, but I've never felt a thing.'

'That's the point, you may not have felt anything, but other people obviously did. The intriguing thing about hauntings is…'

'Are you telling me you believe in ghosts?'

'Is that so strange? Venice is one of the most haunted cities in the world. I'm not talking about… Oh, there's an English saying…Vittore learnt it from *nonna*. He used to quote it at Halloween. Something about ghosties and bumps in the night.'

'"From ghoulies and ghosties and long legged beasties and things that go bump in the night, Good Lord, deliver us".' Anna dredged the ancient prayer from the recesses of her memory.

'Yes, that's it. I don't mean things like that. But I do believe it's possible that particularly strong emotions can produce a sort of energy imprint that somehow impregnates a place. And because that energy is so powerful, those emotions are replayed again and again.'

'You make it sound like a video recorder.'

'Exactly. That's why if you feel, or see something, there's no need to be frightened. It's only like watching TV. You just happen to have tuned into a channel that most other people can't access.'

Anna was not convinced. No television programme could possibly produce that sort of gut-churning terror; that sense of tangible threat.

'The trouble is, virtually all such manifestations are deeply negative,' Raffi continued. 'I suppose because fear is such a strong emotion and always accompanies violent, brutal acts. And we don't expect to walk into a place and be terrified, do we? So when it happens we really notice. But we don't think twice when somewhere makes us feel inexplicably happy… we just accept it. It could be down to the same thing though – that something really good once happened and a positive emotion is being replayed.'

'You've got it all worked out, haven't you?'

'Well, it made sense when I was about sixteen. I'm not so sure now.'

'But why me?' she said. 'And not other women, like Rosina, who have a much closer association with this house? How do you explain that?'

'I can't. Perhaps there's something about you, or your experiences, that resonate with the experiences of someone from the distant past, and that resonation somehow sets the recorder – for want of a better word – in motion. I don't pretend it's a perfect theory, but what other explanation can you offer? It could also account for feelings of déjà vu, don't you think?'

She glanced at him, wondering if Vittore had mentioned the sensations she constantly experienced in Venice, but his comment did not seem in any way loaded.

'Let's change the subject,' she said. 'To something a bit less disturbing.'

Raffi glanced at his watch. 'I must get back to the office, I've a set of drawings to complete before I can leave today. But I'll see you tonight, at dinner.'

'OK. *Ciao.*'

He turned to leave but then stopped, and pulling out one of the chairs, sat down.

'Actually, Anna. Now that we're alone there's something I want to tell you.'

'Oh, yes?' she said, trying to sound casual, as her heart fluttered like a small bird imprisoned within her ribcage.

He patted the seat of the chair next to him and she sat. Looking down at his hands and picking at the plaster on his cut finger, he began, 'Look, this is probably none of my business, but…how's Will?'

'Will?' Whatever else she had expected him to say, she had not thought it would concern Will. 'He's fine…well, apart from having a black eye. Why do you ask?'

'A black eye?'

'Yeah. The night before last he was going into a bar and there were a load of tourists coming out. The first guy was so busy talking that he didn't look where he was going and flung the door open. It hit Will in the face. Broke his glasses too.'

'Ah, so that's what he told you?' Raffi returned his attention to the plaster.

'What's all this about? You're not trying to tell me that Will was in a fight or something are you?'

'No, not a fight, exactly. But someone did hit him.'

'Why on earth would anyone hit Will?'

'Because he accused them of selling sub-standard hashish. And he did it in public, in front of other people. Dealers don't like that.'

'How do you know?'

'I was there. I just happened to be walking through San Maurizio. You probably don't know, but it's an area where the dealers hang out. I heard some guys arguing. One was Will. The next minute he was on the floor. He was lucky to get away with just a black eye. The man who hit him is Aldo Bisceglia. I was at school with him, or at least I was until he was expelled for threatening a female teacher. After that he disappeared from Venice – until last year, when his father died. With him gone, Aldo has moved back home, no doubt terrorising his poor mother.'

'Did Will see you?'

'No, I was going to help him, but someone came out of a bar and took him inside. It looked as though his nose was bleeding, so I guess they cleaned him up. I thought he'd be embarrassed if he knew I'd seen what happened.'

'Izzy'll kill him if she finds out.'

'Who? Will or Aldo?'

'Both probably. Why are you telling me?'

'Have a word with Will…tell him to steer clear of dealers. If he really can't do without a spliff every now and again, he should get in touch with this guy.' He fished in his pocket and handed Anna a piece of paper with a telephone number scribbled on it. 'He's another old school friend.'

'God, Raffi, what sort of school did you go to? Did they give lessons in drug dealing?'

'Gianluca is a respectable civil servant, but his widowed mother suffers terribly from arthritis, has done for years. He also has a small, private and well-stocked garden.'

It took a few moments for the penny to drop. 'Ah, I see. The grass he grows is the sort you smoke?'

'You got it. When he was in our final year at school he read that marijuana could help arthritic pain. Gianluca is the most upright of men, almost naïve, but he managed to score a small amount of the best Thai grass and somehow rolled a joint that he and *mamma* smoked together. It made him sick, never having had a cigarette in his life, but she was fine. And it did help the pain. But they weren't wealthy and drugs, even soft drugs, cost money. But more to the point, Gianluca hated the business of buying them, and mixing with dealers.'

'So he decided to grow his own?'

'That's right. He has – what's the expression? Green fingers? I like his mother;

222

she was great fun when we were little kids. After school we all started our National Service, but Gianluca was exempted because he needed to care for her. I was back from my first leave and happened to be over by San Pietro di Castello where they live, so I called in – unannounced. It was only about ten in the morning but I could smell the drug all over the house. I thought Gianluca must have a guilty secret. I remember laughing and calling him a *fumifero.* Then he told me that *signora* Zinanni needed a joint just to be able to get out of bed. He made me promise not to tell a soul, which, of course, I didn't. Apart from Caterina, you're the first person I've ever mentioned it to. He also asked me did I want any. Well, I quite liked a smoke every now and then, so I occasionally took him up on his offer.'

'Do you still? Smoke?'

'No, I grew out of it – like most of us. Like Will ought to have done by now. But as he hasn't, tell him to call Gianluca. He won't charge him anything, and it's good stuff. Now I really must be going.'

He stood and made for the door, saying before he left, 'One thing. Make Will promise not to tell anyone. Not even Izzy.'

'OK. And believe me, Izzy would be the last person he'd tell. Thank you, Raffi.'

She waited until the sound of his footsteps faded, and then finished laying the table, trying to make her mind a blank. Then she returned to the kitchen and made her excuses to leave. She knew she should have stayed and helped, but she needed a little time alone, away from Magda and Rosina's happy banter.

Thankfully, the apartment was empty. She sank down onto the floor, back against the sofa, arms encircling her ankles, with her chin resting on her knees, making herself as small as possible, as if this would somehow lessen the pain. The onslaught of emotion she had experienced in the kitchen of Ca' Melisa had left her exhausted: the brief exhilaration now faded to a mildewed despair.

'Dear God,' she murmured to herself, rather than to a deity she doubted would be of any assistance. 'How am I going to live without you, Raffi? What am I going to do? What am I ever going to do?'

Venice: April 1516

I would do anything to ease Debra's suffering, but as much as I rack my poor brain I can see no solution. I consider the possibility of her living with us, but I know that *papà* would never agree, nor, I think, would Giacomo. No, Debra must marry and make the best of it, as is the lot of womankind.

The thought of her misery mists my own bright joy, like breath on silver, and I find myself putting her out of my mind. I am, I know, a poor friend and the guilt I feel turns to anger. I am angry with her, and Jakob, and all her people. To Debra I have shown our most resplendent churches; I have told her tales of the saints and explained – as best I can – the sacred mysteries of the Mass, and all to no avail. If she and Jakob were to go to the *Casa dei Cateumeni* and convert to Christianity, they could live in a fine house, Debra should have her pick of husbands, and I would not lose my dearest friend to that dark place they call the Ghetto.

She once asked what the owl signifies in our sacred paintings. At the time, I equivocated for fear of offending her. Now I wish I had told her the truth: that as a bird that only flies at night, it represents the Jews' unwillingness to see the light of Jesus. For to me, her continued blindness to the true faith does indeed seem a perversity. I say as much to *papà*, and know at once that I should have held my tongue.

'How much would you be willing to suffer for your faith, Ginevra?' he asks. 'What privations would you endure?'

I am at a loss to answer, for it is a question I have never considered. I am of the faith that reigns in the civilised world and unless – God forbid – we are invaded by the Turk, there will never be the need for me to be tested. But if it came to it, would I willingly undergo for my breasts to be sliced off, or for my eyes to be put out?

As though he knows my thoughts, *papà* says, 'I do not speak of physical torture. I refer to the small daily losses that grind a people down: the right to live where you wish; to follow your chosen profession; to dress as you choose. Jakob's forefathers came to Venice over two hundred years ago. Accounts of those early days have been passed down by word of mouth. It was not always like it is now, but gradually, due to the power of our Christian Church, the Jews have been excluded from all professions.

We close their music and dance schools; we do not even allow them to farm. Officially they may only be second-hand clothes dealers – or doctors. Or, of course, moneylenders, who are particularly abhorred. And why do you think that is?'

'Because usury is prohibited by the Church,' I reply at once.

'Yet, for business and trade to survive it is imperative that people can borrow money. But the Church is not prepared to grant loans at a zero interest rate, and believe me, attempts to establish alternatives to the Jewish moneylenders have met with little success.' He pauses to allow time for me to absorb his words. 'Think of the tribulations they suffer at our hands. But in the face of it all, they adhere to what they believe. How many Christians would remain as steadfast in their faith under such adversity?'

I have no answer to this. He is right. *Papà* is always right. When I do speak, I sound like a whining child. 'But I love Debra. She is like my sister. And I feel I am losing her.'

'Life is like that,' *papà* replies and then quotes from the Bible, '"The Lord gave and the Lord has taken away". We must learn to live with it. I have.' And I know he refers to the loss of my mother. 'Ginevra, you have me, and you have Giacomo.'

He puts his arm around me and, not to be left out, a raggle-taggle of fur that has been snoozing in the corner leaps onto my lap. 'And Cesare, too,' he laughs. 'Oh, Ginevra. Just think. In less than a month you will be a married woman.'

I look at him and before he smiles I see a little flash of fear; he is afraid of losing me. So I reply, with a shining confidence, 'Married or not, I will always be here for you, *papà.*'

But it is almost as though he does not believe me, and I regret the arrogance of my words, for the Lord can indeed take away.

Over the next few weeks I think of little else but my impending nuptials. The wedding is to be in the church of Santa Maria Abbazia della Misericordia. Debra and Jakob will not be there, for Jews are forbidden to attend Christian ceremonies, but two days before, they come to our house, bearing a gift. It is the finest embroidered bed linen I have ever seen. I think it almost too beautiful to sleep in, and say so. Then I imagine what acts will take place in its soft, secret folds, and feel myself blushing.

I manage a little time alone with Debra, and ask about her new abode, suggesting that I visit. She turns dulled eyes to me and says, 'I doubt you would wish to spend time in such a loathsome place. To accommodate us all, they are building on top of the existing houses, which everyone agrees must be dangerous. In the meantime, the poorer souls have erected temporary dwellings, so the *campo*, being unpaved, is already a quagmire.'

I do not know how to respond. To flaunt my happiness by speaking of our wedding would be unkind. So we, who have talked and talked through the long hours of our young lives, have little to say. However, there are two incidents I can tell her about.

The painting's completion. Yes, it is done and my little part in its creation is over. The final layers of paint will dry quickly in the warm weather, then Giambattista will apply the glazes, and it will leave his workshop forever.

I cried a little on the day of my last sitting, for it marked the end of so much: my friendship with Debra, which will never be the same; my girlhood; and my brief calling as an artist's model.

I do not suppose anyone will paint me again, although I admit that I am surprised how well I look in the picture. It is a thing of most extraordinary beauty, and is all the work of the master himself: our pale faces and hands, our bright shining garments, even the sombre background which, if you look closely, is not a single colour, but infinite variations of deep and deeper browns. The artist was at first uneasy about this, as he prefers to use pure, bright colours, which clearly delineate his figures within their surroundings. But in this painting he has, perforce, had to use darker, smoky tones. All the colours tenderly blend into one another, as though the viewer is looking through the lightest of hazes – a cloud of incense perhaps. He tells me this is known as sfumato, and it is the invention of a great Florentine artist called Leonardo da Vinci who visited Venice many years ago. Bernardo mutters that it is a technique his master should have embraced long since, for it is the modern way. I ignore his insolence. He is piqued because Giambattista is leaving Venice, but he should count himself fortunate as he and his fellow apprentices are to be employed by other workshops.

I begin to describe how sfumato is created, but see that Debra loses interest, so I move onto the other great event in the city: one witnessed by thousands of people – the execution of the monster who violated Agnesina and those other poor girls. He is not a man of mature years but a youth of eighteen. His parents are respectable shopkeepers and protest his innocence even though he was apprehended in the very act of molesting a young woman. Rumour has it that he is a simpleton and acts like a boy of ten, but however stunted his brain, he is a big, powerful lad and can do as much damage with his meaty hands and prick as the most able-minded of men. It is no excuse, for even a child knows the difference between right and wrong, and he must suffer the consequences of his bad deeds. At first he swore that all he wanted was a kiss, but as he was caught with his hands up the girl's skirt, pawing between her legs, no one believed him. Still, he refused to admit any wrongdoing, so they brought in one of the girls who had been sodomised. She swore that he was the assailant. After that, when they interrogated him, he admitted everything.

His punishment will be swift and terrible. Every woman who has feared for her virtue and safety wishes to see it inflicted – myself included. Perhaps I, more than most, because I witnessed the hurt he did to Agnesina.

As is customary, he is taken to where he committed the crime. Here he will suffer the first part of his ordeal. *Papà* will not come, for he says that he sees sufficient human suffering in the course of his work without having to view it on the streets, so Pasqualina accompanies me. When we arrive, there is already a great, greasy press of people, and I can see nothing. Nor do I hear the snap of bone as a mallet severs both his hands. But I hear the animal screams of terror and pain as they cauterise the wounds, so he does not bleed to death and cut short the spectacle. I know that his hacked hands will be hung from chains around his neck and that already flies will be feasting on the unexpected largesse, having abandoned their usual meal of dog shit.

Then we progress slowly to the Piazza. As he stumbles on this last journey, they flog him until his naked back is reduced to raw meat. Beside him, trudge members of the Scuola di San Fantin, a confraternity whose vocation is to accompany condemned criminals to the scaffold. Their chant rises above the crowd's hubbub like a beating drum, but does not quite drown out the man's howling.

Pasqualina chatters happily as we walk. She loves this sort of thing, but perhaps, like *papà*, I am beginning to lose my taste for it. I would turn back if I could, but there is such a mill of bodies around us that I am trapped. A scaffold has been erected between the columns on the Piazzetta and not for the first time I wonder at the bloodshed our winged lion and St Theodore have witnessed. The smallest of the Campanile's bells, the Maleficio, is tolling the boy's death sentence, and as he mounts the scaffold I see him for the first time. He has a big, frightened face, which reminds me of something, but I cannot think what. The priest talks, then the condemned man speaks, but we cannot catch his words. After this he falls upon the block, as though embracing a friend who will release him from his pain, and the executioner separates his head from his body. When they show it, I realise what it reminds me of – a turnip in the winter vegetable market. And I feel very sad. Not for him, but for all the pain we inflict on each other. In truth, he has been fortunate. Had he felt the full force of the law he would have been burned alive, but because of his youth, clemency was shown. His remains, however, must be consigned to the flames, so the bloodied corpse and turnip head are shovelled onto the pyre.

We leave after this, for the smell of burning human flesh sickens me. I fear the melting fat will waft through the air and impregnate my clothes and hair forever. I am soon to be wed and do not care to carry death's odour to my marriage bed.

As we push our way through the crowds I sense their dissatisfaction. It has not been a good end. Free of his interrogators the man, again, denied all wrong-doing and, it is said, reasserted his innocence. It is important that the condemned confess their crimes, for only then are we, the whole city, expiated of the wrong-doing that otherwise will incur the wrath of God. I hear people make excuses: the boy was simple-minded, they whisper; he probably believed in his own lies at the end. Then the crowd begin to feel sympathy for him and I hear mothers murmur, 'Poor little thing.'

But whatever the rights and wrongs of it, one more threat to our safety has been expunged and we can breathe a little easier.

All this I tell to Debra with, I admit, some relish, now that I am not actually there with my stomach heaving. She shows no more interest than she did in the painting. It is as though all the life has been sucked out of her; as if an evil spirit feeds upon that sweet soul.

As they leave, I try to lighten her mood and whisper, 'Come and see me next week, when I am an old married woman, and I will tell you what "it" is like.' For in our happier past we have often giggled together, guessing at the secrets of the marriage bed.

Then I see the pain in her eyes and regret my insensitive words.

Of Wine and War

Being a sensible young woman and not prone to self-pity, Anna managed, in the weeks that followed, to regain some of her natural equilibrium. Nevertheless, her emotions teetered on a knife-edge and she occasionally found tears springing to her eyes, knowing that in four months she would return to England, leaving behind the person she held most dear in all the world.

She reasoned that things would get better when she was back in London, among old friends and familiar haunts, and that she would be able to put this bittersweet interval behind her. How could she remain in love with someone she would never see? Someone with whom she had had only a superficial and platonic relationship? That is what she told herself during the warm September days, but at night, often unable to sleep, panic would seize her with barbed fingers and whisper of the futility of expecting ever to be truly happy again.

She kept her incipient misery, and its cause, secret, surprised at how successfully she managed to conceal her true feelings, even from Izzy, who knew her so well. Her distress was compounded by hardly seeing Raffi. She missed him more than she would have believed possible. It was, she thought, like a rehearsal for the rest of her life.

The reason was apparently quite simple – pressure of work. He was involved in the renovation of a large villa on the Lido and several other projects some distance from Venice. But Anna feared that his absence was partly to do with her behaviour at the dinner following that afternoon in the kitchen of Ca' Melisa. Overwrought and nervous, she had drunk far too much *prosecco*. It had gone to her head, and throwing caution to the wind, she had, for the first time, allowed herself to flirt with Raffi. Looking back, she was not sure why she had behaved in this way – desperation perhaps? The vain hope that the scales would fall from his eyes and he would return her adoration? She suspected that she was not particularly good at flirting, and all she had seen in his face, as she fluttered her eyelashes and allowed her hand to linger on his arm a little too long, was confusion. Seeing his expression, she had realised that she was making a fool of herself, so had slipped away at the first opportunity and spent the rest of the evening chatting to a couple from Eastbourne.

The next time they met she had attempted to laugh off her behaviour, apologising for being a bit tipsy. He was as gracious as always, saying that he had not noticed, and what if she had been a little under the influence – that's what parties were for. But behind his light words she had sensed an awkwardness that had not before existed.

It was consequently with mixed feelings that she looked forward to a Saturday towards the end of September, where Raffi would play an integral part in the proceedings.

Unbelievably, Anna had not yet been to Conegliano, the birthplace of Cima. Vittore had long-promised to arrange a visit, but the summer had come and gone without the trip taking place. However, upon his return from holiday he had made a suggestion. By the end of September, the majority of the grapes should have been picked at his brother's vineyard. Together with an extended family group, Vittore, Rosina and Raffi generally spent the last weekend of the month there, celebrating the harvest. Why didn't Anna, Izzy and Will take an early train to Conegliano? Vittore would meet them at the station, and show them around the town, after which they would all proceed to Fabrizio's estate, which was only a short drive away. Raffi wanted to be in Venice for a christening party on Sunday so he would take them back in the early evening. They had accepted without hesitation.

It was already warm when they left the flat on that Saturday morning and although the early cerulean sky was laced with wispy clouds, an afternoon of heat was promised. Flowers dipped fragrant heads over high walls and butterflies flirted on the breeze. Above them, shutters banged as duvets were hung out to air, and the smell of brewing coffee wafted down. Despite it still feeling like high-summer, Anna noticed that along their path, dried leaves, golden and red, skittered like small autumnal creatures – a reminder that October was just around the corner.

'Bring your swimming costumes,' Vittore had advised. 'It may still be warm enough for you young people to take a dip.'

They bought croissants and coffee from a bar near the station and breakfasted while the train chuntered across the flat countryside towards the Dolomites. An hour later, blinking in the glassy morning sunshine, Anna gaped at a vast range of snow-capped mountains, and realised why Cima, a man born under their watch, took every opportunity to honour this landscape.

Then a familiar voice hailed them and they spied Vittore standing by the exit sign. They bounded towards him like happy puppies.

Conegliano, like many Northern Italian towns, consisted of a small historical centre some distance from the station, around which the modern commercial town had grown, spreading out in all directions. The old *citta* was situated on a steep hill, topped by a crenulated tower surrounded with Cyprus trees. It could have been lifted from one of the painter's masterpieces.

Vittore had devised an itinerary taking them up till noon, when Raffi would meet them with the car. Only Izzy was not voluble in her enthusiasm and Anna suspected that she would far rather explore the shops. However, she tagged along happily enough, despite a yearning glance at a large branch of Benetton.

After crossing a thoroughfare brutalised by cars, they climbed a flight of steps and, passing under a loggia, found themselves transported to a place of graceful arcades, where walls, the colour of a lightly baked biscuit, were adorned by frescoes, and a pair of heavy-breasted sphinxes guarded a neo-classical theatre.

'I think,' said Vittore, taking charge. 'The Duomo first.'

He led them into the cathedral, a building that could have easily been missed, as it lay hidden behind an arcade of arches that joined seamlessly with the adjacent buildings. Inside, taking pride of place in the apse, was the only painting in Conegliano executed by Cima. Six splendidly clad saints stood on either side of the Madonna who, with her baby, was elevated on a high marble throne under a mosaic-encrusted arch. At her feet, two angels played on musical instruments. In a loving murmur, Vittore spoke of composition and spatial configuration, the *contre jour* positioning of the saints' heads against the cloud-streaked sky, and the influences of Byzantium.

'Who's that one?' asked Izzy. 'I recognise all the other usual suspects, John the B, Saint Catherine etc., but what about her…the one in the pink frock next to Mary.'

'Ah, the saint my Rosina should have prayed to a few weeks ago…Appollonia, patron saint of dentists and those suffering from toothache. Look at what she is holding – a pair of tongs. Before she was killed, they pulled out all her teeth.'

'Apparently, one of them is in Porto cathedral,' added Will.

'Gross! What is it with you Catholics and body parts?' said Izzy, glaring at Will, as if he were personally responsible for inventing the cult of the relic.

'Shall we move on to something else that the Catholics did particularly well?' suggested Vittore. 'Flagellation.'

'Even better,' muttered Izzy. 'Lead on!'

And so they visited the Sala dei Battuti, and then climbed the hill towards the castle, stopping on the way, as Vittore pointed out the dilapidated ex-convent of San Francesco, which now housed a school.

'Cima's family sepulchre was in the church belonging to the convent. He was almost certainly buried there.'

'Can we go and see it,' asked Anna, wishing she had a flower to leave in homage.

'Alas, no. It no longer exists. The brotherhood was suppressed in the time of Napoleon and the church demolished in 1812.'

'So there's nothing? No gravestone? No monument?'

'No, only his paintings,' replied Vittore. 'But an enduring enough monument, do you not think?'

They continued to climb, following the steep path that ran along the town's defensive walls. Vittore forged on ahead, like a man half his age as Izzy, trailing behind in her strappy, high-heeled sandals, complained, 'I didn't think we'd be going for a five mile hike uphill. My feet are killing me.'

The museum, housed in the bell tower of the castle, did little to restore her good humour – she had clearly seen enough frescoes for one day, but even she had to admit that the view was worth the climb.

'It's at times like this I know why I live in Italy,' she said, breathing in the air – at this height, cool and clear. 'Just look at those vineyards – all that *prosecco!*'

The descent was easier, and Vittore assured them there was only one more sight on his itinerary – the painter's house.

Number 24, via Cima was an unassuming whitewashed building, arranged over three floors. It was only distinguished from the neighbouring properties by a plaque set in the wall stating, "The town council honours the house of Giambattista Cima, 17th September 1893". Its interior was similarly unremarkable. There was a small collection of archaeological artefacts that had been unearthed during the process of renovation, but the paintings were all reproductions. Everything was pristine. Even the huge fireplace looked as though it had never been used. The only arresting features were inscriptions and old drawings on one of the walls, including a date: 9 October 1492. It was assumed Cima had scribbled these, but why, no one knew.

As the door closed behind them, Anna looked at the same sight that the artist would have seen on leaving his home – a narrow street and the back of the Duomo with the rounded apse where his altarpiece hung.

'Goodbye, Giambattista,' she whispered, disappointed that the house was so empty of the great man. Vittore was right; only in his art did Cima survive. She felt closer to him in the Misericordia, standing before the Madonna, than in the place he had once lived. There were no ghosts here: or at least not ones that cared to speak to her.

With over half an hour to spare, Vittore suggested a walk around parts of the city they had not yet seen, but the sight of more frescoes, and beautifully carved balconies and windows was eschewed by Izzy in favour of the shops.

'Don't be late. We're meeting outside the Duomo dead on noon,' hissed Will, as she cantered off like a schoolgirl let out at playtime.

232

She reappeared at the appointed rendezvous just as Raffi rolled up in a frighteningly large car. They clambered in, Izzy hugging a carrier bag.

'I bought a bikini,' she announced. 'My old one's on its last legs. If I sneeze, it'll fall off me.' She was quiet for a moment, allowing the men to appreciate the implications of this, and then twittered, 'It's so kind of Fabrizio to have us all over. Who else is going to be there?'

In reply, Raffi ran off a string of names: Fabrizio's children, their partners, and some of Rosina's nieces and nephews.

'Has Caterina arrived yet?' asked Vittore.

'Er, no, I'm afraid not,' replied Raffi. 'She rang to make her apologies, but with Milan Fashion Week so soon, she can't get away after all.'

'Oh, what a shame,' said Izzy.

No one else made any comment. Then even Izzy fell silent, intent on the scenery. The suburbs of Conegliano had quickly given way to a lush rural landscape. All around them softly rolling hills basked in rich autumn sunshine, as wave after wave of vines formed an endless sea of sweeping green and gold, here and there rusting to warm orange.

Like most foreigners living for any length of time in Venice, even though its beauty endlessly bewitched her, Anna sometimes longed for trees and green fields, so she was enjoying the novelty of this ride through the countryside, when Raffi slowed down and swung into a road marked "*strada privata*", announcing, 'Here we are. The next bit's rather bumpy, I'm afraid.'

The car laboured upwards, as flocks of small birds flew out of the undergrowth, scandalised by the intrusion. Then the road tapered to a narrow track, lined with fruit trees. Hanging from branches were bauble-bright pomegranates; oranges, still hard and green; ripe golden pears; opulent purple figs; and apples, red as a witch's poisoned promise.

The car turned sharply, scrubby olive trees and terraces of shrubs and bushes, replacing the ribbon of fruit trees. Facing them, atop a gentle slope, lay a long, low house slumbering in the midday sun, its green shutters closed against the glare. White flowers frothed from window boxes and tumbling red roses caressed its ochre walls.

Raffi brought the car to a gentle halt and threw open the door. Crickets sang, and the hot air was perfumed with wild thyme.

'Bravo,' a voice boomed and a man appeared, bounding down the steps that intersected the terraces. He slapped Raffi on the back, almost knocking him over, despite being several inches shorter. 'Got her back without any scratches?' He indicated the vehicle. 'She's my new girlfriend! These Venetians, they are lousy drivers, more at home in a boat than a car. Welcome, my friends…Will? Izzy and Anna? Yes? I've heard all about you, Anna…just like a painting, Vittore tells me… I wouldn't know. I'm the Philistine in our family…Fabrizio Anzelieri, humble viticulturist. Come and meet everyone.'

'You may not live there anymore, little brother,' said Vittore, 'but you are still a Venetian, which is why you too are such a terrible driver. I hope your latest mistress likes rough handling.'

Fabrizio responded with a loud chortle and then, linking arms with Vittore in that easy, unabashed way of middle aged Italian men, led the way up the steps.

Two brothers could rarely have been so different. While Vittore was tall and lean, Fabrizio, although not actually short, gave the impression of being smaller than he really was, due to a distinctly rounded girth – a merlot belly, as Izzy later dubbed his physique. In contrast to Vittore's patrician countenance, Fabrizio's features were small and neat; his raven hair unruly and almost unnaturally shiny. His face was burnt a deep brown, making his eyes seem very blue and his teeth very white. The clothes he wore looked as though he had picked them out of a rag-bag, and although at some point he had, no doubt, tucked his shirt into his trousers, it had long since escaped and flapped happily free. He chatted constantly and laughed a lot.

As they reached the top of the steps, the side of the house became fully visible, as did a group of people sitting around a long table under a vine-covered trellis. A rapid succession of introductions followed. There were all four of Fabrizio's children and their partners plus, in one case, their little girl, who as the first of the next generation of Anzelieri, was treated with almost reverential indulgence. In the faces of Fabrizio's daughters, Anna recognized the vestige of *nonna* Dotty's Gibson Girl beauty. Also present was Rosina's niece, Patrizia, with her husband. Anna accepted her invitation to take the empty seat next to her. Always beautifully groomed, Patrizia looked particularly attractive today – positively glowing. The reason soon became apparent; she was nearly three months pregnant, and evidently enjoying the attention her newly fecund state brought.

'We are making a party,' she said to Anna, naming a date in the middle of October. 'With the baby coming, I think it is the last for much time. Please come. I will send you the invitation.'

Anna was just saying that she would love to, when Rosina and another woman appeared, each bearing a large serving dish. Fabrizio made the introductions. This was his beautiful wife, Claudia; and indeed she was. Her ash-blonde hair was immaculately coiffured and despite having borne four children she was enviably slender. She hailed from Rome and big city glamour still clung to her like gold dust, but she was as welcoming and gregarious as Rosina, exhorting everyone to, '*Mangi, mangi.*'

The first course consisted of multifarious antipasti, as bright as an artist's palette, followed by homemade pumpkin ravioli, swimming in butter and sprinkled with deep fried sage. And then the *pièce de résistance*, an orgy of grilled quail and rabbit portions, heaped on pillows of neon yellow polenta, accompanied by steaming bowls of gently stewed *funghi porcini*. Faced with such a feast, everyone ceased to bother with niceties and resorted to using their fingers to tear tender flesh from tiny bones. Fabrizio's shirt, Anna noticed, was now splattered with gravy, but no one cared. The food was far more important than sartorial elegance. Dessert was mercifully simple: *biscotti*, snowy billows of mascarpone, lusciously ripe pears, and figs – that supremely voluptuous fruit, the most mature of which shamelessly displayed their secret pink fleshiness.

Fabrizio had provided a running commentary on the wines accompanying each course and, after briefly leaving the table, now reappeared, clutching two bottles. He pulled off the wire casings and removed the corks whose expulsion made the gentlest "phuft" sound.

'You won't taste *fragolino* like this in a fancy Venetian restaurant,' he declared. 'This is from our own grapes. We produce just enough for family and friends. Make sure I give you a bottle to take back with you.' This last remark appeared to be addressed to Anna, who nodded enthusiastically, saying that she could not believe a grape tasted so strongly of strawberries.

'You can try them later. The *fragole* are still on the vine. Not due to be picked until next week. Now who would like a glass?'

With the meal finally over, and after plates and glasses had been ferried back to the kitchen, some of the younger people drifted off to change into swimming costumes, leaving the older generation at the table, chatting over coffee.

'Time to show off my new cozzie,' said Izzy. 'If I can still get into it after all that food.'

Claudia had suggested that they change in the en-suite bathroom that adjoined her room. Here, Izzy lingered sufficiently long to ensure that she made an entrance, which given the skimpiness of her new purchase was guaranteed. It consisted of four miniscule triangles of gold fabric held together by almost invisible golden strings, and showed off her pocket Venus charms to perfection. Standing next to her friend, still honey-skinned from her Greek holiday, Anna felt heavy, pale and old fashioned, and regretted that she had not given more thought to the purchase of her own costume. She had bought it when deciding, on a whim, to visit the public beach on the Lido, and had not expected to be seen in it by anyone she knew. It was a simple one piece; navy blue, with a front middle panel of horizontal blue and white stripes. She decided that it did little to show off her slender waistline, and made her look flat-chested.

By the time they emerged into the bright sunshine everyone else had made their way to the pool. The men lounged on recliners, anonymous behind sunglasses. The women sat together on the grass, their brightly coloured bikinis nearly as tiny as Izzy's. They twittered at some private joke, rubbing sun tan lotion onto each other, in a scene that would not have been out of place in a soft porn film. Anna felt like a house sparrow that has flown into a cage inhabited by birds of paradise. No one seemed remotely interested in getting wet.

'Don't want to ruin their make-up,' whispered Izzy. 'And that's just the lads! Italians think you shouldn't swim for hours after eating. Bugger that, it's not going to stop me.'

With that, she ran to the deep end and jumped in, feet first, creating a huge splash, and proceeded to execute an ungainly stroke, taking her diagonally across the pool. Unwilling to share the water with such an unruly swimmer, Anna made her way to the one sun-lounger that was free, which happened to be between Will and Raffi. Will lay slightly propped up, squinting against the sun, as he watched Izzy's golden bottom bobbing up and down.

'She swims like a dog on drugs,' he said fondly. 'Hi, Anna. Come and join us.'

Raffi had been deep in conversation with one of Fabrizio's sons but broke off and swivelled round as Anna approached. His eyes were hidden behind sunglasses but she sensed that they travelled over her body; assessing her she feared. Embarrassed, she sat down.

It was the first time she had seen him anything but fully clothed; his chest was dusted with hair, bleached to a dark gold from holiday sunshine, and he was thinner than she had imagined. When he moved, she noticed that his ribs were clearly visible under the taut, brown flesh of his torso. He looked disconcertingly young, like a skinny schoolboy, both vulnerable and desirable.

They both realised, at the same moment, that they were staring at each other and quickly transferred their attention to the spectacle of Izzy clambering out of the pool. Her bikini top had proved insufficiently robust to withstand the rigours of her vigorous stroke, and one of the upper triangles was dangling free, revealing a rosy tipped breast, startlingly white against the rest of her body. Giggling, she made a great show of retrieving the errant fabric.

'*Che brutta figura!*' she proclaimed, as modestly was restored.

No one, especially the men, appeared to think there was anything *brutta* and looked on approvingly. Fabrizio even applauded. Izzy blushed prettily and dropped a curtsey.

'Let's face it,' she said, flopping down next to Anna. 'This isn't really designed for swimming. I should have known better. You're far more sensibly attired.' And then, addressing anyone who cared to listen, 'Anna really can swim. Used to win all the galas at school. Go on, show 'em, Anna. Don't be shy.'

Anna got to her feet and padded towards the deep end, horribly aware that the cheap costume had ridden up her bottom. Seconds later she executed a graceful dive, swimming the length of the pool underwater, before twisting over and switching to backstroke. The heat of the sun on her arms, and the sight of the deep blue sky filled her with a glorious, almost erotic pleasure. She closed her eyes against the glare, giving herself over to the sensation and thought of nothing but the rhythmic strength of her limbs cutting through the water and the cool droplets falling on her face. It induced an almost hypnotic state and the sound of muted conversation and twittering birds seemed to emanate from far, far away. Then suddenly the calm was shattered: there was the sound of splashing; water washed over her, and opening her eyes, she saw a startling mosaic of rainbow colour that was replaced in an instant by Raffi's laughing face.

'You're like a mermaid,' he said.

Spluttering, she flipped over to face him as he grabbed her around the waist. Gasping in delight they rolled as agile as two baby otters and then breathlessly trod water, their legs entwining like lovers. But without warning, the intimacy of the moment was gone, as splashes and screams heralded more swimmers braving postprandial cramp. A plastic ball bounced between them and Anna hastily escaped from the watery playground, leaving the young men playing a rule-less game of aquatic rough and tumble.

An hour later, showered and dressed, she lay dozing on one of the loungers. While she had been indoors, purple clouds had streaked across the sky and the sun was dragging itself westwards. Soon it would be time for them to leave.

Fabrizio's voice boomed from somewhere behind her. 'Raffi, wake up. Why don't you take our guests on a little tour of the estate? I promised to show Anna the *fragola* grapes, but I'm far too tired. You do it, there's a good boy.'

'Do you want to see?' she heard Raffi ask.

'Yes, of course,' she replied.

'I'd love to, honestly,' Izzy wailed, 'but my feet just aren't up to it.' And she brandished her silly little sandals – the excuse for her inertia. 'I've got blisters already. See.'

Will stirred, making as if to join them, when Anna saw Izzy's restraining hand rest on his thigh and perceived the ghost of a wink in her eye.

Raffi led the way to the back of the house, down through a haphazardly attended garden where nature, rather than man, appeared to be master and which gave onto gently sloping terraces. Oblique shafts of sunlight, filtering through the early evening clouds, daubed the vegetation with bright splashes of gold. Ranks of vines, newly deprived of their burdenous grapes, succumbed to weariness and drooped, the leaves already withering to a papery yellowness. At intervals, red and pink roses studded the rows, as bright as jewels. Small frenzies of sparrows hid in the foliage, chattering and squabbling. Apart from this it was very quiet. They stood, silently viewing the opulent landscape.

'Can anything get more perfect than this?' Anna said after a while. 'I love Venice, but I can see why Fabrizio chooses to live here.'

'He's always been more at home in the country than Vittore. It worked out well; Fabrizio got the vineyard and Vittore got Ca' Melisa. My grandparents came to prefer it here too. I don't ever remember them living at Ca' Melisa.'

'What were they like?'

'Very upright, quite serious. Not like *nonna* Dotty. They were kind enough, but I always felt they disapproved of me because of... you know. The fatherless child born out of wedlock. I came to feel that I was a slight embarrassment to them. They always referred to Rosina and Vittore as my mother and father, even though I never called them that. It was as though they were trying to legitimize me. It didn't matter,' he added. 'Rosina's parents more than made up for it.'

But she could tell that even after so many years, it did matter. That the rejection had somehow leached some of the happiness from his childhood. *Poor kid,* she thought, and instinctively linked her arm through his.

'Vittore would never have wanted to settle here,' Raffi said. 'It holds too many bad memories...war-time memories.'

'Izzy told me that he'd been in the Resistance. Was he really?'

'Yes, yes he was. You see, after Italy agreed to an armistice with the Allies in 1943, Venice was occupied by the Germans. But Dotty absolutely refused to leave Ca' Melisa, so my grandfather stayed with her, and my grandmother and the three children came here, thinking it safer. Vittore was sixteen, and one day he just walked out, without telling anyone – apart from Fabrizio.'

'And joined the Resistance?'

'Yes. *Giustizia e Libertà* – one of the partisan groups.'

'You said there were bad memories. What happened?'

'He's only spoken to me about it once. One night we were sitting up late chatting. I'd just started my national service, and it was my first leave. I found those first few weeks a bit difficult: the discipline...the petty rules, and I guess I was simply homesick. We'd both drunk quite a bit and I made some stupid comment about how lucky he was not to have had to do national service. I knew at once I'd said the wrong thing. And then he told me. Yes, he was lucky: lucky to be alive; lucky to have survived those winter months in the foothills of the Dolomites; lucky not to have been amongst those men, men he knew, who were caught and summarily executed at Bassano; lucky not to have been detected helping people hide in the backwaters of the Lagoon.'

Anna said nothing and looking out across the lush, gilded hills, wondered what bloodied horrors the tranquil landscape had witnessed.

'Then he told me about the thing that still haunts him – even now. It happened only a couple of kilometres from here. It was the spring of 1945, by which time the Germans had been mostly expelled. For days there'd been no sign of them. I don't know what he and the men he was with were doing – presumably something that marked them out as partisans. Anyway, they were walking past an orchard when somebody started firing at them. One of them was hit in the arm, and they realised there was a sniper hiding in a tree. Vittore pulled out his pistol and fired till it was empty. When they found the gunman he was strapped to the branches.'

'Was he dead?'

'Not quite. They cut him down, and then they saw that he was just a kid, probably no more than sixteen. Vittore knew enough German to realise that he was crying for his mother. He held him till he died.'

Anna cleared her throat. 'If Vittore hadn't shot him, he'd have probably killed every one of them.'

'That's exactly what I said. And he knew it too – intellectually. But emotionally, he couldn't reconcile himself to the fact that he'd ended someone's life. He'd still not forgiven himself. He's never mentioned it again and I don't suppose he ever will, but sometimes…I can tell, something reminds him, and I see the pain and guilt in his face.'

'My dad was a bomber pilot,' Anna said. 'Responsible for hundreds… thousands of people dying. He hardly spoke about it either. But it was always there. He once said that no one ever really came back from the war.'

'Well, it was the defining event of their generation, wasn't it? To some extent they'll always be trapped in those years. I'm sorry I never met your father. He must have been very brave.'

Anna felt tears prick at the back of her eyes; for the impossibility of his ever meeting the man she now loved best in the world. She blinked them back and said, 'We're so lucky – not to have had our lives blighted by conflict.'

'And do you think we're any happier?'

'Perhaps not,' she shrugged.

They walked on in silence; the only sound was the soft scrunch of their footsteps, and the breeze worrying the tissuey leaves. Raffi stopped by a row of vines still bearing heavy bunches of blue-black grapes. 'These are the *fragole*. Do you want to taste?'

'Yes, please,' she said, as he snapped off a small, but laden stem. She proffered a hand but he ignored it, lifting the grapes to her face. Instinctively she parted her lips and bit into the purple fruit. A bizarre combination of petrol and strawberry filled her mouth and a spurt of juice, sticky and blood-warm, snaked down her chin. She laughed as Raffi put his finger to the place, catching the fragrant trickle. Their eyes met and she watched him lick the sugary liquid from his hand. He took a half step closer and bent his face towards hers. Her eyelids drooped and then flew open as a piercing call tore the stillness.

'Ciao, *carissimo*.'

Over Raffi's shoulder, Anna saw a willowy figure teetering towards them. Burnished by the dying sun, her hair was a bright halo, but there was nothing saintly about the short white dress or high red sandals.

In the second before he turned towards Caterina, Anna tried to read Raffi's expression: guilt, surprise, annoyance? The moment was too brief, but she was sure that whatever registered on his face, it was not delight at his girlfriend's unpropitious appearance.

Caterina flung her arms around Raffi, planting a shiny kiss on his mouth, as she chattered in Italian. Apart from a brief nod, she ignored Anna.

'Speak in English,' Raffi said.

'OK.' But she made no attempt to include Anna in the conversation. 'So as all the press releases are finished and Guido is going to be driving right past the gate here, I decide to give you a surprise. And here I am! So I can come with you to the christening tomorrow, and we will have a lovely day together, *tesoro*.'

And with that she linked arms with Raffi and led him back to the house. Ignoring his admonition, she had reverted to Italian, but the billing and cooing were comprehensible whatever the language.

Anna trailed behind them. *I hate you*, she thought. *I have no right to, but I do.*

After that, they soon headed back to Venice. With three of them squashed into the back of Raffi's small Fiat, a drive that should have been relaxed was cramped and uncomfortable. It was foolish to feel that the day had been tarnished and spoilt, but that is what Anna felt. No one talked very much on the journey.

Back in the flat, Izzy demanded, 'Well, did he pounce?'

'Raffi's hardly the pouncing type.'

'Any man's the pouncing type. You've just got to make them realise they're not going to be rejected. I bet you gave him no encouragement. Or did Queen-Cat arrive at just the wrong moment?'

'Her timing could have been better,' admitted Anna.

'Do you believe her? This tale about leaving Milan on a whim and someone just happening to be on hand to give her a lift all the way here? I mean, if someone drove you that far, you'd invite them in for a drink, surely?'

'Perhaps he was in a hurry to get home.'

'No, I think it's much more likely that she got wind of the fact that we – well, you – would be here; and took a train and a taxi to make sure that you got up to no good with her property.'

'Well, she could have saved herself the trouble. Nothing happened. I'm sure he just thinks of me as a friend.'

'Bollocks. I saw you in that pool. He'd like more than friendship, believe me.'

'But even if he does – for how long?'

'I don't know, I'm not the bloody oracle. But there's only one way to find out.'

Venice: May 1516

And so we are married and I never do confide the secrets of our bed to Debra, for how can I describe what happens between Giacomo and me in small and silly words? No other woman, I am quite sure, can have ever felt what I feel for my husband. My husband! How I love to say the word. It warms my mouth like honey and sings inside the whole of my head with its sweetness. My joy would conjure the daisies to bloom in the Piazza; persuade the swallows to stay through the winter's ice, and make the very angels of heaven jealous. Our love will keep us young forever, and should death come visiting, we will laugh in his face so that he creeps away like *acqua alta*.

Our wedding is a modest affair, for between us we have little family. The banns are read for the final time and the required legalities observed before the notary. All that is left is for us to progress to church on Sunday and make our vows before God. *Papà* has bought me a fine new gown and Pasqualina weaves flowers and rosemary into my loose flowing hair.

As befits the occasion, it is a day of beauty. The sun capers on the canal and the summer birds swoop and sing, as if just for us. People come out of their houses to wish us well and to throw flowers in our way. The petals fall about us like fragrant snow, catching on our clothes and hair. I feel as though the whole of Venice is in love with our love.

In the church there is a great press of people, and I realise how well loved is *papà*, for it is he who they honour with their presence. The nuns sing from the choir loft, then the priest reminds us of the indissolubility of the marriage bond: we swear love and fidelity, and my ring, with its bright little blue stone, is blessed. Then we are pronounced man and wife. We follow the same path home, which is still strewn with blossom: some people even applaud, as though we have done a brave or a clever thing, which I suppose we have.

At our house all is humming and buzzing. Pasqualina has been preparing our wedding feast for days, but will not countenance any assistance from me. She nudges me, saying, with a naughty giggle, that I must conserve my strength. There are capons and quails; sausages and stuffed hens' eggs; olives and cheeses; great dishes of baked macaroni – a rare treat – and all sorts of salads and fishes. To follow, Pasqualina has made pine nut cakes, marzipan biscuits and many other sorts of fancies. All the people we know and love are here to eat and drink and laugh with us, including Giambattista and his apprentices. Most have brought gifts, the best of which is a spoken promise from Bernardo.

'When I have established myself in Tiziano Vecellio's workshop,' he whispers. 'I will try and persuade my master to let you visit. You may have to flirt a little, for he is most partial to the fair sex.' And then he reveals that he has guessed who Giovanni was, 'So, desist from dressing as a boy, for Tiziano is not that way inclined.' And he winks in a way that on any other man I would think lewd, but on him is comical.

Debra and her father are not, of course, present. Whilst this saddens me, I am too happy and too intent upon enjoying my role as a bride to dwell on their absence. And despite being sorry that Giacomo's parents are not alive to see this day, I am thankful that, unlike most new wives, I will not have to leave the home of my childhood to live with my husband's family. I will be mistress of my own house, beholden to no other woman.

The celebrations continue until the light begins to fail, when our guests, by now silly and sleepy with wine, start to drift away. After they have all left, we accompany *papà* into the darkening garden where we sit quietly together, Cesare snoring at my feet. Sometimes we talk, but mostly we just sit. Then the house falls silent and I hear the sound of night birds calling to their mates, and watch the soundless bat-dance. At last *papà* makes a great show of yawning and stretching and saying how tired he is. He stands, and taking my hand, he places it in Giacomo's open palm. Then he kisses both our foreheads, bidding us goodnight. He looks sad and proud and happy all at the same time, and I suppose that he remembers his own wedding night. At the sight of his face, I want to weep, and stay with him to afford some comfort. But my place is now with my husband, so I watch him go to his lonely bed.

Giacomo and I remain in the garden, kissing under the stars, and I forget about my father and think only of my husband. His hands stray to places where he has never touched me before, but even though my body now belongs to him, he asks me if I mind. As if I could mind his fingers slipping down my loosened bodice to caress my breasts! I hear myself whimper and wonder if this is what a little alley cat feels when she lifts her tail and yowls for a mate. It is a pleasure so exquisite that it borders on pain, and I do not know how much I can bear. Then it begins to rain and although it is a soft, warm rain, it is nevertheless a wet rain, so we scurry indoors, and up to my bedchamber.

We do not close the shutters, so the room remains bathed in shy moonlight, all grey and silvery, just enough for us to see each other. He begins to remove my clothes. I can tell that he is unfamiliar with all the ribbons and lacings of female garb, for it takes him much longer to undress me than I take to do it alone, but that is also because he keeps stopping to plant little kisses on the newly revealed flesh. When all is discarded but my shift, I pull away and scuttle into bed, for although we are wed, I am not ready for him to see me naked. Then he pulls off his clothes, apart from his shirt, for I think he is quite modest also, and he dives under the sheet next to me.

We know quite well what happens between a man and a woman, for it is spoken about openly in our city, and there are all manner of pamphlets in circulation that leave little to the imagination. They purport to show couples the best way to conceive of a child, although I suspect their main purpose is titillation. But we both are virgins, as green as one another, and for all our theoretical knowledge it strikes me that we may not know what to do when the moment comes. However, I need not worry, for nature is the best teacher and when I feel my husband's knee nudging between my own, I sense that it is time to entwine myself around him and let our flesh be united. He finds the place and then 'tis done. I am a maiden no more.

It is over very quickly and I have to admit, does hurt, and although prepared for it, the sudden pain quite kills my desire. I am surprised that this is not the end of things, for I certainly did not expect the jigging about that follows, but despite my discomfort I find myself moving with him, which I suppose must be the correct thing to do. I am just about getting into the way of this unexpected turn of events when he moans a little and shudders. His body goes so limp that I am seized with panic in case he has been struck dead. But then I hear him gasping for air and feel his poor heart pounding.

'Dearest one,' I whisper. 'Are you not well?'

He raises himself onto his elbows and looks down at me.

'You are the most beautiful thing in the world,' he says. His eyes are wet with tears, and the look he gives me! I swear no other woman has received such a look in the whole history of the world. He gazes on me as though I am the brightest star in the sky. It is a great moment for a man and I glow with the pleasure of knowing that I have given it to him, although I am a little disappointed on my own behalf, for I had expected more. He then quizzes me about what I felt. I do not know what to say and try to change the subject, but when you are stark naked in bed for the first time with your husband of less than half a day, this is well-nigh impossible.

Then without warning, he grabs his shirt, slips out of bed and leaves the room, saying that he will be but a moment. He returns, holding a pitcher of wine and two goblets.

'Drink some of this,' he says.

I partook of hardly any wine at our wedding feast, wishing to play the hostess with a clear head, but now I have another role to play, so I do as bid. After two glasses and much more kissing and touching I do not stop him when he pulls aside the sheet and beholds my nakedness. Rather, I revel in the realisation that he finds my flesh so appealing and raise my arms above my head and strike a pose like a Venus. I feel wanton and soft and happy, and very desirous for him. So we try again and this time I know what all the fuss is about. Then exhaustion overcomes us and we fall asleep.

We are woken at first light by the scratch of Cesare's claws as he cries at our door. But we do not let him in, and very quietly, for I can hear that Pasqualina is up and about, we indulge in another act of love – for it will be many long hours until bedtime! And it is even better than I remember from last night and I decide that I like being married very much.

And so I settle down to this new stage of my life. Nothing changes so very much, except that I go to bed earlier but sleep less. During the day I visit Cima's workshop, and I still help *papà* prepare his medicines. What would alter life beyond everything would be a baby. I look at Giacomo's sleeping face in those early summer mornings and think how good it would be to make a small duplicate of his sweet self. Love can addle the minds of the most intelligent of men, so what little chance have I? I run my hands over my flat belly and half hope that another life has been planted there. But my courses come as usual, and I am a little disappointed, which is silly, for I do think that the two of us should be together a while, before we shoulder the responsibilities of a family. However, I do not suppose it so very likely that I will conceive speedily for it is well known that the male seed loses its strength if it is often spent, and hardly a night goes by when we do not prove our love for one another. When we are in church together, he smiles and I remember where his mouth has been so lately, and I realise that I am hot with longing for him. I sense the blush rising to my cheeks, but I feel no shame.

I am so coddled in happiness that I hardly think on Debra. But after a month when she has not come to see me, I make the effort and go to the Ghetto. It is like another world. Apart from a feast or an execution day, when the Piazza heaves with people, I have never seen so many folk in one place. They speak in what I suppose is Hebrew, and I feel quite the foreigner in my own city, which is not a feeling I like. I anticipated that it might not be easy to find Debra, so I have written a letter, asking her to come and visit me, telling her that although I am married I do so miss her. I give this to a boy, together with a small coin and beg him to make sure she receives it. He promises to do so and scurries off.

A week passes, and when I still have not heard from her I begin to think that the boy was negligent and never handed on my message. Either that, or she does not wish to know me anymore. Our girlhood is over, and so perhaps is our friendship. Maybe she is jealous of my good fortune, which she might well be, for I am mightily blessed. And I am so busy and so happy that she slips from my mind. Until one day my work is disturbed by a knock on our door. At last, it is she.

I realise at once there is something gravely amiss. She looks ill, her face is pale with a yellowish tinge and there is a line of perspiration on her upper lip. Although we go up to my room as if nothing has changed, I note that there is none of the old lightness in her step, and she ignores Cesare, who bounces about her feet as giddily as summer hailstones. When I close the door she sinks onto the bed, burying her face in her hands. Then she clutches her stomach, begging me for the chamber pot. I hand it to her and she vomits profusely.

Even without my scant medical training I would know what ails her. I wipe her face with my handkerchief.

'Oh, Debra,' I whisper. 'Who has done this to you?'

Nothing in the World so Well as You

Anna almost did not go to Patrizia's party that Friday in October. Izzy and Will were unable to make it as they had a long-standing invitation to a wedding in Ravenna. Vittore and Rosina were also otherwise engaged and declared that, anyway, it was an occasion for the *ragazzi*. Then Patrizia rang. She so hoped Anna was coming; one of her friends had acquired a new boyfriend who hailed from London, and it would be nice if there was another English person for him to talk to. So Anna promised to be there.

The clocks had gone back at the end of September, so it was dark when she caught the *vaporetto* over to the long, thin sandbar of the Lido di Venezia, but the evening was still warm with a breezeless, almost sultry heaviness. The boat was packed with people: stout housewives whose shopping bags sprouted large vegetables; glamorous office and shop girls; studious business men, their noses buried in newspapers; and a few like herself, dressed for an evening socialising. She stood outside, breathing in the salty air as they sped between the illuminated channel markers, barley sugar bright against the dark waters.

Patrizia and her husband, Renzo, lived on the ground floor of an elegant nineteenth century villa in a quiet road five minutes walk from the Lido's main shopping street, which unlike Venice, was loud with cars and buses. At 7.30 this thoroughfare was also teeming with people, the bars and *gelateria* busy, the last shoppers stocking up for the weekend, and the first diners nosy-ing into restaurants.

When she reached Patrizia's, the party was in full swing. There was no evidence of the Londoner boyfriend, but plenty of other people were more than willing to practise their English and she found, to her surprise, that she was enjoying the evening.

After about half an hour, Raffi and Caterina arrived, affable, smiling, beautifully groomed. The dress Caterina wore was an incredible concoction in shocking pink. Compared to everyone else she was overdressed, but that did not matter. There were women in the room who would have considered, if not actually committed murder, in order to own such a garment.

The couple moved slowly through the room, greeting friends, Caterina looking as though she expected someone to hand her a bouquet. At one point their eyes met and Anna saw the old animosity flicker in those amber irises. Raffi did not appear to have seen her, and then they disappeared into the kitchen. When, after a few minutes, they did not return, Anna assumed they had wandered into the garden that lay at the back of the house. It was hot and stuffy in the apartment, and she wanted to venture outside also, but did not like to, in case she appeared to be stalking them. If Raffi wanted to see her, he could come and find her. Somehow, she knew she would not have long to wait. When he emerged from the kitchen he saw her at once and wove his way towards her.

'When did you get here?' he asked.

'About an hour ago. I saw you come in.'

'Why didn't you say hello?'

'I'm sure Caterina saw me. I assumed she would have said.'

'No, no, she said nothing.'

And then they drifted deep into conversation: about nothing and everything; the past and the future; the silly and the serious things of life. They moved seamlessly from one topic to another and seemed to have been talking for five minutes, yet the clock on the mantelpiece told her it was nearer half an hour. At one point he touched her bare upper arm and she felt a sticky flare of longing that went straight to her groin.

Caterina's entrance, when it came, would have done credit to Floria Tosca. With diva eyes blazing, her high-pitched cry of, 'Raffi, Raffi,' may not have been sufficiently tuneful for La Fenice, but what it lacked in melody was more than compensated for in dramatic force. On her cheeks were two bright spots, almost as pink as her dress. She was both magnificent and pathetic. For a second she stared at them, as if assessing their guilt. Then she filled her lungs and launched into an aggrieved aria.

Although by no means *fortissimo*, her voice was sufficiently loud to make those in the immediate area stop mid-sentence and stare. At one point, a woman put her hand on Caterina's arm, only to have it shaken off.

Raffi did not move, regarding her as though she were a stranger – a mad person berating him on the street for an imaginary misdemeanour. Anna too, remained motionless, as though she were an observer of the scene, rather than a participant. Although she understood only one word in ten, it was not difficult to piece together the reason for Caterina's vitriol. She was livid that Raffi had left her "for hours" in order to talk to another woman. Finally, in a sob-cracked voice, she declared, '*Voglio andare.*'

'OK,' said Raffi.

Suddenly, with a toss of her golden head, she made for the door. Anna heard the words *casa* and *papà*, from which she presumed Caterina intended returning to her father's home, rather than Raffi's flat. No one attempted to stop her. The sound of the front door slamming echoed throughout the apartment, and then people resumed their conversations as if the incident had never occurred.

'I think,' said Raffi, 'I could do with some air. Coming?'

The early evening warmth had disappeared, and the garden was now empty of guests. Raffi and Anna sat together on a wrought iron bench. Unbidden, he took off his jacket, draping it over her shoulders. There was a heady scent of something very sweet; a last burgeoning of summer fragrance before autumn overwhelmed the garden. She leaned back and gazed at the dark sky, now laced with wispy clouds, and the moon nestling in its silvery penumbra. Next to her, Raffi slumped forward, elbows resting on his thighs as he ran both hands through his hair.

'I've had enough,' he said, each word loaded with a heavy weariness.

He did not need to elaborate for Anna to understand. She placed her hand on his shoulder, feeling the tense muscles beneath his shirt.

'She's obsessed with me leaving Venice and coming to Milan,' he continued. 'She let it rest when we were on holiday, but as soon as we got back – nag, nag, nag. For the first time in her life she's not getting something she really wants, and she can't deal with it in a normal, rational way. She just won't take no for an answer, and I'm not prepared to put up with the histrionics and the moral blackmail any longer. It's made me see her in a different light. I no longer feel she's someone I want to spend my life with.'

Anna let the full meaning of his words sink in. The noble part of her thought she ought to say something about compromise and reconciliation. Instead she remained silent, letting him continue.

'Now she's decided the reason I won't leave Venice is because I'm having an affair with someone here.'

She hardly dared ask the question. 'And are you?'

'No, no I'm not. At least not yet.' And he looked up to meet her eyes. 'There is someone, but I don't know if my feelings are reciprocated.'

Please God, let him mean me, she thought. *If he means someone else I'll die of misery*.

'Is she nice, this person?'

'Nice?' He appeared surprised by the question. 'Yes. Yes, she is...*molto simpatica*.'

'Why don't you just ask her? The worse that'll happen is she'll say no.'

'You know, it's ironic. I think Caterina knew before I did. When I first met you

I remember thinking you were really rather lovely, but you were so reserved, so British. Even if I had been unattached I couldn't have imagined anything developing between us. And then...'

He paused as if recollecting the sequence of events.

He does mean me, she thought; too amazed to feel elated. She had fantasized about this moment countless times, but had never envisaged it played out with so prosaic a dialogue – discussing the situation almost as though it was happening to other people.

'...and then,' Raffi said, 'Caterina developed this irrational jealousy of you. I don't know why...I can't remember giving her any reason. But gradually I found myself thinking about you more and more; making excuses to call in at Ca' Melisa when I knew you would be there; you know the sort of thing – like a teenager. And all the time you were still so aloof – so cool. Do you remember the day I cut my hand? God, I felt such a fool. But that evening, at dinner, you were like a changed woman. I didn't know what was going on.'

Anna recalled her execrable attempt at flirting; perhaps it had not been so inept after all.

'Then the next time we met, you let me know that you behaved the way you did only because you'd had too much to drink. Not very flattering.'

There was a long silence, broken by Anna saying in a small voice, 'I didn't think you could possibly be interested in me.'

'Why ever not? I told you, you're lovely.' And he took her hand, raising it to his lips.

His fingers were very cold.

'You're freezing,' she said.

A cool breeze was stirring the leaves of the tree under which they sat, and despite Raffi's jacket round her shoulders, she shivered.

'Come on,' he said, and still holding hands they went indoors.

No one gave any indication of surprise when, after half an hour or so, they left the party together. They had gone into the garden as single people but returned as a couple; their concomitance wordlessly accepted.

And to them too, the revelation was a thing of fragile wonderment of which they did not, as yet, dare speak. They strolled down the quiet back streets, avoiding the busy Gran Viale Santa Maria Elisabetta, their arms loosely round each other's waists, their stride easy and synchronous. A few small drops of rain began to fall, but they hardly noticed.

As they boarded the number 1 *vaporetto*, the soft drizzle thickened to a downpour. During the short crossing they sat inside, and through fuggy windows watched as the rain became so dense it was impossible to see the lights of Venice. The retreating Lido seemed to swim in the deluge, and the illuminated Campari sign, huge and red, quivered and melted into the waters.

Anna's quickest route home would have been to disembark at San Marcuola on the Grand Canal and then nip up through Cannaregio on foot. Instead, when Raffi stood to leave at the Arsenale stop, she also rose, this seeming the most natural thing in the world. Only as they huddled together on the *imbarcadero*, gazing into the relentless rain, did she realise the implication of her actions: that it was a tacit agreement to accompany him back to his flat.

'I could pick up a number 5 at the Campo della Tana stop,' she said.

'You've missed the last number 5.'

'Ah,' she breathed.

'Come back with me. Have a coffee, another drink. The rain won't last all night. If you want, I'll walk you back home when it's stopped.'

'OK,' she said, and then, 'But, Caterina...'

'Caterina will have gone to her father's. She forgot her keys to my place.'

For a few moments more, they watched the rain. It showed no signs of abating but fell with such velocity that each drop ricocheted off the *fondamenta*. It had turned very cold and their light clothes afforded little protection against the plummeting temperature. A sudden fanfare of lightning heralded drum-rolls of thunder.

'Let's make a dash for it,' said Raffi, taking her hand.

They sploshed across the wide deserted Riva, and then along narrow *calli* as quickly as they could, but by the time they reached the Campo de l'Arsenale they were both drenched. Raffi had his key ready and they fell into the building's hallway, gasping and panting, before trailing damply up to his apartment.

'Sorry about the mess,' he said, showing her into a large, white room with a high, beamed ceiling. It was furnished with an eclectic mix of antique and modern, and was far from untidy, although a woman's brightly coloured scarf, together with a scattering of fashion magazines, lay on the brown leather sofa. Raffi immediately swept up the telltale items and left the room. The open door revealed a bedroom and she watched him drop the scarf and magazines into an open suitcase lying on the floor. Then he kicked the case under the bed.

There were the remains of a light meal on the walnut dining table, and a lipstick outline pouted at her from one of the wineglasses. She fancied she could smell Caterina's perfume.

The flat was not warm and she shivered. *I shouldn't be here*, she thought, averting her eyes from the sight of him tidying away the other woman's possessions. She began to inspect his books. Propped up against an Italian/English dictionary was a photo of a much younger Vittore holding a smiling child – Raffi. They stood against a backdrop of pure white and wore skiing clothes.

'Me aged nine,' he said, coming to stand next to her. 'The first time he took me skiing. Do you ski?'

'No, I've never tried.'

'You should. You'd love it. Perhaps we'll go…next year. Look, I'm sorry it's so cold in here. I've put the heating on.' And as if on cue, a radiator made a loud gurgling sound. 'It'll soon warm up. Now, please, don't take this the wrong way but you really ought to get out of those wet things. Why don't you have a shower, get warm and let your clothes dry. I'll find you something to wear.'

Outside the rain still hurled itself at the windows and the room's shadowy corners were shocked awake by another flash of lightning. There seemed no other option, so she padded after him. The bathroom lay off the bedroom, and she averted her eyes from the neatly made double bed, covered with an innocent cream counterpane.

'There's everything you'll need…shampoo…conditioner…' he said, handing her a bathrobe. It was blue towelling and a little threadbare. 'It's mine…quite clean. I only washed it yesterday.' He pulled towels from a cupboard. 'I'll make some coffee. Hang your clothes on the rail, it's heated.' Then rubbing his still dripping hair, he left, closing the door behind him.

She shed her clothes and examined her reflection in the mirror. Staring back at her was a woman with hair hanging in a bedraggled mess and whose face was streaked with mascara that had emigrated southwards from eyes to cheeks.

'What a fright,' she muttered, fiddling with the shower taps. Standing under the steaming water, rubbing the mess from her face she realised that, apart from a lipstick, she had nothing with which to repair the damage. She remembered his choice of word – "lovely" – and hoped he would find the blank canvas of her face lovely.

She found him in the tiny kitchen, pouring coffee. He was dressed in a pale grey jogging suit, and his hair had begun to dry in thick tendrils at the nape of his neck. He turned and smiled. 'Hi. Do you want a hairdryer?'

'No thanks. It's better if it dries naturally.'

He took the cups into the sitting room, placing them on the glass-topped coffee table where a bottle of grappa and two long-stemmed glasses stood. There was also a bowl of sugar and a small jug of steaming milk.

'Help yourself,' he said, indicating the latter. He had remembered that she preferred her coffee macchiato, rather than espresso.

There was another flash of lightning. Through the rain-lashed window, she saw a solitary pedestrian dashing across the *campo*, bowed under the wet onslaught. The floodlit lions at the gates of the great shipyard, safe in their stony impermeability, smirked as he passed. Seen from above, and at night, it was an improbable prospect, giving credence to the old cliché of Venice being one vast stage set.

Raffi came to stand behind her and draped an arm loosely around her shoulders. 'Do you know that the eighth circle of Hell described by Dante is based on the Arsenale?' And bending his head, he murmured into her ear; soft Italian words, seductive and tender.

'That's beautiful. Translation please.'

'It describes boiling pitch – one of the punishments of Hell.' His lips rested briefly on her neck. 'Talking of hot things, come and drink your coffee before it gets cold.'

Curling herself up on the sofa she towelled her hair, sipping the bittersweet macchiato, while he told her more about the Arsenale and the lives of the men who had laboured there. As he poured the grappa she watched the movements of his hands, remembering the day she knew she loved him.

'Is it quite healed – your finger?' she asked.

'What? Oh, yes thanks. My Russian peasant paws have survived intact.'

'Russian peasant?'

The shape of his hands always intrigued her; large, capable and strong with thick, blunt fingers. They could have belonged to a manual worker, not someone whose job included the production of precisely executed drawings.

'My father is Russian – well, the man who my mother assures me is my father. He's actually French, but both his parents were the children of émigré Russians who fled the Revolution. He designs sets for the Paris opera, or at least he did before he retired.'

'Have you ever met him?'

'No. It would only cause upset if I turned up. Anyway, although I've never called him father, Vittore is my *papà*. It's ironic; I have more Russian blood than Venetian. Of my eight great-grandparents, four were Russian; one was American; only three were Venetian. So I reckon these big paws are my legacy from some long dead Russian farmer. Not like yours. These could belong to an artist.'

He took one of her hands in his, placing a kiss in her palm. The innocent gesture sent an outrageous pang of desire through her, honey sweet and sharp as a skewer.

He lifted his face and their eyes met. Then he stroked her hair, twining his fingers into the still-damp curls. 'It's nearly dry; your clothes must be too. So, Anna, would you like to get dressed and I'll walk you home, or…?'

He did not finish the question, which hung in the air like gossamer. Instead he kissed her. They had kissed dozens of times before, in the way that friends do kiss – the swift brush of lips against a cheek. This first kiss on the mouth was as chaste as a child's kiss; their lips met briefly, lightly: a very gentle kiss.

There was still time to go back: time to scuttle away to her own bed; time to test the veracity of his intention to leave Caterina; to not do the thing that would mean being in thrall to him for the rest of her life.

But instead she shook her head ever so slightly, so he kissed her again, not so gently this time, and she knew that there could be no going back. It was imperative that she stay. Tonight might be her only chance. Tomorrow he might be back in Caterina's arms.

Another kiss and the lizard flicker of his tongue. Through the taste of coffee and grappa she detected mint.

'You've cheated,' she said. 'You've brushed your teeth. That's not fair.'

'I do happen to have a spare toothbrush. Brand new. But you do realise that if I let you use it, you're going to have to stay the night.'

'That's blackmail.' She took a deep breath, throwing caution to the wind. 'But I was rather hoping you'd want me to.'

'You're sure, Anna?'

'Oh, yes.'

She traced the line of his upper lip with her finger and thrust her hand into his hair, pushing it back from his forehead. 'I've longed so long to do that.'

'What?'

'Touch you.' She kissed his mouth. 'Taste you.'

He buried his face in her hair, kissing her neck and throat as one hand delved into the folds of the bathrobe. His fingers brushed over her breast and came to rest on her hip. The robe lost its battle to stay tied. One of her legs was bent uncomfortably beneath her and, as she moved, the leather sofa emitted a loud rasping sound of the sort not considered quite polite.

'What an uncouth sofa, you have,' she said as they both collapsed into giggles. 'I hope you don't think that was me.'

'Not for a second, but I didn't buy the furniture with this in mind,' he said. 'Come on, come to bed.'

They got to their feet, ungainly and suddenly rather shy. She pulled the gaping bathrobe round herself.

'Don't cover yourself,' he said, stepping back and looking at her. 'You're beautiful.'

And she believed him. She wasn't, she knew that. But she believed he thought so, and that was all that mattered. Pressing herself against him, she could feel his tumescence through the soft fabric of the jogging suit. She looked down.

He smiled. 'Look, do I need to use anything, because I don't have any…'

'No, no,' she said, grateful for the little coil of metal nestling in her womb. 'It's fine.'

And so he took her by the hand and led her towards the bed. They cast off their single layers of clothing and looked with absurd delight at each other; touched by the vulnerability of the other's nakedness but at the same time driven towards the erotic fusion of that flesh. The sheets were cool and smooth and smelt only of recent laundering, and no long golden hairs shimmered accusingly on the pillow. And Anna quite, or nearly, forgot about the little case lurking beneath the bed; the bed on which their bodies, conjoined at last, moved with a gentle and then urgent rhythm and finally were still. They lay entwined and splayed, replete and congealed in the damp aftermath of that most ridiculous and yet most sublime of human activities, wordlessly marvelling at the miracle of what they had just done, drunk with the aphrodisiac taste of each other's skin. Her hands travelled the length of his back, resting on his buttocks and she pressed him into her, tightening herself around him; an unspoken encouragement for him to stay bonded to her.

Eventually, he shifted his weight, and looking down at her said, 'Your first time in Venice.'

It was a statement, rather than a question. She nodded and wanted to tell him it had felt like the first time ever – as if no one else had ever touched her before. Reluctantly their bodies disengaged and then they began to talk, in the way of newly minted lovers, and to explore each other with fingers and mouths, revelling in the discovery of new found lands.

She felt him begin to harden again and briefly touching him said, 'Hello, what's this? You realise I haven't had my bribe yet – my toothbrush.'

'Later,' he said and then, unable to hide a boyish smugness, 'Unless you have any objection I think I am up to a repeat performance, and this time, if you are a very lucky girl, it may last a little longer. But if you'd rather get up and clean your teeth…'

'I suppose I ought to check if it really was as nice as I thought it was,' she said, as woozy with desire, she shifted her position to accommodate the object of his pride.

'I think, my darling,' he said, sliding into her and beginning to gently thrust, 'that "nice" is a definite understatement.'

And so they made love again: slowly and tenderly as they attuned themselves to the other's rhythms; sometimes stopping and waiting, whispering endearments, kissing and stroking, they shied away from the precipice for as long as possible, until, by an unspoken, mutual accord when they knew it was impossible to hold back any longer their bodies moved hard and fervently, until they exploded into each other, gasping with the impossible delight of it. Then Anna, who with other lovers had found pleasure but always remained earthbound, felt for the first time something that she supposed was a taste of ecstasy. She knew, afterwards, looking into his sleeping face that it was not just what he did that gave her so much joy, but the simple fact of who he was. He was her soul mate: her other half, the love of her life, for now, forever, and always. She anointed his slumbering eyes with a kiss, and fell asleep.

Raffi has taken her skiing, as he said he would. She flies across the snow, screaming in delight, exhilarated beyond belief. And then she is falling. For a few seconds everything is a jumble of colour as she sinks into a soft, white drift, quite unhurt. The snow is very cold on her cheek.

She awoke with a start, her mind scrabbling to put the pieces together. Sun sliced through the shutters and she saw Raffi smiling down at her. He held a glass of chilled orange juice to her face.

'Here,' he said, producing a small object with a flourish. 'A present for you.'

She squinted through sleep-fugged eyes. 'My toothbrush! Wow, you really know how to spoil a girl, don't you?'

'Absolutely. And it'll last longer than flowers. But don't you dare take it away with you. You'll need it tonight.'

'Tonight?'

'Tonight we will eat at my friend Roberto's restaurant and then we will come back here and make love, and tomorrow, when we wake up, we'll make love again, and then we'll have lunch somewhere, in the country perhaps, and then come back here and...' The sheet had slipped down and his mouth found her breast. His voice was muffled but she guessed tomorrow afternoon's activities included making love. He came up for air.

'And tomorrow night we can have a quiet evening in and...'

'Make love? God, Raffi, by Monday I won't be able to walk!'

'That could be a problem. I know...we'll get Paulo from the restaurant downstairs to send us up food.'

'And what about now?' she asked, wanting him again.

'Now, I must shower and go to work.'

'On Saturday?'

'A client who couldn't make it during the week is coming in specially. I'll be late as it is. And this afternoon.' He drew away from her. 'I'll meet Caterina and tell her it's over.'

The breath caught in her throat, all her desire fading at the mention of Caterina's name. They sat quietly for a few seconds, contemplating the day ahead. Tentatively she raised her hand and stroked his cheek. 'I'm sorry. I hope it's not too horrible.'

'It probably will be, but it's been coming for a long time. And without me she can live the life she wants in Milan. She'll meet someone else. It's her pride that'll hurt more than anything. Now, I really must get ready.'

'Shall I make coffee?'

'Please. Here, wear this. You look better in it than me.' And he stripped off his bathrobe, and padded naked to the shower, casting a mischievous glance over his shoulder, confident and easy in his lean, young skin.

A little later, while drinking their coffee, he handed her a card bearing the name of a restaurant near the Rialto.

'Meet me there at seven. Stay here as long as you like. Just slam the door behind you when you leave.'

'OK. Good luck.'

He held her very close, and his kiss was very sweet and very deep, but she could sense his disquiet. Then, holding her at arm's length, he began to speak. 'I...'

Go on, she willed him. *Say it. I will if you do.* Those three tiny words: they were overused to the point of tawdriness, demeaned in bad songs and soured in the mouths of liars, but on his lips she felt they would possess the sanctity of a sacrament. He would not, she knew, renege on their implicit promise. She was glad he had not said them last night as they tumbled in happy abandon. Their utterance would mean more in the cold light of day than in the throes of passion. Perhaps something changed his mind; perhaps he never intended to say them, but as he stroked her hair he said, 'You are very special. This is very special.'

She was only slightly disappointed; there was time enough for the L word.

After he left, she dressed but did not shower, wanting to keep the touch and smell of him on her body. She cleaned her teeth and wondered what to do with the toothbrush; to hang it next to his seemed somehow too proprietorial, so she laid it on the side of the basin, speculating about the whereabouts of Caterina's things, but resisting the temptation to open the bathroom cabinet. Then she washed up and made the bed. Bending down to smooth the counterpane, she caught sight of the suitcase. The end of the bright scarf, trapped outside, trailed on the floor.

She knew she should not do it, but could not stop herself. Pulling the case towards her she yanked it open and saw the pile of magazines, a white cotton nightdress, a packet of tampons, a pink jumper in a plastic bag and curled on top, a crumpled silk bra and pants. The other woman's perfume wafted up in silent reproof.

She imagined the previous evening: Caterina, arriving from Milan in her natty business suit. She would have stowed it in the wardrobe, where it must still hang, cuddling up to Raffi's clothes. Then she would have showered and changed into fresh underwear before squeezing into the pink confection, leaving the bra and pants she had worn throughout the day on the bed, perhaps intending to rinse them out when she returned.

Looking at these most intimate possessions, Anna felt a sudden, sad empathy with Caterina. Would Raffi gather up the girl's other belongings: her clothes, shampoo, face cream – toothbrush? Stuff them in the case? When Caterina saw him with it, would she guess that it was all over? She wondered what Chris had done with the few things she had left at his flat, and then thought about the day when Raffi might be making a collection of her own piteous possessions, in anticipation of returning them.

'It's your own fault,' she whispered, quietly admonishing the case's absent owner. 'You could have kept him if you'd wanted.'

She shoved the case back under the bed. *Anyway*, she thought, taking one last look around the flat, *it might be me. I might be the one to walk away. And there again, perhaps, just perhaps, neither of us will walk away. Perhaps...*and she smiled, imagining all the bauble-bright possibilities the future may hold.

As she walked out into the apple-crisp air her misgivings vanished. On a day that felt incandescent with hope, everything seemed possible. The lions guarding the Arsenale regarded her with benevolent amusement, their stony faces wearing complicit smiles, as if to say, 'We know what you've been doing, young lady.'

'Bye bye, boys. See you tonight,' she said out loud, and turning to leave, could have sworn she saw a whisker quiver and an ear twitch.

It was a day of iridescent loveliness, mild but rain-washed. Last night's downpour, now quite melted away, had left mirrors of water that reflected a forget-me-not blue sky. The canals sparkled and the city glowed with colour. Gaudy geraniums still cascaded from window boxes, and the last of summer's butterflies flitted from hidden gardens, glutting themselves on nectar. In Campo Zanipolo, Colleoni, a long dead *condottiere* immortalised in bronze, surveyed her with a gentle expression, his bellicose features softened. She fancied that even San Michele had thrown off its funereal gloom and gleamed, celebration-cake-pretty. People buying flowers along the Fondamenta Nuove chatted and laughed, as though they were travelling to the island cemetery for a party, rather than to visit the graves of their dear, departed ones.

When she reached the Campo dell'Abbazia, she paused to look across the Canale de la Misericordia at the tottering buildings, rising like glorious cliffs from the water. A boat chugged by, a dog on its prow sniffing the wind. Catching sight of her, it wagged its tail, comic-book face split by a toothy grin. With happiness shimmering around her, she went into the church.

Her Madonna, confined within the ornate rectangle of the incongruous Victorian frame, regarded her lost companion with a barely concealed smile. Looking at the eyes, discoloured by centuries of candle smoke, Anna knew it was purely her imagination, but they appeared a little brighter than usual.

She had long ago ceased to regard the painting as an image of the mother of God. This was a young woman, who had walked the *calli* and *campi* of Venice, as corporal as herself. She held a baby, but had she ever tasted the lychee sweetness of physical love? Lain hot and sticky in the warmth of a Venetian night, her legs wetly entwined with those of her lover? Lover: Anna tried the word out, rolling it around her mouth like a sugarplum. In England, to refer to one's lover would sound pretentious, but here in Venice it seemed perfectly natural.

She said goodbye to the picture, hoping that the unknown girl had, during her years in the sun, experienced the soaring joy that now lifted her own life above the ordinary dust of existence.

The rest of her day was spent in a happy muss of self-pampering and daydreaming, only popping out to the Strada Nuova, to spend far more than was sensible on two sets of lacy underwear. Back at the flat, she half expected a call from Raffi telling her the outcome of his meeting with Caterina, but having heard nothing, she assumed no news was good news.

The restaurant where they had agreed to meet was close to the Rialto, nestling in a corner of a tiny courtyard, near an elaborately carved twelfth century arch, that Will had once told her was reputed to be part of Marco Polo's house. The *trattoria* took its name from the explorer's account of his travels – Il Milion. When she arrived, a few minutes before the agreed hour of seven, she was a little surprised that Raffi had not made a reservation, but Roberto, the owner, must have been told that she had mentioned the name Anzelieri, because he immediately came out of the kitchen to greet her.

'*Buono sera, signorina*,' he said, bowing slightly. 'Are you dining with *signor* Vittore or Raffi?' His voice was as rich as hot chocolate.

'Raffi,' she replied, grinning.

Being a consummate professional, if Roberto was surprised at his friend dining with a woman other than Caterina, he gave no indication of this, but simply asked one of his staff to bring her a glass of *prosecco*. Anna settled back, sipping her drink, relaxed and happy.

Half an hour later, when Raffi had not appeared she was feeling less serene. Roberto offered her another glass of *prosecco,* which she gratefully accepted. He then diplomatically suggested that possibly she had got the incorrect hour. Perhaps Raffi meant eight, not seven.

Eight o'clock came and went. Anna asked if she could use their phone. Roberto consented with kindly solicitude. The phone rang and rang and rang. She imagined it echoing off the walls in Raffi's empty flat. Embarrassed to hold on any longer she returned to her seat, deciding to wait another half hour. Shortly before eight-thirty Roberto approached her again.

'Perhaps you have the wrong date,' he suggested. 'It really would not be like Raffi to miss a…an appointment. You must be hungry by now. Would you like a little plate of something – on the house?'

Anna glanced at the food being served to the other diners; it looked delicious but the thought of eating sickened her. Swallowing her nausea and desperate to get away, she gathered up her things. 'I'm sure you're right. Silly me. He probably meant next Saturday.'

'I'm sure he did,' replied Roberto. 'We'll look forward to seeing you then, *signorina.*'

Standing outside in the now chilly night, Anna had no idea what to do. Going back to her flat was unthinkable, so she began to walk.

When she reached the Arsenale, Raffi's apartment was in total darkness. She was not sure whether to be relieved by this or not. What would she have done had there been light blazing from the windows? Beaten on the door like a fugitive demanding sanctuary? Exhaustion overcame her. Wearily she turned away and caught a *vaporetto* home.

Back in the flat she phoned Raffi once more. Still no reply. Reluctantly, before it got too late, she rang Ca' Melisa. Rosina answered. With studied casualness Anna asked if Raffi were there. No, came the reply. They had not heard from him for a few days. But he and Caterina were coming round for lunch tomorrow. Did Anna want to leave a message?

'No thanks, it's nothing urgent,' she said and hung up.

She began to consider all the awful possibilities. He might have been involved in a car crash; a piece of scaffolding could have fallen at a building site; he may have been taken sick. But then, she reasoned, Rosina would have known of any misfortune. No – the most likely explanation was that he had wavered and

Caterina had persuaded him to stay. They were together somewhere, honeying and making love. She had been abandoned; it was over before it had even begun.

Anna bowed her head in despair and began to weep. She went into the kitchen and grabbed the first bottle that came to hand. Uncorking it, she started to drink, without noticing that it was the *fragolino* from Fabrizio's estate, intended for a special occasion.

Venice: July 1516

The child she carries was conceived nearly three months ago. She knows this for sure because there has been just the one time. At first she prayed that her courses had ceased for another reason, but now there is no denying the signs.

'Is it Enrico's?' I ask, and she nods.

I have not seen the man for weeks. He is with his ships somewhere, making money. So I assume, correctly, that he does not know about the babe growing inside her. There are a hundred questions I wish to ask, but I sit quietly, her small hand clasped in mine, waiting for her to tell me in her own time.

'I could not bear the thought of living in the Ghetto…of being locked up. But neither could I imagine how to avoid it. Enrico is the only person I know with wealth and power, and I hoped he might help. He has such…such authority, such strength.'

Such ruthlessness, such menace, I think, and realise that I knew all along, that despite his creamy words and show of respect, he is a profligate like his father.

'There are rumours that some noble families may take their personal physicians into their households, despite them being Jewish,' she says. 'I thought if I could persuade Enrico to install my father in his family's home…'

I have heard no such rumours. The church is already suspicious of Jewish doctors, purporting that in extremis they prevent patients receiving the last rites. I cannot believe that Jews living in Christian households would be tolerated, however great the family. Debra's hopes are akin to clutching at straws.

'I did not really expect him to be at the house,' she continues. 'But he was. I made an excuse for my call. I asked to see the painting in its finished state.'

I can only imagine Enrico's delight when Debra arrived, unaccompanied, unprotected. He must have felt like the cat when a poor mouse scampers to sit between its paws.

'He has it there, still, you know. In one of the storerooms in the *androne*, ready to take to his father. Then he told me that he could not bear to be parted from it; from the image of me. He stroked my face, and praised my beauty. He was very gentle, but I am not such a fool. I knew where it was leading. But I was tempted, for I thought that if he made me his mistress it would be a way to leave the Ghetto. Then I imagined the shame, and I knew I could not live with the dishonour or the pain it would cause my father. So I pulled away from his embrace and I told him the truth. About who I am.'

Only now does she begin to weep. 'It was as though my words changed him into a different person; all I could see in his eyes was hate. He berated my people in the vilest manner, saying that he was angry because his house is so close to where all the filthy Jews are confined, and that he feared we may contaminate the very air. I knew then that he would never help me, and all I wanted was to go back to my father in the Ghetto, and even the man who has been chosen for my husband, for they are of my blood, and will love and protect me. I realised I had been foolish and ungrateful, so I apologised for wasting his time and said I must leave. But he called me a lying whore and demanded how I dared to presume to sit for Saint Catherine. Then he barred my way, and told me that I may only leave after I had made payment for my lies and deceitfulness.'

I have no need to ask what form this payment took. Nevertheless I say, 'He forced you?'

She nods. 'I screamed for help, but there was no one to hear me. Whilst the house is being rebuilt he keeps no servants. But he still gagged me…I tried to stop him but he is so strong, and he swore that if I fought him he would put such marks on my face that I would not be able to keep my shame secret. So I kept still and, and…let him do what he wanted. And prayed for it to be over. He kept me there a long time,' she adds, burying her face in her hands.

My anger boils to think all this happened just minutes from my own home. Why did she not ask me to accompany her? He would not have been able to overcome two of us. I try to comfort her. 'Debra, you bear no shame. The guilt is all his.'

She shakes her head, rejecting my words. 'He warned me to hold my tongue and assured me that if I did speak out, no one would believe me. It would be his word against mine, and who would countenance the ravings of a Jewish slut – a slut who has committed a grave sin by assuming the guise of a Saint? He said that you too, and *maestro* Cima would be implicated.'

I do not know about the last threat, but I do know that it is always the woman who bears the shame of a bastard child; my platitudes are foolish and hollow. Had he beaten her face to a pulp she might have been believed, but with no marks of violence upon her it will be assumed she was complicit in the act. And now, months later, there is no possibility of her obtaining redress, even with his child in her belly.

What will happen I cannot guess. A Christian girl might be dispatched to a convent, and the child sent to the House of the Innocents. Then, after a suitable period spent in expiating for her sins she may be married to a low status man, willing to overlook her loss of honour for the cash prize of her dowry. Less fortunate are those poor souls who meet a violent end at the hands of an enraged father or brother. And there are some who, rather than live with their shame, take their own life. Many turn to prostitution. It is rare indeed for a dishonoured girl to be kept in the bosom of the family. And this is why we Venetian maids are so mindful of our chastity, for little mercy is shown to those who are careless of it.

But I have no idea what fate awaits a Jewish girl. *Papà* once told me that there are no Jewish whores in Venice. If a Hebrew woman finds herself widowed or orphaned, the community will care for her so that she is not forced to sell her body in order to put food into her mouth. I pray that the treatment meted out to an unmarried girl, who is with child, may be as merciful.

'When will you tell your father?'

'I will not. I cannot.'

Debra must know that even if she manages to conceal her swelling body with tighter and tighter binding, the child will come screaming into the world soon enough; she will not be able to conceal that. Indeed, I am surprised that Jakob has not already guessed, for although childbirth is the province of midwives, rather than physicians, he must be familiar with the signs. But perhaps he cannot see what is under his very nose.

'Debra, you must tell him. You have no choice.'

'Oh, but I do, Ginevra,' she replies.

'No, you cannot,' I whisper. 'It is a sin, a crime.'

'I will not bear this child. Its father is evil. What sort of monster will it be?'

'No, Debra, this is a baby. An innocent. Maybe a little girl. She cannot help what her father is.'

For a second I see her waiver. Then hate carves her features into a parody of her sweet face, as she says, 'No, I would rather die. Every time I looked down at it I would see those cat's eyes of his. But it is more than that; more than what I feel, or what will happen to me. I know my father would not rest until he discovered the man responsible. I do believe that he is capable of killing Enrico, and as much as I would wish him dead, I will not have *papà* swing at the end of a rope, mutilated and beaten because of my sins. And can you imagine the reprisals against my people if a Jew murdered the son of such a powerful man? I will not bear the guilt of that.'

I know that *Papà* is routinely asked for cordials to ease the flow of menstrual blood by those whose courses do not come, for women of all classes will resort to anything to rid themselves of an unwanted child. Few methods work, and those

264

that do, are fraught with dangers. I once saw the result of such desperate measures.

We were summoned to the bedside of a fifteen-year-old girl – the daughter of a notary. Directly *papà* perceived what ailed her, he hustled me from the room, but not before I smelt the stink of putrefaction, as though she were already rotting. *Papà* later told me the cause of her ills, and explained that her body was exacting a revenge upon itself in response to the violation of its natural humours. This had caused a great infection in the womb, so entrenched that even the most efficacious of medicine was rendered useless. Whether she had procured the abortion herself, or had it forced upon her, we never knew. I believe she died shortly after.

I begin to warn Debra, but she brushes aside my words and says, 'I have been told of someone who will help me.'

'Who? Who told you?'

'I asked a woman…one of the street women.'

I am speechless. No respectable girl would speak to these purveyors of flesh. We stick our noses in the air and walk by them as though they are no more than turds on the ground. She sees my expression and continues, 'She was kind to me.'

Kind or not, I am surprised that anyone should divulge such a person's name, for if apprehended the crime merits severe punishment. However, it is said that a blind eye is generally turned, for without the curtailment of unwanted infants, there would be an even greater burden upon the state coffers. Occasionally, in order to satisfy public morals, an example is made of someone reckless enough to get caught. They invariably pay with the loss of a hand.

And then she asks me the question I have been dreading, 'Please, Gina, will you come with me?'

What can I do? At first I refuse: I argue that it is a sin against my God, and her God, and nature too. That it is a crime for which we could be punished in this world and the next. My arguments are to no avail, and as I plead, I ache with guilt, for it is my doing: that she sat for the Saint's picture; that she met Enrico. But I know that if I do not accompany her, she will go anyway, and it is an ordeal I cannot let her face alone. So I agree, taking comfort in the fact that she has yet to feel the child quicken, for this may mean that it does not, as yet, possess a soul and therefore, surely, the crime will be less?

The woman, whose name is Dianora, dwells in the far south-west of the city, an area populated by fishermen and their families. We make the journey on foot, keeping for as long as possible to the familiar territory of "our" side of the city, crossing the Canale Grande by *traghetto* at San Samuele. Some of the passengers look askance at Debra, for she is wearing the distinctive yellow hat that marks her out as a Jew. Before the days of the Ghetto confinement she defied this requirement, but regulations have tightened of late so she cannot risk being apprehended. For my part, I am heavily veiled and, to my shame, sit apart from her. I want no one to witness my part in this vile escapade.

Once on dry land, we pass by the Church of the Carmini, where my favourite painting by Giambattista hangs. It is an Adoration of the Shepherds – the most beautiful and tender representation of the subject that one will ever see. At any other time I would take Debra into the church, but not today. Today it is not appropriate to look upon a picture of the holy mother praying in front of her infant son. But I make a promise to myself that whatever the outcome of this day, I will return to the Carmini, and make my prayers to the Virgin.

The place we seek is near the Church of San Nicolò dei Mendicoli. I have never visited it, so I must ask for directions several times. As we approach our destination, the ground becomes increasingly filthy, and I am grateful for the thick-soled pattens that prevent my skirts trailing in the noisome mess of excrement and fish innards. At last, we enter a small, unpaved courtyard skirted by tiny, one-storey houses. In the doorways women sit on low stools, laughing and gossiping. It is a hot day and they are dressed only in grimy shifts. Their wide-spread legs are bare to the knees, and their breasts sway beneath the sweat soaked fabric, as they gut fish after fish.

As we approach, their joviality withers and they regard us with silent curiosity. Even the half-naked children capering in the filth stop their games. Then a sharp-faced little girl, who is mending a net, runs into one of the cottages. Almost at once, a woman comes out. She is as rodent-faced as her daughter, but is respectably attired. Although her dress is old and patched, it appears clean, and her hair is tucked into a neat cap.

She and Debra stare at one another – two women from such different worlds brought together by the thing that unites all women.

'Are you Dianora?' Debra asks at last.

The woman nods. 'I was told to expect you. Come inside and tell me how I can help.'

At least, that is what I think she says. People in this part of the city speak with a strong *nicoloto* accent, to which my ear is unaccustomed.

The house is almost totally devoid of furnishings and is very dark, with shutters drawn over glassless windows. A scrawny cat, hunched by the door, regards us with vicious yellow eyes and hisses, thinking we wish to purloin its dinner of fish guts. It is oppressively hot, for despite the warmth of the day, a fire burns in a hollowed out hearth in the middle of the room. I realise that this is the only method these people have of cooking their food, which judging by the smell, consists of fried fish and little else. Debra looks as though she is about to gag from the stench, but manages to remain calm as she and Dianora discuss, in veiled words, what must be done. I pray that we will be asked to come back next week, or tomorrow, by which time, God willing, she may have changed her mind. But no…Dianora is beckoning Debra to follow her into what I suspect is the only other room this humble dwelling boasts – the room in which the whole family sleep.

As they go, Debra flashes me a look of such terror that I am tempted to accompany her, but I am too afraid to do so, and I know she would not wish me to witness her indignity. However, I have brought one thing to help; a bag of clean rags that I use myself each month. Although Dianora accepts them, she assures me that they are unlikely to be needed, for Debra will bleed only a little, and feel but small discomfort. I know this to be a fiction, for how will the tiny body growing in my friend's womb disappear, if not in a flood of blood and pain. But when she looks at me with her rat's eyes, I sense that, despite the loathsome nature of her calling, she is not a wicked woman. She is lying, of course, but this is her way of calming Debra's fears.

They leave me, and through a curtain that serves as a door, I hear the chink of coins. Then there is the rustle of clothing and Dianora's soft muttering. Long moments pass. I catch the sound of a shuddering intake of breath and a stifled cry. No longer can I bear to stay in the fetid little house, and I stumble outside into the sunshine.

The women again stare at me, but do not cease labouring. Their carousing grows louder and louder, their voices putting me in mind of seagulls fighting over dead crabs. Perhaps they make such a clamour so as to disguise screams that may sound from their neighbour's house. The thought sickens me and I feel myself sway. Dianora's daughter, catching sight of my distress, indicates one of the low stools. I sink onto it and try to imagine that I am somewhere else, anywhere but here…and I wait.

It is over sooner than I anticipate, and hearing the sound of footsteps, I spring up and see Debra. She is supported in Dianora's meaty arms and her face is wet with sweat, or tears. Her lips are chalky pale but on her cheeks there are two livid spots of colour.

'I fear I will be unable to walk home,' she says. 'For a small payment, Dianora's brother will row us back.'

The little girl scuttles away to summon her uncle, and by taking an arm each, Dianora and I half carry, half drag Debra to the waterside. Here, a huge man wordlessly lifts Debra into his small craft, which stinks of its owner's livelihood.

Rather than take us via the small waterways and along the Canale Grande, he rows around the perimeter of the city. The sun is high and its merciless heat claws through my veil. Debra's face too, is covered, but I can tell by her laboured breathing and the way she shifts in her seat that she is in pain. I long for her to be safely home.

At last we reach the Ghetto, and as Debra is helped out of the boat, I see a dark stain on the back of her dress. I remember then that Dianora did not return the rags to me. Possibly she has stolen them, but I think it likelier that she has swaddled some around her patient. Debra must be bleeding heavily.

We cross the bridge into the Ghetto. I intend to escort her home, but she stops me. 'Do not come any further. Ginevra, believe me, no one could have been a better friend than you, but you must not be implicated in this deed. Please go, now, before anyone sees you. I promise I will send word to you how I fare. And do not worry on my behalf, dear friend. All will be well.'

I try to protest but she will not be moved, and coward that I am, I let her stumble away, alone. Just before she is swallowed up by one of the sombre buildings, she turns and waves. Then she is gone.

Three days pass. Still there is no word from her. So with a great fear in my heart, I go to the Ghetto. I have no notion how to find Debra, but hardly have I progressed a few steps when a small boy cannons into me. He is calling to his friend in what I realise is Veneziano, so I grab hold of his scrawny shoulders, demanding if he knows where Doctor Jakob Solomon resides? He is a handsome little fellow with bright sparkly eyes, but as soon as he hears my question, a shadow passes across his face.

'The Doctor lives there.' And he points vaguely. 'But you will not find him at home. He is burying his daughter.'

'What?'

He repeats the words. To my surprise, I do not faint; I do not weep and wail, or berate the little harbinger of such bad news, but rather, my mind plays tricks and I find myself thinking: *It must be some other daughter of Jakob's. Another girl that he has been hiding away all these years. It cannot be my Debra whom I only saw three days ago, who stood where we now stand, alive and warm...it cannot be...*

'How did she die?' I ask.

He shrugs, eager to be back with his friends and away from this nosy gentile.

'A sudden and fierce fever, so I heard,' he replies. 'She was a very pretty lady,' he adds, as if this makes it better, and then a little frown appears and he asks, 'Are you ill? Shall I fetch my mother?'

'No, thank you. I am quite well.'

And it is true – I am well. I can breathe; my heart beats strongly; I can see and hear and feel the warm sun, but not so very far away, they are shovelling earth onto the face of my dearest friend, who will never again hear a bird sing, or feel a summer breeze kiss her cheek. It is my fault that she is laid in the cold grave and there is no one – not my husband, or my father, to whom I can confess. I think Jakob too, harbours a secret, for he must have guessed the cause of his daughter's affliction, but has chosen to conceal its shameful origin.

In a daze of grief, I stumble home. Although my part in Debra's tragedy must remain unspoken of, my father has to be told of her death. I dread imparting the news, for he has known Debra all her life and loves her as one of his kin. I find him in his workshop with Antonio, the young man who is now his assistant. They are deep in conversation, discussing what conclusions may be gleaned from the colour of a man's urine. Antonio gives me a shy smile. I think he is somewhat in awe of me. Normally I treat him kindly but today I have no time for niceties and ask if I may have a word in private with my father.

I speak quickly, inventing a story about how I heard a rumour at the market, and that upon enquiring at the gates of the Ghetto, it was confirmed that Debra had died.

'Oh, oh. Poor, poor Jakob.' I see the tears begin to form in *papà's* milky eyes, and he holds his arms out to me. In a corner of the room, Cesare throws back his little head and howls as we, father and daughter, weep together.

Hours later, when Giacomo returns from his workshop, he finds us still sitting thus, although we are now calm and dry-eyed. Having recovered a little from the shock, *papà* is pondering whether to call on Jakob. We both know what his old friend will be doing. He will be sitting Shiva for his daughter, wearing torn garments. His friends will bring food, and will try to ease his sorrow by reciting the Kaddish – the memorial prayer for the dead.

It is only right that *papà* should be there, so I ask Giacomo to accompany him. I make my excuses, for Jakob must know me to have been the receptacle of all Debra's secrets, and I cannot bear to think of his accusing eyes – or even worse, his interrogation. But when they return, it is obvious that Jakob has not divulged the details of Debra's death to even my father. Through my grief I feel relief for this deliverance. I will, at least, be spared their reproach.

A Little Brief Authority

Anna finished the bottle of *fragolino* and fell asleep sometime in the early hours. Although her dreams were a disturbing jumble, signifying nothing, every time she felt herself rising to the surface she forced herself back into the depths. No dream could be worse than the reality she would face when she fully woke, even this latest nightmare full of clanging bells.

She was catapulted from sleep by the realisation that the cacophony was actually the doorbell. As she staggered to her feet, it stopped. Seized by panic she ran onto the terrace.

'Hallo,' she cried, leaning over the balcony wall.

'Anna,' came a familiar voice and she saw Raffi on the *fondamenta* below. 'Can I come up – please? I need to explain.'

Pulling on her dressing gown, she ran to the entry-phone. Waiting for him to climb the stairs, she caught sight of herself in the mirror. She looked as dreadful as she felt. Her eyes were red and swollen, there were black smudges of make-up on her cheeks and her skin was sallow and blotchy.

Hearing his footsteps becoming louder, her despair turned to anger. Then she saw him. His clothes were crumpled, as though he had slept in them; there were dark circles under his bloodshot eyes; he was unshaven and as they embraced, she smelt sweat.

'You look all in. Sit down and I'll make some tea.'

'That would be good.'

He collapsed onto the sofa. Anna made the drink, waiting for him to speak. He was so quiet she thought he had fallen asleep.

'So where were you?' she asked.

'It's Caterina…' He stopped, tears welling in his eyes.

Anna sank down next to him. 'What's happened?'

He continued in a voice slurred with exhaustion, 'She was involved in an accident on Friday. A car knocked her down.'

'Jesus. Is she…?'

'In a coma. It's fifty-fifty whether she'll regain consciousness, and even if she does, they don't know if there's brain damage. There's damage to her spine too. She…she' The words fractured into sobs. Anna grabbed his hands, feeling the hot splash of his tears. 'She may not be able to walk again. It's my fault. I should have taken her home, made sure she was safe. I knew she was in a state.'

And then you wouldn't have spent the night with me, she thought. *Are you regretting that too?*

'Do they know what happened?'

'It must have been just after she left Patrizia's. There were witnesses who saw her step right out in front of the car.'

'Was it hit and run?'

'No, the driver stopped straightaway; he's an elderly, respectable man: he wasn't speeding and he hadn't been drinking. It was obviously Caterina's fault. They took her to the hospital on the Lido, but transferred her to the Ospedale here yesterday morning.'

'And no one thought to tell you on Friday night?'

'No one knew who she was. Do you remember me saying she'd left her keys to my place in Milan? She must have forgotten her identity card too. It was sheer chance that a duty police officer at the Ospedale recognised her because he knows Silvio – her father. You know he's a carabinieri officer?'

'Yes. So they contacted him?'

'Eventually – he was at his rowing club all afternoon. He rang me at about five o'clock, but I was out…shopping in the via Garabaldi. I'd been trying to call Caterina all day… from the office…as soon as I got home. I left a couple of messages on the answerphone, but I just assumed she was refusing to pick up. In the end I walked round to their apartment. No one was there, of course, so I came home. I was actually quite relieved…I thought perhaps she'd given up on me and gone back to Milano. I was on my way out of the door when Silvio rang again and told me the news. I did try calling you before I went to the hospital…at about six-thirty.'

'You'd have just missed me,' said Anna, remembering how unnecessarily early she had left home.

'When I got to the Ospedale I rang the restaurant. But the line was engaged and then I went in to see Caterina, and…and, I'm sorry…I forgot about everything else when I saw her.' His voice cracked.

'I understand,' Anna whispered, imagining the broken body, hooked to drips and bleeping monitors. 'It's OK.'

'No, no, it's not. I should have found a way to let you know. But I'd left my address book with your number in it at home. I suppose I could have called Vittore and asked him for it, but my mind didn't seem to be working very well. I'm sorry.'

'It doesn't matter,' she reiterated.

He did not seem to hear her. 'And I was having to contend with Caterina's father. He was…furious with me.'

'Why?'

'He blames me. He kept demanding why the fuck did I let Caterina go home by herself?'

Anna said nothing. There seemed no point in making the observation that Caterina was, after all, a grown woman; that she had been the one to flounce out, and that it had only been a little after nine.

'And I don't know what rumours he's picked up, but he was going on about this "other woman" I had in tow. I can't imagine Caterina saying anything to him about you but...'

But...Anna knew as well as he, that gossip ran through Venice like an infection: he could have heard the tittle-tattle from anyone. Raffi was, in the other man's mind, culpable – guilty of both neglect and infidelity. Listening to him, Anna realised that, in his fragile state, Raffi believed this too.

'Raffi, it's not your fault,' she said.

But guilt had distanced him from her and he stood, suddenly brusque and business-like. 'I'm sorry. I've got to go. I need to shower and change and get back to the hospital. The next forty-eight hours are critical. I have to be there, in case...'

She nodded, hating it but understanding. For an awful moment she thought he was not going to kiss her goodbye, but then he wrapped his arms round her and their lips met. The kiss seemed to bring him back to her a little.

'Whatever happens,' he said. 'This makes no difference to us.'

Relief washed over her. 'Just let me know what's happening, OK.'

The next day, when Raffi again broke his vigil from Caterina's bedside, he was so obviously exhausted that Anna led him into her room where he fell onto her bed, fully dressed, and immediately slept. She watched him slumber, seeing the rapid movement of his eyes under closed lids and wondered of what he dreamt. When he awoke she brought him coffee, and stretching her body alongside his, cradled him in her arms. She felt him trying to respond, but the thought of Caterina, lying in hospital, hung between them like a greasy sheet, smothering all his desire for her.

In the afternoon, Izzy returned from Ravenna.

'Well, how was your weekend?' was the first thing she asked. 'Was Raffi at Patrizia's?'

Anna nodded and their eyes met. She heard the sharp intake of breath as Izzy guessed.

'Oh my God. It's happened hasn't it? You've done the deed at last. Well, how was it? Did the earth move? What did you do with Caterina? Chuck her in a canal?' And then seeing Anna's face. 'What's wrong, angel? Don't tell me, after all that, he's crap in bed.'

'No,' yelled Anna before Izzy could hypothesize further. 'It was fine: it was more than fine...it was...' and she related the whole story.

Duly chastened, Izzy listened until Anna had finished.

'Shit,' she said. 'Poor cow. I knew we wanted her out of the way, but in Milan would have done, not in a bloody coma. Well, whatever happens, you're just going to have to be patient. If she pulls through he's not going to dump her as soon as she's on the mend. He's not that sort of bloke. Look, at the moment he's shell-shocked, but soon enough he's going to need a lot of TLC. So, you just make sure you're there to give it to him, yeah? If you're willing to wait that long?'

'I'll wait for as long as it takes,' said Anna.

Izzy had a pile of marking to get through, so Anna curled up in her room, trying to read. She soon nodded off, only waking when Will returned from work. Not surprisingly, he knew about Caterina.

She lay, listening to him relate some of the wilder rumours that were circulating about the girl's condition. Then he changed the subject. 'That's not the only thing that happened over the weekend. Someone's nicked Anna's Madonna from the Misericordia.'

'What?' Izzy shrieked. 'You're joking.'

'No, it's true...it's all over today's papers. The painting was there when the sacristan locked up after Saturday Mass, and on Sunday morning it was gone – frame and all. No sign of a break in.'

'Wasn't it alarmed?'

'Apparently not. Look, we'd better tell Anna.'

But Anna was already there, pulling on her shoes. 'I've got to see Vittore. He'll be devastated.'

She found him in his garden, surrounded by the day's newspapers, pretending to read. At his side Rosina was checking menus. Whatever disasters beset their personal lives the arrival of another tour group was imminent, with their hungry mouths and minds.

'I'm so sorry,' she said, not sure to which incident she referred.

Vittore shook his head. 'That poor, poor girl. They came and told me about the painting's disappearance almost at once. And then, just hours later, Raffi broke the news about Caterina. It put everything into perspective. The loss of a work of art is a tragedy, but for such a thing to happen to one's only child. I cannot think what her father is going through.'

Rosina muttered something under her breath. Vittore shushed her, putting his hand on her arm, but she shook him off and stomped into the house.

'Rosina is very angry with Caterina. You see, our boy is tearing himself apart with guilt – for something that is not his fault. You were at Patrizia's – what happened? I do not think he is telling us everything.'

Anna skimmed over the events of the evening. She did not tell him everything either. From the look in his eyes, she suspected he had guessed anyway.

'So what happens about the painting?' she asked, changing the subject. 'Have they any idea who stole it?'

'Well, Angelo was under immediate suspicion, even though he has an alibi. It was his wedding anniversary and his daughter was staying for the weekend. She and his wife swear he never left the apartment. The daughter was sleeping on the sofa and would have been disturbed by anyone leaving. Also, they went out to dinner and Angelo was far too drunk to walk, let alone steal a painting. Of course, this does not completely exonerate him as he could have given his keys to anyone else, but the monks, quite rightly, defended his integrity. Also, it appears the locks have not been changed since the 1930s. Dozens of people could have a key that still works.'

'Presumably whoever's taken it will try and sell it on?' said Anna. 'Or perhaps the thief particularly wanted a painting like that for their collection? It can't just disappear?'

'Unfortunately, that is exactly what can, and probably will happen. I remember a Caravaggio nativity being stolen from a church in Palermo in 1969; even after all these years there has never been any sign of it. You must understand, Anna, that it is extremely rare for an art connoisseur to steal, or to commission a theft. The private collector driven by aesthetics is a myth, as is the lone Raffles type cat burglar. It was most likely a gang – very possibly with Mafia connections. They sometimes steal paintings to use as high value collateral in drugs and arms deals. Pictures are easily transportable and take up little room, but in such cases they are cruelly treated and quickly become so damaged that they cease to have any value.'

'Then what happens to them?'

'Then, my dear, they are destroyed.'

'Destroyed? I can't believe it.'

'Well, there is another possibility. Sometimes pictures are stolen specifically with the intention of stripping away the paint. This leaves a blank canvas that can be used by a forger. If the forgery is later subjected to carbon dating, the age of the canvas will support its authenticity. This explains the theft of so called unimportant works of art from country churches.'

'But no one would do that with a Cima,' protested Anna.

'Ah, but remember, although we believe it to be a Cima, that supposition is unauthenticated.'

'So either way the painting is destroyed? I can't believe I might not see her again – it's like losing a friend.'

Vittore nodded in silent agreement, and as he turned his head, she saw the glint of a tear. Further conversation was curtailed by a babbling stream of Veneziano as Rosina reappeared, her beaming face, and the frequent use of the words "Raffi" and "Caterina", indicating that it was good news. Vittore translated. Raffi had just telephoned: Caterina had opened her eyes; she could move a little and was able to recognise Raffi; she could even tell the doctor how many fingers he held up, and what month it was.

Anna excused herself. As she left, Rosina said, 'If Raffi visit you, tell him to come and see us, yes?'

Anna did not ask why they supposed their nephew should call on her, rather than themselves.

Back at the flat, Izzy had already taken a call from Raffi. He would try and see Anna sometime the next day, but for the moment he was going home to sleep. They sat on the terrace, and Izzy said what Anna, to her shame, was thinking. 'I'm glad she's not going to die. But if she had, it would have been easier in some ways. What if she's left as some sort of cripple? How's he going to turn his back on her then?'

'I don't know. God knows what's going to happen.' Anna gazed out over the terracotta rooftops and time nibbled walls. The sun was setting, and ribbons of light, fragile as gold leaf, streaked the darkening sky. Her future was as uncertain as the changing heavens, and she could no more influence it than she could the orbit of the sun.

* * *

Raffi visited every day. They curled up together on the sofa, and he told her of Caterina's slow progress, and despite drinking copious amounts of coffee, he would sometimes fall asleep. She cradled him in her arms, and stroked the still sun-streaked hair from his eyes. On Friday morning she asked did he want to stay with her that night – just to sleep.

'No. It's best if I'm at home. The hospital may ring if there's any change. I'm sorry, Anna. Give me time. It'll all work out, I swear.'

'You know where to find me. Come round whenever you want. I'm not going anywhere. I'll always be here for you, whatever happens,' she promised.

He smiled; the first real smile she had seen since the weekend. 'I know.' Then he stroked her cheek with his forefinger and kissed her forehead. 'See you soon, my sweet.'

She listened to the sound of his feet on the stairs, until the slam of the front door echoed off the walls, telling her he had gone.

* * *

An hour later the police launch came. Hearing the doorbell, she hoped it was Raffi returning, and pressed the entry-phone button without ascertaining the caller's identity. The sight of the young carabinieri officer filled her with alarm, but he at once reassured her.

'Please forgive the intrusion, *signorina*,' he said in perfect English, 'but we would be grateful if you could assist with our enquiries regarding the recent theft from the Church of the Misericordia. Could you please spare the time to accompany me to the police station? The officer in charge of the investigation would like very much to speak with you, but he is a man who has not the time to make house calls.'

'Why do you want to talk to me?'

'Purely routine,' the young man replied. 'The sacristan tells us you are a frequent visitor to the church. We think, perhaps you have seen a suspicious person; someone who may have been...' he hesitated, trying to remember the phrase, '...casing the joint. We can show you identikit pictures.'

Anna had been to the Misericordia twice since the theft, and been surprised to find the usually empty church teeming with tourists and locals, which was ironic, given that its greatest treasure had vanished. However, they obviously derived entertainment from staring at the blank space where the painting had once hung, some of them looking nervously about, as if expecting armed burglars to appear at any moment in search of further plunder.

Angelo had found her sitting before the bereaved wall.

'I miss, very much,' he said, indicating the dirty marks on the brickwork. 'For me, she like daughter.'

'*Per me, una sorella,*' Anna said.

'She come back – one day. God, he help us.'

'*Forse,*' said Anna, but doubting that God was a match for the Mafia. As she watched Angelo waddle away, she thought, *Who do I pray to now? Who do I beg to make it all work out?* There were other Madonnas in other churches, but none of them her own.

It was consequently with some excitement, and a sense of self-importance, that she entered the *carabinieri* station. She was relieved that the authorities were actively seeking the painting's recovery, and flattered that they thought she might be able to help.

Anna had been into a police station only once before, to report the loss of her handbag, stolen when she had left it hanging off the back of a chair in a City wine bar. But then she had infiltrated no further than the front office. Now she was led into the very bowels of the building, through neon-lit corridors painted in shiny cream paint.

The office into which she was shown was startling in its ordinariness. Pale walls, good but utilitarian furniture, a window with a distant view of the water: only differentiated from an English workplace by Christ, gazing in sorrowful disapproval from a small wooden cross. What also set it apart from anywhere she had ever visited was the man seated behind the desk, his uniform and aggressive presence proclaiming his authority. She immediately registered that he did not stand, which struck her as ill mannered. He motioned her to sit, and they regarded each other warily. Even though he remained seated, she sensed that he was tall and strongly built, with a lean frame. His face, however, was pallid and incongruously fleshy, so that puffy folds occluded his eyes.

The young officer who had, till they entered the station, been friendly and chatty had undergone an instantaneous personality change. He stood next to his superior, hands behind his back, staring into space. After what she supposed were instructions from his boss, he said, 'I am going to translate, because *Colonello* Boccardi's English is limited.'

At the sound of the man's name, Anna's heart heaved. Sitting opposite her was Caterina's father.

At last he spoke, his voice cigarette gravelled and quietly intimidating. His minion translated, 'Do you know that an important piece of Renaissance art was stolen last Saturday?'

'Yes,' said Anna. 'And if there is anything I can do to assist in its recovery, please...' She stopped, aware that she was gushing.

'I doubt there is. The painting will probably be out of the country by now. That is usually what happens. But tell me, why do you spend so much time in that particular church?'

'Well, the Misericordia is close to where I live...'

'To where you rent a flat?' The implication was obvious. You do not live here. Your presence, for a few months, is tolerated, as we have tolerated tourists for centuries, but do not, for a second, presume you have the right to call this city home.

'Vittore Anzelieri showed me the painting,' Anna floundered. 'He thinks I'm like the Madonna. I like to look at it, and wonder who this woman was who lived in Venice all those years ago. That's all.'

He was silent. His brown, yellow flecked eyes were inscrutable; one, she noticed, constantly twitched.

'Of course, with my hair like this, and in these clothes, I don't suppose the resemblance is very obvious,' she said.

'No, it is not at all obvious. In fact, you do not resemble a Renaissance Virgin in any way. You look a thoroughly modern…woman.'

Despite not fully understanding what he said, the contempt in his voice was obvious, and she detected a slight hesitation before his mouth formed the word "*donna*", suggesting that something altogether different was in his mind: bitch perhaps, or whore.

'And what were you doing on Saturday night?'

She did not answer. It was what she had been doing on Friday night that interested him, and she guessed that he knew only too well.

He sighed and then, as if he had toyed with her long enough, he cut to the chase and the real reason he had brought her here.

'*Signorina*, you should leave Venice. At once.'

'Leave Venice?' she repeated, wondering whether the young man had translated correctly.

'*Si*,' came the reply.

So great was her shock that she momentarily ceased to be intimidated. 'No, why should I?'

'It would be for your own good. Do you really think it possible to forge a lasting relationship with Raffaele Anzelieri? Surely you are not so naive to think you are the first? No – there have been others, but Raffi always comes back to Caterina. And he will quickly tire of a woman so unscrupulous that she would run after a man whose fiancé is seriously injured – possibly paralysed. Raffi is a young man, with the normal appetites of a young man, and if a woman so easily offers herself to him why should he refuse? But you are not to imagine that such a liaison means anything to Raffi, however adept you are in bed.'

Anna stared at the *Colonello*, who regarded her with an expression she had never before seen on a man's face. She was aware of her colour rising, and glanced at the young translator, who at least had the decency to look away. But he was his commanding officer's creature, and continued issuing threats with a robotic calmness.

'I think,' she said, trying to sound braver than she felt, 'that it is up to Raffi and me to decide what we mean to each other. And we have the right to do that in peace and in our own time. I've no intention of leaving Venice until I'm ready. We've done nothing wrong.'

He laughed – a hard rasping sound, and then spoke, the translated reply swiftly following, 'And do you think what you do is right? You tourists, you come here, thinking you can take whatever you want from us…from our city. You come to plunder and steal. Stealing Venice – that's what you do. You are trophy hunters. But I will see to it that you go back to England empty-handed. You are correct, you have done nothing wrong in the eyes of the law, but that can – and will – change, unless you do as I say.'

She remembered the stories of how the *Colonello's* wife had packed her bags and left with a tourist – a smooth-talking Yank. Thereafter, his life had been forever soured, and now he would stop at nothing to prevent his daughter suffering the same fate because of the moral decrepitude of yet another foreign opportunist.

He withdrew an envelope from his desk drawer. 'In here is a ticket for tonight's Paris train. I advise you to be on it.'

In mute horror she waited to hear the consequences of her not following his orders.

'Your friend, William, has a little habit, does he not? An illegal little habit.' The *Colonello* made a dismissive gesture with his hands. 'Oh, yes, I know William only smokes a little hashish. Many young people do; we turn a blind eye to it. But what if a large amount of a harder drug were found in your apartment – an amount exceeding what anyone could possibly want for their personal use? Drug dealing is a very serious offence. A certain Aldo Bisceglia, a well-known dealer, is currently in police custody. I understand there was an incident between him and William recently. Bisceglia is facing a long sentence and in return for certain charges being dropped, he will swear that you and your friends are involved in supplying drugs to the innocent youth of Venice. If you are determined to stay I cannot stop you, but I do not think you will find the women's prison on the Giudecca very salubrious. And then there is young Anzelieri's friend, Gianluca Zinanni – the one with the well-stocked garden. I know about him too. It would be most unfortunate if his horticultural prowess came to the attention of the authorities. Sadly this would mean him losing his job and pension. And then what will happen to poor, disabled *signora* Zinanni, with her only son in prison? It really will benefit so many people if you are on that train tonight.'

The *Colonello* picked up his phone, barking something into the receiver. He then said, in halting but exact English, 'Good afternoon, *signorina*. Thank you for coming. This interview is over. I hope you have a pleasant journey to Paris.'

A female officer appeared and gestured for Anna to follow her. As they reached the door, the *Colonello* spoke. The translation came. 'One thing more. Do not

279

attempt to see Raffaele. I will know if you do, and anyway, it will be much easier if you make a clean break. I am sure you will soon forget each other. Goodbye, *signorina*.'

Anna was too stunned to further resist, only asking, 'Why? Why are you doing this to me? *Perché*?'

For the first time she saw something resembling tenderness in his eyes. 'If ever you have a child, perhaps then you will understand.'

No one offered to take her home. Clutching the envelope, she found herself wandering through the stinking fumes and blaring car horns of the Piazzale Roma, where coach loads of ill-clad visitors were being disgorged for the day; a few hours roving *la Serenissima* included in their package holiday.

To return to the flat, she needed to cross the Grand Canal, but could not face the heaving crowds around either the station or the Rialto. Instead, she cut through San Croce, aiming for the *traghetto* which would take her to the Ca' d'oro. In the Campo San Giacomo dell'Orio with its pretty church and spindly trees, a long line of tourists filed past, doggedly following their guide, determined to stop for neither man nor beast. One of their number careered into two elderly ladies, not bothering to apologise. The women fixed disparaging eyes on Anna, who was trailing in the tourist slipstream. They muttered to each other and although they spoke in Veneziano, she understood. Their few words were sadly uncomplimentary. Anna wanted to tell them she was not part of the ill-mannered crocodile, but what was the use? And what did it matter?

Not as familiar with this part of the city, and hardly concentrating on her surroundings, she took a wrong turning and found the pavement lurched into a narrow canal, brackish water lapping where she had expected a wide *fondamenta*. It was a common enough mistake. Everyone did it, apart from those born, or so long resident in Venice, that a map of its squirming byways was imprinted on their brain. But it seemed to Anna, who prided herself on rarely needing a map, that it was a reminder of how little she really knew the place. The steps down to the canal were slick with green seaweed. A stench of the urinal – and worse – wafted up, and looking down, she saw that the paving stones sprouted infant stalagmites of pigeon shit. It was low tide and the wall opposite was gouged with gaping wounds inflicted by time and pollution. Something dead, furred or feathered, knocked dully against the disintegrating bricks. Close by, some of the most beautiful buildings in the world flaunted themselves, but here was Venice's putrid underbelly – the real Venice, some might say. Nothing was as it seemed in this city of constant, illusionary reflections and unexpected dead ends; nothing was to be trusted.

She retraced her steps, wondering what the hell she was going to do. That she had to do something was incontrovertible. Although it was possible that the *Colonello* was bluffing, she dare not take the risk. Telling Izzy would serve no purpose and, given her hatred of drugs, could ruin her relationship with Will. Perhaps she could confide in Vittore, but she baulked at the prospect of involving him. Ridiculously, she was reluctant to divulge the new intimacy between herself and Raffi. The interview with the *Colonello* had sullied their union, leaving her unaccountably ashamed, as though she had committed an act of profanity rather than love.

The man had also spoken of other women, implying there had been a stream of lovers. For the first time, she considered the possibility that to Raffi she was no more than a light-hearted, and very temporary, liaison. Perhaps she had made herself too easily available. But that was a ludicrous notion; it was 1987, not 1887. Then she reminded herself that Raffi was Italian with perhaps a different set of mores. He had said she was very special but he had never said he loved her. And had not the *Colonello* referred to Caterina as Raffi's *fidanzata*? Were there things she did not know? Perhaps Raffi had not been altogether honest. Her mind screamed with all the possibilities.

However, there was something else; something more insidious than either the *Colonello's* threats, or whether Raffi was a Lothario. There was guilt. What chance would their relationship have if Caterina did not fully recover? How could they live together in the city, knowing that Raffi's jilted lover was also here – disabled and alone? Guilt would eat away at them like a succubus; it would devour their love, leaving only the bones of remorse. For a moment she imagined Raffi relocating to London, and immediately recognised the impossibility of this. He had said it himself: he would never leave Venice.

As the *traghetto* lurched across the Grand Canal, cliffed with its *pallazzi* of sugar paste and dreams, she knew that Venice would win. The *Colonello* had accused her of stealing Venice, but it was Venice that was the thief; Venice had stolen Raffi from her. The city she adored was now the enemy. It would always hold Raffi captive. He had never been hers; she had stolen him for a few hours – that was all.

He had asked her to give him time; she would give him time, certainly, but it was time he would have to spend alone. She could not risk ruining the lives of so many others by staying. Her mind raced. Even if Will and Izzy were no longer in the city would she, herself, ever be safe here? Would Raffi? Could not the *Colonello* always threaten them with some trumped up charge? There was one hope, and one hope only; that Caterina would fully recover. The restoration of her health was the only thing that would give them the freedom to be together. In the meantime, she had no choice but to flee.

The one saving grace of being banished to Paris was that Tom lived there, still writing his detective stories. By the time Izzy returned from work Anna had already telephoned him and asked if she could stay for a few days. He diplomatically did not ask many questions, simply promising to meet her train.

'What the fuck's going on?' demanded Izzy, seeing the suitcase, and chaos of clothes.

'Mum's not well,' lied Anna.

'What's wrong?'

'That man she's been seeing. Well, he's ended things. She's feeling really, really bad. She needs my support.'

Izzy's eyes narrowed. 'What about Raffi? Doesn't he need your support?'

'I think Raffi's probably best left to sort things out for himself. Look, I'll soon be back. But I'll leave you a cheque covering my share of the rent till January, just in case I get run over by a bus or...'

She stopped, appalled, and then began to laugh. Izzy, perhaps noticing the trace of hysteria in her mirth, asked no more questions.

The *Colonello* had said nothing about telephoning Raffi, so she rang several times. His phone was continually out of order. This did not altogether surprise her. Perhaps it was a coincidence, but she suspected it was further proof of the collusive power the man exerted in the city.

It was inconceivable that she should leave without seeing Vittore and Rosina, but it was a meeting she dreaded. She did not know how she would prevent herself from breaking down. They greeted her warmly, expressing their concern when she broke the news of her departure.

'But I'll be back before you know it,' she said, almost believing the untruths. And then she handed them an envelope. 'I'm sorry to have missed Raffi...'

'He's at the hospital,' Vittore said. 'Caterina's father needed to work, so Raffi volunteered to stay with her.'

'Ah, well. Anyway, could you give this to him.'

The letter did not say much; just the same lies.

She left it till the last possible moment to leave the flat, praying that Raffi would call by or telephone. When he did not, she imagined him by Caterina's bedside, realising that, having nearly lost her, she meant everything to him. Misery seeped into her soul like poison.

Izzy and Will accompanied her to the station. And even then, she scoured the platform, hoping to see a tall, familiar figure. No one appeared and as the train pulled away only Izzy and Will waved farewell.

Anna sat very still, trying not to cry. She felt insubstantial with grief, as though she were dissolving, like sugar in water. She told herself she would be back, if not in two weeks, soon, and all would be well. But remnant memories of another departure, sensed rather than recollected, tore at her mind, and it seemed that with her flight she was abandoning all happiness and hope.

She did not look out of the window, but knew that only a faint miasma of light, barely discernible on the far horizon, marked where the city floated in the dark lagoon – just a glimmer between land and sea. Out of her sight and reach, Venice slipped into nothingness, and was gone.

Venice: August 1516

On the Sunday after Debra's death, Giacomo borrows a boat and we row to the long, sandy island called the Lido. It is a lonely place, for apart from its monastery, it is inhabited by only a few farmers and fishermen. The nobility keep horses here and find pleasure in racing them. To watch this is a treat, as we townsfolk see only these animals' smaller cousins – mules and donkeys. In spring and autumn people often make the journey, but in winter the island is buffeted by cruel winds and, now, in the full heat of summer, it is fiercely hot. There are few shady spots to afford protection from the sun, and on its shores, the canals have silted up, so there is a proliferation of bad air where swarms of biting insects thrive. It is here, next to her mother, that my friend sleeps.

Unlike we Christians, who bury our loved ones in hallowed places near our homes, the Jews must ferry their dead here. They are permitted to use no other burial ground. Over many decades this domain of the Jewish dead has become as crowded as the place that their living descendants are now forced to inhabit. I survey the hundreds of head stones stacked together, and fear that we will never find Debra's grave. Even though it is still early in the day, the heat saps me of strength and calm. Under my clothes I feel the sweat of panic break through my skin; it runs between my breasts, down my legs, and prickles in my armpits. I need to see her resting place to believe that she is truly gone. If I cannot kneel before the earth that holds her, and beg forgiveness, I believe that I will go stark mad.

'I do not know where they have put her. Where is she?' I wail.

I thought to easily locate a freshly dug grave, and the stone next to it must bear her mother's name. But I have forgotten that the inscriptions are in Hebrew. I cannot understand the writing, nor can I see any mounds of fresh earth. Tears mingle with the sweat on my face.

'We will walk all around the edge and slowly move inwards,' Giacomo says, his voice cool and reasonable. 'The grave will not be so far from the outside. Come.'

He takes my hand. As we venture into the forest of stunted stone, I am in dread of graves gaping open. I envisage Debra's vengeful ancestors bursting through the earth, intent on pulling us down to their murky underworld, for assuredly these ghosts must know the darkness of my heart. I chastise myself for these silly, supernatural imaginings, and to divert my tumbling thoughts, I endeavour to remember the shape of the letters that comprise Debra's family name. I saw them only occasionally, but I have the knack of being able to see things in my mind's eye and then…

…it is a very new grave. The soil heaped upon it is still fresh and soft. Next to it is a headstone whose dull greyness is spattered with yellow lichen, the colour of egg yolk. I at once recognize the unfamiliar sweep of those letters. It is the place.

The Jews observe a strange custom – Debra once told me of it: they pile stones upon a grave. This marks the occasion of one's visit and is a sign of respect. I begin to search for a stone. There are none. Previous mourners have taken them all. I cannot even give her this. Giacomo, seeing my distress, promises to find one for me. Whilst he is gone, I kneel by the mound of earth and whisper all the things to Debra that I should have said when she was alive. I am so very sad that my heart feels squeezed to the size of a walnut.

Giacomo returns, and hands me a large pebble. Even in my sorrow, its beauty moves me. It is oval, like the egg of an exotic bird, and is a soft grey-blue, flecked with white. He must have plucked it from the shoreline, for it is still cool, and when I lift it to my face, it holds the scent of the sea. It is not much to give in honour of a lifetime's friendship – but it is all I have. I place it with the other stones already piled there. Then Giacomo leaves me for a little longer, and I pray and weep, but mostly I weep.

At length he returns and we walk back towards the boat. In the distance, Venice glimmers, shivering in the heat. She is confident and proud, mocking us with her beauty, like the cruel mistress she is. She has no time for the poor, the weak, the different. It is men of Enrico's ilk that she fawns upon. For the first time in my life I feel distaste for my native city and all her works.

If I expected to be comforted after visiting Debra's grave, I am cruelly deceived. Knowing that she rots in the ground plunges me deeper into despair and I can find no joy in the world. I even turn away from Giacomo in our bed. I see the look of hurt in his eyes when I reject him, pleading that the nights are too hot, but he knows there is more to it than this. On other nights, as sultry as these, we have united our flesh, straining towards mutual pleasure until the sweat on our bodies sweetly mingles, and we are as drenched as if we had bathed in the lagoon. But now, when he takes me in his arms and attempts to nudge apart my legs, I think of the violence done to Debra and feel guilt that the only love she ever knew was cruel and brutal and led to dusty death. Then all my desire fades. Giacomo understands my grief, but he must not know of the guilt that trammels my happiness. I am sure that he thinks I have ceased to care for him. How can I explain that he is my sun and moon, my soul's desire; but for all that, I seem to have forgotten how to love him with my body? Perhaps it is the end of our sweet romance, for if this continues he will tire of me, I know he will. But I cannot help it; I am being smothered by guilt. Also, there is something else that bedevils me, both waking and sleeping, and that is hate. When my mother died, I thought I hated my brother, but it was nothing to what assails me now. My hatred for Enrico Sartorani could strip the leaves from the trees. I dream of flaying him alive; of tearing away his flesh with red hot pincers; of holding his head under the murkiest of canals and leaving his foul flesh to be gorged by crabs, until only his grinning skull remains. And even that, I would dredge from the filth, and pound into a powder to be spread upon the winds. It is as if hate has left no room in my heart for love. Even my little dog looks at me with uncomprehending eyes and avoids me, for he must sense the blackness festering inside my soul, and stays clear of such a poor companion. I am alone in my anguish.

Perhaps, at last, this is my punishment for wishing my brother dead. But now I am deeper in sin, for I have helped snuff out a new life. And by refusing my husband, I am denying life to my own offspring. Should I have a child, I am sure that its birthing would kill me, and in my present state of gracelessness I would plunge down to Hell and eternal torment.

I go to confession in the distant Church of the Carmini, near to the place where Debra's child was ripped from her. I consider finding Dianora and confronting her with the result of her butchery. But this would take a courage I lack, and what good would it serve? It would not stop Dianora peddling her foul trade, for beneath the gilded surface of this city, life is very cheap.

Before I confess, I kneel before Giambattista's Adoration of the Shepherds. It is an image of perfect motherhood, and is at such odds with my own sinful nature that it tortures rather than comforts me. Looking at it, I imagine what the painter would think if he knew the secrets of my heart. He is not even aware of Debra's death. Why tell him? Of late, he is as happy as a child, packing up his workshop, putting the finishing touches to paintings, and preparing to leave Venice for his hometown. I spend as much time in the workshop as possible, for only here, with brushes and paint, can I find the balm to ease my agony of mind. When he is gone I do not know what I will do to calm myself. The priest who hears my confession is shocked, I can tell from his voice, but then I say something that reveals Debra was Jewish. All concern for her and the unborn baby vanish from his mealy mouth. Of a sudden they are lesser beings, and my sin is reduced, although I do not see how this can be. I hardly hear my penance, for I do not believe in his absolution. As I stumble out of the cool church into the scorching day, I nurse the hope that Debra will be an angel in Paradise, whilst he kicks his heels at Heaven. Thus I cut myself off from even God.

July drags itself into August, then shortly before the Feast of the Assumption, we have a visitor to our house. His name is Matthew Shelborne, and his conviviality dispels my sorrow a little. He hails from the distant country of England, and is a learned man who, in his youth, studied medicine at the University in Padua, where he met *papà*. Although Matthew knew Latin, the language in which lectures were conducted, he was unable to converse in the vernacular, and consequently struggled with all manner of things. *Papà* befriended him, and in return earned Matthew's everlasting gratitude.

Master Shelborne has long since abandoned the practise of medicine. His primary interest was surgery, but in England this is, apparently, the province of men who are often no more than illiterate barbers, so it is not a profession suitable for a gentleman. (Venice is, so I am told, one of the few places where men such as my father combine the skills of both physician and surgeon.) So upon the death of his father, Matthew took over the family business and makes a great deal more money from trade than medicine. He resides near an ancient town called Totnes, where there is an abundant supply of tin. This metal is not as precious as gold or silver, but being an essential component of bronze, is much sought after in our Italian states. It is transported to Venice on Matthew's ships, and when he returns to England he takes with him a cargo of glass and mirrors, sugar and silks.

I look forward to his visits, for he has a wealth of tales, not least those concerning his monarch. King Henry is said to be the handsomest prince in Christendom, but he seems to suffer the same misfortune as the Sartorani when it comes to progeny. His queen has given him five children and only the last born, a girl of six months, still lives. What would happen, I ask, just out of curiosity, should there be no sons? Would there be a queen?

Matthew knits his brow. That would fare very badly for his poor country. A woman would be swayed and manipulated by all. To maintain England's fragile peace, after the long and bloody civil wars, a strong male ruler is essential. I, who have never known anything but a republic, make the observation that for affairs of state to rest upon the fickleness of a woman's womb is a foolhardy way to run a nation. Matthew confesses that he is inclined to agree, but would never venture such an opinion at home, for fear of his head ending up on a spike!

The talk then turns to medicine, in which Matthew still takes an active interest. He and *papà* compare the ruthless progress of the vile condition that we know as *mal franclosati*, and which the English call the French disease. (How, I wonder, do the French describe it?) It has claimed many victims since it first appeared twenty years ago, for however skilled the physician, and however ingenious his treatments, it always kills – in the end. Many succumb to it, the poorer of whom lie rotting on our streets, detracting from the wholesomeness of our city. Thus, there is talk of founding special hospitals where these incurables may die away from the public gaze. It is now acknowledged that the condition spreads as a result of coupling, for the first signs appear on the sexual organs. No one knows from where the disease first came, although as Matthew now reminds us, it has long been rumoured that the Jews introduced it, a suggestion that my father roundly discounts as gross calumny.

The subject changes again as Matthew fishes in his bag and places a small bottle on the table. 'Here, Francesco. I have brought something that may interest you.'

'What is it?' asks *papà*, trying to focus on the offering.

'A drug, that in England, we call dwale.'

'Ah, yes,' *papà* says. 'I have heard of it. Did it not fall out of usage because so many died after taking it? Surely it is the preserve of village quacks and has no place in modern medicine.'

'No, no, quite the contrary. In unskilled hands it was, as you say, often deadly. It contains hemlock, mandrake, henbane and the juice of poppy flowers, any one of which can kill. But if the quantities are exactly measured and mixed with other ingredients to mitigate their strength, and if the potion is dispensed with regard to the weight and age of the patient, it has truly miraculous results. There is a woman who lives near my home. I have seen her give enough to render a man quite insensible whilst his leg was amputated, and when he awoke, he swore he had felt no pain. She has the uncanny ability of knowing the exact quantity of each component to use. I do not know how she does it, I do not think she knows herself, but if a common village woman can succeed in this, think how much more we educated men could achieve.'

Papà looks doubtful. 'But how do you propose we perfect the dosage, Matthew? No physician wishes to see his patients in agony, but nor can we administer something that may well kill them.'

'Resort to its use only in cases where the patient would almost certainly die without surgery.'

'One day, perhaps,' says *papa* gently. 'But I do not think the world is yet ready for such interventions. And I am not prepared to take such risks.'

'Well, let me know if you have a change of heart,' Matthew says, his enthusiasm not in the least dampened.

Papà nods. 'Now I think we must all take to our beds for young Giacomo is working very hard and has no need of dwale or any other drug to send him to sleep.'

'Ah, young lovers,' Matthew laughs, winking at us. 'They possess the best medicine for sweet slumbers!'

Giacomo takes my hand and we smile lovingly at one another, but as he leans towards me to drop a kiss on my forehead, I see the sadness in his eyes.

I have some domestic tasks to complete before I can retire, and by the time I join him, my husband is asleep. Perhaps my coolness has so diminished his desire that he would rather be in the embrace of Morpheus than the arms of a frigid wife. I lay awake for a long time, listening to the gentle rhythm of his breath, as my tears soak into the pillow.

Exile

That night, Anna did not even try to sleep. Standing in the train's corridor, engulfed by the dark nothingness of the vast countryside, she watched the wind whistling through midnight stations, until dawn and Paris approached, grey and wet and devoid of hope.

On the news-stands, English papers showed a London devastated by the previous day's storms. She vaguely wondered if her flat was OK. It did not seem to matter.

Tom was there to meet her, but they hardly spoke as they metro-ed to his home in Asnières, a place famous for having been painted by Seurat and van Gogh.

The spare room was cupboard small, its tiny window framing a landscape of grey mansard roofs sprouting TV aerials. But the narrow bed was comfortable, and there was a cheery bunch of flowers on the sill. Left to herself, Anna managed a few hours sleep. In the afternoon they visited the area's other claim to fame, its extraordinary Cimetière des Chiens, the last resting place of the film star dog, Rin-Tin-Tin.

'Are you going to tell me what's happened?' Tom asked, as they stood before a monument commemorating an unknown stray, mown down by a car outside the cemetery gates.

'Later, when I've had a drink, or three or four,' said Anna, thinking how horribly apposite was the gravestone, given the circumstances of her being here.

That evening, however, their conversation was sidetracked. One of the characters in Tom's latest wartime novel lived in Vichy France, and he planned to describe the village of her birth. Having chosen the approximate location, he now felt compelled to visit the area, and also fancied a break in the country before winter set in. He suggested that they go together. Anna could think of no reason why not, so they spent the rest of the evening pouring over the *Gîtes de France* book. The next day Tom made a few calls, and early on Monday morning, blissfully unaware of the world's plummeting stock markets, they piled into his battered Citroën and headed south. They shared the driving and made good progress, arriving at their destination while the golden autumnal sun still gilded the mellow roofs and treetops.

Their *gîte* was a two bedroom self-contained annex of a spacious stone built house belonging to an English couple who had fled the rat race to open a B & B. That first night, Tamsin, the owner, provided them with a meal *en famille*. Her husband, Roger, was a fan of Tom's books and they spent a pleasant evening consuming a large amount of wine.

Still buzzing from the long car journey, Anna and Tom decamped to their quarters, and Anna, her tongue loosened by the alcohol, at last told Tom the full story.

When she had finished, he was quiet for some time and then said, 'For an intelligent woman you can be bloody stupid at times. Why didn't you go to the British Consol or someone?'

'I didn't think. But even if they could have helped us, what about Raffi's friend?'

'The one with the marijuana plants?'

'Yes. Short of him pulling them up double quick, he'd have been stuffed. I couldn't let that happen. Anyway, the more I think about it, the more I'm sure things couldn't work out between Raffi and me. Whether or not she gets better, Caterina will always be there, like some sort of glamorous spider, waiting to ensnare him.'

'Perhaps. But you should give it a chance. And you must tell him what happened. The man at least deserves that. Phone him for God's sake.'

'OK. Tomorrow. And promise me one thing. Never mention this to Izzy. She's so happy with Will, but this could really screw things up. You know what she's like about drugs.'

But instead of phoning, Anna composed a letter to Raffi, describing the *Colonello's* threats. She wrote that she did not know when she would return to Venice, but that their time together had been very special and she hoped they could find a way, if that is what he wanted, to be with each other in the future. She gave him the *gîte's* number and, in case he preferred to write, her mother's address. What she did not divulge was how much she missed him; that hardly a minute went by when he was not in her thoughts; that wakened by their one night together, she existed in a restless state of arousal and constantly imagined his hands on her body, his mouth on hers. She was with a dear friend, in a beautiful place, but without Raffi, the world was a joyless chasm. Instead, she wrote, "lots of love, hope to see you soon", and three large Xs.

'I couldn't face ringing,' she told Tom over breakfast. 'This way, if he wants to ignore my letter, he can. I'd rather that, than one of those awful, embarrassed silences on the other end of the phone.'

'Coward,' said Tom.

She opened her mouth to defend herself, and then found she could not. 'I am aren't I? I think I always have been. And my father and uncle were so brave; I don't know how I dare call myself their relative. Do you know, that's why I didn't apply to university all those years ago? I was afraid of not getting the grades. Afraid of leaving home. Pathetic!'

'We always suspected that was why,' said Tom. 'But, hey, you've done OK.'

'Till now, perhaps. Do you think I'm being punished for being such a wimp?'

'Punished?'

'Well, the last two years have been pretty awful. Losing Dad; the house in Putney; my job; Chris – OK he wasn't the love of my life, but even so…and now this thing with Raffi. You know, I really thought that it might all work out. I don't mean wedding bells and all that but…'

'But you wouldn't say no?'

There was a small silence.

'No, I don't suppose I would.'

Tom put his arm around her. 'Poor old you. I don't think you're being punished. It's just that, at times, life can be rather fulsome in its random spitefulness.'

'You're telling me. You know, there's this phrase that keeps going round my head…something to do with the President of the Immortals and…and his sport.'

'Ah yes, it's from the end of Tess of the d'Urbervilles.'

'Oh, of course.' And she remembered standing amongst rustling vines, Raffi feeding her strawberry flavoured grapes and the touch of his fingers on her mouth. 'Oh, well, it could be worse. Even if I commit murder, at least, I'm not going to be strung up, like poor Tess.'

By the next day it was obvious that Tom's muse had joined them. Although he was happy to explore their surroundings for a couple of hours each morning, all he wanted to do after lunch was write, and he would apologetically abandon Anna for his typewriter.

Left to her own devices, she struggled to fill her time, until on their fourth day, rummaging through a cupboard containing paperbacks left by previous guests, she came across a box of watercolours, a selection of brushes and a large supply of paper. Outside, it was a glorious day, the garden still a riot of gaudy colour, and she felt an irresistible urge to try her hand at capturing it.

She found Tamsin engaged in transforming anything left in the vegetable patch into chutney, hoping that it might approximate Branston Pickle.

'All the paints and stuff in the *gîte*, do they belong to anyone?' Anna asked.

Tamsin stopped chopping. 'No, they were all left by a guest…oh, ages ago. I didn't take them away in case anyone else fancied a dabble. Feel free.'

Anna settled herself at a rickety wooden table opposite the pool house. It had once been an outbuilding and was constructed of mellow, ochre coloured bricks. Some sort of green creeper clung to it, and against its walls nestled a haphazard arrangement of pots, containing herbs, geraniums and other late blooming shrubs.

Bees and insects, attracted by the flowers, gently hummed. In the distance she could hear Tamsin singing and the tap-tap of Tom's typewriter. Dipping a brush into the jar of water, she experienced, for the first time in days, a sort of peace.

She painted for hours, intent upon the task, all other thoughts banished. Only when Tom came to ask if she would like an aperitif, did she stop. She had painted the same view four times – not compulsively, but simply endeavouring to get it right, and to make the unpredictable medium behave.

'Wow!' said Tom, looking over her shoulder. 'Not bad at all. I'm really impressed. I remember now, how good at painting you were when we were kids.'

Anna squinted at her work, silently conceding she was a little impressed herself. It was over ten years since she had picked up a paintbrush and it amazed her that she remembered techniques learnt so long ago. But also surprising was how right it felt and how content she had been.

Over the next few days she painted constantly. While she worked all the pain vanished, and it was one way to keep sane, waiting for a phone call that never came.

* * *

On the last night of their holiday they joined Tamsin and Roger at a local restaurant. Roger began by quizzing Tom about his next novel, but in the face of continued circumspection, turned his attention to Anna. 'So what about you? Back to the world of high finance?'

'No,' she said. 'I've got other plans.'

Just then their main courses arrived and the conversation moved on, but she could see Tom eyeing her with curiosity.

He did not mention it again until the next day when they were driving back to Paris. 'So what are you planning when you get back to England?'

'In Venice, something amazing happened to me. And I don't just mean Raffi, and all that. But being there, being shown around by Vittore, it was as if I was seeing, you know…really seeing, for the first time: light, colour, shadows – all those things – the magic of paint. How a flat piece of canvas or wood can be transformed into something vibrant and alive. It's what I want to do, Tom. It's probably what I've always wanted to do. I just never would have had the guts – or the wherewithal to do it before.'

'Do you have the wherewithal now? You'd probably get a grant – you could do a foundation year somewhere and try for art school.'

'I don't really fancy being with a load of kids ten years younger than me. I thought I'd try some evening classes instead. There'll be dozens to choose from. That way I can concentrate on the things I really like, and I'll do temp jobs to earn a crust.'

'It's a big step. Chucking in your career and everything.'

'I know, but I should be able to pay off my mortgage with the money Dad left. I know it's not what he'd planned for me. He wanted me to travel. But quite honestly I don't think I'm up to gadding off to places by myself. I want to be at home. And anyway there's more than one way to travel. I reckon this could be a pretty amazing journey.'

'Absolutely. I think he'd be really proud of you.'

'Yeah…after all, it's quite a brave thing to do, isn't it? And I'll be in good company. I read a biography of Van Gogh when we were at the *gîte*. Do you know how old he was when he made the decision to become a painter?'

Tom shook his head.

'Twenty-seven, only a year younger than me. And he was virtually self-taught.'

'Just promise me one thing, Anna. However bad life gets, don't cut your ear off.'

'I promise.'

'Actually, while we're dropping bombshells, I've been thinking about my future too. I've decided to rent out my flat, and come back to London. I should just about be able to afford a shoe box in Hammersmith or somewhere.'

'Oh, Tom, that's fantastic. It'll be brilliant having you home again. Almost like old times.'

'It might be more like old times than you think. I've a feeling it won't be that long till Izzy's back too.'

'What makes you say that?'

'Dunno,' said Tom. 'Just one or two things she's said when I've phoned her. Well, it's only right isn't it? Whatever else happens, it's where we three belong… London.'

Venice: August 1516

For the first time since Debra's death, I have tonight felt something approaching peace, sitting amongst, and listening to, the men I love, but now all my old miseries return. I lay, willing sleep to come, and then something makes me open my eyes.

She stands at the end of our bed, her face and body glowing like an angel's. She lights up the whole room, and in her arms is a child, as beautiful as the dawn.

'Debra, is that your baby?' I ask, and then I am standing next to her. I can see my sleeping self, lying beside Giacomo. We have thrown off the sheet, and our naked bodies look like marble statues. I watch myself stir; my hand finds his, and our fingers entwine.

In reply to my question, she shakes her head, saying, 'No, it is yours. But although her body will grow in your womb from Giacomo's seed, her soul will be the soul of my baby. She is only waiting to be born. Gina, you must not turn from your husband. He loves you so much. And only by your union can the soul of this little one be free. Do this for me. And for your own happiness. Please.'

I have never heard of such a thing before, but I do not, for a second, doubt the truth of what she says. I will do as she wishes, but there are things I must ask. 'When the child is born, will I live or die of it?'

'Everyone must die, Gina. But there is nothing to fear.'

'Will I see you in Heaven? Or are you in a different Jewish Heaven?'

The question plagued me when she lived, but now she dismisses it with her laughter. I am surprised that the sound does not waken my husband...or my sleeping self. But we remain oblivious to this unearthly conversation.

'There is just the one Heaven, and just the one God. He loves us all as equals. I will see you there. But for now, find joy in your bed again.'

I sense that she is about to leave me but I have one more question. 'Do you forgive me? If I had not made you sit for the painting...'

'There is nothing to forgive, my dear friend.'

The baby makes a little popping sound with its rosebud mouth and squirms in Debra's embrace.

'Let me hold her.' I open my arms to take the child, but then I am clutching at nothing and I feel only air as its little body melts into the night, even as Debra too, dissolves.

'Don't go,' I wail, and then I am awake, stifling a scream. But it is not a cry of terror that dies in my mouth but one of joy. It was only a dream; of that I am certain, but the dark thing that has long oppressed me has taken flight. I am at peace, and yes…yes, I am happy. I have forgiven myself, and know that God has also.

The unworldly glow that illuminated the room has gone, leaving only a narrow shaft of moonlight resting on Giacomo's face. I yearn for the touch of his hands and to feel him inside me, so I bend towards him, intent on waking him with a hundred little kisses, starting at his mouth and working slowly down his body until…and then I stop. He is toiling all hours to complete the carving of choir stalls for one of the smaller *scuole*. I do not wish him so weary that he spoils the work or injures his hands. Tomorrow night we will take to our bed early, and I will make amends for my coldness.

I stretch my body alongside his and close my eyes, knowing that my sleep will be dreamless and sweet. And then I hear it: a whining and scratching at the door that goes on and on.

Cesare has grudgingly accepted that he may no longer share my bed, for he does not understand what goes on between a man and wife, and wishes to join in, thinking it a great game. Consequently, although he has been banished, he remains determined not to be far from me, and lies sentinel outside the door. Although he usually makes no complaint, tonight he is insistent in his whimpering, and I guess what ails him. Matthew is very soft hearted and despite my telling him it is folly to do so, he insists on feeding Cesare titbits. And now, my little dog, who is unused to rich food, is suffering from a pain in the guts and urgently needs to relieve himself.

I have no wish to be clearing up the results of his gluttony, so I clamber out of bed, pull on my shift and creep from the room. As I tiptoe towards the street door, Cesare twirls and pants around my feet, and I realise that I must have slept for hours either before, or after, I dreamed of Debra, for it is nearly dawn. Soon the place will be buzzing with folk. I do not wish to be seen standing in the doorway so scantily dressed, so I slip on my sandals, and finding my cloak, pull it about me, for the modestly it affords, rather than its warmth.

As soon as I have granted him his freedom, rather than evacuate his bowels, Cesare is off, scampering down the *fondamenta*. He has deceived me. It is not an ache in his belly that afflicts him, but an ache in his heart. He is in love with a little spaniel that resides close by, and is in search of his sweetheart. Unless I prevent him, he will sit yowling outside our neighbour's house and be rewarded with the contents of a chamber pot over his head. So I give chase, but he is intent upon his amorous adventure and treats my attempts to catch him with typical canine disregard. Only when he comes to the house of his beloved does he stop, gazing upwards, quietly whimpering. I have not the heart to chastise him, for as I well know, love has the power to make fools of us all.

'Silly creature,' I whisper, crouching down to gather him up. And then, in the grey light, I see a flash of white as he bears his teeth and growls. Cesare never shows me malice, however much I may thwart his desires, so the sight of his aggression shocks me, even as I realise that it is directed not towards me.

He must have approached with the stealth of a cat, for I heard no sound. As I lift my head a familiar odour pricks my nostrils and I know, without looking, who has found me, alone and unprotected in a deserted and sleeping city. I hear the faint rustle of his garments, feel the heat of his breath on my neck and smell again, that scent – more animal than man. Then a hand encircles my elbow and hoists me, unresisting and weak-kneed, to my feet.

'Ginevra,' he purrs. 'You seem to have a fondness for being abroad at night. Do you enjoy courting danger?'

'My husband is only a few steps behind,' I lie, willing it to be true.

'Married then? The artist's nephew no doubt? Yes, I saw those hot looks you gave him. So at last you have someone to tend the itch between your legs? You were well ripe for it.'

The moon has slipped from behind a cloud and he must see the shock on my face, for his mouth curls into a smirk. I am outraged by his disrespect. My head tells me to take to my heels and run, far, far away from this creature. But it is my heart that speaks. 'How dare you insult me. You are not fit to walk the streets of this city, of any Christian city.'

'And what, pray, have I done to so outrage you?' His voice is as treacherous as a dagger sheathed in silk.

'You know what you have done. Debra…she is dead, because of you.'

'Because of me? Oh, I think not. When I saw her last, her heart beat as strongly as mine own. I felt it under my hand, like a little bird.'

'You forced her. You know you did, and she conceived a child by you. A child that she could not bear to carry so…'

'And so, what did she do? Throw herself into the lagoon, or get a filthy hag to cut the brat out of her? Either way, she was a sinning Jewish slut and will burn in hell.'

'She was no slut. And whatever she did, she is better than the son of a jumped up Venetian trader. A man who is no better bred than an alley dog and whose mother is a whore. A man who is a bastard, conceived out of lust…'

The blow is so violent that it sends my head reeling and knocks me off my feet. My knees meet the *fondamenta* with a crack that shoots such pain through my legs that I cry out. Cesare falls from my arms but lands soft and unhurt. I think he begins to bark but perhaps it is just the ringing in my ears. Enrico yells at him and through streaming eyes, I see him aim a kick. He misses, but Cesare is a coward, used to only sweet words, so at the sound of Enrico's voice he gives a little yelp and runs away, with his tail between his legs. I watch his small body, bobbing into the gloom and feel that with his desertion all is lost. He could not have protected me, but somehow when he was in my arms I felt brave, but now…then I sense a shifting of the air above my head, and another punch sends me flying sideways. The damp coolness of the *fondamenta* stings my cheek. Then darkness falls over me, thick and dark as mud.

I am unable to cry out, unable to move, only aware that I am being hauled from the ground. Rough hands claw under my armpits, digging into my breasts and then my feet are scraping painfully along the pavement. One of my sandals falls off. I want to tell Enrico to pick it up but my mouth cannot form the words. The shoes were a present from Giacomo and I do not wish to lose one. There is a soft, plashing sound as it lands in the water. But we cannot be crossing the canal for there are no bridges close by. Then I remember: a few planks of wood have been thrown from one bank to the other at the site of Ca' Sartorani. We are bound for his house. Terror rises in my throat like bile and somehow I manage to scream. But even as my cry fades into the creeping dawn, I am aware that it will avail me nothing. No one will stir themselves, for it is an acknowledged truism that a woman is more likely to receive help if she cries, "fire" than "rape".

I hear the scrape of keys in locks and then a sudden chill swallows the warmth of the early morn. Without warning, his hands relinquish their hold and I fall to the floor, as though I have no more value than a sack of flour.

I can sense that he is moving about the room, and through my eyelids I detect the warm glow of lamplight. For a long time I remain quite still, curled up in a little ball of fear and pain. If I wait long enough, surely Giacomo will come to my rescue, but even as this hope springs in my mind it is smothered by the realisation that he will not know where I am. Why should he ever imagine I will be in Ca' Sartorani?

Perhaps if I plead with him, Enrico will let me go, and leave me unmolested. I pray to God, to our Lady, to all the Saints. I pray harder than I have ever done in my life, before forcing open my reluctant eyes. The sight that greets me is not what I expect. Despite this being a patrician house there are no fine wall hangings or splendid furnishings. There is the sound of lapping water, and through the open door I see the sleek blackness of a *gondola*. We are in one of the storerooms on the ground floor *androne,* where the spoils of trade would normally be kept. This room is, however, empty of all wares. There is only a table and a chair, in which Enrico sits. And the painting. It is propped against the wall, at a level with my eyes. It seems broken in some way, disjointed and out of kilter with itself. I fear that the blow to my head has damaged my sight. Then the truth dawns. It has been hacked in two.

'It offends me,' he says, seeing my amazement. 'She offends me. I thought to throw it in the canal. What do you think I should do with it?'

To relegate such a beautiful thing to murky waters is an affront to God, but if by agreeing, I can appease Enrico, and save my skin, I willingly will do so.

'But I think,' he says, rising and sidling to where I cower. 'I think I will save the Madonna – save you. My father and his betrothed unite their flesh next month. Do you like the thought of watching them in their bedchamber?' He crouches down next to me, and runs a finger across my cheek. Although his touch disgusts me I try not to flinch. 'Would that excite you?'

I nod, evading the question. 'It would be an honour.'

'Oh, I do not think so. There is no honour in fucking,' he says. 'And even less in watching others transport themselves like beasts.'

Then, to my surprise, something like a sob tears at his voice, and his face contorts, as he continues, 'Our weak flesh forces base, filthy actions upon us. Why did God create women, only for them to be such whores? If my slut of a mother had kept her legs closed she would not have brought me into the world with all the calumny that is heaped upon me. I cared for her, you know.' I assume he speaks of his mother but then I see that his eyes are fixed on Debra's portrait. His voice softens and he sounds almost tender. 'But she only wanted to use me for her own ends. She deceived me.' His attention again shifts to me. 'And you colluded with her to make a fool of me. Do you know what it is to be deceived?'

His head droops, and for long moments nothing is said. He is caught up in his own thoughts, his mood changed in an instant to sadness. Here is the opportunity to make my escape. Gingerly, I rise. He watches me take two, three, four steps towards the door. Then, just as I break into a run, with freedom in sight, he launches himself across the room, grabbing me by the hair. The next moment I am slammed against the table, its hard edge biting into the small of my back, all the air knocked out of my lungs. His body is pressed against me and I know what is coming, and coward that I am, I reason that if I do not fight him, he may not hurt me so very badly. I let my body go limp, as I feel his hand pulling at the fabric of my shift.

The loss of honour is a terrible thing, but unlike poor Lucrece in the old Roman story, I would not take my life, and if I could hide the truth from Giacomo maybe I could live with the secret shame. But then I remember my dream. Perhaps fate has decreed that tonight I will conceive a child. It is a horrible thought – Enrico's seed taking life in me. I know I could no more carry his offspring than could Debra. I would rather die than succumb to that fate.

My arms have been pinned to my sides but somehow I manage to release one, and I pummel his back, and try to claw at his face. Rather than discouraging him, my struggles excite him and I feel the growing hardness in his groin. He begins to rave and it occurs to me that he is quite mad. I hardly hear what he rants as his spittle falls on my face: he rails against me; against his mother; against all womankind. I am fighting now, kicking and screaming, resisting his efforts to force my legs apart, when, somehow, he flips me over, so that I am splayed face down over the table. I hear the crack of my head against the wood, and as my teeth cut into my lip I taste the metal-sourness of blood. I think all my ribs must be broken, and I mewl like a kitten.

'God speaks to me,' he hisses in my ear. 'He tells me how to deal with sluts.' His tongue slides down my neck. It is like a slug. 'You squeal and protest, but it is all pretence. You cannot fool me. Which way would you like it first? Go on, tell me how you want to be fucked? Like your little friend Debra, and all the others? She pretended not to want it, but I knew she did. Like this?' He is clawing at my buttocks, and I realise the violation that he intends. In that instant, I am sure that it was he who attacked Agnesina and those other women, and that it was here that he brought them all. That poor boy I saw die in the Piazzetta with his lumbersome, vegetable head was innocent of no more than stealing a kiss from an hysterical girl.

'Oh, God,' I wail through tears and snot and blood. This is the end for me, I know it. I am not a humble girl dragged from the street, unaware of the identity of her assailant. If I point my finger at him, I may be believed. He dare not let me live. When he has used my body in whatever vile way he wants, he will extinguish my life with his bare hands, dump my remains in one of the lagoon's deepest channels, and I will never be seen again. I will die unshriven, without funeral obsequies and my soul will…

And then the weight of his body suddenly vanishes and the pawing of his hands cease. I sink to the ground. My sobs, and the ringing in my ears, have obliterated anything other than Enrico's voice, so I did not register the sound of footsteps, or hear the furious yapping of a small dog, but when I open my eyes I see a sight that is at once both wonderful and terrible. Enrico is sprawled across the floor and standing above him is Giacomo. I look at my husband. He is little more than a boy, not yet twenty and, compared to his adversary, is as slim as a reed. Only the element of surprise has enabled him to pull Enrico from me. He is no more used to fighting than I, whereas Enrico, I am sure, excels in the brutal art.

Time, and everyone, stands still for a moment. The snarling Cesare is the only creature that moves, and then Enrico springs. On the wall, his shadow leaps – a huge, black parody of himself. Something flashes in the lamplight, and I see that he brandishes a knife. Still, Giacomo does not stir but stares, as if in a trance, at the small tongue of steel that promises to be the instrument of his death. At the sight of the weapon my fear evaporates, and my only concern is to save Giacomo. I launch myself at Enrico, screeching like a bird of prey, latching myself onto his back. He shakes me off, as though I am no more than a burr on his coat. I skid across the room, landing heavily. But my intervention has roused Giacomo from his stupor, and I can see that he is scanning the room, looking for a weapon. His eye lights on a heavy silver candlestick. At that same moment Cesare throws himself at Enrico, fastening his small jaws around his ankle. While Enrico is distracted, Giacomo grabs the candlestick. Although a poor defence against a dagger, it is better than nothing.

Enrico kicks at Cesare with his other foot, almost unbalancing himself, but my little dog hangs on, his terrier blood roused; he is trying to shake Enrico's leg as if it were a rat. But, Enrico, alas, is better armed than any rodent. With one swift movement he lashes out, slicing through fur and flesh. Dark blood stains the blade. Cesare howls as his teeth unfasten. The next instant Enrico grabs him by the scruff of his neck and hurls him across the room to where I am still crouched. I hear the crack of bone, as Cesare slams into the unforgiving wall, and I watch his small, broken body hit the floor. An obscene daub of red smears the white plaster. His head is twisted at a strange angle and a trickle of blood escapes his mouth; then his eyes flicker, still, and glaze over.

Somewhere a wild animal screams. It yells obscenities that would shock a Chioggia fisherman. I do not know where I have learnt such profanities, but a white-hot rage has taught me curses dredged from Hell. This man is responsible for the death of two of the living creatures I loved best in the world. He will not take the life of a third. I rise, ready to fling myself at him once more. But this time there is a difference, this time I am armed. When he threw me from him, I landed on my discarded cloak and my hip struck something hard. It is the knife that I secreted in my pocket all those months ago when I sought to defend myself against the danger that roamed the byways of Venice.

301

The two men still face each other, as motionless as wary dogs, each waiting for the other to make the first move. Enrico, confident of his superior strength and ability, is enjoying this. My attack takes him off guard. I aim for his face, for those mocking animal eyes. Too late, he sees the blade flicker; too late he tries to deflect it with his hand, but somehow I get behind his defences, and then comes the awful moment when his flesh is sliced. He screams, blinded by blood spurting from his eye. I raise my arm to strike again. This time I aim for his heart, but before my weapon finds a home, he crumples to the ground, felled by a single blow from the candlestick that Giacomo brandishes like a club. He neither cries out nor moans, and all I hear is the soft expulsion of his breath as he hits the ground.

All is silent. I fall into Giacomo's arms. I am bruised and bleeding but not greatly hurt. We allow ourselves only seconds to regain the equilibrium of our breath and heartbeat, for at any moment the monster on the floor may rise and fall upon us once more. I extricate myself from Giacomo's embrace and go to the pathetic little heap of bloodied fur.

'It was he who alerted me to your absence,' Giacomo says. 'He would not rest until I had left the house and found you. He led me here.'

And I had thought my Cesare a coward. I stroke the rough fur. Already, he is growing cold. I want to howl, but my sorrow must wait until we are out of harm's way.

'I will go and summon my father and Matthew. They will know how to deal with him,' I say, looking at Enrico who lies, motionless, face down in a pool of blood.

Outside, it is almost light. The pearly grey sky is streaked with pink, and as I race down the *fondamenta*, I pass a water carrier. He is weighed down with his heavy burden but pauses to look at me with undisguised curiosity, no doubt noting my bloodied face.

Matthew and my father are deeply asleep, and when I summon them, they fuss and dawdle in the way of old men. I tell them what has happened as quickly as I can, and seeing my cuts and bruises, *papà* wishes to attend my hurt. Brushing him aside, I make for my room, where I dress.

When I return, Matthew asks, 'Where is your dog?'

'Killed by Enrico,' I reply. 'And if you delay, he may kill my husband also.'

This spurs them into action, and together we return to Ca' Sartorani. Enrico, thank the Lord, is still motionless in the spot where he fell. Sitting cross-legged against the wall is Giacomo, as white faced as a ghoul, the inert and bloody corpse of my dog stretched over his lap. It is a sorry sight, and there are tears in my husband's eyes. Then, looking at the mess of matted fur, I fancy that a black eye blinks, and the tip of a pink tongue flickers. Surely I am seeing things?

'I believe his leg is broken,' says Giacomo. 'But the cut is not deep. He must have been merely stunned when he hit the wall.'

'Cesare,' I whisper, and falling on my knees, I am rewarded by the feeblest of tail wags.

'I will take him home and *papà* will set his leg,' I say, brushing away my tears.

Giacomo lifts Cesare off his lap and places him very gently on the floor. Then we join *papà* and Matthew, who are kneeling either side of Enrico. They have turned him over so that he lies on his back. Blood drools from his face.

'I assume he received a blow to the head?' says *papà*.

Giacomo indicates the candlestick. 'Yes, with that.'

Papà rests his head on Enrico's chest, listening for a heartbeat. 'He is still alive, but is quite insensible. He may stay thus for hours, or even days. Or he may awake at any moment. I cannot see well enough to determine the extent of his injuries. What is your opinion, Matthew?'

'He will lose the sight of that eye, for sure. It is so damaged that the only course is to remove it before it festers and poisons his whole body.'

Nobody speaks as we consider the gravity of this. Then my father says, 'Ginevra, I think it best if you tell us everything. And I do mean everything.'

And so I do, omitting nothing. When I finally speak of my suspicion that Enrico was responsible for the assaults upon the women of our city, *papà* sadly shakes his head. 'That boy they executed was just a common lad. Agnesina said her assailant spoke like a noble. I had thought she was mistaken, but now I am not so sure. The attacks ceased after the execution, but perhaps that was because Enrico was absent from the city.'

We all look at the man stretched on the floor. There is a small gurgling sound from his throat.

'I knew he was evil,' I say. 'I should never have let him set his filthy eyes on Debra. Her death is my fault.'

Giacomo takes me in his arms. 'Shush,' he whispers.

'There will be time enough for reflection and penance,' says *papà*. 'Who knows what any of us would have done in your situation, Ginevra. Hindsight, alas, is a gift possessed by no man. For the present moment, we must decide what to do about…this.'

Again, we all look at Enrico, and watch as the fingers of his left hand move, clawing at the flagstones. Then Matthew speaks. He is a small man, thin and pale, with sandy hair hardly covering his freckled scalp, but his eyes are as bright as a blackbird's. His voice, even with its strong accent, is deep and steady. 'You three must leave here. Francesco, take Ginevra and her dog home. See to their injuries and leave this fellow to me. I will play the stupid Englishman who does not understand your language, and say that I followed the sounds of a fight, found him injured and attended to his ills. I will do as neat a job as any in Venice, I warrant. And then, my children, I think you must leave this city.'

I open my mouth to protest, but he silences me. 'If you report him to the authorities I doubt you will be believed. And if he is as vile as Ginevra attests, then he will seek revenge. He may not cut your throat with his own hands but he will pay someone else to do it. Francesco, you should also consider fleeing.'

My father brushes aside the suggestion. 'No. I will not let him force me from my home. But, Giacomo…yes…please take my daughter to a place of safety. Perhaps you can go to Conegliano, to Giambattista's house.'

'No, Enrico would guess that is where we are,' says Giacomo. 'But Giambattista's son, my cousin, fra Niccolò, is a monk at San Giustina in Padua. That would be the safest place.'

'Then that is where you must go,' says Matthew. 'Wait until dark. It is best that as few people as possible see you. I have something to ensure that our friend here does not awake until you are far away.' And he produces the bottle of dwale.

'No, Matthew,' my father protests. 'It is too great a risk.'

'Ah, a young, strong, healthy man – he will suffer no ill effects. And I certainly do not wish him to wake whilst I am dealing with that eye. Now, go – all of you.'

There seems little choice, so with Cesare in my arms, we make to leave. Then I see the painting, so cruelly hacked in two, and I cannot bear the thought of abandoning it.

'Please, Giacomo, let us take it. If we do not, Enrico will destroy it, I know he will. And wherever we are bound, I should like to have Debra's image with me. Please.'

So Giacomo picks up the two pieces, and we walk back to our home, trying to look as though we have not a care in the world. I know it is a foolish notion, but stealing my portrait from Enrico gives me hope that I also will escape his filthy clutch.

The rest of the day is spent in preparing for our self-imposed exile. Giacomo at once hurries to see Giambattista. I have every intention of accompanying him, for God knows when I will see my teacher again, but as *papà* is tending my cuts and bruises I am overcome by a fit of shaking and sobbing. *Papà* gives me a sleeping draught, and orders me to bed, where I doze fitfully with Cesare at my side. His wound has been bandaged and his broken leg fixed in a splint. He is so happy to be permitted onto my bed again that he forgets to feel sorry for himself, and wags his tail and smiles as much as a dog may.

At some point in the afternoon, Matthew returns. Whilst he was tending to Enrico, the men who are working on the restoration of Ca' Sartorani returned, and finding their master being so well attended have hailed the Englishman a hero. Enrico's father was summoned and embraced Matthew, pressing bags of money onto him, weeping with happiness that his son had been saved. Then he took Enrico back with him to his own house on the Canale Grande.

'So, you have only a few hours before he wakes, and a Sartorani henchman comes looking for you,' Matthew warns. 'As soon as night falls you must leave. Henceforth, I intend to lodge at an inn, for the connection between us must remain secret. But your servant is a good person and to be trusted; likewise your father's assistant. Between them they will take care of him until it is safe for you to return.'

A gondola is hired to carry us to Fusina where a horse drawn barge will take us along the Brenta on the eight-hour journey to Padua. We stand on the shoreline, watching our possessions being loaded. I cannot believe this is happening. It is surely a dream from which I will awake. Only my husband gives me the strength to leave this city of my birth, for the thought of any harm befalling Giacomo is more than I can bear.

'You will soon be back,' says *papà*, but something tells me this will never be. We are facing an exile that will last unto our death. I try to be brave, but as I kiss Cesare goodbye my salty tears fall onto his face. He licks at them, and at my hand, not knowing that this is farewell.

And then we are bobbing on the indifferent waters, and the figures of my father and Matthew become smaller and smaller, until they disappear into the darkness. I think I hear Cesare whimper. It is a thin, sad sound that rides on the breeze, but they are now so far away that it can only be the call of a bird; nevertheless, it tears at my heart.

Giacomo holds me close as I stare into the distance. My home fades from sight, until I can see only the faintest light on the far horizon marking where the city floats in the dark lagoon – just a glimmer between land and sea. I watch Venice slip into nothingness, and then it is gone.

The Swift Foot of Time

Sidmouth, Devon

21 November, 1987

Dear Raffi,

I do hope you are well and that Caterina is making good progress.

I'm back from my French sojourn and as you will see from the address, am now in Sidmouth. (In case you don't know, it's a quiet little seaside town in Devon.) Tom's granny had a hip replacement a couple of weeks ago and needs someone to help her until she gets back on her feet (literally!) and as I'm homeless until my tenant moves out, it seemed the perfect solution. I've lots of spare time on my hands, so I've taken up painting – just watercolours – but it passes the time. There are beautiful coastal views here, but I seem to be gravitating towards painting the townscape. It must be the city girl in me! When I'm back in London I'm going to sign up for some proper lessons.

Perhaps you didn't get my last two letters? (I know the Italian postal system leaves a lot to be desired.) In them I explained why I had to disappear so quickly. I know now, I was stupid to run away because of *Colonello* Boccardi's threats. I'm sure there would have been a way round things, but at the time I felt so threatened and confused. Thinking about it though, maybe it's not such a bad thing, as it has given us time to think about what we want, and how we truly feel. You said what we had was very special. I think – will always think that too, and whatever happens will never forget our time together.

Love from Anna xxx

* * *

Venice

10 December, 1987

Hello Precious – and Happy Christmas,

I can't belief that Raffi still hasn't replied. What a bastard!! To lose one letter may be regarded as a misfortune; to lose two is carelessness, but to lose three is beyond belief – even in Italy.

I can't promise not to say anything if I see him, but there's not much chance of that. Caterina is out of hospital and staying with her Aunt in Treviso, and apparently Raffi is there too, so he hardly comes to Venice. I bumped into Vittore yesterday. He asked after you.

And how's your mum? Look, I can't believe there wasn't more to you up-ing and leaving than her dodgy love life. Please tell me…I may be able to help.

Anyway, I hope the festive season isn't too miserable for you…Ding, dong merrily on high, cut your throat and wish to die and all that.

Lots of love and big supportive hugs.

Izzy x x x x

PS: Will sends a big, wet kiss – yuck!!

PPS: NO man is worth it – especially one who hasn't got the decency to reply to your letters!!!

* * *

Venice

27 March, 1988

Hello Angel,

I did try phoning, but you were out, and hadn't switched on your answering machine. (God, I hate not having a phone in the flat.)

Anyway, there's no easy way to say this. Raffi and Caterina were married yesterday. I heard about the impending nuptials a couple of weeks ago, but kept hoping someone would turn up and stop it – like in Jane Eyre. (Even a mad wife up in the attic would be better than him marrying Caterina.) But no such luck. Everything went swimmingly. I snuck into the church so I could give Raffi the Rat my best dirty look, but I don't think he saw me.

Caterina is still a bit wobbly on her pins, so she was supported up the aisle by her dad AND a cousin. All the old ladies in the congregation were twittering on about how brave and beautiful she is. I suppose she did look gorgeous – although her dress was definitely OTT.

You were right. They go back so far and are so wound up with each other that nothing is going to split them up. I thought he had more sense, but obviously not. I hope you're not too upset. Don't be – there's lots of other fish in the sea (as I can testify – more on that later).

I spoke to Vittore very briefly. He asked if you were coming to stay with me again soon. I said I didn't think that was very likely because I'M LEAVING VENICE TOO!!! Well – that's my big news. It's all over between me and Will. I've met someone else.

Things haven't been great between us for a while. For one thing, I really want to come home. The new flat, as I've told you already, is crap – it's getting more and more difficult to find anywhere to live at a reasonable rent, and I've decided that I need to start earning some proper money. I don't want to end up an old lady, freezing in front of a one bar fire, wearing a tea cosy and living off cat food. We're both thirty next year and I think it's time to grow up. But Will is stuck in Peter Pan land and won't even consider coming back to England. So – three weeks ago we had a massive row, which ended up with me storming off to Paradiso Perduto. None of the gang was there, but I got chatting to a group of English tourists – two couples, and a bloke by himself. One of the women was celebrating her thirtieth birthday with a long weekend in Venice, and Edward – the bloke by himself – is her brother. Well, Edward obviously fancied me and to cut a long story short I ended up back at his hotel. Come the morning I'm expecting it to be, 'OK, so long, bye bye,' but, no, he asked if he could take me out for dinner that night. Will was out when I got back to the flat, so I grabbed some clothes for the evening and left a note saying I was staying with Paola. I had a brilliant night with Edward – we went to Fiaschetteria Toscana, and it was SO nice to spend time with someone who is such a gentleman – and solvent. (He works for some sort of investment bank.)

I had planned on playing hard to get (yeah, yeah a bit late, I know) but of course we ended up in bed – again. Then he told me that although he was going home the next day, could he come over in a couple of weeks for the weekend. Well, what is a girl to say? This one said, 'yes please', still not believing he really would. Suffice to say, I didn't tell him I'm living with someone. Then three days later I come home from work and there's Will sitting by this humongous bunch of red roses from Fantin's. For a second I thought he'd bought them and then he asked, 'Who's Edward?' and handed me the card that came with the flowers, which said, "Darling Izzy. My flight and hotel booked. See you on the 18th. Please phone to arrange where to meet".

There didn't seem much choice but to tell him the truth – so I did. And it was extraordinary, he came over all Victorian. Said that if I phoned Edward now, and told him I couldn't see him again, then he would overlook my infidelity (he actually used the word "infidelity") and he'd forgive me and we would pretend it never happened. There was no discussion about WHY I had gone off with another man. Well, I saw red and said a lot of horrible things I shouldn't have said and told him that I'd rather try my luck with Edward than hang around with a pathetic waster (yes, I know I'm a cow).

And that was more or less it. He's staying with a friend in Mestre and we've not spoken since. It's a horrible way to end a relationship. We've been together for two and a half years and I used to love him SO much, but I've just had enough of living in grotty flats and having no money, and I REALLY want to come back to London. I felt awful, but you know me…instead of moping I went to Paola's, rang Edward and we talked for over an hour, after which I felt a LOT better. Anyway, he did come over, and we had a wonderful time. On his last night he asked me had I thought about coming back to England, so I explained that I wanted to, but it's difficult because I've no job and nowhere to live etc. etc. and then he just came out with it – "Move in with me!!" He said that he's never felt like this about anyone before and he thinks he's fallen in love with me and it was all so amazingly romantic that I said, "all right". I'm not sure if I should live with him so soon, so I may stay with Mum and Dad for a while, but the main thing is, I'M COMING HOME.

I've told the University some elaborate lie about why I've got to leave. I don't think they believe a word, and I don't suppose I'll ever get a reference, but what the hell. (Edward has said he'll help me find a job.) And I've informed the landlord that he can keep his lousy deposit on his lousy flat. And on the 8th April, Edward is going to drive down here and bring me and my few pathetic possessions back to England. I CANNOT WAIT!!

Oh, God, I'm sorry. I really didn't mean to go on about me so much, but I'm sure Edward will have some lovely friends I can introduce you to, and you'll soon forget all about Raffi the Rat. And if things don't work out with Edward, you and me can go out on the razzle together!

Anyway, as I can't cram anymore onto this page, I'm going to stop and put it in the post NOW, so you'll get it asap. Can't wait to see you. I'll call as soon as I'm back.

PLEASE try not to be sad. Everything will work out – I promise.

Lots of Love

Izzy x x x x

* * *

Ca' Melisa, Venezia

Christmas, 1988

My dear Anna,

I am sorry not to have written since Raffi's marriage, but it has been a busy, and somewhat trying, time for us all.

First, I have some good news. Caterina gave birth to a little girl in September. They have called her Marietta (do you remember that this was the name of Tintoretto's daughter?) She is the most beautiful child, although in my role as doting "grandfather", I am perhaps biased.

Sadly, only a month after her birth, Caterina's father committed suicide. He let himself into one of the cells at the station, and put a revolver to his head. The note he left explained that he had been diagnosed with motor neurone disease eighteen months ago and although, at first, the symptoms were only slight, he had, of late, been aware of his condition rapidly deteriorating. He could not bear the thought of suffering such a debilitating illness and therefore chose to end his life with, as he put it, dignity. It seems he was only waiting to see his grandchild. Caterina is, of course, devastated. She was very close to her father. We all pray that she will find comfort in her daughter.

Anna, forgive me for asking, but why have you never returned to Venice? It is something that has never ceased to mystify me. Now that Raffi is married, and a father, whatever happened between you two, if indeed anything did happen, must necessarily be truly in the past. Perhaps I am being presumptuous, my dear, but I do think we have a right to know.

Very best regards Vittore and Rosina

* * *

Ca' Melisa, Venezia

6 January, 1989

My dear Anna,

Thank you for your letter, and for being so frank. At last, we understand. I was shocked and sickened to hear of your treatment by *Colonello* Boccardi. But I believe his illness explains his behaviour. He saw his daughter facing the prospect of coping with severe disablement alone, and consequently he did everything he could to ensure that Raffi would be there for her.

It was inexcusable, but in spite of everything I cannot help but feel sympathy for him. One will do anything to protect the welfare of one's child. But, at the same time, I do so wish that you had confided in me. However, as you say, it is too late for regrets.

I will respect your wishes not to tell Raffi any of this. Like you, I see no advantage in doing so – at least not at the present. He does so love little Marietta.

I believe that the baby will exert a calming influence upon Caterina, and I hope that she will make my boy happy.

One thing puzzles me. You say that you wrote to Raffi. I took the liberty of asking him if he had ever heard from you and he confirmed that he had not. I know you will think I am biased but I really cannot believe that he would have ignored your correspondence. But perhaps I do not know him as well as I imagine.

If it is any consolation, I am certain that he cared for you very deeply but I suspect that the bond between him and Caterina was too strong to sever. I pray that you are not bitter. You must not let this blight your life.

I am so pleased to hear that you are painting. The immersion of oneself in art can be a great comfort, as I am sure you have already discovered. I had no idea that you had such aspirations. It is a brave course for you to take, and I look forward to seeing your work. Please let me know if I might assist you in your new career. I do have a few contacts, you know!

Finally, please come and see us. You will always be very welcome, here at Ca' Melisa.

Very best regards Vittore and Rosina

* * *

South Kensington, London
Christmas, 1990

Dear Vittore and Rosina

Well, another year nearly over. I am keeping well, and managing to attend lots of art classes.

I'm sure you will be pleased to hear that Izzy and Edward were married in the spring, and she is already expecting a baby. I'm going to be a godmother!

Thank you for the photo of Marietta. What a poppet! Do send them all my best wishes.

Love from Anna

* * *

South Kensington, London
Christmas, 1991

Dear Vittore and Rosina

Thank you for all your news. I was sorry to hear that the Misericordia has closed.

311

I suppose when the restoration project fell through, there didn't seem much point in keeping it open, especially as there are now so few monks. Do you know what will happen to it? Admittedly it's not the most beautiful of churches but I always thought it had such a lovely atmosphere. I assume that nothing has ever been heard of the Madonna?

I am still happily painting. I'm now working mainly in oils, and concentrating on London townscapes. This city may not be as ethereally beautiful as Venice, but for me it's an endless source of inspiration.

A couple of months ago, I put some of my pictures into an exhibition at a local library, and sold every one of them! At long last I feel I am making some real progress.

Love from Anna

* * *

South Kensington, London

Christmas, 1992

Dear Vittore and Rosina

I do hope this reaches you before Christmas. It's been an exciting six months work wise. I'm now renting studio space in Fulham. This means I can produce much larger paintings, and I think my work has already benefited. In the summer I pooled my resources with some other artists and staged an exhibition. I entered six canvases and sold all but one. If this goes on I might be able to give up the day job!

Yes, I am still single, or at least, there is no one special in my life. But lots of other people seem to be tying knots. My mother has moved to Scotland with Leslie, her "boyfriend". (He wanted to go up there to be near his daughters.) But she won't marry him because she would lose my father's pension. I call her the Scarlet Woman, which I think she secretly rather likes.

Also, Tom got married to my friend, Zoë. (He's the one who writes the crime novels.) He's been besotted with her since I introduced them four years ago. She's a paediatrician and rather wonderful.

Izzy is having another baby (due in May). She's hoping for a little brother for Chloë.

Please give my regards to Raffi and family. No sign of a brother or sister for Marietta?

Love from Anna

* * *

South Kensington, London

Christmas, 1993

Dear Vittore and Rosina

I'm sorry not to have been in touch for so long. But I've been very busy with commissions and my latest exhibition – again shared with other artists – which was at the Bishopsgate Institute in the City.

Also, I've been seeing a very nice man called Jeremy. He works near the Institute, and came in a few times, so we got chatting. He ended up buying two paintings, and when he came to collect them on the last day he asked me out to dinner. The rest, as they say, is history.

Tomorrow we're off to Joshua's (Izzy's little boy) christening party. Another godchild!

And you say Edie is expecting? Gosh! She must be well into her forties, so that's very brave of her.

Much love from Anna

* * *

Ca' Melisa, Venezia

Christmas, 1994

My dear Anna,

We were both so pleased to hear that you have enjoyed such a successful year professionally. Please let us know, in advance, about any proposed exhibitions. We may well come over. Rosina hates flying, as you know, but it would be an excellent excuse to try the new Channel tunnel.

Last week I heard from Edie. Her baby was born, very prematurely, in the spring. She did not mention anything at the time, but now it transpires that the little girl has cerebral palsy, although it is apparently too early to ascertain to what degree the condition will impact upon her life.

Graham is devastated, but Edie, as is her wont, is determined to be positive. Already she is working with a cerebral palsy charity that helps children and their families who could not otherwise afford assistance. She tells me that because of this she no longer has time to be actively involved with Save Venice. This will be

313

a great loss to everyone, but I do understand. Also, she is very reluctant to leave little Bryony, so I doubt we will see her in Venice very often, although she plans to keep her apartment.

I hope we will see you in 1995. If we cannot manage to come to London, why do you and Jeremy not visit us? We would so like to meet him.

I must conclude this now. We are about to attend a nativity concert in which Marietta is playing an angel, a most appropriate piece of casting in my humble opinion.

Very best regards Vittore and Rosina

* * *

South Kensington, London

Christmas, 1995

Dear Vittore and Rosina

Thank you for your card. I'm afraid I've been very late sending out mine this year. To be honest, life has been a little fraught. I split up with Jeremy two weeks ago. It was all very amicable and by mutual consent, but nevertheless upsetting.

I may not have told you, but he's nearly three years younger than me, and wants to settle down in the country and start a family. I'm thirty-six, and I really don't want to change my life so very drastically. For a start, I can't bear the thought of leaving London – I know it sounds pretentious, but it's my muse. The countryside is all very beautiful but I'm just not inspired to paint it. I love the animation and the mercurial quality of the city. Oh, listen to me! I suppose it comes down to preferring painting people and buildings, rather than sheep and trees. So for all these reasons Jeremy and I had to go our separate ways. I'm sure that he'll find someone else very soon, and I hope we can stay friends. I think I'm destined to be an old maid!

Love from Anna

* * *

South Kensington, London

6 September, 1996

Dear Vittore and Rosina

As promised, enclosed is the catalogue for my exhibition. I'm really sorry you won't be able to make it.

314

I am SO nervous about it all – it being my first solo venture. Obviously I've put a lot of money into it (mostly courtesy of a very generous loan from my mother) and I'm really hoping that it'll enable me to get representation with a London gallery. Fingers crossed!

I'll let you know how things go.

Much love from Anna

* * *

Chiswick, London

4 August, 1997

Hello Anna

Just to say thank you for such a scrummy dinner. And once again, CONGRATULATIONS on your news, you clever, clever girl.

Edward wants to know if you being represented by this Bond Street gallery means that we have to insure your paintings for thousands and thousands of pounds. I said that we'd better buy some more, pronto, while we can still afford them!

See you when we get back from hols.

Lots of Love

Izzy xxxxxx

PS: I really like Mack, and he obviously adores you!!

* * *

South Kensington, London

Christmas, 1998

Dear Vittore and Rosina

Thank you for the photo. I cannot believe that Marietta is ten. How time flies.

Great news that you are getting a computer. I really must organise myself a website (you'll be able to check up on me then!)

I've been very, very busy working for the exhibition next year. I'm amazed at the prices that the gallery will be charging for my paintings. I don't suppose you can expect anything else in Bond Street. I only hope they sell some!

I'm so fortunate being able to share Mack's studio. His house is a little end of terrace in Fulham. It's tiny and the studio is an extension that takes up half the garden. But it backs onto a school playground, so although it's a bit noisy at times, it does get fantastic light all day long.

If you can't make the exhibition, perhaps we will see you in Venice. Mack is constantly nagging for us to go there!

Love from Anna

* * *

THE LONDON MONTHLY ART REVIEW: JULY 1999

London Lives, currently showing at the Miles Babington Gallery, is an affectionate hymn to our capital city. Amongst the exhibitors there are some familiar names, but the rising star of this paean to London is undoubtedly Anna Fleming, whose bold and assured canvases belie the fact that she is largely self-taught. Her technical mastery of oils, and keen sense of composition draws the viewer deep into the picture, giving us iconoclastic images such as windswept and be-wigged barristers struggling against the elements in the courtyard of Lincoln's Inn; young lovers buying plants at Columbia Flower Market, and children paddling in the fountains of Trafalgar Square. Much of her work has a nostalgic, yesteryear quality to it, typically exemplified in *Last Bus Home* featuring the beloved Routemaster. With a dramatic use of light and shade, she takes us through sheltered archways, along quiet backstreets and out into the glittering sunlight of the city's open spaces.

These paintings combine the grittiness of Hopper, and the commercial appeal of Vetriano (although currently at a fraction of the price) but with a tender regard for the human condition. Never mawkish or trite, she paints real people and records incidents that you suspect she has personally witnessed on the streets she knows so well.

Fleming's love for her home town shines out, and residents and visitors alike will find a deep resonance in these works. Buy now – the price can only rise, as the talent of this poet of the city becomes common knowledge.

* * *

Ca' Melisa, Venezia

From: Vittore Anzelieri
Subject: That which was lost
Date: 6 April 2000
To: Anna Fleming

My dear Anna

Something quite extraordinary has happened. Our Saint Catherine, the lost half of the Misericordia Madonna, has been found.

I have just returned from confirming its authenticity, and although it must now be subjected to various tests, they will, I am sure, support my judgement.

I am not cognizant with the full facts of its recovery, but I gather that it was discovered in a village close to Domodossola, which, if you remember, was the home of the Raimund Thalberg collection. It was in the house of an elderly farmer who had recently passed away. The painting had been in his possession for as long as his children could remember, and they had no idea how he came to "own" it. As he was far from wealthy, they assumed it had little value. But after his death, his daughter-in-law had it valued – just to make sure. The valuer she approached, upon seeing Cima's signature, contacted me. We have alerted the authorities and what will happen to it now, I do not know. I suppose it depends upon whether Thalberg has any living relatives.

Whilst I am, of course, delighted that it has been found, it does make me grieve even more for the Madonna. I can only hope that if it is still intact, it will spur whoever has it, to return it. I will let you know if I hear anything further.

Regards to Mack.

Kind regards Vittore and Rosina

* * *

South Kensington, London

From: Anna Fleming
Subject: Mack
Date: 8 November 2001
To: Vittore Anzelieri

Dear Vittore and Rosina

I have some very sad news to tell you. Last Friday Mack died. He had a massive heart attack. I was downstairs making breakfast and could hear him pottering about. Then there was a thud and everything went quiet. The paramedics were here in no time, but it was too late. I still can't believe it. He was only 58.

Everyone is being amazingly supportive, especially Izzy. In fact, this is my first day back home, as I've been staying with her in Chiswick.

The funeral is next week. His kids are organising most of it but there is still so much to do.

I am so sorry that you never met him. Somehow we just did not manage to get to Venice.

Love from Anna

* * *

Fulham, London

From: Anna Fleming
Subject: Change of address
Date: 10 July 2002
To: Vittore Anzelieri

Dear Vittore and Rosina

Having recently made a major decision, I thought I would fill you in on the latest development in my life.

I'm leaving my little flat (although I am renting it out, rather than selling).

A year or so before he died, Mack told me that he had changed his will and had left me his house. He said that he loved the idea of me carrying on working here, even if he was no longer around. I remember laughing and saying that it wouldn't be an issue for years and years – Mack always seemed so fit and well. But, of course, I was wrong. I was also quite shocked because he does have two grown up children, not to mention a wife. But apparently, when his mother died, he settled all the value of her estate on his kids, so he reckoned that they had been well provided for already. His wife, well off in her own right, will get his pension. I thought it might cause a few problems, but they are all really lovely people, and seem to really want me to have the house.

Although I know there's no actual obligation for me to move in, and I could sell up if I wanted, I've found it's where I really want to be. It's a very happy little place – and I would never find a better studio.

Mack's kindness has given me financial security too. Painting is such a precarious existence. You never stop worrying about people ceasing to want your work or, God forbid, what would happen if an accident or illness meant you couldn't paint. But now, the rent from my flat will mean that I'll always have an income.

I'll send you one of my change of address cards, which is a painting of the house.

Much love from Anna

* * *

La Columba Internet Café : Venice

From: Izzy Henshawe
Subject: Greetings from Venezia!!
Date: 15 December 2003
To: Anna Fleming

Ciao Bella

Well, so much for my dear husband staying incommunicado on hols. Even as I type this, he's stuck on a conference call at the hotel. Sod you, I thought, I'm off for a bit of retail therapy. 600 euros later (not all for me – honest) and here I am, sitting in this nice little Internet café, supping a rum punch.

Anyway…an AMAZING thing happened y'day – well, three amazing things.

First. La Fenice opened!!! (Do you remember when it burnt down and we all sat round saying, "Oh, it'll never open again. Not in our lifetime etc, etc?" How wrong were we?) Edward, bless him, thought he could get tickets!! In fact, according to the concierge at the hotel, they were all given away to celebs or sold in some sort of complicated Internet auction. So they'd put up a big screen to relay the concert (not that I had any intention of freezing my arse off in the middle of December). But we were meandering through the Piazza and on the screen there's this really grim opera production. Or at least that's what I assumed it was – Fidelio or something, 'cos they're dragging up this poor prisoner. And then I realised it was the NEWS, and it wasn't Placido Domingo scruffed up, but Saddam Hussein!!!

SO – we're all galvanised to the screen, when I hear this voice say, "Hello, it's Izzy isn't it?" And bugger me, but there's Raffi! And his daughter. She's lovely, with one of those huge Julia Roberts smiles! He looks really well, hair's a bit shorter, a little bit grey, and he's wearing specs, but apart from that, hardly changed (bastard!) Anyway, we chat away and I can tell ('cos I always can) that he is DYING to ask about you. So I say, all casual like, "Anna's very well. She's really getting quite famous," and his eyes go all sort of soft and misty – honestly, they really do. And I'm just wondering what wifey would think of this when, talk of a she-devil,

Caterina swans up. All fur coat and leathery cleavage (meow). Actually, I hate to admit it, but she looked pretty good.

Well, after she arrived the conversation fizzled out, and they wandered off, and that was that. We ended up eating at a little restaurant near our old flat, in the building where the fruit and veg shop used to be. The one where you got the word for fig wrong and asked for a bag of c**ts. Oh, how we laughed!

I'll tell you more about the trip when I see you. Don't forget our drinks party on the 21st. And thanks again for looking in on Mum and the kids.

Lots of love Izzy xxxxxxx

* * *

Ca' Melisa, Venezia

From: Vittore Anzelieri
Subject:
Date: 6 June 2004
To: Anna Fleming

My dear Anna

Thank you for your last email, telling us all your news. I am sorry not to have been in contact sooner, but it has not been an easy time for any of us of late. Raffi and Caterina have separated. It was not a very great surprise, and I think we all saw it coming. I do believe they would have parted long ago, but have stayed together for the sake of Marietta. Caterina has left Venice and is living in Milan. Although Raffi has not told me so, I suspect there is another man. She, of course, wanted Marietta to accompany her, but Marietta refused. I am not surprised, all her friends are in Venice and naturally she does not want to change schools at such a crucial time (she hopes to study medicine at Padova). We are naturally delighted not to lose her, but it is very difficult for the child, having to choose between her parents. However, I am afraid that Caterina always did put herself first. At long last I can say that, and not feel disloyal.

I do hope you are well, my dear. Have you started Izzy's painting yet? I agree – you must be firm with Edward, and let him know it has to be your own creation, and not just a copy. Do let me know how the work progresses.

Kind regards Vittore and Rosina

Mr and Mrs Henshawe and a Glass of Champagne

Looking up from her palette, Anna glances towards the window. Sunlight slants through the white shutters, painting bars of yellow across the figure slouched on the retro dining chair. Izzy is nodding off again. Agreeing to her posing with a glass of champagne in her hand was a mistake. Anna fears that this entire project is a mistake. Nevertheless, she is thankful to have company today; thankful for anything that distracts from the sharp nip of memory; thankful to be in this elegant family home in leafy Chiswick.

The house was spacious when its first owners took possession, during the final year of Queen Victoria's reign, but extended by both Izzy and the previous occupants, its 2004 proportions are almost grand. Despite this, Izzy wants to move: she fancies one of those squares off the King's Road. Edward refuses to budge. In Chiswick, the kids can walk to school (not that they often do, preferring to rely upon Izzy and the 4 x 4); there is a health club around the corner; plenty of restaurants and shops; people they know. And he nearly always gets a seat on the train that takes him, still half asleep, to his temple of Mammon, as Izzy uncharitably describes his workplace. Why move? Why spend hundreds of thousands for a smarter address?

Izzy is not even sure herself: she says something about wanting more room. Edward suggests a basement conversion. They are quite the rage, and for less than £100,000 will give her all the extra space she could possibly require. Izzy agrees: she has no choice. Edward holds the purse strings, and although it is a sizeable purse, it cannot indulge his wife's every whim. Out of the ensuing chaos of builders, carpenters and plasterers, Edward's desire for the painting is born.

Edward is not particularly interested in art, but one evening he attends a "do" at the Tate Gallery. After dinner, for those who can tear themselves away from the port and brandy, there is a private tour of the collection's highlights. The guide is a pretty little thing, and Edward is enjoying looking at her as much as the paintings. Then he is stopped in his tracks. He vaguely recognises the huge canvas, so assumes it must be "famous". Closer inspection reveals that it is *Mr and Mrs Clark and Percy* by David Hockney. Edward guesses Percy is the cat, but as he knows even less about fashion than art, he has no idea that the handsome couple staring out from a sun-drenched room are the designer, Ossie Clark and his wife Celia, depicted in their 1970 heyday.

'She's a dead ringer for my Izzy,' he says to anyone who cares to listen. And then informs them that the Clarks' sitting room is also uncannily like his own: the same French windows leading onto a balcony; the same white balustrade; wooden shutters rather than curtains; even a vase of lilies – Izzy loves white lilies.

By the time a taxi drops Edward at his front door he has hatched a plan. Their new basement requires an impressive piece of art. Why not commission Anna to produce a smaller copy of Hockney's painting, but with Izzy and himself as the subjects? He is so excited he has to wake his wife to tell her. She is a bit too drunk to appreciate his proposal but is gratifying enthusiastic the next day. The only person with reservations is Anna.

'I'm not a portraitist,' she says.

Edward is nonplussed. She tries to explain. 'I daresay I'll manage a fair likeness, but I haven't got that knack of capturing the essence of a person. It's a very particular talent, you know.'

Edward pooh-poohs, and Izzy says, 'I don't care about my essence. Just make me beautiful – and ten years younger.'

Anna does not say, but this is the main reason for her misgivings. She likes to paint things as she sees them, warts and all. Izzy is approaching forty-five, and although not warty, over consumption of white wine and yo-yo dieting have taken their toll. Anna is afraid of upsetting her friend by too strict an adherence to the truth. Edward mistakes her reluctance for a ploy to exact greater payment and ups his offer. In the end, she agrees: it seems churlish not to, and it is a challenging project.

'It's OK to harken back to the original, but I don't want to produce something that's just a bad copy with your and Izzy's faces,' she tells them. 'For a start, I suggest we reverse the couple's poses, so Izzy sits, and Edward stands.'

Mr and Mrs Henshawe agree. Anna calls round one Saturday morning to help them decide what to wear. Izzy has chosen a shot silk dress in a shade of blue identical to the colour of Ossie's jumper. But when Edward bounces into the room, Anna's heart sinks. The jeans are too baggy; the jumper too tight. The outfit reveals that his belly now coerces his belt to rest just above his groin. Posing with hand on hip, in these over casual clothes, he possesses none of the insolent dandyism of the young Mr Clark. In fact, he reminds Anna of a fat schoolboy. Then she has a brain wave.

'Go and change into your dinner jacket, Edward. And take off your shoes and socks.'

Edward is stunned into obedience. Five minutes later he pads into the room – a changed man. He spent a lot of money on this DJ, and the cut is superb; it hides a multitude of sins.

He holds out a bow tie. 'Tie it for me, Iz.'

'No,' says Anna. 'Just drape it round your neck. Do you have a bottle of champagne, Izzy?'

'Silly question!' Izzy scuttles off.

Anna is about to call not to open it (it is only ten o'clock) when she hears the pop. Izzy reappears with the bottle and a carton of orange juice. She mixes bucks fizzes. In her glass there is only a token splash of juice.

'Edward, you hold the champagne bottle. That's it…in your right hand,' instructs Anna. 'And put your left hand on your hip.'

She takes some photos that they view on the computer. The effect is startling; disarmingly similar to the original and yet quite different. The couple look, even Edward, almost rakish, and a little Bohemian.

'It's like,' says Izzy, 'we're waiting for guests to arrive. Or they've just left…early in the morning, after some all-night bash. I think, in the absence of a friendly cat, I can have a nice glass of bubbly on my lap.' A few clicks, and she zooms to examine her face. 'But you will get rid of my eye bags, won't you?'

Anna has already decided to forgo her scruples and perform some virtual cosmetic surgery, although looking at her friend on this June morning, she is struck by her youthful appearance. Izzy usually tortures her hair into a sleek bob, but for the purpose of the painting she has abandoned her straighteners. With the rebirth of her corkscrew curls she really does bear an uncanny similarity to the twenty-nine year old Mrs Clark. It is one of life's little ironies that this was Izzy's exact age when her future husband first caught sight of her across a smoky Venetian bar. Ironic also, that Mr Clark bears more than a passing resemblance to a man whom Anna has not seen for nearly seventeen years. Paint a pair of geeky glasses on his face, and it could be Will staring out from the canvas. It is extraordinary that she has not seen it before.

That night, compelled to check that memory has not deceived her, she rummages in a cupboard and pulls out a box filled with silly keepsakes, ancient scribblings and photos. She finds the faded image snapped by a young German student on that long ago morning in Venice. Yes: Will is, or was, a dead ringer for Ossie. She wonders if Izzy has noticed.

Deeper in the box there are photos of another man she has not seen in all those years, but who has seldom left her thoughts. It is foolish, she knows, to hang onto these faded snapshots of someone who is, by all accounts, a happily married father and who, she is sure, rarely spares her a passing thought. She had intended to destroy them when she and Mack became lovers, but could not bring herself to do so. With an effort she stops rifling through the past, puts the box back and tries, unsuccessfully, to banish Raffi from her mind. The next day she receives Vittore's email.

* * *

A sudden gust of wind seizes the closed shutter, slamming it open.

'Shit,' exclaims Izzy, jolted awake. 'Sorry, must have nodded off. It was so hot last night, I hardly slept.'

Anna also is tired, her sleep having been disturbed by one of those ridiculous Venice dreams. It took the usual form: sitting outside a bar near the Accademia, she waits for Raffi. Then the scene switches and she is transported to a small, dark place, terrified by something or someone. And still she waits for Raffi. On waking, she knows that the coming day will be smeared by the past.

Driving to Chiswick, her mind is like a laden sponge: the slightest pressure drips memories into the present. She recalls not only her time in Venice, but the years after, and the events and people that have shaped her life.

Those first months back in London, she threw herself into work with a steely resolve, audio typing in windowless offices, and skivvying in restaurants. Boring and poorly paid though these jobs were, the flexible hours gave her the freedom to attend as many art classes as possible. Her constant occupation also meant there was less time to think about Raffi. Even when she heard about his marriage she did not quite relinquish the dream of a future in which he would somehow figure. Then came the Christmas card bearing the news that he was a father.

While festive merry makers revelled in the streets, Anna lay on her bed feeling as though some dark, nocturnal creature had invaded her body, clawing through her guts; shredding her sanity. This marked the total dissolution of hope. Marriage was not irrevocable; mistakes happened and people left their spouses. But she knew that Raffi, marked by his own fractured childhood, would never abandon his daughter. She had lost him, if not to Caterina, to a tiny scrap of humanity called Marietta.

The realisation tore away the boundaries of her life, and she strayed into what she later thought of as her wilderness years. Not even to Tom and Izzy did she confess the extent of her devastation. Even they, she was sure, would not understand this obsession for a man with whom she had spent just the single night. They would tell her to get over it and move on. This was a wisdom she could not dispute, and so she did anything to put him out of her mind. She worked too hard, drank too much, and occasionally spent nights in the beds of strangers, most of whom she had no wish to see again. And she deliberately distanced herself from

324

those who could help her most, reasoning that they were immersed in their own happy lives. The persona she showed to the world was one of brittle cheerfulness, and few suspected the internal misery that was fast becoming habitual.

It was Izzy who provided the motivation to reassemble the pieces dismantled by loss. Little Chloë Henshawe was being christened, and Anna was a godmother. The night before the ceremony, she went to a party in Islington, and woke up at ten-thirty in a scruffy north London flat, next to a man whose name she could not recall. She could not even remember whether they had had sex. The christening was at midday. She left her snoring bedfellow, and spent a fortune she could ill-afford on taxis, sneaking into the church at ten minutes past twelve. Creeping into the pew next to Izzy, she whispered, 'I'm so sorry. I think I've got this gastric flu thing that's going around. I've been up half the night.'

Izzy peered over her lace festooned child. 'Pull the other one. I can smell the alcohol from here. And to think people used to say I was the soak. Do you think you're really fit to be a godmother?'

And then it was time for a hymn.

Later, Izzy sidled up to her. 'Anna, I'm sorry. I didn't mean what I said. I was just worried you weren't going to be here…'

'No, you were totally justified. It was unforgivable to be late.' Anna took a swig of mineral water. 'Oh God, Izzy. I'm so unhappy.'

'I know. We all know: me, Edward, Tom, Zoë. Why have you shut us all out? Look, I've got to play mine hostess now, but tomorrow night, cancel whatever you're doing: work, art class – whatever. Edward can look after Chloë, and you and me'll go out and talk. Really talk. Promise me.'

'OK. I promise.'

And so, with admission, the slow process of healing commenced. Grief has its own agenda and does not care to be hurried, but it can be coerced into submission. She sobered up, made new friends, occasionally dated men she met, but remained stoically single. And she continued to paint, driven by an insatiable resolve to improve. She pounded London's streets, a tourist in her hometown, constantly seeking inspiration. The city's architectural glories were woven into the stories she conjured: from the fantastic Gothic monuments of Victoriana, to the Burano bright cottages tucked away in Chelsea; from its ancient seats of learning and government, to the South Bank where the starkness of weather stained concrete was jollied by crowds of culture seekers. People complimented her work; some even bought it. Life began to acquire meaning once more, and her first waking thoughts ceased to be always of Raffi. Gradually, she became reconciled to not being part of his existence; gradually ceased to feel devalued by his absence.

Not that she got over him, any more than she got over the death of her father. The loss simply became part of what she was, and therefore less painful. But it left its mark, like a brand on hidden skin, invisible to all, except those who knew her best.

Jeremy came into, and out of her life, and although their parting saddened her, he left her a stronger and happier person than he found her. Eighteen months later, when she bumped into him at the theatre with his very pregnant wife, she was truly happy for him. And by this time she had received a proposal from another man – but not of the romantic variety. Miles Babington, who owned a prestigious London gallery, offered to represent her. Professionally she had arrived. During that same summer, fellow artist, Tristram Mackenzie, commonly known as Mack, asked if, rather than renting studio space, she would care to work at his house in Fulham.

Mack had abandoned mainstream teaching at a Notting Hill comprehensive, and to supplement the modest income from the sale of his paintings now taught at various adult educational establishments. Once he had been Anna's teacher but declared that she had more talent in her little finger than he possessed in the whole of his hairy body.

It soon became obvious that he wanted to make more than art with her, and one night, after hosting an impromptu meal for Izzy and Edward, Anna and Mack ignored the washing up and climbed the narrow stairs to Mack's bedroom.

She was very fond of this lumbering Scot, many years her senior, who was kind, gentle and possessed of a ribald sense of humour. Life with Mack was without complication: he did not ask for commitment. His children were now in their twenties, and he had no desire for more "sprogs". She doubted he would ever suggest marriage, as there was still a Mrs Mackenzie, alive and well in Chichester. His estranged wife had lived with an antiques dealer for five years, but divorce had never been mooted. All this suited Anna very well, for reasons she did not care to examine too closely.

'I like my freedom,' she told her mother, who fretted about her daughter's lack of security.

When Mack died, felled by a sudden heart attack, she mourned him sadly and sincerely, but with the sure and certain knowledge that her life would go on. Weeks later, as executor of his will, she was going through his papers and found a letter dated a month before his death. It was from a solicitor, referring to a meeting in which Mack had sought advice on initiating a divorce from his wife. Anna could only draw the one conclusion and wondered what her reply to Mack would have been.

Now, nearly two and a half years after Mack's death, Izzy has decided that it is high time for Anna's "widowhood" to end. She suggests Internet dating, and when Anna recoils from the prospect, commences a campaign of not very subtle matchmaking. Although available suitors are few and far between, her efforts are rewarded when one of Edward's colleagues, recently divorced, asks Anna out. Anna rather likes him, but their fledgling relationship comes to a precipitous end when he bursts into angry tears over dinner, while relating the saga of his bitter divorce. It appears that his wife left him for "a little oik who runs a haulage business". Anna politely refuses his suggestion that they meet again.

'Perhaps it's only to be expected,' she tells Izzy. 'At our age most of us carry around a bit too much baggage. If I'm going to meet someone it'll happen. And if it doesn't, so be it. So no more matchmaking, please.'

Ostensibly, Izzy agrees, although Anna suspects she still hatches plans. Partly because of this, she does not mention the news contained in Vittore's email. In fact, by one o'clock they have hardly spoken to each other about anything. Izzy is lost in her own thoughts; Anna in her work.

'Shall we have some lunch?' Izzy suggests, as the grandfather clock in the hall chimes the hour.

The back of the Henshawes' kitchen is all glass, and leads onto a leafy garden. Once it had featured handcrafted wooden units with curtains and blinds fashioned from sunny fabric brought back from Provence. Then in a fit of modernity, inspired by house make over programmes, Izzy replaced everything with stainless steel and granite. Rows of murderous knives stand to attention and an army of shiny pans hang from butcher's hooks. It reminds Anna of scenes in television dramas where pathologists perform autopsies. The only food visible is a vast bowl of lemons. Izzy has forgotten to replace them and a couple are growing mouldy. She rarely cooks now, having discovered that the surfaces show every finger-mark. Instead, she buys "bung it in the oven" meals. For dinner parties she decants them into serving dishes and swears no one is any the wiser. Even today, rather than create crumbs, the sandwiches are from Waitrose.

'I thought I'd get one of those mutli-gym thingies,' she twitters. 'I want to shed a few pounds so I'm bikini fit for the summer hols.'

She shows Anna a brochure. The preferred model costs thousands. Anna feels a sudden exasperation and says, not altogether kindly, 'If you want to lose weight, go to the gym. You spend enough on the membership.'

In reply Izzy wrinkles her nose and refills her glass.

'And try cutting back on that stuff. You really are drinking too much, you know.'

Izzy hangs her head like a penitent. 'Yes, I do know. But it does so help.'

'Helps what?'

'Oh, everything. Life just seems a bit empty at the moment. My forties are nearly half over and I've done nothing.'

'Don't be daft. You've got two lovely kids for a start.'

'Who scarcely acknowledge my existence unless they want something.'

'Come on, Izzy. They're teenagers.'

'Don't get me wrong. I love them to pieces. And I know how lucky I am, having Edward and…and all this.' She gestures the top of the range Lacanche cooker and Smeg fridge; the professionally landscaped garden, where a discreetly camouflaged hot tub hides. 'But it's not like what you've achieved. Or Tom. OK, he's never going to win the Booker, but a string of bestsellers is no mean achievement. And now I'm getting old and it's too late to do anything worthwhile.'

'You're not old, Izzy.'

'Soon will be.' She picks up her glass, draining it. 'No one ever tells you, do they?'

'Tells you what?'

Izzy leans back and closes her eyes against the probing sunlight. 'When you're living through the best time of your life. If you did know, you'd bottle it somehow, wouldn't you? Remember every tiny, little detail. Ask me now what the happiest day of my life was, and I wouldn't be able to tell you. But it'd probably have been during that summer you were with us in Venice. Just some ordinary, forgotten day with…with Will.' She sits upright, looking at Anna, eyes brimming. 'Oh, God, sometimes I think I'd give anything to be twenty-odd again and back in his bed.'

Anna is shocked by the admission, and yet not that surprised. She remembers a night, long ago, Raffi and Will walking either side of her. They are celebrating her twenty-eighth birthday. The sky is high and cloudless. Izzy bounces on ahead of them, skipping over moonlit puddles, intent on finding an ice cream. Then she turns and looks at Will, her face starry with happiness. Edward Henshawe is a sweet, clever and kindly man, and he has given Izzy the emotional and financial security for which she had always hankered. But not once, even on their wedding day, has Anna seen Izzy grace him with the adoration that illuminated her eyes when she looked upon Will.

'I'm sorry,' Izzy says, wiping her nose with the back of her hand. 'Actually, I'd give anything to be twenty-odd and in *anyone's* bed. Oh, don't mind me…I'm just pining for my lost youth – literally. It's the picture – it's stirred everything up. Old Ossie really is the spitting image of Will, isn't he?' She is quiet for a moment. 'I've tried looking for him…Will, I mean….on the Internet…'

'And?'

'Zilch. Disappeared into the ether. Just as well really.'

'Yeah…just as well.' Anna resolutely snaps the shutters on her own past.

'I don't suppose it would have ever worked out between us, but some days, when I'm feeling sentimental,' Izzy continues, 'I'm convinced that I let the love of my life slip through my fingers. And for what? For a stainless fucking steel kitchen.'

Anna takes a deep breath and faces the truth. 'If it's any consolation, Izzy. So did I. But not even for a kitchen.'

They fall into each other's arms, giggling and crying; slightly tipsy, bound together by flotsam memories, guilt and regret. Then Anna confesses, 'I got an email from Vittore yesterday. Caterina and Raffi have separated.'

'Oh my God! I knew there was something up with you. Did Vittore say why?'

'Not really. He thinks Caterina may have another man, but he didn't say anything about Raffi. It's so stupid, but just hearing it, brought everything back.'

'Well, if you've got any sense, you'll be on the next plane out there. Help him pick up the pieces, and stake your claim.'

'Don't be ridiculous, Izzy. I can't just pitch up after all this time.'

'Why the hell not? Vittore would be over the moon to see you. And you are an artist, for God's sake. Every other bugger who's ever picked up a brush goes to Venice. In fact, it's bloody peculiar you haven't been there in the last seventeen years. Look, if you don't nab him, somebody else will – pretty damn quick, and this time it'll probably be someone with enough sense to hang on to him.'

Anna has long since told Izzy about her interview with Caterina's father and its consequences. It explained some things, but not everything.

'Izzy, he got her pregnant just weeks after I left. He ignored all my letters. And not once did he pick up the phone. It was a one-night stand. End of story.'

'Only if you want it to be the end.'

'It's too late now.'

'No, it's not. It is for me, I couldn't change my life, even if I wanted to, but you can. Go there…see him. You'll be sorry for the rest of your life if you don't. Do you want to know what I think? I think the reason you never married Jeremy or Mack…and don't give me all that bollocks about not wanting to leave London, or Mack already being married…it was because you just could not stand up there and swear lifelong fidelity, while there was the tiniest hope, however remote, that one day Raffi would come back into your life. Look, I'll even come with you. I'll get Mum to look after the kids. At least think about it.'

'Well…perhaps. When the painting's finished,' Anna says, but only to keep Izzy quiet. She has no intention of going. Mack had kept the demons at bay, but with him gone she refuses to court the hooligan stuff of life again.

Anna completes *Mr and Mrs Henshawe and a Glass of Champagne* early in October. The spindly little trees that were a tender green when she started painting have yellowed, and their leaves now confetti the pavement outside Izzy's house. A week later, Josh breaks his ankle, skateboarding, and Izzy is too preoccupied to think about trips to Venice. Vittore, since telling her of Raffi's floundering marriage, is unusually quiet. When Christmas arrives without his usual greetings card, she is a little concerned but reasons it was probably lost in the post; it would not be the first time. She will email him in the New Year.

For the festive season Anna flies to Edinburgh, spending it with her mother and Leslie at the home of Leslie's eldest daughter. She is very fond of her gregarious "step-family", and after twelve days in their convivial bosom, is not looking forward to being alone again. Even though the weather is unseasonably mild, her house is cold and unwelcoming when she returns. Of late, she has felt Mack's presence fading from its little rooms. Now, when something catches in the corner of her eye, she no longer thinks, for a split second, that it is he.

Still wrapped in her coat, she switches on the computer, guessing correctly, that there will be a wealth of emails. Clutching a whisky and ginger, she scrolls through them. There is one from Vittore, dated 31st December, no doubt wishing her a happy *capodanno*. She clicks on it. Then it is as though something shudders in her rib cage and flaps up towards her throat. It is not from Vittore, but from Raffaele Anzelieri.

From: Raffaele Anzelieri
Subject: zio Vittore
Date: 31 December 2004
To: Anna Fleming

Dear Anna

I am so sorry to be the bearer of bad news, but I gather that Vittore has not disclosed his ill health to you. Over two years ago he was diagnosed with myeloma, which is a cancer of the bone marrow. It is not curable, only treatable. However, the treatment is gruelling and unpleasant. In August he decided that he wished to end all medical intervention and let nature take its course. He enjoyed a few weeks of fragile, if not exactly good health. But without the drugs and blood transfusions, his condition is now rapidly deteriorating. It is unlikely that he will live for many more weeks, and at any time could succumb to an infection that would be the end. Many old friends have visited him and he remains in good spirits. However, he would so much like to see you. Could you find the time to come and say goodbye? Even if it were for only a short visit, it would mean so very much to him. I will arrange your accommodation.

Whatever you are doing, have a happy New Year celebration. We are hosting a small party at Ca' Melissa. I would rather not, as I worry that Vittore will pick up a cough or a cold, but he insists and how can I refuse?

Fondest regards Raffi

It is inconceivable that she should refuse the request, but she cannot understand why Vittore should so wish to see her. Over the years they have spoken only very rarely and their correspondence has generally been little more than superficial. Yet, she acknowledges the debt she owes him, for it was he, who by showing her Venice, kindled her desire to paint. But she dreads the possibility of a deathbed vigil, and other inevitable encounters fill her with trepidation. Not just a reunion with Raffi, but also meeting his daughter, and whatever woman may be newly part of his life, for surely there will be a significant other by now?

A week later, on the afternoon Anna flies into Venice, the city has hovered in a daylong sea of fog, as thick as buttermilk. She does not dislike flying, but hates hermetically sealed airports, the delays, queues and security checks. Only when the plane leaves the ground does she ever feel relaxed. This journey, however, affords no such respite. Take-off is nearly two hours late, and once in the air, she remains so on edge that it is an effort to restrict herself to the one glass of wine. As they touch down, her stomach is churning and she feels faintly nauseous.

Raffi has promised to meet her and take her to the apartment where she will stay – a spacious studio in Dorsoduro. Normally, it is let out to tourists, but is currently un-booked until *Carnevale*. She has not liked to ask why she cannot be put up at Ca' Melisa. As is the modern way, she and Raffi have not spoken to each other, but have communicated solely by email. Even when she contacts him about her delayed departure she sends a text.

Walking into the arrivals hall, after waiting an age to reclaim her baggage, she registers that the airport seems to have undergone a complete transformation. It has doubled in size and is all marbled halls – shiny and new. She scans the sea of people for a familiar face. And then she sees him. At least she assumes it is he; there is no other explanation for the tall, bespectacled man hurrying towards her, his dark overcoat flapping like a cloak. In the brief interval before he is at her side, she tries to view him dispassionately, and not as the boy who ripped her heart out.

Would she give him a second glance if she saw him running for the train at Fulham Broadway? Perhaps not. He is nothing so very out of the ordinary, she decides. To her surprise, the short sprint has left him breathless.

They take each other's hands, and stand for a few moments, saying nothing – an island of stillness and quiet amongst the waves of people lapping around them. *We could be strangers, meeting for the first time,* she thinks. *It's as though none of it ever happened.* It is she who pulls away first. Then they kiss the air, and against her face she feels his cheek, cool and a little rough, the scent of his cologne – not the one he used to wear – and the faint smell of coffee on his breath.

'Thank you so much for coming, Anna.'

'That's OK.' She waves his gratitude aside, fiddling with the handle of her case. He takes it from her. Together they make for the exit, chatting about her journey, the awful weather, the changes to the airport.

'They're planning to expand it even further. Venice is truly international now. I'll be interested to hear what changes you see in the city.'

He stops mid-stride and looks at her. 'Have you really never been back here since...?'

'No.' She waits for him to say more. When he does not, she babbles on about being busy; the pressure of work; personal issues, at which he murmurs, 'Yes, I was sorry to hear about...' His voice trails off and she suspects he has forgotten Mack's name. This, unaccountably, angers her.

'Yes, well,' she says. 'Time just flew by and I never got round to it...'

'You look so well. The years have hardly touched you.'

She smiles, but cannot return the compliment. Izzy had said how little he had changed. That was just over a year ago. Perhaps recent events have taken their toll, because the man at her side looks every one of his forty-six years. Lines that used to appear only when he smiled are now permanently etched down his cheeks, and his forehead is tramlined. The thick glossiness of his hair is dulled, streaked with grey and has surely receded and thinned. He is not as tall as she remembers and she realises that he has acquired the slight stoop so often appropriated by those who tower above most of their fellow men. Yet it is more than a mere change in appearance. Gone too, is that shiny confidence of youth. He is careworn, slightly diffident. There is not a vestige of the boyish flirtatiousness that had won her heart.

You are a different person now, she thinks, with a relief only slightly tinged by disappointment. *Everyone was right. I should have returned years ago and laid your ghost to rest.*

It is only when they are slowly driving past the fog shrouded conurbations lining the road to Venice, that she addresses the reason for her visit. 'And how is Vittore?'

'Not good. He just about got through our little party on New Year's Eve, but since then he's hardly been out of bed. He's eating next to nothing. Then last Thursday they started to give him morphine. It makes him tired but at least he has no discomfort anymore.' He pauses for a moment. 'I don't think I told you. We've moved him to my place.'

'That must be easier for everyone.'

'It is. Just trying to keep him warm at Ca' Melisa was impossible.'

'And all those stairs. How's Rosina coping?'

For a second Raffi takes his eyes off the road, turning to look at her. She registers the surprise on his face. The car swerves, only a little, but enough to provoke an angry blare from the driver behind.

'Ah. Something else Vittore obviously didn't tell you?'

'What?'

'For the last eighteen months Rosina's been in a nursing home.'

'He never said a thing. What's wrong with her?'

'Alzheimer's. It started five, six years ago, but only got really bad halfway through 2002. Even then, Vittore was doing fine looking after her, with support from us all, but then he got sick and couldn't cope anymore. Rosina was…well, still is, as fit as a fiddle. She'd get up in the middle of the night, wander off, half-dressed and end up in all sorts of places. No harm ever came to her, but it was only a matter of time before something did happen. In the end we had no choice but to find somewhere where she would receive twenty-four hour care.'

'Why didn't he ever mention it?'

'I don't know. The same reason he never told you he was ill, perhaps? Denial…?'

'Does she know how ill he is?'

'She hasn't known *who* he is for over a year. She doesn't know any of us anymore.'

'I'm really sorry. It must be awful,' she says, imagining the burdens he has had to bear.

'No, it's not easy. But I'm lucky having Marietta here with me. If she was in Milan with her mother it would be very hard.'

'I'm really looking forward to meeting her.'

She glances at him and sees him smile, his face suddenly animated. For a moment he looks like the young, carefree man she once knew.

'You'll love her,' he says with the supreme confidence that only a parent can feel. 'It never ceases to amaze me how one's child can be such a source of strength.'

They lapse into silence until, through the mist, the ghostly whiteness of a winged lion is caught in the headlights. It stands in stone relief, high above the road, guarding the entrance to the Ponte della Liberta. Venice is only four watery kilometres away. Opening the window, just a fraction, she smells the sad, salt sea-fret of the Lagoon and is gripped by a visceral excitement.

'Nearly home,' says Raffi: for a second she almost believes him.

The route from the car park takes them through not the most scenic part of Venice, but she has never before seen the city veiled by fog; lights hover in a sfumato haze and the usual bright colours are muted and shy. It is eerie and unnerving, but undeniably beautiful, with thick tendrils of moisture conjuring a soft focus palette, as if Monet's water lilies have been transformed to stone. By the time they reach their destination, Anna feels newly seduced by her surroundings, her mind reeling with the challenge of translating it into paint.

The apartment is carved out of the building's roof space – all sloping ceilings and exposed beams. Even though the heating has apparently been on all day, it is still chilly. The main window overlooks a canal, and through the gloom she can just make out a small *campo,* and a church fronted with an unusual porch construction. Unless she is mistaken, it is San Nicolò dei Mendicoli, the church used in the film, *Don't Look Now.* She also remembers that in this part of the city she always, unaccountably, felt slightly uncomfortable. These rooms, however, are bland and functional, quite indifferent to her presence, and anyway, she will not be staying long. For a few pounds she has purchased a ridiculously cheap plane ticket, leaving from Treviso in four days; a quick get-away.

Raffi ferrets around in cupboards: he gives her keys; demonstrates how the heating works; shows her the provisions he has bought. The fridge is packed; there is fruit on the table and flowers on the sideboard. In the shower room stands a row of unopened bottles: shampoo, conditioner, shower gel, body lotion. A note is propped against them: "I hope you like lavender. Marietta XXX".

'She decided you might need some, some…bits,' says Raffi. 'Look, I never asked, how long are you planning to stay? Have you booked a return flight?'

'No,' she lies. Seeing Marietta's note, with its childish handwriting and the big "X"s, she senses that these people, this man who is all but a stranger, and a teenage girl she has never met, really want her here; even need her.

'I'll stay as long as you – and Vittore – like.'

'Thank you,' he says. 'It means a lot to him. I'm very grateful.' He glances at the clock. It is nearing ten. 'I should be getting home; make sure Marietta gets to bed. School started today. If your flight had been on time we could have eaten together but…'

'It's fine. I'm pretty tired. Perhaps tomorrow?'

'Oh, most definitely tomorrow. At the moment I'm finishing work at around two. I'll call for you…it's on my way home.'

'OK. See you then. Thanks for…for all this.'

'No problem. Give me a call if you need anything. Goodnight.'

'Goodnight.'

As he opens the door, he says, 'It's so good to see you again, Anna.'

A Sad Tale's Best for Winter

It is seven o'clock when the church bells wake her. She lies, toast warm, listening to the unfamiliar sound. Only very occasionally does an errant breeze carry a faint Sunday summons into her Fulham house, but in Venice, of course, there are always bells; day and night, near and far.

The heating has been blazing for hours, so the flat is now sweltering, although the terrazzo floor is cold on her feet as she skips to the window. Outside it is still dark and the streetlights' glow hardly penetrates the fog. When she opens the window, mist creeps into the room, cold and clammy pawed.

She remembers loving Venetian early mornings, for in those few hours before the invasion of day-trippers, the city belonged to those who lived there. But that was during a long ago summer, when the skies were blue and Venice was window-dressed in sunshine. This dank pall is less inviting. Nevertheless, there are seven hours to kill before Raffi will call for her, and she is too on edge to stay in the flat. If her visit is going to be longer than three days she should use the time productively. She has packed a box of watercolours and some favourite brushes, hoping to produce some small, wintry studies. Pictures of Venice always sell well, and the departure from her usual London scenes would please the gallery. But she will need paper, and remembers a shop off the Strada Nova, that sold art supplies. The owner had been a great Anglophile, constantly talking about London. He may still be there. The prospect of a friendly face heartens her.

Immediately she steps outside, it is obvious that painting *en plein air* will be out of the question. The cold is of the type that gnaws at the joints and stiffens the fingers into uselessness. Nevertheless, she presses on, keeping close to the walls, for the fog is so dense that she can hardly see the edge of the *fondamenta*. The city is blurred at the edges, and within minutes she is lost, having twice ventured into *calle* that are nothing but watery dead ends. Changing direction, she heads towards the Zattere with the intention of taking a *vaporetto*. When she reaches it, the wide waterfront promenade is strangely empty. There are other people abroad but they are hardly visible, and she senses their proximity by perfume or tobacco trails, footsteps and muffled voices.

Many of the restaurants and bars are closed, their shutters and walls scrawled with graffiti. The sight shocks her; not the content, which is, for the most part, the usual English four letter vulgarisms, and drawings of male genitalia, but the fact that anyone should deface any part of this city.

At the *vaporetto* stop, a notice is tied to the ticket machine bearing the message, "*Chiuso a causa di nebbia*". A small huddle of tourists turn uncomprehending eyes upon her.

'The boats aren't running, because of the fog,' she explains. 'If you want to go anywhere you'll have to walk.'

Unimpressed, they return to their hotel. Anna heads for the Accademia, but not before noticing that the cost of a one-way *vaporetto* journey – for visitors – is now six and a half euros: residents pay one euro. In London, a bus journey, for tourists and residents alike, is about a pound. No one has ever pretended that Venice is a cheap holiday destination, but such extortion seems excessive.

After crossing the Grand Canal, where the fog has lifted a little, the territory becomes increasingly familiar. Even so, she is constantly surprised by small changes: the lack of greengrocers, butchers and ironmongers; the proliferation of mask shops; the transformation of old-fashioned bars and restaurants into slick, trendy establishments. She easily locates the site of the art shop but in place of the inviting little emporium of yesteryear is a shining beacon of modernity, selling *telefonini* – mobile phones. At least the bar next door appears unchanged. If she remembers correctly, it used to sell hot chocolate, as sweet and thick as treacle. Pushing open its door she finds the interior reassuringly shabby, exactly how she remembers it. Although she has no recollection of who previously ran the place, it certainly was not this young Chinese couple. They are pleasant enough, but appear to understand neither her perfect English nor her imperfect Italian. The chocolate is nothing special, and she leaves, disappointed and strangely deflated.

It is probably a mistake, but her old home and Ca' Melisa are so close that she feels impelled to go there. She reaches the flat first. The front door is slightly ajar; unless banged shut it never did close properly. Peering inside, nothing seems to have changed: the wrought iron staircase; the worn steps and faded Canaletto print on the wall are all as they were. She has a bizarre notion that if she climbed the stairs and pushed open their apartment door everything would be just as she had left it. Then she hears footsteps from above, and scuttles away, afraid of being caught snooping.

The short walk to Ca' Melisa is achingly familiar. The *portone*, set into the wall of the narrow alley, is firmly closed; the bell push is tarnished, and the door itself is in need of a fresh coat of paint. She imagines the still and sleeping garden on the other side of the crumbling bricks, remembering it brightened by party lights – alive with happy music.

Viewed from the fondamenta, the house makes an even sadder picture. With every shutter tightly closed, not a chink of light peeks out, as the building shifts and loses itself in the swirls of mist. Even the stone lions perched on the balconies appear dejected. The summer geraniums have not been cleared, and their frost blackened remains droop miserably down the walls, like corpses of oil smirched seabirds. It exudes such an air of melancholy that Anna can hardly believe it is the place where she partied on countless summer evenings; the place where she first felt such outrageous pangs of love. For a few moments she allows herself the exquisite self-indulgence of remembering; then she retraces her steps to the Strada Nova where, despite the fog, there are people and bustle, and air that is not heavy with nostalgia.

Back at the flat she has just finished a light lunch when Raffi arrives. He looks exhausted. As they walk to his house, he explains, 'Vittore had a bad night and I only got a couple of hours sleep. So from tomorrow I've hired a night nurse. Marietta has important exams this year; I can't have her being tired at school.'

His home is a converted boat builders, and affronts a *rio* branching off the Zattere. It is accessed via a private courtyard that is surprisingly peaceful and scented by tubs of early flowering mimosa. A small entrance lobby, busy with coats, umbrellas and boots, leads into a spacious room overlooking the canal. The ceiling is crossed with wooden beams, and seams of exposed brickwork relieve the cream marmorino walls. Despite the fog, light floods through three large, steeply arched windows. In the wake of a passing motorboat, the pallid water erupts, smattering the glass. It is like being on the bridge of a ship, and Anna almost expects to feel sea-sway beneath her feet.

Recessed into the far wall is a glass-fronted fire, and before it stands a large sofa. There is a faint rustling and over its back, a tousled head appears. The girl's eyes are bleary, her cheeks flushed from sleep.

'*Ciao, babbo.* Hi, you must be Anna. I'm Marietta.'

Anna only has time to say, 'Hello,' before Raffi mutters an expletive in Italian and then switches to English. 'What are you doing out of school?'

'I fell asleep on my desk. *Signora* Baldini told me to come home. They all know what's happening,' she adds, smiling widely, but with eyes beginning to brim.

Even without the self-introduction, Anna could be in no doubt who she is. While she has her mother's dainty nose, this could, otherwise, be Raffi's face, aged eleven or twelve: high cheekbones, wide apart hazel eyes, a soft spill of light brown hair.

If things had been different, she could have been my child. The thought careers into Anna's mind before she can stop it, bringing with it the heart-stopping regret that can assail even the most resolutely childless.

'Well, go to bed…get some proper rest,' says Raffi, gently extricating a textbook from his daughter's grasp. 'How's *nonno*?'

'Asleep. Well, he was when I came in.' She turns to Anna, grabbing her hands. 'He's so looking forward to seeing you. He was telling me…'

'Bed,' reiterates her father, taking her by the shoulders and guiding her towards the door. He plants a kiss on the top of her head. 'You can talk to Anna all you like over dinner, but for now, get some sleep.'

'OK,' she says, and pads out of the room. They listen to the schlep of her footsteps on the stairs. Then comes the sound of low voices.

'I think Vittore must be awake. The day-nurse stays till three. Do you want to see him now, or wait till she leaves?'

'No time like the present,' Anna says with false brightness, trying to hide her dread of the sickroom and its clammy hopelessness. It was a lifetime ago that she spent hour after weary hour by her father's bedside, but time has played its mind-tricks and that earlier vigil could be but yesterday. She almost expects to see Hugh propped up amongst the mountain of pillows, but it is, of course, Vittore who smiles and holds out his arms to her. She embraces him, feeling the sharp bones under his pyjamas, and despite a determination not to cry, her disobedient tears anoint the old man's face.

'Anna, Anna.' His voice is tremulous and husky, robbed of the vibrant timbre that once so enraptured audiences. 'My dear girl, why the tears?'

'Because I'm so happy to see you,' she lies, unable to explain her remorse at having excluded him from her life. Only now can she acknowledge how much she has missed him, and that whatever time they have left, it can never make up for so many lost years.

'And me, you. Now let me look at you properly. I am so sorry that I have become such a feeble old fellow. Am I quite unrecognizable?'

Age and illness have indeed left their mark on the patrician face. The fine nose is whittled to a sharp beak, the cheeks sunken. His once tanned skin is dry and grey like old parchment. The hands she holds are liver-spotted and cord-veined. And yet he still possesses that rich sweep of silver hair, the same bright eyes.

'But you are as lovely as ever, Anna. Now tell me all about your next exhibition.'

They talk for hours. Raffi brings tea and cake. Anna wolves them down, feeling guilty that Vittore can only manage a few sips of nutrition drink. At some point, he says, out of the blue, 'I do apologise for not telling you about Rosina. I kept hoping the diagnosis was incorrect and that she would come back to us. Well, at least she has been spared seeing me like this.' He closes his eyes and Anna thinks he has succumbed to sleep. Then he murmurs, 'But it really is all for the best.

Although I doubt very much that there is any sweet hereafter, if there is, it is only right that I should be there first – to pave the way for her.'

He rallies a little after this and asks, 'Will you come tomorrow, my dear? If you can spare the time, there is something I should like you to do for me. I have been re-reading the plays of Shakespeare, but the print is too small for my poor, old eyes, and I find it difficult to hold a book for long. Could you read them to me?'

'Of course, but I don't think I'll be much good.'

'Nonsense. Your voice is ever soft, gentle and low, an excellent thing in a woman. And now I fear I must sleep a little.'

For a while she sits in silent watch, then creeps out of the room, feeling unexpectedly calm and at peace. Somewhere in the house there are voices, and she follows their source into the kitchen. Father and daughter are preparing a meal together. Marietta is speaking in Italian. Raffi's response to whatever she has said is an emphatic, 'Non.'

As Anna enters the room, a look of childish calculation passes across Marietta's face. 'I think I should buy dinner on my way home from school each day. It's not fair that *papà* has to worry about it…'

'And *you* have enough to worry about with your studies, without having to trail around the shops.'

The two glare at each other, their obstinate expressions identical. Anna comes to the rescue. 'Why don't I do it? I'll cook too. That is, if you don't mind me eating with you.'

Raffi looks doubtful, and she fears she has overstepped the mark.

'Only if you really want to,' he says. 'When it gets to five or six o'clock you might be only too glad to get away. It's not going to be easy here over the next few…'

'I know, I know what to expect. And I also know that you two need to eat properly, even if you don't feel like it. I'm not a bad cook if you remember. After all, I did have an excellent teacher.'

'So you did. The very best.'

'Who?' pipes Marietta.

'*Nonna*,' replies her father.

'*Nonna* Rosina?'

'Well, it certainly wasn't my mother,' laughs Raffi.

Marietta's eyes flash from Anna to Raffi. 'Why? When?'

'That,' says her father, 'is a long story.'

The next morning, Anna makes her way to Billa, the supermarket on the Zattere. Here, behind its unlikely façade – it could easily be taken for a private residence – she buys the ingredients for tonight's dinner, plus fruit and vegetables, cheese and chicken. She will make Jewish penicillin – chicken soup. Vittore may be able to manage a little; it has to taste better than those nutrition drinks. When the contents of the trolley are decanted into bags, she can hardly carry them back to the flat. Only now, as she lugs her purchases up the three flights of stairs, does she remember what a chore shopping was in this city, and how the old couple in the flat below worshipped Will because he would carry up their bags.

Raffi calls for her at two-thirty and, laden with shopping, they walk to his house. The fog has lifted a little, and as they approach Angelo Raffaele, she sees a group of women shuffling in front of the church, vainly trying the closed door. They gaze up at the niche, in which the winged archangel, Tobias and a rotund little dog reside, as if imploring the stone figures to grant them access.

'This church was ignored for years; now it's a place of pilgrimage,' says Raffi, bypassing the tourists who all clutch the same book – *Miss Garnet's Angel*. 'Have you read it?'

'Not yet.'

There is a copy on her bookshelf. Mack bought it in the hope that it would encourage her to visit the city with him. A few weeks later he was dead. She has not had the heart to pick it up since.

Raffi stops by the wellhead. 'I used to love it here when I was a kid. I thought they'd named the *campo* after me. See this wellhead, most people don't give it a second glance, but it's very, very old. You can just make out the carvings.'

Anna bends to look. She can see the angel and boy, both faceless from the ravages of time. 'But there's no dog.'

'Yes, there is. Here.' He stoops next to her, his finger tracing a tiny form at Raffaele's feet.

'Oh, it's weenie, like a Chihuahua.'

'I called it Little Jack,' he says. 'I used to pretend I had a dog.'

'And did you ever have one?'

'No. I don't think Vittore and Rosina even knew I wanted one. I certainly never asked. I don't remember ever asking for anything as a child. I think I was too afraid that everything I already had would be taken away if I made any demands.'

The tourists have drifted off, and apart from the plangent cry of a seabird, it is very quiet.

'Did they ever guess? How afraid you were?' she asks.

'No. But when Marietta was about three she occasionally had nightmares. I mentioned it to Vittore, and he said he remembered how I used to wake in the night, crying. They assumed it was because I was missing my mother. It was only then, so many years later, that I told him what I was really afraid of: that I was crying in case she came and took me away. They did everything to make me feel secure, but it was a long time before I felt I really belonged.'

'What? In Venice?'

'No...no, I always felt I belonged in Venice...no, with them, I mean.'

When they reach his house, she hastily chops a few vegetables and puts them with the chicken to simmer.

Marietta is at school, and Raffi disappears into his study to work. The day nurse, a Polish woman called Krysia, has helped Vittore get out of bed. He sits in a high-backed chair, resplendent in a silk dressing gown.

Krysia used to live in Liverpool, where she met her Italian husband.

'You must not be getting Signor Anzelieri too tired,' she warns Anna in extraordinary Scouse tinged English, before exchanging goodbyes with her charge. They speak in Italian but there is no mistaking the affection she feels for him.

'You old flirt,' says Anna. 'Still making all the girls fall in love with you?'

'Till the very end, my dear.'

Ignoring the implication of this superficially light-hearted remark, she picks up a volume of Shakespeare's comedies. 'Where shall we begin?'

'What about *A Winter's Tale*? A story of a love lost and found, after...oh, sixteen or seventeen years, if I remember correctly.'

His voice is syrupy with meaning, but when she meets his eyes, they are as innocent as a child's.

It takes until the next day to finish the play, as he frequently interrupts to discuss the text, or some other quite unrelated topic. When she finally lays down the book they are both silent. He has not got out of bed today and is clearly exhausted with the effort of staying awake. His eyes are closed and Anna suspects he may be asleep. Her mind drifts not to the final scene of the play, with a statue made in the image of a woman, but to a painting. That very morning she trekked over to the Misericordia church. Even knowing it would be barred and shuttered, she had been unprepared for its dilapidation. The entrance is now a makeshift door of rough-hewn wood, spawning graffiti; the white marble steps sprout moss, and most of the small bottle glass windowpanes are broken. Its walls haemorrhage plaster.

She waits until Vittore stirs and then says, 'I walked by the Misericordia today. Will it ever re-open, do you think?'

'Never as a church, I am sure. It is privately owned now.'

'And have Save Venice completely abandoned the restoration project?'

'Sadly, yes. Edie found something in New York to keep Graham busy, and without her impetus, financial input was transferred to the Miracoli's renovation. As you know, she has gradually distanced herself from the charity.'

'And the Madonna? Still nothing?'

He waves his hand as though shooing away an insect. When he does speak the subject has been changed. 'You ought to talk to Edie. She may be able to help you get a show in New York.'

'I can't imagine I'll be running into Edie in the foreseeable future.'

He opens his eyes. 'She came to say her goodbyes to me before Christmas, but I am sure she will be here for the funeral. Talking of which, will you read? The piece from *Cymbeline*, you know, "Fear no more the heat o' the sun".'

She nods and then says, 'I'm so sorry.'

'Whatever for my dear? For the fact that I am going to die? Do not be. I am not so very sad. Life, without Rosina…well, I prize it not a straw. But I have been very blessed. To have found her; to have been given Raffi and Marietta. To have lived in this wonderful city. You know, if there is a heaven, I suspect I may find it a little disappointing…after Venice.'

'I'm sorry for not having visited you before. That it's taken…this to get me back here. I just couldn't come before because…because…'

'I know, I know,' he says, taking her hand. Their fingers entwine. 'No need to explain. Life can be very unfair at times. My only wish now is that Raffi is given the happiness he deserves. And you too, of course. You know, it is never too late, and you are both still young enough.'

But it is too late. They have both changed; even Venice is not the same. Soon she will return to London, and although she may visit this improbable city from time to time, it will never be home. As for Raffi, although he is not the golden lad he once was, she has seen the way women look at him; he will not be alone for long. In the face of her silence, Vittore lets go of her hand and points to a small chest of drawers.

'In there, in the top drawer, is a letter. I wrote it before I knew you would be coming, so some of it is not relevant. Take it now, but please do not read it until after I am dead.'

As she rummages in the drawer, she hears him say, quite distinctly, 'Raffi never did receive those letters you sent to him, you know.'

But when she turns, his eyes are closed, his mouth has grown slack and he is fast asleep. She finds an envelope with her name on it, and creeps from the room.

343

The next day Vittore is much weaker. At his request, Anna reads from *Much Ado About Nothing*, although she doubts he hears much of Beatrice and Benedick's sparring. But as she nears the end of the play and speaks the line, "I do love nothing in the world so well as you", his hands claw the bedclothes, and then he says, 'Look after Raffi for me.'

Marietta sits on the other side of the bed. Neither of them knows to whom he speaks. The girl leans towards her great-uncle, the only grandfather she has ever known, and whispers in Veneziano, some sweet conspiratorial secret. Her eyes never leave Anna's face. Vittore chuckles before sleep steals him away once more.

These are his last coherent words. After this he hardly wakes, but at one point he speaks in what Anna guesses is German. Marietta, who is proficient in the language, translates, 'He's saying, "Forgive me"'. And Anna remembers Raffi's account of a young sniper, gunned down in an orchard near Conegliano. The next time he briefly opens his eyes, they are calm, his expression serene.

Early on Monday morning, the doctor pronounces that the "end" can be no more than two or three days hence. Marietta pleads to be let off school but Raffi insists she goes. He stays at home and with Anna, takes his place at Vittore's bedside. Occasionally, they attempt to give the dying man a little water, but it trickles from his mouth. All they can do is moisten his lips. They play music: Vivaldi, Monteverdi, Venetian folk songs, ballads popular in the 1940s and '50s that he and Rosina would have sung in their youth. Every now and again, Anna picks up the book of Shakespeare sonnets and reads aloud, but his face remains impassive. He is already in a place where they can no longer reach him. Krysia hovers around; there is little for her to do, but she washes and changes his nightclothes, dresses the angry bedsores and whispers comforting words in a sonorous mix of languages.

Outside, the city still wheezes under the blanket of fog. Anna's bones ache from the unremitting dampness. With stiffened fingers she paints small watercolours from memory. Little wonder that Titian was crippled with arthritis. It is no climate for an artist, however incandescent the light. While she works, Raffi ploughs through sheaves of paper. He is itemizing every bill, every receipt pertaining to Ca' Melisa.

'Why?' she asks.

'In preparation for putting it on the market,' he says, as if she should know. And then in response to her shocked expression, 'Nobody, apart from Hollywood film stars or Russian oligarchs, can maintain a *palazzo* these days. Even when he was making a good income from the art vacations, Vittore had to borrow against the property, and since Rosina became ill...well you can imagine the nursing home fees.'

'I'm so sorry. To have to leave such a beautiful place must be heartbreaking.'

'Well, there's an outside chance I might not have to. I'm hoping to get the backing to form a company that'll buy the house. Then we'll convert it into apartments, and if I sell them to Venetians at a reasonable price there should be some public funding. If it all works out I'll keep one for myself, but as you can imagine, it's complicated. Whatever happens, I'll have to leave this place.'

'To do with splitting from Caterina?'

'Yes. It's jointly owned, bought with the proceeds of my apartment and her father's home. But we've agreed not to do anything until Marietta goes to university. She's had enough disruption without having to move out of the only home she's ever known.' He looks around the room. 'I'll be sorry to go. It was a wreck when we bought it. I designed and oversaw every bit of its renovation. Still, it'll be good to be back at Ca' Melisa.' He is quiet for a moment and then continues, 'It was the final straw – for Caterina – hearing about the debts.'

'She had no idea?'

'No. She really thought I was going to inherit it unencumbered. I suppose I should have told her, but by the time I knew the full extent of the borrowing, things weren't going too well between us and…well…'

'It's none of my business, I know, so tell me to shut up if you want, but what did go wrong?'

He stares into the distance, chewing his thumbnail. '*Differenze inconciliabili.* It was inevitable. We'd outgrown each other long before we married. But you of all people know that.'

It is the first time he has made any reference to what happened between them. She averts her eyes, and braves the question. 'I can understand why you needed to give her support after her accident. But if you felt like that why…why… become close enough again to…to have a child?'

'We'd been a couple – on and off – for so long. It's difficult enough to break those sort of ties under normal circumstances, but when something like Caterina's accident happens, it changes things. It changed her – for a while – back to the young girl I'd first known, not the hard-bitten career woman she'd become. She was convalescing with her aunt in Treviso, and one night we were alone. While she'd been in hospital they'd shaved part of her head, so she'd had all her hair cut short. It made her look very young, like a little sprite, and very beautiful. Looking at her, just being with her again, I wanted to love her, protect her. I wanted things to be how they were when we were kids, I suppose. Or just put it down to lust. Because of the accident she hadn't taken the Pill for months. She didn't tell me that, otherwise I would never have…it was just the once, but it was enough.'

345

'So you had to get married?' She is aware of how archaic and judgemental she sounds.

'No, we didn't *have* to,' he replies. 'Caterina suggested a termination. I persuaded her to keep the baby; convinced her that we could be a family; convinced myself that I loved her, because as soon as I knew she was pregnant I wanted that child so much. And it was the one thing I did that was right. When I held Marietta in my arms for the first time I knew she was the best thing that had ever happened to me. So I can't really have any regrets about my marriage. Actually, the first few years were OK: creating this house together, bringing up Marietta. Then Caterina started working again, and we drifted further and further apart. Despite that, we were both determined to stay together, for Marietta's sake. I suppose because of what happened to us as kids…you know that her mother walked out on her when she was only eight, don't you? But I'm afraid neither of us were true to our marriage vows. Caterina was the first to stray, but it could just as easily have been me. No one was ever hurt,' he adds.

'It sounds like one of those telly programmes,' she quips. '"No animals were hurt in the making of this film".'

'They all knew the score – that I would never leave my family. Anyway, they were mostly attached too.'

'Gosh, "mostly". You have been busy.'

He is silent for a moment. 'Have I shocked you?'

'No, of course not,' she bridles. 'I've not exactly lived like a nun, you know. But now you really are going your separate ways? So what happened, apart from her learning that Ca' Melisa is mortgaged up to the hilt?'

'Daniele Genduso happened. He's the CEO of a PR company in Milan, and despite the fact that he's stealing my wife, I rather like him. Thank God, otherwise I wouldn't want him anywhere near Marietta. Then Caterina had a breast cancer scare. Fortunately, it turned out to be nothing sinister, but it made her focus on what she really wanted in life. And that's Daniele. The court granted the *separazione formale* last July, so as Daniele is already divorced, they'll be free to marry in the summer of 2007.'

'And you? Is there a significant other in your life at the moment?'

He shakes his head. 'No, not at the moment.'

For a second she thinks he is going to tell her more, and then they hear the front door slam, followed by the sound of Marietta's voice.

'Time I was thinking about starting dinner,' Anna says.

She is aware of his eyes following her out of the room. But when she turns, he is again immersed in his paperwork.

346

The next day the fog lifts and there is even a little sunshine. But by noon, the sky is broody with un-spilt snow, and as dusk creeps into the city, fat, silver flakes begin to fall. They dance sleepily in the lamplight, before being swallowed by the black canals. They settle on pavements and roofs and on the moored boats; they rest on the window boxes outside the bedroom, shrouding the corpse geraniums still languishing in their summer home. After less than an hour the sugar frosting has thickened to a pall, and the dead plants look like bizarre Arctic creatures peering into the house. Because Vittore always loved snow, Marietta opens the window. She scoops a handful and takes it to him.

'Smell the snow, *nonno,*' she whispers, holding her cupped hands to his face. His eyes remain closed but his brows lift a fraction, as a tiny smile tweaks the corners of his mouth, then he recedes once more to his own private place.

It snows for over six hours. By ten o'clock, the time when Anna would normally leave, it lies thick in the little courtyard garden, buffeted up against the doors and windows. The initial whoops of delight from the bar across the *rio* have ceased, landlord and customers alike having long since departed for home. The city is eerily quiet without the usual click-clack of footsteps and the chugging of motorboats. The four of them are isolated on this small island of frozen silence.

'You can't go back in this,' says Marietta, peering out of the window. 'Can she, *babbo*?'

'I think not,' agrees Raffi. 'I'll make up the foldaway bed in my study.'

'No. Anna can share with me. You don't mind, do you, Anna? I'll find you something to wear.' And before Anna can reply, Marietta scuttles off.

'Don't keep Anna up all night gossiping,' Raffi calls after her.

They have been sitting in the kitchen, Marietta engrossed in her homework, already in her nightclothes, Anna making stock from the chicken they ate for dinner. Because the night nurse has been unable to travel from the mainland, Raffi is keeping vigil over Vittore.

'I'll say goodnight then,' he says. 'See you in the morning.'

She listens to his footsteps on the stairs and the sound of his voice as he speaks to his unhearing uncle. Then, when all is quiet, she creeps up to Marietta's room.

It is the typical domain of a teenage girl. Soft toys rub shoulders with schoolbooks; a dressing table is scattered with a clutter of make-up and hair ornaments. The walls are adorned with a mix of posters: Kylie Minogue; an androgynous boy band, unknown to Anna; Francesco Hayez's *Il Bacio*; a pin board covered with photos of Marietta's friends and family.

The Venetian princess herself sits cross-legged on her bed. She is wearing pyjamas, emblazoned with a cartoon mouse and the words, "*sogni d'oro*". Piled on a chair is a nightdress, a cotton waffle dressing gown, a couple of towels…and a toothbrush. Anna picks it up, remembering another night of inclement weather spent with this little girl's father. *Bloody stupid getting sentimental over a toothbrush*, she thinks.

Marietta misinterprets her expression. 'I'm sorry. It's only one of those they give you on the overnight trains.'

'It's perfect. Thank you, sweetheart.'

When she returns from the bathroom, Marietta is in bed. Her hair streams over the pillow like melted caramel. She stretches an arm out to Anna. 'I'm so glad you're here with us. It's…it's…making the unbearable, bearable.'

Anna takes her hand, and slips into bed. 'It's a privilege, being here. Vittore did more for me than I can ever tell you.'

'Like what?'

'Gosh, how can I explain? He taught me to see…to really look at things. He opened my eyes. And after that I've never been able to close them…never been able to stop painting what I see. Without him, I'm sure I'd never have become an artist.'

'Wow. That's so cool.' Then Marietta's eyes mist over. 'I'm going to miss him so much.'

'We all will,' says Anna and recites the usual comforting platitudes.

The girl listens, hugging a soft toy. 'I worry about *papà*. *Nonno* is like, like his rock. *Nonna* just isn't *nonna* any more – she doesn't even know who we are – and *mamma…*' Her voice trails off.

'I know. It's rotten. All the bad things seem to have come at once for him. But I'm sure he'll be all right. After all, he's got you.'

'You know I want to be a doctor, don't you? *Papà* assumes I'll live here while I'm studying, and I suppose I will, at first. But later I'd like to live in Padova, near the university. And then he'll be all by himself.'

Anna does not know how to reply. Surely Marietta cannot think that her father, still an undeniably attractive man, will be alone for long? Perhaps she cannot countenance the thought of another woman replacing her mother. Then Marietta says, almost casually, 'But I suppose he'll get a girlfriend soon.'

'Er…yes. Perhaps. How do you feel about that?'

'I don't mind – if she's nice. But my friend, Tanya, her father's new wife is… well, she doesn't get on with her at all. Tanya can't wait to leave home.'

'I'm sure whoever your father chooses, it'll be someone nice.'

'Hmm.' She sinks down into the pillows. Anna thinks she has fallen asleep. Then, with eyes still very deliberately shut, she says, 'Were you and *papà* ever… ever…you know?'

'Whatever makes you think that?'

The girl raises her eyelids. 'Just watching you together. The way he sometimes looks at you.'

'Marietta, your dad and I, we were only ever friends. And all the time I was in Venice he was with your mother. If he's looking at me, he's probably only thinking how ancient I've got.'

'No, it's more than that…and you're not ancient. You're fun and nice, and we'll miss you. Will you come and visit us?'

'Yes. If you want me too.'

'And perhaps we can come and see you in London. I love London, it's such a cool city.'

'You'll always be welcome. My house isn't very grand though. It's only got two bedrooms. One of you'll have to sleep on the sofa-bed.'

Marietta considers this and then smiles. 'You don't have a boyfriend at the moment, do you?'

The look on her face is so innocently calculating that Anna almost laughs.

'We ought to try and get some sleep,' she says, turning off the light.

'Anna?'

'Yes?'

'Do you remember when *nonno* said to look after *papà*?'

'Yes.'

'He was talking to you, you know. Not me.'

'I doubt it.'

'Oh, yes, he was. If he'd been talking to me, he would have said it in Veneziano. He thinks it's really important to keep *il dialetto* alive, so we always speak it to each other. Why would he ask you to look after *papà*?'

'I don't know, Marietta. People say funny things when they're…when…Now go to sleep.'

Anna wakes sometime in the night and for a few seconds wonders what has disturbed her. Then she realises that it is rain beating against the windows. Wanting to see the snow once more before it is washed away, she creeps out of bed. The landing is very dark and she is feeling her way to the stairs, when a slant of light falls across her path. A figure appears, silhouetted in the doorway of Vittore's room.

'Anna, is that you?' whispers Raffi.

As soon as she reaches his side, she knows that it is over.

'Is he…?'

He nods. 'He just slipped away. So quietly, I didn't even realise he was gone.'

She watches a tear snake down his cheek, and instinctively takes him in her arms. His body convulses against hers, and she senses that it is taking a huge effort for him not to sob. They stand motionless for a long time, until he slightly pulls away. 'I must tell Marietta. She ought to see him as soon as possible before…'

'Of course. While you tell her, let me say my goodbyes. Then I'll leave you both in peace with him…just family together.'

They both hear the door open, followed by a strangled little cry. It is Marietta. She does not move but the mouse on her pyjama top executes a bizarre dance as her body heaves with emotion.

'You are family, Anna,' she whimpers.

Raffi seems glued to the spot, his body heavy with shock, so it is Anna who reaches her first. The girl falls, knees buckling, her breath hot and rasping. Then Raffi is by their side too, and the three of them cling together, united in grief.

Eventually, Raffi extricates himself. He is calm now and takes one of Marietta's hands. Anna takes the other, and in unspoken accord they prepare to make their farewells to the grandfather, uncle, father and friend who has finally left them.

We Come to Praise Him

For much of the next day, Raffi is absent, attending to the necessary formalities. The funeral will take place on Monday. By British standards, rather speedily, but there is not so very much to arrange. Vittore has forbidden funeral posters to be plastered around the city, and the church is all but booked. Even though it is winter, a busy time for death, his mortal remains do not have to tarry long. He has chosen to eschew Venice's island of the dead in favour of the municipal crematorium in Mestre. At some unknown point in the future, his ashes will be mingled with those of Rosina, and scattered on the outskirts of Fabrizio's estate near Conegliano.

By late morning the phone calls begin; word of Vittore's demise has crept through Venice like mist. Marietta, who has been granted leave from school, glares at the answerphone, refusing to pick up. Anna feels obsolete: the girl has withdrawn into her own sad little place and anything that threatens to drag her away is an intrusion. Nor is there any need to shop or prepare food; the first of the neighbours' largesse has already arrived – a huge lasagne. This is followed by casseroles and cake and more lasagne. Soon the fridge and freezer are packed with edible condolences.

At four, Raffi returns, grey-faced and exhausted. He has emailed his mother in New York, and now shows Marietta her response.

"Hi baby. Me and Edie leaving JFK Saturday night. Arrive 16.45 Sunday. Sorry not able to come sooner – Edie at a big charity do on Sat afternoon. Don't worry about accommodation. I'll hunker down with Edie. We'll come to you first to say Hi. Big kiss to Marietta. Stay strong both of you.

Love you lots. Mamma."

Marietta is cheered by the news of Lucia's arrival, so Anna seizes the opportunity. 'Well, I think I'll head back. Give you guys a bit of peace.'

Raffi nods but Marietta turns to Anna, her face skewed by consternation. 'No, don't. Please stay.'

'But I need to get a change of clothes and things.'

'OK. But come back,' she pleads, once more the clingy child, disarmed by grief, and then adds, 'Stay the night. Please.'

Anna glances towards Raffi. She rather dreads a solitary evening but feels that father and daughter ought to spend time alone.

'You're welcome to stay as long and as much as you want,' he says.

'OK,' she concedes. 'If you're sure. But isn't there anything I can do to be of some real use?'

'There'll be a reception at Ca' Melisa after the funeral. Rosina's sister, Letizia, is organising things. She might need some help, but probably not till Sunday. Until then, just keep Marietta out of mischief. Take her shopping. I think you need a smart, new coat don't you, *cara*?'

Marietta beams, the prospect of new clothes momentarily assuaging her heartache.

As it turns out, outside caterers have been hired, so Anna's assistance is not required. Nevertheless, she accompanies Marietta when they visit Ca' Melisa on Saturday afternoon, while Raffi meets with the priest who is to officiate at the funeral.

Letizia is in the kitchen, checking that silver is polished and plates are clean. She is eleven years younger than her sister, and so like her in manner and appearance that Anna feels it could almost be Rosina herself, presiding as of old. But the sensation of time standing still is an illusion; the kitchen is badly in need of refurbishment, and Anna suspects the rest of the house is equally down at heel. The majority of its bedrooms have been unused for years, but so many people are travelling such long distances that it seems churlish not to provide them with accommodation. A bevy of helpers have been conscripted to prepare the rooms. Their clattering footsteps dispel some of the gloom that has seeped into the walls.

'It's so long since I was here,' says Anna. 'Do you think anyone will mind if I look around?'

'Of course not. Where shall we begin?' replies Marietta.

'Let's start down here.' And she leads the way from the kitchen, across the *androne* to the storerooms.

Marietta makes no comment, not even when they are both standing in the small place. For Anna, nothing has changed. Although she is not poleaxed with terror, the air is stagnant with ancient horror.

'I wondered if it had all been my imagination,' she whispers, instinctively reaching for Marietta's hand.

'*Mamma* hates it too. To me, it's just a cold little room. But we certainly won't have our apartment down here, just in case! Come on, let's go upstairs.'

They start in the dining room, still graced by Sargent's portrait of Marietta's great-great-grandmother; then the *sala*, with its nymph adorned ceiling; next,

Vittore's study. As they enter this little sanctum, they feel the closeness of the man who will never again sit before the bulky 1990s computer. It is here Anna first notices the marks on the walls, testimony to the removal of pictures; she suspects that over the years they have been sold. The Sargent would command a handsome price, but it has been promised to Ca' Pesaro, the museum of modern art. Dorothea Anzelieri will remain in Venice, smiling on multitudes of admirers for years to come.

At last they reach the topmost storey, and Marietta pushes open the door of what had once been her father's room. There, where it has always been, is the painted cradle-end. As they stand before it, Anna's nostalgia for the past is so intense it feels as though she is being torn in two.

'It's so pretty,' says Marietta.

Then, for Anna, history seems to repeat itself, as a small sound disturbs them, and they turn to see Raffi standing in the doorway.

'I thought I'd find you here,' he says, coming to stand between them. He puts an arm around each of their shoulders; the room is suddenly warmer.

'You won't be present for the formal reading of the will, Anna,' he says. 'So I'll tell you now. Vittore has left it you.'

'Me? But I couldn't possibly take it. I mean, you really like it too, don't you? Both of you?'

'We have plenty of other lovely things,' says Marietta.

'And after all,' her father continues, 'it did come from Bruges, which is nearer London than Venice. Perhaps we can come and see it in its new home. He left you a letter. I'll give it to you when we get back.'

'Ah. I already have it. Or at least I did.' She makes her confession. 'He told me not to open it till after he died. I remember taking it, but later I couldn't find it. I think it must have fallen out of my bag when I was shopping.'

'Don't worry. It's on his computer. I'll run you off a copy. It doesn't say much. Just that he thought you had a special affinity with it. Anyway, Letizia has finished here for the day, so shall we head off?'

On the way home, Marietta asks if they can have pizza for supper. She has consumed so much of the rich food brought by well-meaning neighbours that she craves something simple. Rather than eat out, they call at the supermarket. As well as the pizzas, Marietta piles cabbage, carrots and mayonnaise into the basket.

'Coleslaw,' she explains. 'It's the American in me.'

'She'll be gorging McDonalds next,' says Raffi, in mock despair.

Back at the house, Marietta grates carrots. Then she turns her attention to the cabbage. A moment after she picks up the knife, her father walks in.

'Careful with that,' he says, taking it from her. 'Let me.'

Anna looks up from the English newspaper she is reading, watching as the vegetable is transformed into thin, white slivers. Without thinking, she says, 'You be careful too. Look what happened when you chopped those onions for me.'

He stops and laughs, remembering.

'What?' demands Marietta.

'Your father was trying to impress me with his knife skills. Nearly sliced a finger off.'

'I still have the scar.'

Raffi shows Marietta, who crinkles her nose, making a sympathetic "ow" sound. Then he holds his left hand out to Anna, but too close for her to focus, now she has grown a little far-sighted. She takes hold of his wrist, moving it a few inches away. Her thumb presses into the soft flesh of his palm. She recalls the shock of his spilled blood, the smell of onions, the sight of Rosina kissing the bandaged finger. And then it happens – an irresistible urge to bend her mouth to the place and rest her lips on the faint, white scar. There is nothing maternal in the impulse – rather, she feels compelled to feel the roughness of his finger against her tongue, to taste his skin, kiss the warm hollow in his hand, then press it against her cheek and move it down to rest on her heart…

She drops his hand as though scalded, and presses her spine into the back of the chair. He steps back. The whole episode has taken just moments; moments during which Marietta stares at them, her mouth falling into a little O of surprise. Then Raffi resumes shredding the cabbage, and Anna turns her attention back to the newspaper, not absorbing a word of the day old news.

The next morning, being Sunday, they drive to a restaurant overlooking the Brenta canal. In summer it would be idyllic, but under a battleship grey sky it is draughty and unwelcoming. Their attempts at normality crumble under the prospect of what the next day holds. And Anna is unnerved by something more than the funeral blues. The air squirms with things unsaid. She watches Raffi, and sees the boyish twenty-odd year old rather than the careworn father. Her eyes travel to his mouth, the memory of a long-ago kiss brushing her lips. She recalls the touch of his hands; the fullness of him inside her.

Grow up, she tells herself as they head back to Venice. *You're only hankering after the past.*

When they reach the city, she announces her determination to return to the flat. This time Marietta makes no objection. She is looking forward to seeing her glamorous grandmother; excited about the promised gift of the latest tiny iPod. Raffi, also preoccupied, only reminds her of the time that the water-taxi is booked to take them to the funeral service.

After a few hours she is screamingly lonely, and takes herself out for a solitary dinner. The sole she thinks she has ordered turns out to be veal, drenched in a creamy sauce. Not liking to protest, she ploughs through the rich dish and is later punished by insomnia. When she does sleep, her dreams are a confused mush, culminating in the familiar scenario. Alone and frightened, threatened by something or someone, she waits for Raffi. She wakes, sweating and distressed, longing to be back in London, back in her comfortable little house, warm with its happy memories. Pressing her tear-slicked face into the pillow, she mutters, 'Why the fuck did you go and die on me, Mack?'

* * *

When Anna arrives at Raffi's house, a small party has already gathered to take advantage of the taxi bound for Madonna dell'Orto, where the obsequies will take place. Despite the gloom of the occasion the air snaps with the excitement of being transported by *motoscafo* – a prohibitively expensive mode of travel for ordinary people.

The sleek little craft whisks them to the other side of Venice in a fraction of the time it would take a *vaporetto*, so that when they disembark there is three-quarters of an hour before the service is due to start. Nevertheless, they are not the first to arrive. Groups of friends and relatives huddle in front of the pink brick church, watched by a coterie of white, carved apostles, residing in sloping galleries. Inside, the first few pews are already occupied. Anna cannot remember seeing so many fur coats outside of a zoo. Marietta marches towards them and, somehow sensing her daughter's presence, an immaculately coiffured woman turns her golden head. Mother and child are re-united and Anna is seemingly forgotten.

She is just wondering where to sit when a deep, New York voice says, 'Hi honey, it's Anna, isn't it? Remember me?'

The auburn hair is now streaked with silver and worn in a neat chignon, but apart from this, Edie Singelmann has hardly changed.

'Edie, yes, of course. How are you?'

'Fine. Just fine. Look, why don't we sit together? I'm by myself too.'

'Aren't you with Raffi's mother?'

'Yes, but she'll be sitting up at the front, with the rest of her folks. I'd rather not intrude. She's outside with Raffi and Fabrizio – you know, Vittore's brother? He's just arrived.'

'That would be great,' says Anna, relieved to have found a companion. 'But I better not be too far at the back. I'm supposed to be reading a poem.'

'Yeah, me too. Well, not a poem. When the Mass is done, it's traditional in Italy for people to get up and share their memories. I'm going to say a few words. Lucia'll translate. Oh, talk of the devil, here she is. Lucy, this is Anna.'

It is difficult to believe that this petite, glamorous blonde is Raffi's mother. In her mid-sixties, she looks ten or fifteen years younger. She hugs Anna, twittering gratitude for all she has done for her son and granddaughter. Then she bursts into tears and is ushered away by a man Anna recognises as one of Fabrizio's sons.

'She's a lovely girl, despite the drama queen antics,' Edie whispers. 'And she is genuinely devastated about Vittore. Well, we all are, aren't we?'

The two women take their seats. Edie slides gracefully to her knees and silently prays, leaving Anna to reacquaint herself with her surroundings. The star turn of this church is Tintoretto. Both he and his daughter, after whom Marietta is named, are buried here. It is crammed with his vast masterpieces, but there is also a Cima altarpiece and a Bellini Madonna. But no – if she remembers correctly the latter was stolen ten…twelve years ago. Vittore wrote to her, describing how the thieves just walked off with it. The theft was so similar to that of the Misericordia Madonna that he had suspected the same hand was behind both crimes. She cranes her neck to look behind her into the last chapel on the left. Sure enough, only the empty frame remains, and propped against the back of the altar is what she assumes is a reproduction of the purloined original.

The main tourist attraction is, perhaps, a stumpy Madonna, carved in stone. Found in a nearby orchard over six hundred years ago, it was reputed to work miracles, and is still in the church. Halfway through the Mass, Anna is aware of a shuffling and whispering, as a group of tourists make their way past the mourners to the chapel where the statue resides. She, along with others, stares in disapproval. The Venetians, she notices, do not bother. They are so used to such indelicate behaviour that they resort to the simple expedient of ignoring the intruders.

She tries to concentrate on the service, but even allowing for the fact that she understands very little, the Requiem Mass is uninspiring and formulaic. But at last it is over and Fabrizio addresses the congregation, inviting those who wish to eulogise his brother to step forward.

'Let's go stand at the front,' Edie whispers.

Raffi is first, followed by Marietta, who stutters through a tearful little homage. She commences in the lilting Veneziano dialect, but concludes in English, saying that she has lost "the best grandfather in the world". Letizia says a few words on behalf of Rosina, who is heartbreakingly conspicuous by her absence. Then the baton passes to a respected member of the art establishment, an Englishman, famous from the occasional television appearance. Next, an elderly gentleman who was at school with Vittore says a few words, making people laugh; and finally an ex-student adds her praise.

'My turn now, I think,' says Edie and makes her way to the lectern where she is joined by Lucia.

Although she is a woman used to public speaking, Edie appears nervous. Clearing her throat and shuffling her notes, she pauses every few sentences, so that Lucia can translate. 'I am going to talk to you about a part of Vittore's life that I'm guessing most of you are unfamiliar with,' she begins.

Anna can sense the unrest. Even those most devoted to Vittore are now longing to flee this sepulchrally cold church. They are hungry, cold, in need of the loo. Whatever this American woman is about to say, it had better be good.

'Vittore rarely spoke about his war-time experiences,' she continues. 'Partly, I guess, out of modesty, but mostly because he was genuinely traumatised by them. He tried to forget, but I believe we owe it to him to remember: to remember his bravery. Me – perhaps more than anyone here today.'

A few people look uncomfortable. To many, it is ancient history; to those who lived through the conflict, it is something on which they would rather not dwell. But Edie is not so easily discouraged. She forges on, recounting how the teenage Vittore abandoned family, home and studies to join the resistance fighters. She talks of cutting down Nazi flags in hilltop villages; aiding the Allies; helping those under threat to escape. She does not mention a young German boy killed in a hail of bullets, fired in fear rather than fury.

By the time she is nearing the story's conclusion, her audience are enthralled, amazed, humbled.

'So, what's my personal involvement in all this? Well, my name is Singelmann, from which you may guess, correctly, that I have Jewish blood. My dad, however, was not a religious man and married a Baptist, so I was brought up in that tradition. But I have relatives who are practising Jews. One such was my great uncle Karl, although he too married a Christian. He was an artist, and in the '30s, he and his wife, Jenny, left Boston to live in Venice for a few months. When Karl suddenly died, Jenny stayed on. Like so many, before and since, she had fallen in love with your city. Even with the rise of Fascism and the outbreak of war, she refused to leave. She kept her head down and tried to live a quiet life, but by 1944, as an American and the widow of a Jew, it was becoming increasingly likely that she would be sent to an internment camp. She had never enjoyed robust health and may well have not survived the incarceration. To cut a long story short, a young Venetian man helped her escape, needless to say at great personal risk. That boy was Vittore. Somehow, Jenny managed to later discover his real identity, and always meant to return to Venice to thank him personally. Sadly, she was dogged by ill health and never made it. Although Jenny was not our blood relative, I came to regard her as the dearest of my aunts. And it was her influence that engendered my love of Italy. By the time I was studying for my History of Art Degree she had gotten very frail, but when she heard that I would be spending time in Venice as part of my course, she asked me to look Vittore up and convey her thanks. I did just that, and he became one of my dearest friends, and over the years taught me more about art than I ever learned at Yale.

'Well, that's about it. Thank you for listening. I don't know if Vittore would approve my telling you all this, but I felt it was my responsibility to let you know what a brave man he was.' Her voice cracks and she moves away, dabbing her eyes, while Lucia finishes translating.

One or two people begin to clap, very quietly at first. Others join them, and soon the sound has built to a great crescendo of praise, swirling around the marble pillars and rising up to the rafters, so the vasty church creaks like a boat. When the noise subsides, Fabrizio invites Anna to read the piece from *Cymbeline*. Then it is over. Raffi and five of his cousins, heave the simple coffin onto their shoulders, and proceed out of the church. Only he and Fabrizio will accompany it on its final journey to Mestre.

The reception at Ca' Melisa is not as gruelling as Anna anticipated. She busies herself helping to hand out food and drink, and Edie makes an effort to include her in conversations. Even Caterina makes a point of speaking to her.

'Thank you for looking after my little girl,' she says. 'I wanted to be with her, but…well, you understand, it is so…difficult. I am grateful to you.' There is a calmness and sincerity in the woman that Anna has never before seen. Perhaps, at long last, she is content.

When Raffi returns, the first of the guests begin to drift away, including Caterina. Anna watches the estranged couple and their daughter hug. She hears Marietta say, '*Ci vediamo sabato, mamma.*' The girl will be visiting her mother in Milan at the weekend.

By seven, most people have left. Anna is exhausted and her throat is sore, either from an incipient bug, or constant small talk. She finds her coat and makes to leave. Edie has collared Raffi, and on seeing Anna, beckons to her.

'Raffi's coming over to my place tomorrow, about six o'clock. There's a couple of things I need to discuss. Just to do with Vittore's books…the ones we publish. Why don't you join us?'

'There's a concert in the Frari that I thought I might go to.'

'Oh, that won't be starting till nine, will it?' says Edie. 'We'll be finished way before then.'

'OK,' says Anna, feeling it would be rude to refuse.

And so, the next evening, she and Raffi find themselves in Edie's penthouse apartment on the Fondamente Nuove overlooking San Michele. Although night has fallen, it is impossible not to be drawn to the view: the treacle-dark lagoon swirled with spirals of light, on which small boats skid like fireflies; the jagged smear of the cemetery island against the sky; the bright pinpricks of colour marking where Murano hovers on the horizon, and the rhythmic coruscation of a distant lighthouse splitting the night.

Lucia takes a bottle of *prosecco* from a crystal ice bucket and pours the sparkling liquid into elegant flutes. She is flushed; her hands flutter like nervous birds.

They chat for a while, then Edie drains her glass, announcing, 'I have to confess, I got you here on false pretences. There's actually nothing I need discuss with you regarding Vittore's books.'

She and Lucia exchange looks, obviously complicit in some drama of their own making. Edie stands. 'Come with me,' she says.

As they follow the two women, Raffi glances at Anna. He would, she knows, so much rather be at home with his daughter, than be drawn into his mother's little games.

To their surprise, Edie leads them out of the flat. On the landing are three doors. The one facing them is the entrance to another apartment. The other two, laying to their right, are stout and unnumbered. Beside both, is a numeric keypad. Edie punches a long series of numbers into one. There is a click as the lock is released. She pulls open the door and switches on a light. A huddle of coats sway, the hangers creaking as Edie pushes them to one side. Then she moves back, motioning Anna and Raffi to step into the cupboard. It is surprisingly deep, and behind the coats, a black curtain hangs.

No one speaks. Anna knows that something extraordinary is about to reveal itself, but her brain is laggard and she cannot, or dare not, fathom what it might be. She stands slightly in front of Raffi; his left hand rests on her shoulder, and with his right he reaches forward and draws aside the curtain.

Without the protective glass, the fissures and tracery of cracks criss-crossing the painting are only too evident; the patina of years, testimony to its great age. Gone is the nineteenth century frame, so the frayed edges of the canvas are now visible, revealing the fingertips of the Madonna's long lost companion, eternally extending her hand towards the baby Jesus.

Anna and Raffi stand before the painting, like pilgrims at a votive shrine, neither speaking. Centuries fall away; seventeen years fall away, and Anna is transported back to a sunlit morning with Vittore at her side, meeting her Madonna for the first time. She can almost smell the incense, hear the lap of the canal, feel the finger of warmth that points its way through the church's windows.

Feeling slightly unsteady on her feet, she remembers fainting all those years ago. But this time Raffi is here to support her. His breath is warm against her face as he softly swears, 'Gesù bambino. Mamma, Edie, I think you owe me an explanation.'

'I think we're all owed another drink,' says Lucia. 'Come on Edie, lock that damned thing away and tell these poor kids the full story.'

Back in her apartment, sipping bourbon on the rocks, Edie explains, 'What you must understand, is that I adored Vittore. When we first met, I fell head over heels in love with him.'

Beside her, Anna senses Raffi tense, in dread of further revelations.

'Not that anything ever happened of course. Vittore was far too much of a gentleman to take advantage of a gawky twenty-year old, and anyway, he was totally devoted to Rosina. So in time I grew out of my silly infatuation and came to love him as a friend. But I'd have still done anything for him.

'I thought he'd be over the moon about the restoration of the Misericordia and the Madonna. I did everything to push that goddamn project through, but in the end it was like I'd opened Pandora's box – two of the people I cared most about, fighting over how a painting should be restored.'

'They certainly had very different ideas,' says Raffi.

'Too right they did. Vittore was absolutely convinced that Graham's methods were wrong, and he let Graham know that he would do everything within his power to stop him. Vittore had a great deal of influence in Venice, as Graham well knew, so he decided to pacify Vittore, you know, play along with him. But all the time he was determined to do exactly what he wanted. As he said, once he had the Madonna in the restoration studio there was sweet FA anyone could do about it. I wanted to support my husband…of course I did, but I couldn't help thinking Vittore was probably right. So I did a bit of research. I'm older than Graham, a lot richer than Graham, and I had contacts. I spoke to people at the Louvre, the Uffizi, the Met. They all agreed with Vittore; agreed that Graham's methods were too innovatory and could cause lasting damage.

'I don't know why that painting was so important to Vittore. I don't think he knew himself, but it was. So somehow I had to find a way to pull the plug on the project.'

Edie falls silent and then Raffi asks, his voice spiked with disbelief, 'Surely you didn't just take it? Walk out of the church with it under your arm?'

'Yeah...pretty much, although I didn't actually walk out the front door. Even I don't have that much chutzpah. You see, I knew someone – Emilia was her name – who lived in one of those little houses along the Fondamenta de l'Abazia, just up from the Misericordia. Vittore had introduced me to her, years ago, because during the war she'd been in cahoots with him. She was actually instrumental in helping my Aunt Jenny escape from Italy. Emilia's terrace opened onto the cloisters, and they hid her in the church's *campanile*, of all places. Of course, by the time I first met her in the sixties, she was getting on a bit, and by 1987 was really quiet gaga. But she was a sweetie, and I always visited her when I was in town.' She smiles and falls silent, recalling the old lady.

'But how did you get into the church?' Raffi prompts.

'Oh, well...years ago, Emilia used to help clean the place, so she had a key to the sacristy door, which also is accessed from the cloisters. No one had ever asked for it back. So I waited till after the monks turned in for the night, let myself in, and...and took the painting. I knew that it wasn't alarmed, but I really didn't expect to be able to unhook it from the wall – just like that. It was all so easy. Then I went back to Emilia's, wrapped it in a tablecloth, and left. Emilia had nodded off and didn't see a thing. When the police questioned her she'd forgotten I was ever there. I remember walking back to this apartment, like it was yesterday, my arms aching from the weight, and amazed that no one gave me a second glance.'

'But what about Graham?' asks Raffi. 'What did he...?'

'Graham! Oh, believe me, Graham knows nothing about all this. I was in Venice by myself. I'd come over for a few days to move in. Before I returned to the States I had reinforced doors and new locks put on both the closets. Graham thinks that only one of them belongs to us. He's never gotten to speak anything but the most rudimentary Italian, and the neighbours don't speak a word of English, so my secret's pretty safe.'

'But to leave the painting in a cupboard, on the landing. Aren't you afraid someone'll steal it?' asks Anna.

'No, not really. Believe me, that closet's pretty secure. And when you think about it, I reckon that it's probably the safest place. After all, what do most people keep in closets? Galoshes, umbrellas, all their old junk. Thieves wouldn't bother breaking in. Isn't that right, Raffi?'

'I suppose so,' says Raffi. 'And when did you tell Vittore? You did tell him, I assume?'

'Eventually. That was the hardest part – Vittore thinking that the painting really had disappeared. You see, I meant to return it as soon as Graham had something else to work on. But then they changed the lock on the sacristy door and I couldn't figure how to get it back. Whatever I did, it would be a risk – more of a risk than when I took it. Every time I came to Venice I thought, this time I'll do it, but either Graham was around, or the time wasn't right, or I just chickened out. I took it on impulse, but its return had to be planned. And I guess I was just scared of being caught. Not so much of criminal charges being pressed, I could have probably bought my way out of that…no, I was most scared of Graham's reaction. He'd have regarded it as the worst of betrayals. It would have been the end of my marriage, I'm sure. Then the Misericordia closed, and I reckoned the painting would have probably just been stuck in a storeroom at the Accademia. Or, even worse, sold to a private collector on the quiet – such things do happen you know, so I didn't feel too guilty. And by that time I'd sort of gotten used to having it around. I'd sneak out of the apartment at night to look at her. She'd become like a friend.' Edie fixes Anna with a knowing look. 'Do you understand?'

Anna nods. *Oh, yes*, she thinks. *I understand only too well.*

'Then, out of the blue, Saint Catherine pitches up. And Vittore, for some reason, SO hopes this means the Madonna will be returned. I just couldn't bear lying to him anymore, so I told him everything.'

'And what was his reaction?' asks Raffi.

'God, I'm surprised the poor man didn't have a heart attack,' Lucia says. 'Like I nearly did when she told me on the plane coming over here. Just think, all along, my goody-goody brother was in league with a common criminal. I wish I could tell the old devil how proud I am of him.'

Edie ignores her and continues, 'He was shocked…delighted. Then he began wracking his brains to find a way to return the Madonna that wouldn't land me in it. Things weren't made any easier because my little girl was going through a bad patch, so I was hardly coming to Venice. Then about eighteen months later he phoned me with a solution. He'd received his diagnosis and knew he didn't have long to live. He suggested that after he passed away the painting could be "found" at Ca'Melisa.' Edie picks up some envelopes and hands them to Raffi. 'Here's a letter for you, Raffi, confirming everything. And ones for his lawyer and the police.'

No one speaks for a long time and then Raffi says, 'Edie, correct me if I'm wrong, but you want me to agree to the man I regarded as my father being branded a thief – to bear the ignominy of your irresponsible behaviour?'

'Raffi!' snaps Lucia. 'Don't be like that. OK, Edie was a bit impetuous, but it does mean the wretched painting wasn't ruined.'

'Read his letter,' Edie says calmly. 'It explains what'll happen next.'

Raffi tears open the envelope, taking out a single sheet of paper. Despite the letter's brevity, several minutes pass before he puts it down. He rakes his fingers through his hair, shaking his head, as though unable to digest what he has just read.

'I think the shock must have affected my brain,' he says at last. 'I'm finding it hard to take all this in. He writes here that you now own – legitimately own – the other half of the painting; the part depicting St Catherine. Is this true? How?'

'Well, it took a while,' says Edie, 'but the Holocaust Art Restoration Project managed to track down Thalberg's nearest relative – a second cousin. She lives in San Diego with her husband. They're elderly, have no children, and aren't particularly well off. They didn't want to keep the painting…they couldn't even afford the insurance. What I paid them for it means they'll never have to worry about money for the rest of their lives. I was quite upfront with them…that I couldn't promise that they wouldn't get more at auction. But what I did promise was that the painting would be donated to a museum in Venice in memory of Thalberg and also themselves. They liked that. I guess it's a sort of immortality. And nothing else of the poor man's collection has ever turned up. You know, it can't all have been destroyed. There's stuff out there, there has to be. It's scandalous that…'

Raffi interrupts her diatribe, 'Let's just think about the one painting for the moment. So, when I "find" the Madonna among Vittore's possessions, together with his "confession", you miraculously come forward and offer to donate St Catherine. How are you planning to orchestrate that, Edie?'

She hands him another letter. 'This is also for you to "find". It's from Vittore to me. In it he asks if I'll consider loaning my newly acquired St Catherine to the Correr, so that it can be displayed with its other half. Naturally, I will agree to this, and then, in a gesture of philanthropy, offer to donate the picture permanently – on the condition that Vittore's involvement in the acquisition of the Madonna is not made public.'

Raffi stares at her with reluctant admiration. 'You seem to have thought of everything.'

'Hopefully. I really don't think there's much likelihood of Vittore's name being dragged through the mud, especially as he's also gifted the Sargent. All in all, Venice will have done very nicely out of the Anzelieri. And as a last resort, I wouldn't be above greasing a few palms,' she says, rubbing her thumbs against her first two fingers. 'Look, there's no need to make a decision straight away. We're not leaving until Saturday. But remember, I'm putting my whole future in your hands.' She glances at Anna. 'I even invited an independent witness, so if you can't face going along with all this subterfuge, you have someone to back you up.'

'Please, don't involve me,' protests Anna.

'Yes, it would be best if you pretended you never heard this conversation, Anna,' says Raffi. 'You've left me no choice, have you, Edie? This,' and he waves the letter, creating a slight breeze, 'is obviously what Vittore wanted. I can hardly go against his wishes, can I?'

'Oh, thank God for that,' Lucia jumps up, clapping her hands. 'I knew he'd see sense.' And she throws her arms around her son's neck. 'Now, who wants to eat? I'm sure Edie will rustle up her famous spaghetti *vongole* if we ask her nicely.'

Raffi shakes his head. 'No, I need to get back to Marietta. I don't like leaving her for too long.'

'OK,' says Edie. 'And thank you, Raffi. There aren't words to express my gratitude.'

All three women sense he wants to be alone. Anna is not sure what to do, then Lucia comes to her rescue. 'You don't really want to go to that concert in the Frari, do you? Stay and eat with us.'

'If you're sure? Thank you, I'd like that.'

She watches as Edie helps Raffi into his coat. He kisses them all goodbye. 'I'll see you both on Friday, seven-thirty at Montin's. And I'll see you tomorrow evening, Anna.'

In acknowledgement of her last night in Venice, Raffi has suggested that he, Anna and Marietta eat out together.

He is hardly out of the door before Lucia links her arm through Anna's, and says, her eyes glittering, 'My little Marietta seems to have taken quite a shine to you, Anna. We hardly got to speak on Monday, so tell me all about yourself...'

I morti verze, i oci ai vivi

The following evening, when Anna arrives at Raffi's house she finds Marietta curled up on the sofa, clad in pyjamas and dressing gown.

'What's up, sweetheart? Aren't you coming out with us?'

Marietta shakes her head. 'No, I'm not feeling very well.'

'Oh, poor you. Are you starting with a cold?'

'No, no, it's just… you know.' The girl casts a shy glance at her father, who manages to look suitably solicitous of what is presumably a covert reference to the mysteries of the female cycle.

'Will you be all right by yourself?' he asks.

'Yes, of course, but,' she springs from the sofa and launches herself at Anna, 'I won't see you again for ages. Thank you, thank you for everything.'

'Hey,' says Anna. 'Summer will be here before you know it.'

It has already been agreed that, during a July trip to New York, Raffi and Marietta will stop off in London for a few days. For one thing, Raffi has to deliver the cradle-end to its new owner.

'Yeah, I know,' sniffs Marietta. 'Look, off you go or I'm going to start crying.' And she flaps her hands in front of her face in an effort to ward off the tears.

'I'll email you as soon as I get home,' promises Anna, realising how much she will miss the girl.

Raffi has booked a table at a restaurant in the Campo Angelo Raffaele. He has been going there since he was a student, and it is one of those rare things in Venice – an unpretentious, neighbourhood *trattoria*, unspoilt by tourism, serving simple but excellent food. But it is about to change ownership; it may be superb when it re-opens, but it will not be the same.

A dog-eared menu is displayed in the establishment's window, but Anna suspects that this is only for show, as the owner, a lady of indeterminate years, who greets Raffi like a long lost son, simply recites the bill of fare. They choose mixed fish antipasto, one portion of prawn and zucchini lasagne between them, and sea bass.

There are only two other people in the restaurant – a young American couple, who appear to be in the midst of an emotional crisis. The girl, clearly struggling to hold back the tears, hardly touches her food.

Raffi surveys the deserted room. 'I'm sorry, it's busier at lunch time.'

'No, I love it,' says Anna, grateful that their first course has arrived almost immediately.

The restaurant is dismally quiet, except when the kitchen door opens, and English pop music from the '70s and '80s blares out, in stark contrast to the prevailing gloom.

Apart from discussing the food, they seem to have little to say to each other. The past, by unspoken mutual agreement, is taboo, and there is no point in discussing futures in which they will be wrenched apart. The present is the only landscape in which they can communicate, but neither dares discuss yesterday's revelations – even in such a sparsely populated setting.

The dank misery of the young American girl curdles the air; Anna can almost smell her desperation. In an attempt to dispel its contagion, she chats about her day – spent sightseeing. *Carnevale* is imminent and the city is swelling with visitors, their boisterous presence a contrast to her sombre mood. She does not say, but she suspects that she will not visit Venice again for a very long time. It is too laden with memory; and anyway, there are countless other cities still to explore. Edie has invited her to New York; perhaps now, so many years after his death, she will do what her father wished – see the world. Her attention strays as she imagines the future – where, and what, she will paint.

'So, how have you found Venice this time? Do you think it's changed much?' asks Raffi.

'What? Oh…yes. Yes, it has. Not the…the bigger picture perhaps. It's true what they say: you could plonk Titian outside his house, and he'd still be able to make his way to the Rialto. But so much has been smartened up, or…or sanitised. Like the Sacca della Misericordia. I used to love it there, standing on the little bridge, looking out over the lagoon. It was peaceful, and a bit eerie, but now there's a whopping great marina, full of boats. And what about all the shops selling masks, and tourist tat? I mean, where do you get your shoes heeled, or buy – I don't know – a frying pan?'

'Or take your kids to school?' says Raffi. 'It's a vicious circle. Young people leave because it's such an inconvenient place to bring up children. They move to Mestre where you can get to the school without having to drag up and down dozens of bridges. Then yet another Venetian school closes because there aren't enough pupils to justify it staying open, so the kids who do stay, end up having to walk even further to another one.'

'No, it can't be easy. But it's not so great being a tourist here anymore, you know. A lot of the time you're not made to feel very welcome. And things like…like the plinths around the columns on the Molo. I remember, one night, sitting on them with a load of Izzy's students, having a whale of a time. You can't do that anymore, can you? They've put iron railings all around them. And I went into the Basilica today. You're just herded around. It was like being on a conveyer belt. And…'

'And why do you think that is, Anna? The columns were literally being worn away by people's bodies. And do you know how many day-trippers trail through the Basilica during the high season? Some of them have absolutely no respect for the building. If most of it wasn't roped off, they'd be pawing the walls – scratching their names into the marble, probably chipping bits off for souvenirs.'

'Oh, come on…'

'It's true. If you want to know what it's really like, stay another few days and experience *Carnevale* in all its tawdry, drunken inconvenience. As well as using doorways for lavatories, they steal things: doorknockers, name plaques, clothes from washing lines – anything. Then when it really gets busy, when there's about three times as many visitors here as residents, the police close the causeway and enforce a one way system throughout the city.'

'I thought Carnival was fun. Izzy used to love it.'

'Oh, it's fine if all you want to do is party. But try getting to work or school with all that going on. It's our own fault, of course. 1979 it was, and when someone suggested reviving it, just for a long weekend, to liven up February, we all thought it was a great idea. And it was, and the next year's Carnival was fantastic. Too fantastic: word got round and the rest of the world decided they wanted a piece of the action too. So the city began to look for outside help to cover the cost. Before long, corporate sponsors were allowed to advertise: car sized helium balloons, laser beams, non-stop music blaring out. It's become one big trade fair that's got absolutely nothing to do with Venice, or the Venetians. Most of us try to get away. Those that can't, are virtually prisoners in their own homes.'

'Makes tucking into a solitary pancake sound positively appealing,' says Anna, realising why the city is newly upholstered in advertising banners. 'But it's only a few days…'

'Over two and a half weeks now.'

'OK. But it's not as bad the rest of the time, surely?'

'Almost. Every year there are more tourists. They come in from the beach resorts and camping villages, or cruise liners. Have you seen those ships? They're so vast that people living near where they anchor can't get television reception – not to mention the damage they do to the lagoon's eco-system. And they're all day-trippers, spending next to nothing. They just trail around San Marco and the Rialto, leaving their garbage, sneaking into bars to use the lavatories without paying the couple of euros it costs to have a drink, and…'

'Wow! You're really angry about it, aren't you?'

'Yes. Yes, I am. And it's going to get worse. Islets in the lagoon, uninhabited or used as dog sanctuaries, or whatever, are being bought up so that hotels and conference centres can be built on them, bringing in even more visitors.'

The arrival of their main course is heralded by another blast of '80s greatest hits, and for a few minutes, conversation ceases, as they bone the fish. It is succulent and sweet, stuffed with fronds of rosemary. But neither has much of an appetite and they make only a token effort to eat.

'Is it any wonder the city's population has more than halved in the last fifty years?' Raffi says. 'That's what upsets me. That young people like Marietta, born and bred here, won't want to make it their home.'

'No. I don't think I'd want to live here, anymore.'

'But you did once. You adored this city.' His tone is almost accusatory.

'That was a long time ago. I was young, on holiday. Of course everything seemed magical. Don't get me wrong. Venice is beautiful, fascinating…totally unique.' She pushes her plate aside, struggling to find the words, conscious that she is talking about something more than simply her feelings for the city. 'Part of me does love it…still, but…but. Years ago, I read a description of Venice, comparing it to an ancient countess, all decked up in her jewels and faded silks, still lovely but very, very frail. And it's true. It's not like London, where…OK, I know parts of it are really skanky, but it's…young, vital, full of life. Just go to Trafalgar Square on a summer's day and watch the kids playing on the lions. London's a proper, working city. Not like here, where everything has to be kept under wraps because it's all so precious.'

Seeing their abandoned plates, the *signora* clears the table. She is solicitous, concerned. Anna can tell that she is commiserating with Raffi about Vittore's death. Moments later, she brings a plate of *biscotti* and two glasses of dark, red wine.

Anna picks up her glass and breathes the unmistakable scent of strawberries. 'Oh, it's *fragolino* isn't it? Can you believe it, there's a shop on Fulham Road that sells it? I bought a bottle once, but it wasn't the same.'

'Neither's this,' says Raffi. 'You can't buy real *fragolino* anymore.'

'No?'

'It was "outlawed" by the EU, five or six years ago.'

'Why?'

'Well, the *fragola* grape's not indigenous; it's originally from America, and its introduction may have been partly responsible for bringing phylloxera to Europe – you know, the aphid that destroys vines? So although it's been grown here for a hundred and fifty years, or whatever, the wine that's made from it can't be sold. So most vintners have replaced their *fragola* vines with other varieties. A few, like Fabrizio, continue to make it for personal consumption, but these days all you'll find in shops or restaurants is cheap merlot, flavoured with strawberry syrup.'

'Still, it's quite nice,' says Anna, making an attempt at cheeriness. 'Especially if you've never had the real thing.'

Raffi takes a sip and grimaces. His eyes glint in the candlelight. 'Yes. But if you have experienced the real thing…it's impossible to forget, isn't it?'

Now it is he who hides under the veil of euphemism. She senses, rather than sees his hand travel across the table towards hers, and feels the brush of his fingertip. He waits for her response, but she remains mute, unable to speak or even think the appropriate words. He moves his hand away.

They watch the young Americans struggle into layers of coats, fleeces, scarves and gloves; seemingly reconciled, or perhaps only wrapped in the fragile security of a temporary truce.

Raffi leans back in his chair, regarding the wine. 'Yet another thing we've lost. We're like a people dispossessed – all living in the past. It's crazy, we still call the bridge near san Giovanni Crisostomo the Ponte dei Giocattoli – the toyshop bridge – even though the toyshop's gone. I'll probably still be calling it that in twenty years.'

'And yet you wouldn't live anywhere else would you?'

'No. No, I wouldn't. Living here is like being in love. You know all the bad points, but you accept them because you are in love and nothing can change that. So, that's that isn't it?'

'What is?'

'I had hoped,' he says, 'there might be the smallest possibility that you would consider trying to…to pick up where we left off, all those years ago.'

Something, somewhere in the region of Anna's heart performs a small somersault and then constricts in on itself. She can hardly breathe, let alone speak. In the face of her silence, Raffi continues, 'I do believe that there was between us something very…very precious. And if we could only find the courage to trust one another, who knows what may happen. If you came to live here…I can't leave Venice, of course, not while Marietta still needs me, and my work is here too, but you…'

She finds her voice. 'But you think I can just pack up and leave. Move lock, stock and barrel, on the vague possibility that this time things may work out between us? And what if they don't? What then?'

'Anna.' This time he does take her hand. 'I can't promise anything. No more than you can. All I'm saying is, why don't we give ourselves a chance? We'll only know if we spend some real time together. You're an artist; you can work anywhere. And just think what you could create here in Venice.'

For a moment she is tempted to say, 'Yes, why not?' But then she thinks of her home, her friends, her life – forged and fought for over the years. And of the city that made her. 'I'm sorry, but I don't think I could be happy anywhere but London. It's where all my memories are. It's the backdrop to my life. It's what I am.'

But it is more than that. Although he is trying to do the decent thing by not swearing everlasting love and fidelity, the remembrance of his earlier betrayal is still razor sharp; the wounds newly opened. She knows they would have to retrace those first tentative steps they took seventeen years ago, but what if, after revisiting those places together, they are not enough for each other?

'I hope we can be friends,' she says.

'Yes, yes, of course. I'm sorry. It was stupid of me to even think...' He lets go of her hand. The kitchen door flies open, unleashing a robotic drumbeat, sweetened by an ethereal keyboard, and a heart-rending vocal. Lyrics from the year she turned twenty-one: "And love will tear us apart, again". She wonders if Raffi knows the song; is aware of its appositeness.

He is gesturing for the bill. If she does not ask him now, she never will.

'Why did you never reply to my letters? I'd have understood if you'd explained that you didn't want to leave Caterina, after all. I wouldn't have liked it, but I'd have accepted it. But just not hearing from you made me feel cheap...used. Could you just not be bothered to write?'

The music is killed as the door slams shut. He turns to face her, takes off his glasses and rubs his eyes. 'Vittore told me everything...eventually. That you wrote three times? I never received a thing.'

'Oh, come on, I know the post is crap in Italy but it's not that bad.'

'Anna, you may not believe me, and the only person who could confirm it one way or other put a bullet through his brain in 1988, but...'

'What? Who do you mean? Caterina's father?'

'Yes. I've no proof, but he could have easily arranged for a few letters, with foreign postmarks, to go astray.'

'Oh, God. So you really did never get them?'

'No. I swear I never received a thing. All I knew was that you'd packed your bags and left. How do you think I felt? Only that morning, you'd promised that you weren't going anywhere; that you'd always be there for me. I remember your exact words.'

'I left a letter for you with Vittore. Don't tell me you didn't get that one?'

'Oh, I got it all right. But it didn't ring true and I didn't believe a word of it. Do you remember, Anna, the last time we saw each other, you asked me to spend the night with you? And I said no. I just assumed you'd had enough…that you felt rejected in some way. That you weren't willing to wait after all. Then when I spoke to Izzy she said you'd be back in two or three weeks. But of course you weren't. I thought she was covering up for you.'

'Izzy didn't know what was going on. I didn't tell her the full story until after she'd split up with Will, and by then…'

'Why didn't you phone me?'

'I don't know…cowardice…fear of rejection. Would it have made any difference?'

'Yes…yes, it would. We'd have sorted things out. My father-in-law was a bully and a xenophobe, but he wasn't corrupt. Intercepting letters was as far as he'd have gone, I'm sure. He was gambling on being able to frighten you away.'

'Well, he certainly succeeded.'

'I was an idiot. I should have contacted you. I could have got your mother's address from Izzy. But it was such a difficult time. I was a real mess.'

Like the images that a drowning man is supposed to see, pictures flash into her mind from a life she never had: Raffi by her side before an altar in a Venetian church; children – a girl, aged perhaps thirteen or fourteen – Marietta, but not Marietta – with dark curls rather than a honeyed mane; a little boy with the face her father wore as a child. She feels sick with regret. 'We're both as much to blame. It obviously just wasn't meant to be, and anyway, it might not have worked out. After all, we hardly knew each other. Look, can we go? I need to finish packing.'

Raffi walks her back to the flat. They keep their distance. She catches him glancing at his watch, no doubt worrying about his daughter. There are few people about and no one gives them a second glance. What is there to see? A tall, middle-aged couple, elegant and unassuming. But anyone looking into their eyes would see something exceptional there: something that lifts them above the ordinary. It is the remembrance of their single night together; a night of such heartbreaking sweetness that, despite their best efforts, neither have ever been able to quite forget. Why, she wonders, from a litany of so many nights, should this one shine so bright? It is, she concludes, down to the merciless chemistry of love. And yet, would that love have been enough? Had they made a life together, would she have been content – her days filled with whatever Venetian wives and mothers do? Most significantly, would she have become what now defines her, above all else – an artist?

They reach the apartment. An aimless breeze picks up pieces of litter, scattering them about the *campo*.

'I'll see you tomorrow,' he says.

Her check-in time at Marco Polo is just after nine, and Raffi has offered to take her to the airport before he goes to work. The thought of a public goodbye, amongst harassed travellers, to the accompaniment of public address announcements, fills her with gloom.

'OK,' she says, but resolves to telephone him first thing in the morning to insist that she makes her own way. Piazzale Roma, with its half-hourly bus service, is hardly any distance. Unaware that this is goodbye, Raffi drops a kiss on her cheek. He walks away, leaving her cowering in the doorway. It takes all her self-control not to run after him. Only when his footsteps fade to nothingness, does she make a weary ascent to the apartment.

The little flat is no more welcoming than on her first day. She switches on the television and starts to pack, but canned laughter howling from virtually every channel grates on her nerves. Whatever else she will miss about Venice, it will not include the trite titillation of Berlusconi controlled TV.

She turns her attention to cleaning out the kitchen cupboards and fridge. Much of it ends up in the bin, but the olive oil, pasta and packs of biscuits are untouched. The apartment is booked from Saturday evening, and she knows that someone will be coming in tomorrow to scrub the floors and change the linen. She has no idea who the visitors are, but they will undoubtedly be wealthier than the woman preparing their holiday venue. It seems fairer that the cleaner should have the provisions.

In front of one of the windows, recessed into the roof, there is a small, but chunky writing desk. Here she settles, and writes a note: "*Per favore. Prendere il cibo*".

Suddenly she feels bone-crushingly tired. Her head begins to droop. She will close her eyes for a few moments, and then take a shower.

Outside, a group of locals are talking and laughing in what she recognises as Veneziano. There is something comforting about their chatter, and in particular one of the voices, a voice that has unaccountably switched to English, a voice at once achingly familiar and yet almost forgotten. Opening her eyes, she sees three men, huddled under the church porch. Two have their backs to her, and the third is hidden by their greater height. Then the silver-haired man moves, enabling her to focus on his companion's face. Her heart heaves into her mouth. She is looking into her father's eyes. He raises a hand in greeting as the other men turn: Vittore, restored to vibrant health; Mack, wild-haired and scruffy in his duffle coat and long multi-coloured scarf. They all smile and she knows that they want to tell her something important.

Then her head snaps back as her right hand jerks forward, sending the pen rolling towards the wall. For a second her attention shifts. She watches the pen disappear, registering the sound of its descent. When she looks back, the men stand in the same spill of lamplight, continuing their conversation. But it is now inaudible through the closed window. Although their faces are no longer visible, she knows they are strangers, their similarity to those she loved, the stuff of dreams. But their appearance, albeit only in her mind's eye, has so unnerved her that she hears the breath catch in her throat, and feels the accelerated beat of her pulse. Unable to move, she wills some puckish alchemy to transform them again. Only when the men part company and meander away does she think to retrieve the pen.

It has fallen in an upright position, wedged between the back panel of the desk and the wall. The only way to extricate it is to move the piece of furniture which, jam-packed with brochures and guidebooks, is surprisingly heavy. Leaning all her weight against one of its sides, she pushes. It shifts, only slightly, but enough. Just enough to dislodge the pen…and an envelope. She assumes that it has been hiding there for years, and so is unprepared to see her own name on it. Then she recognises the writing. It is the letter Vittore gave her two weeks ago and which she presumed lost. Raffi has already run off a copy. It is a brief, business-like note advising her that she has been bequeathed the cradle-end. Knowing its content, she is about to put it in her case, when something impels her to tear it open and extricate the two sheets of thick cream paper. It is a quite different epistle; handwritten and far lengthier. The date at the top of the page is 3rd December, 2004.

My Dearest Anna

I write this, not being entirely sure that you will ever read it. Perhaps we will meet once more before I die, and I shall be able to speak the words. Then again, I may choose to relegate both this letter, and my hopes, to the flames. But I suspect not. There are some things that must be said, even if the voice comes from the grave.

I do not think you will be surprised that it is the Bard of Avon who has inspired me to put pen to paper. As I sit here in my little study, I have at my side the complete works of Shakespeare, for I had the intention of re-reading them. Alas, I make slow progress, for I find my eyes either closing or drifting from the page to watch the rise and fall of the rio, the evening light as it plays on the buildings, or the dancing step of a pretty girl walking along the fondamenta. Ah, as you see, even now I digress.

I am, however, justified in abandoning my books for a moment or two, having just completed As You Like It. You will laugh, I am sure, but I could not help but see you as Rosalind. And, indeed, the bard has given to her the lines that I find most pertinent to you, although they relate to Celia, rather than to herself. Do you know them?

– "for your brother and my sister no sooner met, but they looked; no sooner looked but they loved; no sooner loved but they sighed" –

You know of whom I speak, and before you admonish me for being a foolish, fond old man, remember that I was there at the instant you and Raffi met. If I had ever doubted the existence of love at first sight, watching you two, I was, at once, convinced of its absoluteness.

I confess now that this was one of the reasons I sought out your company, hoping that your relationship would blossom. I knew that Caterina would never make Raffi happy. She is too much like his mother – my little sister. But despite all my machinations, the course of your true love never did run smooth.

And now, after so many years, is there the smallest chance that the flame could be reignited? Well, only you can know. I realise there are many obstacles to overcome, but none are insurmountable. Yes – you have your life, and he has his. You are both emotionally and physically bonded to your hometowns, and for the moment Raffi must be in Venice for Marietta. But there are aeroplanes from London to Venice – cheap and frequent. I know of other people who divide their time between these two great cities.

However, these practicalities are nothing, I imagine, compared to your inner turmoil and misgivings. Why, you must wonder, did he so easily allow you to leave his life; why did he not fight for you?

There were many reasons, some of which you understand. But I do not think you are aware of what I believe is the most significant. Neither was I, for many years, and I suspect Raffi himself is still uncomprehending.

I must ask you to cast your mind back to his early childhood. I do not believe that he ever consciously regretted leaving his mother, but what he experienced could not help but leave scars. I had a great friend – a psychotherapist – who, watching Raffi as a child, warned me, "There will always be a part of him that expects people, especially women, to leave him. He does not feel that he deserves their love".

I dismissed my friend's words as psycho-babble, but years later, I remembered them. We were entertaining an English friend – well, acquaintance really. He and his wife were telling us how much easier their lives were now that their son, a child of seven, was attending boarding school. Raffi said nothing at the time but later, when they had left, he picked up a photo of Marietta, who was about five at the time and said, "How could they do that to their little boy? Seven years old, still a baby – only two years older than Marietta". And then he looked at me, as though it had occurred to him for the first time. "Only two years older than when my mother sent me away. How in God's name could she do that?"

I realised then, that now he had a child of his own, whom he loved more than his very self, he could not imagine how his own mother came to abandon him. I suspect, however, that he did not blame her. He blamed himself, and subconsciously always had done. If he lived in America he would no doubt "be in therapy", but Raffi does not, I am sure, need therapy. He only needs you; you and Marietta.

I know that you have been the beat of his heart for the last seventeen years, and I believe it has been the same for you: that whoever you are with, or whatever you do, not a day goes by when you do not, in some small way, miss him. If I am wrong, tear this letter to shreds, go back to London, and forget the meanderings of an interfering old man. But if there is an iota of truth in what I write, I beg of you, my dear, to find the courage to give yourselves the chance of happiness.

There is an old Venetian proverb: "I morti verze, i oci ai vivi", the dead open the eyes of the living. I pray that I have been able to open yours.

Goodbye Anna and God bless.

Vittore

She starts to read it once more but there is really no need: everything he has written she already knew, in some small place, deep in her heart or head. The jagged pieces of the jigsaw fall into place: things Raffi has said, the small insecurities so expertly hidden.

The letter rests on her lap, but now there is something wrong with the words: they blur and roll about the page. Then she realises that the paper is wet from her tears: the ink has smudged, running in black rivulets. She moves, sending the sheets fluttering to the floor. They tremble from the heat of the radiator, as though they are living things with a beating pulse. Watching them, she senses that the cold, alien thing that made an icy nest in her heart so many years ago, is melting.

Tomorrow she will be on that flight to London; there is no doubt about that. The question is, how soon will she board another plane bringing her back to this city. And what, if any, promises will she make to the man who may be waiting for her.

She thinks of her studio and the stack of empty canvases. And of her life – a great empty canvas also, begging to be daubed with bright splashes of colour. Then into her mind comes a vision of a painting: two women, not unlike younger versions of herself and Izzy, are caught in the moment their full skirts are tugged and billowed by the wind. It is a scene reminiscent of Bert Hardy's 1950s photograph, but the girls sit on a Venetian bridge, rather than Blackpool sea-side railings. Passing by, and smiling over his shoulder, is a young gondolier. More images tumble and whirl, demanding to escape from the obfuscation of her mind and be given life. They are daring pictures, a mixture of the prosaic and the magical. Stone lions, petrified for centuries, quicken and pace moon-drenched streets; golden angels abandon high pinnacles and walk with men. Their creation will demand a new vocabulary of colour and sciagraphy that can be inspired only by this city. Here is her future. There is, after all, no choice. Everything in her life has led to this, like perspective lines converging in a single vanishing point.

She picks up her phone, and finding his number, presses CALL. It rings for a long time. Then a sleepy voice says, 'Pronto.'

'Hi, Marietta. It's me…Anna. Can I speak to your dad?'

'I think he's in the shower. Shall I get him to ring you back? Oh, no, here he is.'

She hears a muffled exchange, the sound of a door closing and then his voice, 'Anna. Is something wrong?'

'No, no, nothing's wrong. Everything's all right. More all right than it's ever been…I can't explain over the phone. Can I come over?'

'No, no. I'll come to you. Give me fifteen minutes.'

'OK. But there's no need to rush. Get properly dry. I'm…I'm not going anywhere.'

'Promise?'

'Yes, I promise.'

* * *

Raffi puts down the phone. He knocks on his daughter's door. She is plugged into her new iPod, singing along to its tinny hiss.

'You shouldn't play that thing so loudly. It'll damage your hearing.'

Pulling off the earphones, she gives him one of those indulgent smiles that teenagers reserve for their antediluvian parents.

'Will you be OK if I pop out for an hour or so? Anna needs to speak to me about…about something?'

'Sure. Nothing's wrong is it?'

'No, no. Just some last minute stuff. I won't be long. Promise.'

'It's cool. Be as long as you like.' She fiddles with the iPod and then looks up. Her expression is beneficent. 'It's all right, babbo. I give you permission.'

For a moment he suspects that she has listened in to his conversation, but then he realises that she does not need to. She already knows; has probably known longer than he has.

* * *

376

Anna puts down the phone. She sits by the window and picks up a novel, brought from home. From its pages flutters a piece of paper she has been using as a bookmark. It is a flyer for her last show: she scans the potted biography, rereading the final sentence: "Anna lives and works in London". Taking a pen she scribbles out the full stop, and in a bold hand adds just two words: "and Venice".

Then she leans back in her chair, calm at last, and waits for Raffi, knowing that this time he will arrive – as he was always meant to.

Bruges: Winter 1520

Today it has rained since dawn and the canal beneath my window is as dull as pewter. The rain drums on the roofs and pavements with long, dark fingers. This is more than mere wetness; more than liquid cloud. Its dampness seeps permanently into our bones, for even in summer this country is never sufficiently warm to wholly dispel the cold. I yearn for Venetian sunshine, and yet I am grateful to live in a city built on water, even if it is cold, northern water.

I sit, as I do every day, making the most of the reluctant light, before dusk forces me to lay down my brushes and paint. Closing the shutters, I see that the waters have risen. They burgeon, like my belly, which is full and round with our first child.

We, Giacomo and I, have lived in this city for more than four years. That I should be here at all confounds me, for I felt myself so much a part of Venice that I thought never to leave her. But unless Enrico Sartorani dies, we can never return.

I have, of late, ceased to pray for his demise, for whilst the baby grows within me it is unwise to dwell on bad thoughts. So I try not to think of him, or of the long journey north that brought us here.

We had at first hoped to settle near the monastery in Padua, but when *papà* and Matthew arrived we knew we would have to travel much, much further. They sat with us in the shaded cloisters and broke the news. *Papà* had been absent from our house, visiting a patient with young Antonio. Only Pasqualina was at home. She heard them break in but could do nothing to stop the thugs. They rampaged through every room, smashing all they could. They slashed mattresses and clothes; they tore the pages out of books; they emptied their bladders onto our beds, and terrorised poor Pasqualina almost to death. As they left, they promised to be back with more medicine for the good doctor, thinking this a fine jest.

It was then that Matthew persuaded *papà* to leave Venice, for the violence wreaked upon our home left him in no doubt that Enrico would stop at nothing to extract the secret of our whereabouts. For the sake of everyone, *papà* must also flee. So he packed his belongings, gathered together his money, and allowed Matthew to take him to the same sanctuary where we hid.

There he remains, for the holy men welcomed so talented a physician into their midst. It is a religious house where many pilgrims from the North break their journey, so he is kept busy. He writes to me often, although one of the monks must act the scribe, for now he is almost completely blind. He seems content enough, although I know that he sorely misses me. It breaks my heart that I will not be there to comfort him in his old age, and that someone else will close his eyes when God calls him away.

I would have happily stayed at the monastery but, unlike *papà*, we had no useful skills to offer, and a woman could not remain as part of their community. We had to move on, and to a place far from the range of Enrico's malice. Giambattista had given Giacomo letters of introduction and names of Flemish artists whom he knew. So when a group of pilgrims arrived on route back to Bruges, we decided to travel with them, there being safety in numbers.

Had I known how arduous the journey would be, I do not think I would have willingly undertaken it. Even now, the remembrance of it causes my heart and stomach to churn: the filthy inns; the foul food; the fear of being attacked by brigands; the discomfort of travelling in a small cart, (neither Giacomo nor I could countenance riding a horse) and being so shaken about that even my teeth hurt. But worse of all was my terror of the alien landscape. I was born in a city; the nearest I ever came to a mountain was to see them in the far distance, snow-capped and magical. I imagined them to be like Giambattista's paintings, green and lush, inhabited by jolly folk and gambolling animals. But the real thing, the mountains they call the Alps, are the most horrible of places. They are vast beyond belief: at times our path was so high that we teetered above the clouds. It was enough to make me doubt the very existence of Heaven. For where is it, if not in the firmament? *Papà* had taught me not to believe in monsters, but at night, listening to the inhuman cries that echoed up to the stars, I believed in all manner of fearsome things, and did not know whether I heard ghosts, or dragons, or wolves. And it was in the mountains that the dreams first came. Night after night I woke sweating in terror, as I relived that time in the storeroom at Ca' Sartorani, waiting and praying for Giacomo to arrive and save me. The dreams do not come so frequently now, thank God, but sometimes when I am tired or unwell, they tear my sleep to shreds. No, I do not believe that any sane person would choose to cross the Alps, and even if I heard that Enrico had met his maker, I do not think I could countenance that ordeal again, especially now that I have another life to consider.

The light has all but gone. I stretch and rub the small of my aching back, thankful that Giacomo will soon be home. Two years ago *papà* appointed an agent to sell our house in Venice, and having no need of the money himself, gave half to the monastery and sent the rest on to me. This meant that Giacomo, who is now a master woodcarver, could set up his own establishment. There is work aplenty and we find ourselves quite prosperous. Even I bring in a modest income, for here in Bruges a woman may be an artist, and I am a member of St Luke's, the artists' guild. My small devotional pieces and painted furniture are becoming sought after, and in time I may make quite a name for myself.

And what of the other players in the drama of my life? After *papà* and Debra, the living creature I miss the most is Cesare, for it was more than books and mattresses that were destroyed when Enrico's thugs broke into our house. This time Cesare did not survive their vehemence. They took a cudgel and shattered his skull like a nutshell.

When their life is through, animals are usually cast into the lagoon, but *papà* took my little dog into the courtyard at the back of our house and made a grave for him there. For this I am grateful: Cesare never could abide water.

Giacomo has carved a cradle for the baby, and I am painting it with all manner of pretty things. I have summoned into my mind the image of Giambattista's painting of the Nativity that hangs in the church of the Carmini, and on one end of the cradle I have fashioned my own humble version. The face of the Virgin is Debra's; Giacomo has provided the likeness for the angel; *papà* is the shepherd and the dog is, of course, Cesare. He, together with these good souls, will, I am sure, protect my sleeping child. There could be no better guardian, for I am sure I owe my life to him.

My baby will be born astride the old and the new year, and for this reason I have left the date incomplete. To do otherwise, would, I believe, be tempting fate, for who knows whether my child will live, or indeed whether I will be spared. When we are both safely delivered and I sit with my son or daughter in my arms, then I will take up my paints, and inscribe either a nought or a one. Until then, the cradle bears just the three figures: 1, 5, and 2. If I die, and the child survives, perhaps Giacomo will add the final number. It is not something of which we speak. I mentioned it once, but the look he turned on me was so stricken that I have never referred to it again.

As for my kind teacher, Giambattista, he did not long enjoy the quiet of Conegliano's mountain shadowed streets. About a year after we fled Venice we received word that, following a short illness, he had died. He was greatly mourned in the city of his birth, for he was, and must always be, the greatest of its sons. I do so regret not seeing him before we left; I loved him dearly and the pattern of my life has been determined by knowing him. For the good parts, I thank him; for the bad, I acknowledge these as my own doing. It was my vanity that demanded I be painted, and my obstinacy that I insist Debra should share my adventure. If I had refused Enrico's request, we would all be happily living together in our little house in Cannaregio. My foolishness spread across our lives like a stain, and can never be erased.

The instrument of all our sorrows, Enrico, thrives. His father married the little Mocenigo virgin and nine months later she presented him with a son. But before the year was out, both mother and child succumbed to a virulent fever and went to their graves within days of each other. It is said that the old man was so grieved that he suffered a violent seizure. He survived, but his face is distorted, his speech incomprehensible, and perhaps his manhood can no longer rise to the occasion. Either this, or he finally accepted that it was God's will that he should beget no more sons, for he married his concubine. Poor Alphonso Sartorani has been declared an imbecile, so Enrico is now the legitimate heir. In deference to his newly elevated position, a noble bride was speedily found. Already he has two fine sons, so the perpetuation of the Sartorani is assured, for at least the next generation. I pray these boys are not as heinous as their father, for I am sure that Enrico was the assailant of whom we lived in dread. I believe there have been no further attacks in the city, so perhaps with the acquisition of his shiny new respectability, he does not hate we poor women so much. I will never know. I try not to think of him, although it does give me some satisfaction to know that when he looks into the glass and sees his damaged face, he must think of me.

And finally there is the painting, which for all that it is mere canvas and coloured pigments, is as much a part of the cast as we poor mortals. It is certainly the cause of all our ills, and yet I cannot but love it. The half with my picture is with *papà*. Although he can no longer discern my features, he says that it gives him comfort to know that it hangs on the wall of his little cell. I have asked him to leave instructions that one day, when we are all dead and buried, the painting is donated to Santa Maria Abbazia della Misericordia. It is the church in which I was married and where I was so very, very happy. I do not know if this will happen, but I pray that it will. I miss the city of my birth so much it hurts, and it gives me comfort to think that one day "I" may return.

I hear the sound of Giacomo's footsteps, and in my last seconds alone I meet Debra's eyes. The other part of the painting is here with me, and of late I spend a deal of time in its contemplation. It is thought that when a woman is with child, beholding things of beauty will ensure that she gives birth to a well-formed baby. Certainly, there can be few sights as fine as this picture, and my child should be strong and comely.

Debra and I will never meet again in this world, and who knows whether we will encounter each other in the next. But perhaps, just perhaps, in a distant future, of which I can only dream, her picture will find its way back across the Alps, and our images in paint will once again smile at one another under the bluest of Venetian heavens.

Giacomo steps into the room, wet from the rain, and the air dances with love. Things between us are as sweet as they have ever been. He kisses me, and I cease to think of Debra, or the past, or the future, but only of him. Kneeling before me, he places his head on my belly and whispers endearments to his unborn child. Later, he will take me to our bed and ever so gently love me. Then we will fall asleep, listening to the lap of small waves against the bank, imagining that it is the soft murmur of the rio de la Sensa. And in my dreams, I steal back to Venice.

Bibliography

Patrick Bishop: *Bomber Boys – Fighting Back 1940 – 1945*, Harper Perennial

Robert Bonfil: *Jewish Life in Renaissance Italy*, University of California Press

Patricia Fortini Brown: *Private Lives in Renaissance Venice*, Yale University Press

Patricia Fortini Brown: *The Renaissance in Venice*, Everyman Art Library

Patricia Fortini Brown: *Venice and Antiquity*, Yale University Press

Patricia Fortuni Brown: *Venetian Narrative Painting in the Age of Carpaccio*, Yale University Press

Stanley Chojnacki: *Women and Men in Renaissance Venice*, The Johns Hopkins University Press

Carlo M Cipolla: *Public Health and the Medical Profession in the Renaissance*, Cambridge University Press

Ellizabeth S Cohen & Thomas V Cohen: *Daily Life in Renaissance Italy*, Greenwood Press

Elizabeth Crouzet-Pavan: *Venice Triumphant: The Horizons of Myth*, The John Hopkins University Press

Giorgio e Maurizio Crovato: *The Abandoned Islands of the Venetian Lagoon*, San Marco Press

Elizabeth Currie: *Inside the Renaissance House*, V & A Publications

Satya Datta: *Women and Men in Early Modern Venice*, Ashgate Publishing

Robert C Davis and Benjamin Ravid: *The Jews of Early Modern Venice*, The Johns Hopkins University Press

Robert C Davis: *The War of Fists*, Oxford University Press

Robert C Davis: *Shipbuilders of the Venetian Arsenal*, The Johns Hopkins University Press

Robert C Davis & Garry R Marvin: *Venice, The Tourist Maze: A Cultural Critique of the World's Most Touristed City*, University of California Press

Richard Goy: *Chioggia and the Villages of the Venetian Lagoon*, Cambridge University Press

Richard Goy: *Building Renaissance Venice*, University Press

Daniela Hacke: *Women, Sex and Marriage in Early Modern Venice*, Ashgate Publishing

Paul Hills: *Venetian Colour*, Yale University Press

Deborah Howard: *Venice and the East,* Yale University Press

Peter Humfrey: *Cima da Conegliano,* Cambridge University Press

Peter Humfrey: *The Altarpiece in Renaissance Venice*, Yale University Press

Patricia H Labalme, Laura Sanguineti White and Linda L Carroll: *Venice: Cita Excelentissima: Selections from the Renaissance Diaries of Marin Sanudo,* The John Hopkins University Press

Frederic C Lane: Venice – *A Maritime Republic,* The Johns Hopkins University Press

John McAndrew: *Venetian Architecture of the Early Renaissance*: MIT Press

Stefania Mason, translated by Andrew Ellis: *Carpaccio: The Major Pictorial Cycles,* Skira Editore

Jan Morris: *Venice,* Faber & Faber

Edward Muir: *Civic Ritual in Renaissance Venice*, Princeton University Press

Stella Mary Newton: *The Dress of the Venetians,* Scolar Press

John Julius Norwich: *A History of Venice,* Penguin Books

Brian Pullan: *Rich and Poor in Renaissance Venice,* Wiley-Blackwell

Dennis Romano: *Housecraft and Statecraft: Domestic Service in Renaissance Venice,* The Johns Hopkins University Press

Dennis Romano: *Patricians and Popolani,* The Johns Hopkins University Press

Cecil Roth: *History of the Jews in Venice*, Schoken Books

Guido Ruggiero: *Binding Passions,* Oxford University Press

Guido Ruggiero: *The Boundaries of Eros,* Oxford University Press

Guido Ruggiero: *Violence in Early Renaissance Venice,* Rutgers University Press

Nancy G Siraisi: *Medieval and Early Renaissance Medicine,* University of Chicago Press

John Steer: *Venetian Painting,* Thames and Hudson

Sarah Walden: *The Ravished Image Or How to Ruin Masterpieces by Restoration,* Weidenfeld & Nicolson

Jonathan Webb and Julian Radcliffe: *Stolen : The Gallery of Missing Masterpieces,* Herbert Press Ltd

Evelyn Welch: *Shopping in the Renaissance,* Yale University Press

Garry Wills: *Venice, Lion City, The Religion of Empire,* Washington Square Press